AFTERWORDS

STEPHEN BIAS

Printed in the United States of America
First Printing, 2023
Paperback ISBN-978-1-9620190-4-0
Hardcover Isbn-979-8-9866027-4-5

The Henlo Press
P.O. Box 1694Ashland, KY 41105
WWW.THEHENLOPRESS.COM

For Max, Andrew, Lillian, and especially Rachel
Without you I don't exist, much less this book.

To the Kickstarter backers thank you for every ounce of support and
patience you showed. Have a wonderful trip to the After.

To Henlo Press for taking a chance on me. Courtney, and Chandler
you were magical, I can't wait to see where we go next.

1

NOVEMBER 18TH, 1804
CLOVER, VIRGINIA

Clayton Shaw blew out the candle on the nightstand and watched the string of smoke rise from where the tiny flame had been. The moon was full, and there wasn't a cloud in the night sky. It left the room awash in a natural glow that seemed to reflect off of every surface. He'd extinguished the flame since the lighting was more than sufficient. He was exhausted. All he wanted was to sleep. His body ached from head to toe. Clayton paced to loosen up. He was stiff from sitting in the chair he'd brought up from the dining room. He sat down and gave a small groan as his back protested.

He stared down at his mother, who was wrapped in several blankets, shivering. The fever had ravaged her for several days now, and he wondered how she was hanging on. She hadn't eaten in what seemed like forever, and any attempt came right back up. The rash had completely engulfed her neckline, chest, and face, leaving them a bright red. It reminded Clayton of a terrible sunburn, with splotches a deeper shade than the rest. The part that disturbed Clayton the most was her lips. They were ghastly white, and he felt uncomfortable when he looked at them. She didn't look like Emma Shaw anymore. His mother was always so full of life, sparkling, really. Seeing her in such shambles broke his sixteen-year-old heart.

He had prayed hourly in the beginning for her to pull through, but it was too late. She was too far gone. He was praying now for her to go peacefully. Doctor Brown had warned the family, "It won't be long now," two days ago.

He'd never heard of scarlet fever; he knew she'd cut her hand in the kitchen a couple of days prior. A nasty slice while peeling a potato that bled profusely. Her voice became raspy the following day, and then the cough came swift and brutal. Every exhale ended in a hacking fit, leaving her gasping for air. Shortly after she took to bed, the red lines started to form on her neck. The fever came that evening, and getting her to eat or drink was impossible. She lacked the energy to sit up, much less stand. So, she spent her time in bed while her breathing shallowed and a slight rattle became audible. Clayton refused to leave her side once she was bedridden.

As a reward for his loyalty to his mother, Clayton had to stay in the room with her. Doctor Brown had explained that Emma was contagious and Clayton could be the next to fall ill. He wasn't afraid. Clayton's only thought was for his mother. He did not want her to die alone. If he got sick, he would fight his way through. He wanted to be with her. She had done so much for him; he wouldn't abandon her now. He brushed a strand of sandy blonde hair away from her face, which was coated in sweat. He reached to the nightstand, picked up the cloth, and wiped her forehead. Emma's hazel brown eyes opened and looked upon him. She smiled weakly and coughed.

"You're alright. I'm still here," Clayton whispered to his mother as he patted her brow.

"So good," she gasped.

"Shh, don't talk, Momma."

"I'm going to die." A tear streamed down her cheek.

"Don't say that. You..." He shifted in his seat and looked away, struggling to come up with a plausible lie. "You just need to rest."

"I-" she coughed, and a little blood splattered on her lower lip, which Clayton quickly wiped away. "I never told you." She tried to clear her throat. Clayton didn't want to break down in front of her. He wanted her to see him strong and capable of handling the worst. He didn't want her to worry that he wouldn't be able to make it without her. She was always thinking of others instead of herself. Clayton always admired that about her.

"What did I say? You need to rest. It's my turn to take care of you," he said to her. She gave him another weak smile.

"You need to keep it up," she wheezed, trying to catch her breath after every word.

"Keep what up?"

"This farm." Her cough was much harsher this time, and he wished she would stop talking. "It's really your farm. You work so hard."

He wanted to thank her, but another hacking fit had taken hold. He leaned her forward off her pillows and placed the cloth over her mouth. He could hear the fluid in her lungs as she violently convulsed against him. He kept his eyes closed. If he saw her in the act, he knew he would lose control. A minute passed, and after she gagged a few times, her body settled. He laid her back against the pillows stacked behind her head to keep her elevated. The cloth was damp with mucus and blood, and he tossed it to a stand near him where the washbasin sat. She was staring off into a dark corner of the room. Clayton followed her eyes.

"So good," she repeated. Clayton Shaw was good. His mother never had to scold him or have Jonas, his father, take a switch to him. Clayton never sassed her. He wouldn't dare. He was polite and well-mannered and did precisely as he was told. No one in the small village of Clover ever came to their door to complain about him. Mischief just wasn't in his nature. His days were spent completing chores and helping his father with the sheep. Afterward, he was in the house assisting his mother with the cooking, setting the table, cleaning up the dishes, and keeping his younger sister, Eve, entertained.

Clayton was too busy to make friends. He didn't have time to chase after the other boys in town or head to the river for a swim. That was fine by him. The boys loathed him. If one of them did something unsavory, his moral compass would start spinning, and off Clayton would go to tell their families. So, no boys came to the Shaw homestead to ask for Clayton, which he preferred as there was work to be done. He felt there was only so much time before the sun went down, and anything not done today would be extra work tomorrow.

Clayton only spoke to one other child, a girl named Amber Ward. They had been friends from the time they could walk. They only spoke fleetingly on Sundays at church, but they didn't see each other as much as they used to. Clayton stayed on the farm during the week, consumed in his work, but the bond they formed as toddlers stayed strong. She was the only person that seemed to get conversations out of him. Clayton was quiet and mostly spoke only when spoken to. It wasn't that he was shy, far from it. He just had a routine, and he adhered to it. Six days out of a week, from sun-up until sundown, unless harsh weather stood in his way. He still had to go outside and check on the sheep on those days.

This time with his mother was the most he'd ever spent missing his chores and time out in the field. Clayton didn't take extra days off. He already had one built into every week. The seventh day, Sunday was for the Lord. That day began with the weekly baths in order, Jonas, Emma, himself, and finally little Eve. They'd have a nice breakfast, dress in their best, and off they'd go to church service from Reverend Price. Clayton would be there, clean, attentive, and thankful for the week that passed. The rest of his day was for reflection and ease.

He found himself looking to the Lord now, as his mother lay dying. He didn't want to be left alone without her. Yes, he would have Eve and Jonas, but Emma was the foundation of this family.

Eve was only four. What did Clayton know about raising children? Emma was the one that he turned to if he had a problem. The most common phrase his father used was "go ask your mother." She always seemed to have the answers, and if she didn't, she would have a Bible quote ready. Emma knew the scripture front to back. Jonas and Clayton would spend some evenings listening to her recitations. Clayton knew her soul was strong, her life was led as a strong Christian woman, and the kingdom of heaven awaited her. That gave him comfort, but it wasn't nearly enough.

He had gone through denial, in the beginning, sure she'd pull through. He told himself that God wouldn't take her and recounted her good deeds here with them. The anger phase was short-lived. That just wasn't in his nature. He was past bargaining now. He begged God to take him instead, offered everything he could think of, but received no answer. She only got worse. He felt a mixture of sadness and acceptance in the room with her. He knew she would leave him, and he felt sorry for himself and everyone around him. He didn't want her to go, and before the sun had set, he talked to her while she slept. He told her he didn't know what to do and wanted her to stay. When he finished, he saw Jonas in the doorway, leaning on the frame, his eyes filled with sorrow.

"Son, when it's your time to go, you have to go," that was all he said, and then he left. Clayton took no offense. He actually took solace in his father's words. Clayton had overheard Jonas the day before talking to Doctor Brown. They were in Clayton's room discussing Emma's condition. Jonas was pleading to go in to see Emma, to comfort her.

"What if you get sick, Jonas?" Clayton heard through the wall.

"This ain't right, Doc. I can't hold her hand. I can't sit there and read the Lord's Word to her."

"And if you catch it, and you go too? Clayton isn't old enough to run this farm or raise that girl."

"It ain't right," Jonas repeated.

"Listen, you can stand in the doorway, call her from there. Talk to her."

"Clayton doesn't need to be hearing that stuff. Bad enough seeing his Momma die, but to watch his Pa blabber on like an idiot?" There was a pause as Jonas' words hung in the air.

"Maybe he does, Jonas," Dr. Brown said quietly.

Clayton stared out the window to the south. It had snowed the week before, followed by some unseasonable warmth. It left everything wet and muddy. Tonight was mild too, and he was thankful for that. His parent's bedroom could get cold during the November chill, and in his mother's condition, she was already trembling.

He stood watching the night. All was silent, except the wheezing from his mother. He looked up towards the barn where he spent most of his time. His breath fogged up the window as he leaned in.

Clayton felt he was instrumental in the success of his father's farm. For as long as he could remember, he helped Jonas with the sheep. After turning ten, he was allowed to care for them mostly independently. That was his specialty, sending them to graze, bathing them, shearing them, and protecting them. His skill at soaking cut wool was unmatched. It didn't felt after he washed and dried it, a feat that his father could never replicate no matter how many times Clayton demonstrated his technique.

The only thing Clayton dreaded while working were the moments he'd see Jonas coming to him in the field, his stride long and his pace quick with purpose. Clayton knew it was to tell him to bring a freshly skinned carcass and that they would eat well that next evening. It also meant Jonas would sell the rest of the meat and bones to the other thirteen families in the village, giving them money between wool harvests. He hated watching his father stroll nonchalantly up to him, look him in the eyes, and say the words, "Give us one."

Clayton never let on how much this bothered him. He'd nod to Jonas and turn back to the flock.

Clayton always chose the oldest or the weakest. One that stood away from the flock or lagged. He would lead the animal out, talking to the creature as he led it to the barn, saying words of encouragement and apology. His father had constructed a small pen where Clayton would guide the doomed creature inside. It needed to be inside this enclosure for an entire day to ensure its rumen was empty, making the whole process less disturbing. Confused and unable to turn around or move forward, the sheep would cry out in what Clayton thought were quizzical bleats.

Clayton would have trouble sleeping that night. He knew the job that awaited him in the morning. It wasn't the gore that bothered him. It was the act of killing that did. He understood why it had to die, the family needed money, and they needed food. Still, it was defenseless in a pen, trapped, waiting to be slaughtered. Clayton felt a bond between himself and the animal. He was with it out in the field protecting it, he would fetch it when it wandered away, and he was the one to take it out daily to eat. Clayton interpreted it as a trust between them, one he was about to betray.

He would enter the barn the following morning. The sheep would be angry from being left there overnight. Letting it be known through its cries and huffs that it wanted out of the tiny cage. Clayton would rush over to the workbench and grab the six-inch hunting knife. He paused at this moment; he didn't know why. He would turn and approach the animal, speaking softly, his right hand reaching out and petting it on the back of its neck. Once it calmed Clayton swiftly jammed the knife into the animal's throat.

He always turned away, not watching death take its hold. He made a mistake once and kept eye contact as an animal bled out before him. The images haunted him for weeks. So, he stood with his back to it as it died. He would wait for the sounds to stop, and even longer still, before finally opening the latch and retrieving the carcass to hang and skin. Clayton reminded himself to slow down during the skinning process on numerous occasions. His need to be out of the barn had led to blunders in the past. When he was finished, he would wheel the skinless husk down to his father before going back to the barn to retrieve the large bucket of organs and bring that to him as well. Jonas was always pleased with Clayton's work.

"Boy, you outdid yourself again," he'd tell Clayton every time. Jonas would run his hand through Clayton's hair and pull the remains out of the wheelbarrow by its hind.

"Thank you, sir. If you need me, I'll be at the house." And with that, he would take his leave. He would clean himself and spend the rest of the day with Emma, helping with her housework. Then later, he'd be with Eve, talking about the things outside of Clover, of which he knew very little about.

The sight of his reflection brought him back to the present. He barely recognized himself anymore. He was becoming a man. He was already tall and muscular like his father. Even at sixteen, with the work he did, he was becoming defined and strong. There wasn't much special about him outside of one thing. Clayton had the most peculiar shade of blue in his eyes. His eyes stood out from every other feature he had. Emma always told him that God was so pleased when He made him. He bestowed something unique upon him. Every other part from his brown hair to his thin face was plain.

"Have you come to take me?" Emma rasped from the bed. Clayton turned around and saw his mother staring off into the corner behind his shoulder.

"Shh, what is it, Mother?" Clayton rushed back to her side. She was wide awake now, her eyes glossed over. He hadn't seen her like this in three days. She usually was in and out, but her gaze was fixed off into the dark.

"I don't want to leave my babies, and I don't want to leave Jonas," she forced out.

"Momma," Clayton said as he knelt beside her and took her hand. "I'm here. We don't want you to leave either." He could feel himself losing control. He would start crying soon.

"This is my son. His name is Clayton." She lightly squeezed his hand.

"Who are you talking to?" He asked, looking around the room.

"The angel in the corner, the man." Her eyes never lost focus. Clayton sighed; he knew of fevers making people hallucinate. He stayed there for a long time, holding her hand, listening to her gasp for air.

"He hasn't?" She asked.

"What's that?"

"He said you haven't left my side," she croaked. A tear slid down Clayton's face.

"Of course, I haven't, but you should close your eyes and rest. You need to sleep."

"You are so good," she sighed. He let go; tears ran down his cheeks and off his chin. He could barely speak, choked as he was. He couldn't help her, and it was crushing his very soul.

"It's going to be alright, Momma. There's no one there. You just sleep."

"So good." She closed her eyes. Clayton looked to the empty corner one more time.

2

Clayton was half asleep, sitting up in his chair when it happened. He awoke, was uncomfortable, and went to take his spot on the floor where his pillow and blanket lay. He knew when he saw her face that she was gone. He watched her lifeless body for a long moment, wondering why this had to happen. He got on his knees and prayed for her, thankful that she could rest in peace.

He got it all out right then, he told her in whispers how much she meant to him, that no other person in his life would matter as much as she did, and he cried till his body was completely drained. There were no tears left to fall from his eyes, and his body ached. He was exhausted, but he knew no amount of sleep could fix this. It was as if he was disconnected from the world; everything was covered in a dense fog. Clayton's head was pounding as if someone was squeezing it every few seconds, and his stomach was in a tight knot. He couldn't concentrate, much less speak. He sat and wheezed, knowing this was the last real moment he would have with his mother, even though it was just her body. What made her wonderful was gone, and he thought it would be an eternity before he saw her again.

Clayton spent an hour grieving in the room with his mother before calling for his father. Jonas didn't enter the room; he stood in the doorway staring at them before telling Clayton he'd go and fetch Doctor Brown. He turned and walked away. Clayton sat in the corner his mother had been staring into and waited till sun-up. His father left and retrieved Doctor Brown, who came with another man he didn't know to take Emma's body away. Clayton had to take the sheets, blankets, and pillows outside and burn them. He didn't want to, but the doctor had suggested it to Jonas, so he asked Clayton to do it. He watched blankly as her bedding was reduced to ash.

Clayton was still quarantined in his parent's bedroom the next day, there was still the fear he may contract his mother's illness, but he showed no signs or symptoms. He was told by Doctor Brown he could attend her funeral as long as he stayed back from the people attending. If he felt ill in any way, be it a sore throat or a cough, he was to head home straight away.

Her funeral was presided over beautifully by the Reverend Price, who made Emma out to be a saint. He was powerful and pounded on the pulpit several times. He even stopped halfway through "God-fearing" because his emotions had taken hold, and he began to cry. He couldn't heap enough praise on her as a person, wife, and mother. There were many Amens from the village folk. They all respected her. Not one ever uttered an ill word about her. Reverend Price reminded everyone that Emma was best friends with his wife Mary, who had passed the winter before and that the two of them now were in God's arms.

Clayton had forgotten that Mary Price died only last year. It seemed so much longer. She was Emma's best friend, and Emma was crushed by the loss. Mary had been in her home, getting ready to cook supper, when she clutched her left breast and fell to the floor. Emma and Doctor Brown arrived simultaneously, but it was far too late. Emma had mourned her friend in her room for days.

Clayton didn't cry during his mother's funeral, and he didn't cry as they put the dirt over her casket. He was spent. The only things that kept him sane were the memories of her calling him down for breakfast, her crooked smile, and her hair that had just started showing gray. It began in a small streak by her temples, and she joked that Eve was the cause. That made him pause and smile, and he promised himself silently that he would make her proud as she watched him from the heavens.

They had food to last for days. It seemed like every family had cooked a meal for them. The evening after the funeral, every family in town stopped in one by one to pay their respects. He sat on the steps out back so they could come in the house and talk to Jonas and Eve. Clayton didn't want to scare anyone. The whole town knew he'd sat with her until the end. He knew people would be wary of him, plus he wanted to be alone with his thoughts.

The last of the village to visit right as the sun started to set was the Wards. John Ward was a small-framed man. His wife, Ruth, was a good three inches taller than him. Jonas always picked on John by calling him "little fella ." John would give it right back, usually insulting Jonas's intelligence. They were the best of friends. They were around each other every chance they got. With John being a fantastic carpenter, a practical magician with tools and wood, he always had work in town. He often took Jonas with him as his helper.

The Wards were one of the oldest families in Clover. They also had the largest to boot, Ruth had given birth to seven children, ranging from twenty to seven in age, but the one that mattered, the one Clayton went out of his way to speak to, was Amber, their third youngest, born two weeks before him in March. Clayton spoke to Amber at church, when their families got together for an outing, or when they visited. Amber would talk about how her father had promised to take her into Richmond the next time he had a job there, and Clayton would talk about herding the sheep. Clayton liked talking to Amber. She was humorous and beautiful, with long curly red hair and honey-colored eyes. Jonas also loved to point out that she was already taller than John.

Clayton was sitting on the back steps watching the sun pass behind the trees when he heard John speaking inside the house. He wanted to go in and say hello but knew he still could be a danger. So, he sat there, still dressed in the suit he wore to the funeral.

"They're still not letting you around anyone?" He heard from his left. He knew it was Amber.

"Nope, your family is last, though. Everyone else has already come and gone." He looked up at her. She was in a thick yellow dress with her hair up in a yellow ribbon. She looked fantastic. Nothing seemed out of place. "You look really pretty."

"Oh, this old thing?" She joked. "I just threw it on to hang out here in the mud with you."

"I'd invite you to sit beside me, but..."

"I know. I was told to stay away from you, but I think I'm far enough back." He watched her wrinkle her nose at him, and he smirked. He stared back down at his dress shoes. Her demeanor changed instantly, and she started forward but stopped.

"Clayton, I am so sorry about your Momma. I wanted to come and see you. They told me you sat with her through the whole thing. If they had let me, I would have come and been there for you. You know that, right?" She said. He nodded. He knew she would have. That was the kind of person she was, just like his mother said about him.

"Good," he said out loud.

"Excuse me?" She asked.

"Nothing," he answered. They stood in silence.

"There is so much I want to say to you." She looked away. "I just don't know how. I can't imagine losing my mother." Clayton looked over to her, but she didn't return his gaze.

"Go on. Just say it." He dropped his head and stared at the ground. "I think I kind of need someone to talk to me right now. I was with her for days, but we only spoke for a moment or two."

He sighed. "At the funeral, I couldn't go near anyone. Father and Eve have to stay away. I couldn't even go out and work. At least that would have kept my mind off things." She started towards him again, but he stopped her by saying, "Don't. The last thing I need is everyone upset that I didn't listen and you could get sick."

She froze in place, and he could see the frustration across her brow. She tightened her fists and took a deep breath.

"You're my friend, Clayton. Really my only friend," she stated matter of fact. She paused. He could tell she was embarrassed by her cheeks flushing. "I know what Emma meant to you. I feel helpless here. I want to do more than make you food." He smiled at her. To hear her call him her friend meant more than she could possibly know.

"You don't get out much, do you? If I'm your only friend."

"Not many girls our age here. Most are Eve's age, and they are a little hard to talk to." They shared a chuckle, and she continued. "You aren't childish like the other boys, Clayton. You work hard. You're respectable. You treat me like a lady."

He put his hand up and nodded. Amber had hit a soft spot with him. If she had been anyone else, he would have started crying, but he wouldn't do that in front of her. He wouldn't dare. He wanted her to say more. He couldn't explain how wonderful it made him feel, but he was exhausted. He couldn't take anymore.

"Amber got in trouble!" Alvin teased, appearing behind Amber. She turned around to her youngest brother, who was only seven.

"Hush now, Alvin. He doesn't care about that."

"She's in big trouble, Clayton! She hit Tom and hurt him bad!" He sang while bouncing around.

"Alvin, I swear. Do you want the switch?" She asked, annoyed.

"What did you do?" Clayton asked. "Why did you hit Thomas?" Thomas Brown was Doctor Brown's grandson. He was a little older than them both.

"It's not important," she waved him off.

"It is. Why did you do it?" Clayton asked. She paused.

"He thought it was cute to say to some boys that with your Momma dead, you didn't have anybody to run and tattle to anymore. So, I spun him around and hit him right in the eye."

"She blacked it good. It's all swollen! He ran away and told his grandpa, and he came to the house and yelled." Alvin chimed in. Clayton stared at her, and they locked eyes. Amber was biting her nails.

"She's too old to switch, but Pa is gonna make her work real hard this week. He told me she needs to act like a lady." Alvin spouted with pride, his tiny arms outstretched.

"He said nothing to you. He was talking to Mother." She corrected him sternly. Clayton burst out laughing. He couldn't help it.

"Stop it, Clayton. It was wrong." That only made him laugh harder.

"The thought of Tommy getting knocked for a loop by you is the only thing good about today," he snickered.

"I said quit," she started to grin. The laughter was infectious, and she broke down too. They both tried to stop, but their eyes would meet, and they would start all over again.

"What's so funny?" Alvin asked them, completely confused.

3

DECEMBER 1804

December was horrible that year. Just when Clayton thought the snow was going to let up, the sky dumped more, and it was bitter cold. The kind of chill that hurt his insides, deep into the bone. The farm was covered in thick white, and getting the sheep hay and taken care of wasn't easy while traipsing through a foot and a half of snow. None of them mentioned how much they missed Emma. To say her name would have brought complete despair down on the household, and that was the last thing they needed. On the days when the elements would let up, sometimes two or three in a row, Amber would stop by to help Clayton fix dinner or play with Eve. They would talk about the weather, about the farm, and casually mention what an asshole Thomas Brown was. They were becoming closer with each visit, and Clayton could feel a change in his feelings towards her.

Christmas was different for the Shaw family. Usually, Emma woke the family, and they sat by the fire. Things felt off without her around. Clayton tried his hardest to be cheerful for Eve, but not having his mother with him on Christmas was devastating. There was only one gift given out that morning; a doll for little Eve. One that John and Ruth had poured their hearts and souls into. It was exquisite, with a lovely red silk dress and a carved wooden face; they'd even whittled her hands. There probably wasn't a nicer toy around for miles. It looked like something a wealthy child would own. Clayton was certainly impressed. He had no idea Eve would be receiving it, and seeing her joy made his first Christmas without Emma a little less painful. As they prepared for church, Jonas called Clayton to his room and asked him to shut the door.

"Something wrong, sir?" Clayton asked.

"No, son, it's just Amber has a gift for you. I wasn't supposed to tell you, but she's going to give it to you after church." Jonas said. Clayton felt a twinge of panic.

"I have nothing to give her."

"I know, come here." He patted the side of the bed. Clayton paused but then sat down beside him. Jonas pulled a silver pendant necklace from his pocket. It shined in the morning light coming in through the window. It looked like an inverted teardrop with flowers engraved on it. Clayton had never seen it before.

"What is this?"

"It belonged to your mother."

"I don't remember-" he began.

"She never wore it. It was her mother's. She has a box of jewelry she never wore. It's mostly things from her side of the family."

"We don't talk much about them...have we ever talked about them?" Clayton asked.

"They didn't like me much and told me to stay away from her," Jonas chuckled. "They were an uppity bunch that thought I was a lower class of man, way beneath their baby girl. So, we saw each other in secret, and one day we left together and came here."

"Why would they think that?"

"I was a completely different man back then," Jonas said. Clayton had never heard his father speak this way before. He shuffled a little uncomfortably, wanting to let that end the conversation. Still, his curiosity got the better of him.

"How's that?"

"My life was going to send one of two ways, in a prison cell or by a bullet. My father was a horse thief and a card cheat, a real piece of work. I don't think he ever wore a shirt he didn't steal off someone else's back."

"Is that why we never met him?"

"I left him behind. I have no idea if he's even still alive." There was an awkward silence. Both of them didn't look at each other. They kept their eyes forward to avoid making it worse.

"I..." Jonas rubbed his hands together, lost in thought for a moment. "I was following in his footsteps. I was stealing everything that wasn't nailed down."

Clayton felt like he'd been punched in the stomach. He'd always seen his father as the most honorable man he knew. At times Jonas could be temperamental with the animals and get frustrated. Still, he never got the impression that he was anything but an upstanding family man.

"I met your mother in Richmond. I was going to rob a feed store. The man was old and brittle and wouldn't put up much of a fight. I'd kept watch on it for three days. On the fourth day, the day I was going to do it, the old man wasn't the one working. It was his daughter."

Clayton finally looked at his father. Jonas' face was filled with sorrow and regret. Clayton could tell it hurt Jonas to tell him about the man he used to be.

"I was going to hold her up, son. I had every intention. I was already in a foul mood. I was laid out drunk the night before. I had a raging headache, and I was low on cash, so I needed that money."

"Father, I don't think you should be-" Clayton started.

"Quiet, son, let me finish. This is important." Jonas stood with his back to Clayton, who sat and said nothing as he was told.

"She greeted me, and I looked into her eyes," Jonas ran his

hands through his dark black hair. "She was the most beautiful thing I'd ever seen. I told her I was just browsing." He paused and tilted his head ever so slightly. Clayton didn't want to speak up and interrupt, but he could tell Jonas was having a hard time finding the words. Jonas walked to the window and stared out of it, leaning against the frame.

"She asked me who on earth browsed a feed store," he chuckled. "She wanted to know what kind of animal I was buying food for," he turned his head back towards Clayton and smiled. "You know I never asked her if she thought I was there to rob the place? I wonder if she knew. I bet she did. She was the smart one."

"What happened next?" Clayton asked. Jonas turned back to look out the window.

"I told her I didn't have any, and she suggested sheep. Told me they were the easiest to take care of."

"Is that why we have sheep?" Clayton laughed. Jonas turned and looked at Clayton for the first time since he started.

"I just told you she was the smart one." Jonas walked back over and sat beside Clayton, this time facing him.

"I stayed in that feed store all day talking to her. She was the only person that ever made me laugh. I knew halfway through the day that I was going to marry her, or I was going to die trying."

"Really?"

"You bet. I made a promise right then and there that if I got that woman, I'd straighten up. Be a man."

"Well, you kept your promise."

"Wasn't easy. Your mother's family hated me. They had her life all planned out for her. She was to marry a family friend's son. She was to do as they said, and that was that."

"How did you get around that?" Clayton asked, enthralled.

"We'd sneak and meet. Her father found out about it and sent three men to talk with me."

"They beat you up?"

"Well, no," Jonas smiled, "I didn't get beat up." Even now, he was a large man, standing well over six feet with a thin but muscular frame. His cheekbones were high, and his jawline was square and clean-shaven. That was the first feature people noticed, how strong his face looked. His eyes were as dark as his hair, both nearly black. The eyelids narrow as if he was in a constant squint. Jonas had a very commanding presence, and his voice was low and scruffy. He could make anyone uneasy by just staring at him. Clayton knew that all too well.

"Things didn't go as planned?" Clayton asked, grinning back.

"I broke one man's jaw. The other I had to pull out of a mud puddle, or he'd have drowned. I knocked him out. The other fella ran away."

"What did you do then?"

"We had been sneaking around for weeks, but I'd hurt those boys pretty good. Her father would obviously get the law involved. That was one way to get me out of the picture. So, I asked her to leave with me."

"She left with you?"

"Emma told me that if we did this, I was going to marry her the second we got where we were going. We left that night. We had no idea where we would end up," Jonas shook his head. "We stopped here in Clover to start our life together, as husband and wife. Reverend Price married us. John helped me build this house. I got the sheep, and then we had you."

"I had no idea."

"It's not something we talked about. How would you have known? She was filled with dreams of being away from Richmond and her family. She wanted her own life. One she chose, one that made her happy. I made..." He placed his hand on Clayton's knee. Clayton could see the pain in his eyes.

"I made her happy. We couldn't wait to have kids and grow old side by side, and up until she took ill, everything was working that way." The room was; still Jonas had finished his story, and it was the most he'd ever let his guard down. Clayton had a newfound respect for his father. Not that he didn't have it before, but his perception of Jonas was different. He'd walked away from a life of deceit and villainy to one of a family man with honor and class.

Clayton's thoughts drifted to his mother. She changed this man and did it for the better. Her influence alone kept him out of jail or worse. Clayton loved her now more than ever. He was proud to be her son, and he was happy she got away from the people who held her down so that she could live the simple life she yearned for.

"Did her family ever come looking for the two of you?" Clayton asked.

"No," Jonas slapped his leg. "They were much older and passed on right before you were born. They didn't want to see her anyway. They claimed she disgraced them," he handed Clayton the necklace. "This should go to someone who deserves it, instead of wasting away in a box here. It's nice. I think she'll like it." Clayton stood and held the necklace up. It was a perfect gift.

"Do you think this is a little much? I mean, what will she think?"

"I see the way you're starting to look at her. She brightens you up, and the Lord knows you need it. She means a lot to you, and a gift like that shows it."

"I don't know what to say. Thank you, Father." Clayton felt embarrassed and looked away from him in an attempt to hide it. If Jonas could take all that just from Clayton's glancing at her, what was she noticing? What was the village thinking?

"I'm glad I could help you, son. Now one last thing. Do you know how to wrap a gift?"

"No."

"Shit," Jonas put his hands up to his lips and looked over at Clayton. "Sorry, boy." Clayton snorted a laugh.

"It's okay, Pa."

4

Clayton was nervous throughout church that morning. He kept peeking over at Amber, wondering what she possibly could have gotten him. She never matched his gaze. It looked like she was staring at the floor for the entire proceedings. She looked incredible though, her dress was blue with white frills. Jonas had to nudge him several times to pay attention to Reverend Price. He was thinking about what his father said, and it made sense. When she stepped into the room, it seemed brighter. The bitter cold didn't feel as harsh if he knew she would visit. He found himself looking out the front window on days she didn't arrive, wishing she was there. His mind was always wandering to her, things they did the day before, or something she said. Was this what a man felt for a woman? He was so confused. He didn't understand it in the slightest, but he knew being with her made him feel whole, and he cherished that.

Clayton approached Amber through the small crowd after the service.

"Hi, Merry Christmas," he said. She smiled at him

"Merry Christmas, Clayton. How was your morning?"

"Well, Eve got her doll. She couldn't be happier," he said. She looked him up and down.

"Yes, but how are you doing?" She asked seriously. He wasn't stupid.

"You mean my first Christmas without my mother?" He asked. She nodded, a little abashed. "It's quiet, different. It felt," he paused, thinking of how to say it. "I don't know, wrong?" Amber stood for a moment in silence, and then her face lit up.

"Oh! I got you a present." She rushed back to her pew, returning quickly with a package wrapped in brown shop paper.

"You didn't have to do that, Amber," he said as he held the gift in his hands.

"I know," she smirked, "but I like making you uncomfortable." He tore the paper to reveal a thick buckskin coat. It was heavy and perfect for the weather they were having.

"Oh my! Did you have your mother make this for me? This is amazing!" He exclaimed, holding it up. Ruth was well known in the village as a talented seamstress.

"Mother didn't make it. I did. Sure, she showed me, but this is all me. I started on it in November. Do you like it?" He stared at her, his mouth open.

"Oh, Amber, I don't know what to say. This is...this is too much."

"Do you like it?" She emphasized the question.

"It's one of the best Christmas gifts ever. I can't thank you enough." He removed his suit jacket and threw it on the pew in excitement. He put the new coat on and stared down at the arms. He hadn't been expecting such a wonderful gift, and he was amazed again that she made it by hand.

"Oh, I have a present for you too," he told her awkwardly, his face starting to flush. He noticed her smirking.

"Oh, really? You shouldn't have."

"Yes, I didn't have time to wrap it all fancy, but..." He removed the coat, placed it on the pew next to him, fumbled around inside his suit pocket, and pulled out the necklace. "I hope you like it. Merry Christmas, Amber." He took her hand and placed the pendant in her palm. She stared down at it for what felt to him like an eternity in utter silence.

"I thought you were joking. Where did you get this?" She was pale, and her voice was hushed.

"It belonged to my mother." He scratched the side of his head and stared at the necklace in her hand. "I wanted you to have it."

She let out a soft cry. Clayton hadn't expected this reaction. What had he done wrong? He thought of his father saying, "Shit," when he didn't know how to wrap. Was that it? Clayton didn't think wrapping it meant that much to her. She was weeping, and he could tell she was fighting to hold the tears back, unsuccessfully so.

"I'm sorry, Amber. If you don't like it, I can take it back."

"No!" She shook her head violently. "I love it. I-I'm sorry. Excuse me." She turned and rushed towards the back of the church, far away from him. He contemplated going after her, but Reverend Price stepped up beside him.

"Everything alright?"

"I think I messed up, sir."

"How so?"

"Well, Amber gave me a present, this coat here, she made it," Clayton picked it up and showed him. "My father gave me a silver necklace that belonged to my mother to give to her, and she started crying. I think I should have wrapped it."

Reverend Price was a heavy-set, older man with bushy gray hair, a solid beard that looked almost white, and an eyepatch on his right eye. He'd lost it in a fight against the British during the war. He was a loud man but pleasant enough. He'd known Clayton since the day of his birth. Clayton noticed the reverend's suit was getting too small for him as if his stomach might pop out any second. He looked silly. His eye stared down at Clayton, brown and hazy, and his cheeks were crimson. Clayton could smell whiskey on the reverend's breath. Reverend Price had taken a liking to the bottle after Mary died.

"Well, Clayton, maybe she was overcome with joy. With everything that happened in your family recently, she probably wasn't expecting a gift from you."

"I guess."

"It was a nice gesture. Would you like for me to talk to Amber?"

"Please, sir?" The reverend walked by Clayton and off in her direction. Clayton took his coat, met up with his father, and asked to go home.

5

JANUARY 1805

Amber stopped by during January when she could and acted as if nothing had happened. She was back to being herself, so Clayton didn't want to mention it to her. He enjoyed her visits. They ate and talked when they weren't being interrupted by Eve. He was becoming closer to her. Clayton let his mind drift to her whenever he could.

February had a smattering of snow here and there, but mostly the temperatures stayed up. Amber came by nearly every evening, making the ones where she didn't excruciating. He rushed through his work during the day to get up to the house, to make it more presentable for when she arrived. Clayton would always greet her at the door, and off they'd go to start dinner for the family. She was teaching him how to cook, and he was getting to the point where he didn't have to ask what to do next.

Amber was already an essential part of Clayton's life, but now she was impacting Eve and Jonas as well. Eve would follow Amber around, reminding her that she'd promised to pick flowers with her when they came in bloom. She'd bring her doll and tell her all about their adventures together. Clayton would eventually have to shoo Eve away. He was a bit selfish when it came to Amber. There just didn't seem to be enough time during her visits. It was as if she had arrived, and before he knew it, she was leaving.

It was the last day of February, and they sat at the dining table talking about the Richmond Enquirer she'd brought with her. John had purchased the latest issue on his trip to the city. It mostly contained political articles that neither Clayton nor Amber could follow properly. Still, the Lewis and Clark expedition story was what she was excited to share. Clayton listened attentively as she read aloud about the dangers they would face and how the writer wondered if any of them would come back alive. He could tell how much it meant to her by how passionately she read to him. Her fingers followed along as she went. He cherished moments like this, watching her eyes flow left to the right and how she'd slow down on the difficult words, pronouncing them phonetically. He'd grown to appreciate every tiny detail about her.

Once she finished the article, she wanted to discuss it, and he was astonished at how much it enthralled her. She had a sense of adventure when they were younger, but he chalked that up to their age at the time. She hadn't outgrown it, and if Clayton was being honest, it was only getting stronger. It was then that he'd noticed the sun was down, meaning she had stayed later than usual, and he insisted on walking her home. It wasn't too far, but he didn't want her roaming around alone after dark. The conversation was mostly about what she'd read to him, but he decided to change the subject once they neared her home.

"Our birthdays are right around the corner," he reminded her.

"Mine is first," she mocked. "You're just a baby to me."

"Shut it," he joked. "Will you be stopping by on your birthday?"

"I can't. Mother has plans for me. Did you need something?"

"Eve and I were thinking of baking you a cake."

"Oh, Eve planned that out?" She raised an eyebrow and grinned at him.

"Alright, I wanted to do something nice for you on your birthday." He admitted trying to hide his disappointment at the thought of her not coming.

"Why?" She was almost on her front porch.

"Because I messed up Christmas."

"What are you talking about?" She laughed.

"I made you cry. I should have thought of something else. I'm really sorry," Clayton stared at the mud.

"Oh," her face fell. "No, not at all." She reached down in the neckline of her dress and produced the inverted teardrop. "I wear it every day. I rarely take it off. It's the best Christmas present I've ever gotten. I didn't know I made you feel that way, Clayton," she said. He let out the breath he didn't realize he was holding.

"That's a relief."

"I'm sorry, I should have said something. I was just a little taken aback by it."

"I thought it was where I didn't wrap it." He said shyly with his eyes locked on the porch to avoid looking at her. After a few moments, he heard her speak.

"Clayton, I... I think I'm in..." He looked up, noticing the change in her tone. She wasn't facing him. Her hands were clutching the front of her dress near her waist. The smile that adorned her face all day was gone. Something was troubling her.

"Are you alright?" He asked with growing concern. The front door opened behind her, and Ruth stood in the doorway.

"I thought I heard you. I'm glad you're home. Hello Clayton, dear, how are you?"

"I'm great, Mrs. Ward. Yourself?"

"Not so good right now. I'm afraid we got a bit of stomach trouble in here with John and the boys," Ruth sighed.

"Oh no. I'm sorry to hear that."

"Amber, I could use your help. Alvin is throwing a fit." Ruth sounded desperate, and with the circles under her eyes and her hair unkempt, Clayton could tell she was having a rough go of watching after everyone. Amber looked back at Clayton.

"Sorry, I have to go. I'll stop by soon."

"Sure. You all try to have a good night. I hope everyone feels better," he said. Amber walked through the doorway; Ruth stepped aside before nodding to Clayton.

"Good night," Ruth said and shut the door. He didn't see Amber Friday, Saturday, or in church. She wasn't around the following week either. As the sun was setting on her birthday, he walked to her homestead and knocked on the door. Her brother, Alan, answered and told him she was ill. She had caught what the rest of the family had suffered from and was still queasy. He asked Alan to give her his best and went home upset. When he got home, his father shook his head.

"Clayton, son, you have it bad," he said. She wasn't in church the following Sunday either, and now Clayton couldn't get her out of his mind. On his birthday, he walked back to her home and found her father sitting on the porch.

"I know why you're here," John teased coyly.

"Hi, Mr. Ward, is Amber available?" He asked as he climbed the steps.

"How many times have I asked you to call me John?" He scoffed at Clayton. "You aren't ten anymore."

"You know I won't do that," Clayton said. John nodded his head in agreement.

"I swear, your father should hit his knees every night thanking the Lord for you. My boys couldn't find manners if I drew them a map."

"Thank you, sir," Clayton said, feeling a tinge of pride.

"You're welcome," he stared at Clayton as he picked up the mug sitting beside him on a barrel, "but I have some bad news for you." He took a drink from his cup. "She's still sick. I've told her to stay away from everybody. She'll be alright one minute, but the next? She can't even hold water. I've had Doc over a couple of times. Says she's kept the illness we've passed around."

"That's terrible." He let his disappointment show across his face. "Could you give her my best?"

"I sure will." John thought for a moment and then looked around sneakily to see if anyone was listening. He held out his cup. "Want a tug of this?"

"What is it?" Clayton took the cup from him and looked inside.

"Some shine from the Cyrus boys. This batch ain't too bad. Last one burned the hair off my chest."

"You have hair on your chest?" Clayton joked.

"Woah, like father like son, eh?" He slapped his knee and laughed. "That was a good one!" Clayton shook his head at the offer of the cup and handed it back. John shrugged and took a drink.

"Well, tell her I stopped by, please? She's been in my thoughts." Clayton said. John grinned from ear to ear.

"I'm sure she has," he taunted. "I'll have her Momma tell her. I ain't going around that. I had that sickness a few weeks back, and I spent practically two days in that outhouse. It's no joke."

Clayton stepped off the porch and started the trek back home, only turning back to wave goodbye. Amber was all he thought about. He didn't know if he could make it another week without her. Not seeing her was maddening. Did she miss him half as much as he yearned for her?

6

MARCH 24TH, 1805

Clayton finished putting the sheep away for the evening, the sky was darkening, and a nasty storm was brewing. He could feel the electricity from the clouds, and the wind had picked up. Clayton was wiping the sweat from his brow when off in the distance, he saw Amber beyond the fence, walking the road towards his house. He could tell it was her the second he squinted. He was overjoyed. She was finally back. He started towards her, as he didn't want her stuck out in the downpour that was coming. He called out her name, but she didn't seem to hear him, so he trotted towards the fence and hopped over it. He had a nagging sense that something was off, a prickling feeling at the back of his neck. He picked up his pace. The grass was high but offered no resistance as he rushed towards her at the edge of the field.

"Amber!" He yelled when he was sure she was in earshot. She turned to the sound of his voice, and he saw her face, pale, almost ghostly. He stopped for a moment. She looked so sickly, he was taken aback. She had been moving slowly but was now at a complete stop, only swaying back and forth. She looked as if she might topple over. He ran towards her again, his left hand outstretched to catch her.

"Amber!" He raised his voice over the wind as he took her arm, "Are you okay?" She faked a smile.

"I'm fine. I'm just still under the weather, is all. I thought the fresh air would do me good, and I hadn't seen you in forever."

"It's about to storm. I need to get you inside. Can you walk?"

"Oh," she grinned. "I'm not so sure." He guided her to sit on the grass.

"You stay right here while I go get the horse. Will you do that for me?" He said sternly.

"I promise, I'll be right here when you get back."

Clayton broke into a sprint, his heart pounding as he raced back to the barn to get Charley. Charley had been part of the family for most of Clayton's life. A bay quarter horse that was the offspring of one Jonas brought from Richmond, Charley was muscular for his size and quite timid. The saddle was a gift from the Reverend Price from his time during the Revolutionary War. It was oversized, faded, and chipped but did the job. The last thing Clayton did every workday was remove the saddle if his father had forgotten. Clayton prayed that this was one of those times. He reached the barn, and his hands were shaking as he opened the door. Charley looked up at him.

"Charley, come," Clayton ordered, keeping his voice monotone to not frighten him. Charley trotted over to where Clayton was standing, next to where he kept the blankets. He used them sometimes to take a break from the cold during the winter. Clayton breathed a sigh of relief. The saddle was still on. Clayton picked up a few of the heavier blankets and sniffed them. He found one that wasn't soured, folded it, and threw it over his shoulder. Clayton placed his foot in the stirrup and swung his leg up and over the horse. Charley seemed not to mind. Clayton was good to him, overfed him, and talked to him constantly when they were stuck in the barn together.

Clayton thought again of Amber in the field and felt a renewed surge of panic. She didn't look well, and he didn't want to leave her alone. He gripped the blanket. He would use it to keep the rain off of her. He didn't want her to get soaked, especially if she had a fever. "Boy, what in the world are you doing?" Jonas called to him as Clayton emerged from the barn. Clayton turned to see him standing next to the door.

"It's Amber. She's down by the south fence and can barely walk. She's real sick, sir. I'm going to get her and take her home."

"Well, go on," he slapped Charley on the buttocks. "Get!"

Clayton galloped along the road up into the tall grass on the south side of their property. He could see her in the distance. She was standing again. Charley wasn't used to going this fast and let it be known that he didn't like it, but Clayton edged him on.

"Woah!" He yelled as he came up beside her. "You okay?" He grabbed the blanket and hopped down from Charley. "I was hoping you wouldn't move."

"You don't have to do this."

"Nonsense, you're not well. You need my help."

"Clayton, I don't think I've recovered yet. I should have stayed home," she looked at him and smiled. Clayton took her arm and guided her to the horse's left side. With what little strength she had and his guiding hand, Amber mounted Charley. She seemed to sway, and Clayton kept his hands on her to keep her steady. He handed her the blanket.

"Take this. The storm will hit soon, and I wouldn't want you to add a cold on top of it."

"Always a gentleman."

He placed one foot in the stirrup and swung his leg awkwardly over Charley's back, trying not to disturb Amber. He steadied her with his hands before reaching around her to take the reins. He was sitting to the back of the saddle, but he wasn't worried about his comfort.

"You alright?" He asked her.

She nodded.

He needed to get her home before this storm hit, and he needed to be sure she was going to be alright. She looked up into his eyes and smiled weakly.

"Want me to take it slow?" he asked her.

"Please," she said. Clayton gently nudged Charley, who was quite happy to be going at this pace.

"I'm already feeling better," she proclaimed.

"Thank the Lord. You had me worried for a spell."

"I'm just not over whatever father brought back from Richmond."

"I'm sorry. I wish there was something I could do." A sprinkle began, and she wrapped herself in the blanket. She gazed back at Clayton and nestled up close against him. His stomach did a small flip. He had never been so close to her, and her smell was heavenly. *Even in sickness*, he thought, *she's an angel*. She was leaning hard against him. They rode for a while in silence, and as they got to the small dirt road that led to her home, she finally spoke again.

"You do care about me, don't you? What would you consider us? Friends? Best friends?"

He didn't know what to say, he didn't want to sound childish or silly, but he also wanted to answer her. He didn't want to show this side to her yet. He didn't even know what this side was. A best friend didn't do his feelings justice, so he thought about how his mother would want him to answer her. She would like him to tell the truth. So he did.

"You're my everything," he said. He heard her gasp in surprise. He hadn't meant for it to come out like that, but it was too late. He could feel her tight against him. She was looking up to him with an expression he didn't recognize. She took her hand and guided his face towards hers. Their lips met, and the outside world was gone. The kiss was slow, deep, and he felt through this tiny connection they were made for one another. She pulled back and stared deep into his eyes like she was looking at everything that made him, him.

"You are a good man, Clayton Shaw," she whispered.

They arrived at her house, and Clayton jumped out of the saddle. He hurried around to hold both her hands as he helped her down. She went up to the porch and tossed his blanket back to him.

"I am feeling much better, Clayton. Thank you kindly." She turned to leave, paused, and looked back at him over her shoulder. "Can I come to see you tomorrow? If I feel better?"

"Please do," he said over the rain. Amber smiled and went inside. It took him a second to get his senses. He mounted Charley and adjusted himself in the saddle.

"Let's get home," he told Charley. The ride home was quick, and Clayton kept reaching up and touching his lips. He could not remember a time in his short life where he experienced such happiness. He rode in a daze till he made it back to the barn. He put Charley back in his stall, patted him.

"Don't tell anyone, alright?" He told Charley as he unsaddled him.

He skipped dinner that evening. He couldn't have eaten if he tried. He stood by the fire, drying off the rain, lost in the memory of their kiss. He was off to bed as darkness fell but had trouble falling asleep because his mind wouldn't shut down. He replayed the moment over and over again in his thoughts. The storm was pounding now, which would make tomorrow's chores harder, but he didn't care. There was nothing that could break him tonight.

He hoped she would be fine for tomorrow. She could come to see him, and maybe, just maybe, he could kiss her again. No, that was too forward, he thought. Perhaps he could hold her hand. That put a smile on his face.

He tossed again, this time remembering his mother and how she always spoke of proper ladies. Amber was a lady. She was beautiful and classy, and he knew now that he loved her. He believed in love, and at the young age of seventeen, he thought he'd found it. It was always right there in Clover, just down the road. His best friend, who would one day be his wife. It gave him a warm feeling of comfort. His body relaxed, and he was finally able to close his eyes and doze off.

7

"S on," Jonas spoke softly. Clayton's eyes opened, and he looked towards the window; noticing where the sun was, he shot straight up in bed.

"I'm sorry, Father, the rain kept me up. I didn't mean to oversleep." He hadn't just laid in bed too long. This was inexcusable. Clayton looked at his father, standing at the foot of his bed, hat in hand and his face practically buried in his chest. He was dressed, but not for work. He was wearing his best church clothes.

"Son," he continued. "Get up, put on your best, and meet me out on the front porch."

"Is everything alright, sir?"

"Do as I ask, Clayton." His father marched out of the room with purpose, and Clayton rose out of bed and began to disrobe. His best was in the open closet to the left in his room, not that he had much of one. A nightstand, a bed, an oil lamp, and a footstool.

Clayton quickly put on his suit that felt a little snug and hurried to meet his father outside. On his way through the house, he didn't see Eve, and a lump formed in his throat. What if something happened to her? He quickened his step. When he reached the doorway, he saw his father sitting in his chair, and Eve was standing in front of him in one of her best dresses. Jonas stood the second he saw Clayton, but Clayton's eyes were on Eve. He was relieved to see her. She looked like a doll in her white dress. That's when everything dawned on him. Why in the world, on a Monday, were they in their church clothing?

"Father, is everything alright?"

"No, son, it isn't." Eve let out a small moan. She was starting to cry. Clayton understood something terrible had happened.

"Who?" He asked, knowing full well why they were dressed up. It was to visit a family, to pay respects. His father stumbled over his words. He hesitated and glared around out into the field. Before he could get the words out, Eve turned to face him, her cheeks wet from tears.

"Amber died," she whimpered.

8

THE AFTER

Feme was beautiful. In fact, at one point, it could be said she was the most beautiful woman on planet Earth. One would be hard-pressed to find anyone who would argue that fact. Men had murdered for her, stolen for her, and started wars for her if rumors were to be believed. Many paid money just to sit in her chambers to speak to her while she lay naked in her bed. To be allowed to touch her at the height of her notoriety was divine. At that point in her life, one couldn't pay her for her affection. One must be chosen, then one could pay her for affection. Countless had lied and claimed they'd been selected. She gave the rumors, not a moment's thought. Most of the stories they told would have been better than the actual act itself, and it only added to her legend. She was adored by many and worshipped by even more.

Feme owned one of the nicest upper-class homes in all of Egypt. It sat at the edge of the city of Shedet, with three luxurious floors and decorated with gifts given by the men who visited its halls. She made sure everything was clean, in order, and spotless. This was not a house of ill repute but an oasis. A place for a man to escape, where she and her proteges would take the lonely, the tired, the stressed, and the wealthy to heights of pleasure they had never seen before. Yes, it is called the oldest profession, but Feme was the one who perfected it.

There is no place in man's history books for her, but there should be volumes given the things she knew and the stories she could tell. Men at their most vulnerable would tell her their most intimate secrets. Confessions they never told their wives, comrades in arms, and children. People revealed their deepest secrets to her, and she always kept them. She never betrayed anyone who was a client. That was part of her code and one of the reasons her brothel was chosen by so many.

Her parents had passed very early, and Feme had to fend for herself. She was always stunning. She turned heads wherever she went, but she had no talents or real skills. She wasn't going to make an exceptional wife. She was too sassy and wouldn't cook, even for herself. She did odd jobs for people who felt sorry for her loss, cleaning mostly, for the wealthy, the ones she wished every night to be. She was charismatic and had an unnatural level of charm. Finding work, food, and places to lay her head were a nonissue. The turning point came when she gave herself to an older man who handed her a silver ring afterward. He came back two nights later and, upon leaving, gave her more silver. He came back many times over the next month, bringing her all sorts of gifts. She assumed this would lead to courtship and her being wed. He was the captain of the night guard. She could do much worse.

She soon found out he was already married and had four strapping boys. Instead of rushing home to his so-called beloved, he was coming to her and giving her his pay, plus anything else he could fleece off people roaming the night streets. He was addicted to her. She was dumbfounded when his wife came to her and gave her a family jewel, begging her to stop. She understood then how powerful her body was, and not only that, she was brilliant. A great deal more intelligent than almost everyone who darkened her door. She made friends with women in the same profession, learned from them, listened to their tales, forged an aggressive but tender style, perfected her craft, and built an empire.

The difference between herself and several other women who were paid for their company was her highly selective nature. She learned quickly how to sell herself. She built a myth about her being the greatest lover in all the lands. Was it true? Probably not, but that wasn't the point. What mattered was that every man believed it, and most did. As her legend grew, so did her wealth, which afforded her the home, jewels, fine clothing, wine, and protection. Along with all of the luxuries, the one she coveted the most was her power. She never abused it, but knowing she wielded it was more than enough for her.

She brought in other women to her home. Some were down on their luck, some abandoned, some just lost. She took them in and gave them swagger and style. She taught them to be unique and have the confidence to look a man in the eye and tell them what they wanted to hear. She allowed the rumors of her teaching these women the art of love to spread throughout the kingdom. She loved them, and she protected them. They became her daughters since she could not bear children of her own.

All she had to do was walk through the sitting room and passionately kiss one of her girls. She didn't have to speak, just make sure the men waiting saw, and then that girl could command almost any price she wanted for her company. As the sun would come up, the women would laugh and jest at how easy this was. She allowed them to keep their coin, their presents, for she loved to see them happy. She trusted them because most of them had nothing when they arrived. She believed these women felt the same for her. She thought that they were family. She had given them a new lease on life and got them paid for something they would have done for free in marriage to men.

But she was betrayed by one of her own, Amisi. One of the first to live with Feme and one of the originals to still be with her at the time of her death. Amisi held a lot of power in the home. Her opinions and words had weight. Things Feme didn't have time for, she would let Amisi oversee. Feme had great respect for her. They had been so close. She was the last one Feme or anyone else that knew them would expect to hurt her.

Amisi, and the man that had poisoned her mind with whispers of betrayal, poisoned Feme during an evening's festivities in honor of the goddess Beset. Amisi had been the one to give Feme the wine laced with the powder her lover had asked her to mix in. Feme knew instantly something was wrong. She stumbled back into the courtyard and fell against a small stone bench. She sat in the sand, with her senses failing, wondering how this could be her end. It was then Amisi knelt beside her, a wicked grin across her face, and Feme knew.

"Why?" Feme choked out. Her throat was closing shut. It wouldn't belong.

"I deserve so much more," Amisi whispered.

"I gave you my world."

"You only gave me a fraction of it." Amisi stood, smiling as her lover came to her side and wrapped his arms around her. He was the captain of the night guard. The man Feme turned away for a jewel a few years earlier. Feme floated off into death, watching them embrace.

Once Feme ascended to her position in the After, she checked on Amisi's fate. It was a perk of her job. She was able to review anyone's life entirely. She was killed by her lover the same night Feme was. That man had betrayed them both. He took control of her empire and sold most of her girls off into slavery. The ones who resisted or tried to escape were murdered. It infuriated her when her mind drifted to these thoughts, but it did bring her a sadistic joy to know Amisi's plan had failed.

Feme sat at her desk, looking through papers for any irregularities. This was the worst part of her day, if one could even call it that. It was just time smashed together. Day and night were meaningless, along with hours and minutes. She hated checking and double-checking to see if anyone had made a mistake. Mistakes were not an option here, everything had to be perfect, or the consequences were extreme. Her time here had turned her cold and bitter. She arrived angry over her death, and it had festered for millennia.

The office was large and mostly bare, except her desk and its fading, chipping wood. The walls were a nasty yellow. She was sure they had been white at one point, but age had given them a sickly hue. No pictures adorned the walls, and there were no windows to gaze out. There was a lamp here from a period utterly foreign to her, and her pen and quill had seen better days. This was as good as it got, checking paperwork and telling people what to do. She only left to go to someone else's office, and usually, that was only to raise her voice. Their offices were always worse than hers, and that was just depressing, so she put it off as long as she could.

At one time, her hair was the darkest black, nearly iridescent as a crow's wing, and envied by every woman she'd ever met in her life. Now it was gray from root to tip. She refused to trim a fraction of it, so it still flowed down to her waist. There was a brush in her desk, and when she had lulls in her work, she would pull it out, close her dark brown eyes, and brush it. She would pretend she was back in her room, and she had a moment before going downstairs to entertain. She brushed slowly and thought of the taste of wine, bread, and a kiss. She would give all her memories for a kiss and someone to tell her how special she was. She had no time for brushing now. The paperwork had to be completed.

She stared down at her hands. Her skin was loose, and her fingers thin and boney. The dark, beautiful skin that commanded gold just to touch it was wrinkled and dry. She hated the way she looked, the lines under her eyes, her breasts sinking on her chest.

Age had been cruel to her. And that was the real issue for her. She stopped counting after she passed two thousand years. She knew she was being punished and had no idea for how long, but was it fair to age her?

At the time of her murder, she was twenty-nine. She had no idea how old she was now. Time seemed to flow slowly for her. She believed she was somewhere that the sun and moon did not exist. There was no release in sleep. She couldn't; she'd tried on several occasions to nod off at her desk. All she had was her work. It was frustrating to her because the rules here weren't set in stone. They varied from person to person. She dealt with people in the office constantly, and none of them seemed to age as quickly as she was at first. Then it stopped. She was trapped in this elderly body, a shell of what she used to be. She hated the sight of herself. She'd gained weight even though she'd eaten nothing and her skin felt leathery and dry. She was so vain in life. She knew she was beautiful, and for her to lose that beauty was the worst punishment of all.

She'd seen enough in her long time here to know that this was part of the plan. Feme had feared growing old; in her lifetime, she would constantly check her appearance, she loved to look at herself. She had a bronze metal disk polished to shine, which she kept by her bedside. She would pick it up several times a day just to look at herself. A similar disk was in one of the drawers to her desk, and she hadn't looked at it in ages. The last time she glanced at herself, she was mortified to see an older woman staring back at her. She thought how unnatural she looked and wept for hours. She refused to touch it. She'd always assumed she wouldn't age here. It was bad enough she was dead, but to have aging thrown on top of it all was cruel.

Her thoughts drifted to when she passed over. She remembered how painful it was. When the string that held her soul to the mortal world was severed, it was as if her spirit was ablaze. Her own death was nowhere near as painful, and once she got here? She stubbed her toe on the edge of the very desk in front of her now. She remembered crying out.

"Motherfucker!" She reached out towards her foot. Jawara, her predecessor, laughed at her the entire time. "This isn't how this is supposed to be!" She yelled out to him, shocked and angry, that she still felt pain even after death. There was enough of that while she was alive. Jawara was an ancient African tribal chief. For all the time they spent together, she couldn't remember exactly what part of Africa he hailed from. She was appreciative of how he tried to help her come to terms with her death, but she was angry over the betrayal. She would snap at anyone that looked at her cross, including him, and the centuries had only made her worse.

So, here she was in this office with no windows and no way to tell time, just paperwork and the occasional visitor she summoned. She rarely got to get out of her tiny space in the After. She didn't like people to see her, and she much less enjoyed interacting with anyone. All she had were these assignments and a prayer that she would pay off all her sins and be promoted soon to transcend. A piece of paper appeared on her desk as if by magic. She had seen it happen a thousand times before, but this paper was red with black lettering, which meant this took precedence. She picked it up and scanned it over. The contents were surprising and unexpected.

9

"**T**akis!" She called out to the air. A few seconds later, there was a knock at her door. "Come in! I called you, didn't I?" She said, already irritated. In stepped a mountain of a man. Bald, with a dark brown beard past his neck, his leather sandals barely made a sound as he shuffled in front of her desk. His large stomach almost touched the edge of it. He was easily six foot four and 370 pounds on his best day. Everything about him seemed enormous, from the size of his feet to his voice; even his brown eyes looked unnaturally large.

"Hey, Feme," he said brightly. "My, you look lovely today."

"Shut up, Greek, I've had enough lips on my ass today. I don't need to add yours. Are you still wearing that silly Chlamys? You look ridiculous. Go ask Astrid to get you something more modern. You'll frighten people. It's already confusing enough without you showing up in a greek cloak covered in wine stains. Times have changed, and you've been warned," she hissed. He looked wounded by her remarks.

"Feme, it's all I have left. Don't take that from me."

"It smells, and you look stupid."

"Well, I have nothing else."

"That's why you are going to march down to Astrid's office and get new clothes. Today. As in when you leave this office," she demanded.

"Okay." He looked down at his stomach, defeated.

"Good, besides today is your lucky day." She slid a document across the desk towards him and leaned back in her chair. His immense hands picked up the sheet slowly. He looked at her with astonishment.

"A promotion?"

"Yes, you are getting a partner. You need to show him the ropes. He will be on baby detail, which I am sure he'll love," she sighed, "and no, I don't know for how long, but every person that's ever gotten a partner transcended next time up. He's a seventeen-year-old boy by the name of Clayton Shaw." She studied his face for a moment. She thought he would be ecstatic to get a partner. This was the first step to his transcendence, but he didn't let it show if he was excited. She expected more from him. He wasn't his usual animated self.

"By Zeus, is he American?"

"Yes, is that a problem?" She could sense the disappointment coming from his large Greek brow as he shook his head no.

"Spit it out, man. I have things to get done."

"Americans get really depressed when they get here. They have this idea of-" he started. She held up her hand.

"You don't get to pick your partner."

"That isn't what I meant, Feme."

"Sounds that way to me," she snapped back. She was itching for a fight. She raised her eyebrows and placed her hands flat on the desk. She was being confrontational for the sake of it.

"No, he's perfect. When will I get him?" He straightened up and looked down at the paper in his hands.

"He dies today. You are to bring him directly to me once he's able."

"Why? I can handle it." Takis asked.

"Because this is important." She told him frankly.

"And so is the rest of my work. What makes this any different," he snarked.

"Because I do not want another fuck-up like you. If previous experience has taught us anything, you are more than likely on your way out. What I need is someone better than you. Someone who takes things more seriously, and that starts with me telling this boy the rules."

Takis opened his mouth as if to speak but stopped himself.

"You were saying?" Feme sneered.

"Where's his life list?" He held out his hand, waiting for a stack of papers.

"You're holding it."

"What?" He asked, shocked, turning the lone piece of paper over in his hands. "This is only one page."

"I know, everyone has a novel to sort through anymore. Even though he is only seventeen, it's light on content." He checked the list up and down.

"Feme, this boy doesn't belong with me. This boy doesn't belong here. This should be a straight trip to the River." He paused. "For Aphrodite's sake, he's never played with his front tail."

"Look at the end," she said. Takis's eyes darted to the very last thing on the page. His mouth gaped open in shock. As he slowly looked up at Feme, she nodded her head.

"Kills himself!" He barked. "What for?"

10

MARCH 25TH, 1805

CLOVER, VIRGINIA

No one spoke on the way towards the Ward homestead. Clayton sat in the back of the cart in disbelief, the reality not dawning on him yet. He hadn't said a word since finding out Amber passed away in the middle of the night. His sister was staring at Jonas, who was guiding Charley up the road. Jonas didn't dare look over at her. He knew if he did, she would begin to cry again. Jonas hated to hear Eve cry, he didn't know how to handle situations like that and normally ushered her off to Clayton, but that wasn't an option now. Jonas' mind wouldn't stop playing the scene from this morning over again in his head.

When the sun had barely been a thin line in the east, Jonas was awoken by a knocking at his door. He didn't want Eve waking, so he hurried to the door to find Reverend Price standing there without color in his face.

"What's happened, Donald?" Jonas asked. The reverend was shaking almost uncontrollably.

"I'm sorry to get you up this early. I wouldn't if it wasn't important," Reverend Price stuttered.

"Are you alright?" Jonas stepped out into the cold in his gray greatcoat and long underwear. Reverend Price didn't hesitate.

"Amber Ward bled out in her bed last night. They tried to save her, but she didn't make it."

"Bled out? Wait, she's dead?"

"Yes, I heard the commotion during the night and woke up." The Wards lived across the road from Reverend Price. "Ruth was screaming. I made it to the house and stood outside with the family while Doc tried to save her life." Jonas put his hands on his head.

"Clayton said she was sick. She was here on the road last night, and he took her home. Right before the storm." Jonas paced back and forth. "You don't know how he feels about that girl, Donald. He just lost his mother, and now this! What should I say to him?"

"When he came back from taking her home, did he say she was in that bad of shape?"

"No," Jonas still paced. "He was happy. He was so uppity he didn't eat dinner."

"I was with the family when William came outside and told them. It was awful. No parent should bury their child. It's times like these I have to trust in God. I had no idea she was that sick."

"I'm sorry, Donald. I have to get ready to go to John, and I have to think of what I'm going to say to Clayton when he gets up. I can't tell you how much I appreciate you stopping by."

"It's okay Jonas, I just came by hoping to get some answers. I've prayed all morning, and I've shed some tears. I'll see you later," the reverend said.

Jonas missed his wife terribly. He had no idea how to handle this. She would have been so comforting to Clayton and Eve. She always knew the right things to say in moments like this. How many times, he wondered, had she calmed him down or made him laugh when things were at their worst? He silently prayed to her now, asking for her guidance, begging her for help.

This ride, which was a simple five-minute trip, had already felt like hours by the time they neared the Ward's home. Jonas pulled the reins at the crossroad leading to their destination, and he turned to look back at Clayton, who had not moved or spoken at all.

"Son, I know you are upset. I know this is a shock." He paused for a second, choosing his next words carefully. "John and Ruth are going to be devastated. I don't know what I would do if I lost either of you. This is going to be rough. Offer your condolences, don't say anything to offend. We won't be staying long." Jonas didn't wait for a reply. He gave a quick flip of the reins, and Charley started down the dirt road.

Jonas didn't want to do this, but he loved John Ward like a brother, and he wanted to show John the same courtesy he showed Jonas when Emma passed away. John was the one he wanted to talk to after Emma was gone, and he made sure to let the family know that if they needed anything, all they had to do was ask. He stopped the cart short of their massive front porch and stood up. Jonas helped Eve down first and leaped down to the ground.

"Are you up for this ?" He walked around to the back of the cart where Clayton was sitting. Clayton didn't answer, only stared off into the distance. Standing on the porch was Amber's eldest brother, Alan. His hands were in his pockets, and he was looking at Jonas with fear and nervousness. He ran his fingers through his red hair and stared at the front door, then back to Jonas. He came down from the porch quickly and hurried toward them.

"Jonas, I don't think this is a very good time," Alan said. Jonas felt confused for a second. He took his hat off and held it in both of his hands.

"I'm sorry, Alan. We came to say we are sorry for what happened, and if there is anything we cou-" he started.

"Is that a joke?" Alan said, trying to hide his anger. His blue eyes narrowed, and the corners of his mouth pinched in disgust. Jonas was taken aback.

"Excuse me, young man?"

"Haven't your family done enough? What are you trying to do by coming here?" Alan spat. Jonas looked at Eve and asked her to walk away for a second.

"Listen, Alan, there is no need to insult me. I came here to offer help."

"My sister is dead, Mr. Shaw and your son-" Alan stopped short, and both he and Jonas turned to the sound of the front door opening. Ruth emerged, heading straight for them, her eyes puffy and her face red with anger. Her dress made a swoosh sound as she glided down the steps. She was staring straight through Jonas. Jonas had never seen her so angry; he'd never even seen her slightly upset. He went to speak to her, but she sailed right past him to Clayton sitting on the edge of the cart. She brought her hand up and slapped Clayton as hard as she could across the face. He tumbled off the cart and into the dirt.

"How dare you!" She screamed. "How dare you show your face here!" Jonas rushed over to pick up his son.

"Ruth, what in the name of God are you doing?" He yelled. Clayton was holding his face. He was staring at her with tears welling up in his eyes, his mouth open wide in shock.

"You brought her home to die!" She continued. "You didn't come in and tell us what was going on! You just left her to die in her sleep!" Her rage boiled over. Her eyes darted from Jonas to Clayton.

"He had no idea she was going to die, Ruth! You need to calm down, now! And don't you dare touch my son again." Jonas noticed Alan tense up. He watched as Alan reached out and placed his hand on his mother's shoulder.

"Careful, Momma. You know what he was before he got here," he said. Ruth's face soured.

"He doesn't frighten me. I don't care what he's done. What his boy did is unforgivable."

Jonas couldn't believe the nerve of this woman; he understood she was grief-stricken, but to blame his teenage son for their daughter's death when Clayton was as upset as they were, if not more so? Alan stepped in between Jonas and his mother.

"Just leave. No one wants you here."

"We came here to pay respects, and you insult us this way? You're lucky I don't kill you," Jonas growled. He clenched his fist and held it up for Alan to see.

"You owe me, Jonas!" John called from the porch. Jonas looked up to the top step of the porch to see his friend, disheveled and eyes filled with sadness.

"Will you please tell me what the hell is going on here, John? There's no need for this. We're friends, by God, we're family." Jonas' fists were still balled up tight. John stepped down off the porch.

"Why don't you ask Clayton?"

"John, the boy, is a wreck. He loved that girl. I loved that girl."

"She was with child!" Ruth wailed. "She miscarried and bled to death in her bed!" The silence was deafening, no one moved, no one said a word, it was as if the wind had stopped, and time was still.

11

"**B**oy?" Jonas asked. He did not turn to look at Clayton staring blanking into the distance. Clayton didn't answer. Jonas was silent, he could imagine Clayton struggling, and that's when he heard it.

The boy is ignoring you.

The anger took hold instantly. How dare his son dismiss him.

"CLAYTON!" Jonas bellowed.

"Y-yes, sir?" Clayton gasped in shock. Jonas still had his back to him, so he couldn't get a read on the boy's face.

"What do you have to say about this?" Jonas heard Clayton step forward.

"Nothing, sir, I didn't know," Clayton said. Ruth hissed, and Alan shook his head in disgust. John stood very still, his face a mask.

"I asked you a question; I want an answer," Jonas growled, rounding on Clayton.

"And I answered it," Clayton insisted. He recalled to everyone the exact details from the night before; he left nothing out, including what he told Amber and the kiss. "Mrs. Ward, you must understand. I would never, not before we were wed, and I wouldn't ask for her hand without asking Mr. Ward's blessing first. I don't know what's happening here, but I swear to you, on the grave of my mother, I loved her. I would never do anything to sully her name or reputation. I kissed her yesterday, and for that, I'm sorry, but *that* never once crossed my mind."

Ruth started to cry again, and Alan held her against his chest. John walked towards Clayton, his eyes watering, and Clayton took a step back.

"I don't believe you!" Came the slurred speech of Reverend Price. He stumbled across the road, obviously intoxicated. "Amber cried and ran away from you at Christmas, remember?" The reverend had his finger pointed directly at Clayton. It seemed as if he could barely hold himself up.

"Yes, I thought the present upset her, but she said that wasn't it." Clayton's voice was rising. He put his hands up defenselessly, palms towards the reverend.

"You had me go after her, and I did." Reverend Price continued, his bleary eyes fixed on Clayton.

"You said you would go talk to her, and I left with my family," Clayton snapped back. Reverend Price stumbled forward a step.

"And I did, and she told me you gave her a necklace from your mother, and she felt you were trying to force her into a relationship."

"No. We were best friends. I wouldn't do that," Clayton stammered as he frantically backed away.

"She said you were becoming aggressive," Reverend Price finished shaking his head with resentment.

"That isn't true," Clayton began to shake and turned to face Jonas. "She told me the gift was perfect. She was constantly wearing it. If she felt that way, she never spoke of it."

Jonas heard it again.

Lying little shit. This is what happens when you raise them soft.

He wasn't just angry; he was infuriated. Jonas backhanded

Clayton across the mouth, blood bloomed on his bottom lip. He fell into the dirt again.

"You lie! And on your mother's grave? What kind of boy did I raise?" Jonas screamed. Clayton scrambled to his feet, his hand on his mouth. Jonas had to catch himself; he hadn't been this angry in decades. He wanted to hit him again and again. Jonas knew if he started, there would be no chance of stopping.

"I didn't do anything wrong!" Clayton cried out through his fingers. Jonas reached down, picked Eve up, and placed her on the wooden seat.

"Papa, what's going on? Why are you mad at Clayton?"

"Nothing, sweetheart, everyone is just upset," he told her as he climbed up into his seat. He glared down at Ruth, who was crying again. His heart sank for a moment, she was heaving uncontrollably, and Jonas' rage waned.

"Ruth, John, I am so sorry for what has happened here today. I know I can never make this right, but I damn sure will punish this boy, and believe me, he will suffer for what he's done."

"Just go," Ruth sobbed. Jonas took the reins in his hands.

"Come on, Clayton." Jonas looked around, but he wasn't there. Clayton had disappeared.

12

THE AFTER

"**I**s there anything else?" Takis asked Feme.

"Why would there be?" She asked in return. Takis breathed a loud sigh.

"Feme?"

"Takis?"

"Can I just say," he looked her in the eye, "I know you don't think too highly of the Greeks, and I know you've been here a long time. Longer than I have." Feme leaned back in her chair. "This place is draining; it takes something from you the longer you're here. Zeus knows it's driven me to the brink of madness," Takis continued, and she smiled. "So, why is it you and I never have a kind word for one another? Everything is always right on the edge of a fight. Can't you and I have one meeting where we exchange pleasantries?"

"Takis, I don't know what to say," she replied, and Takis smiled back. "So, maybe we can go sit down and have a nice lunch? Talk about our day? Oh, wait, no. No, we can't do that because if we don't do our jobs, we're stuck in this shit even longer." Her voice raised, and she slowly stood. Her expression turned to anger. "What are you, lonely? Do you need a friend? Go cry on that

57

naked monster's shoulder. Here there is work to be done. This is not a vacation, you Greek dumbass."

"There she is," he glared at her in disgust. She pressed her hands down on her desk.

"You have something else to say to me?"

"No, Feme. I've got nothing left to say to you," he sneered.

"Then get out of my fucking office!" She yelled into his face. Takis stepped out of Feme's office and shut the door to the sound of her still cursing. He couldn't stand being around her. It was like being forced to sit in a chair made of solid ice. She didn't break him today though, he was wearing a grin from ear to ear. He'd not gotten a promotion the entirety of his time served so far. He was sure Feme was angry about it, which made the day a little more bearable. Sure, he'd been shifted to other jobs, but they were lateral moves. If what Feme said was true, this may be his upward turn out of this place. He started down the hallway, trying to contain his excitement. No one showed happiness here. People were miserable, at the very least depressed by their workload, and jealousy ran rampant inside this building. He just wanted to go get Clayton, and for once, have someone with him to pass the time while he worked.

Takis felt a tingle of excitement for the first time in what seemed like forever. Could this be the way home for him? The chance to see his wife and son and finally atone for his mistakes? Takis had been stuck in this place for almost two thousand years, a prisoner of his sins as a living man. He had watched so many souls cross over, excited to see a loved one on the other side. Now he was one step closer to having that feeling himself. He stopped in the middle of the hall and took a deep breath. He couldn't wait to get out of this place.

"Okay, so what did you do this time?" A voice asked from behind him. Takis turned and saw his friend, Nix, almost upon him. He hadn't seen Nix since somewhere around the 1300s, and it was just recently he'd thought about Nix and wondered if he'd moved on.

"It must have been bad. I've called your name three times. I was about to hit you," Nix jested. Nix was a Denisovan, an ancestor of modern man that predated even the neanderthals. He was the oldest person in this place when Takis arrived in 177 BCE and was one of the few people who said hello to him in the hallway. No one knew much about Nix. When Takis would ask, most would say Nix had always "been" there. Which led to the burning question of what he'd done in life to be trapped here for so long.

He was a scary sight to behold. Seven feet tall and extremely muscular, a nose taking up half his face and his tiny chin made him look like a caricature. His hair was pulled back in a ponytail, coarse and grey, and receding from his gigantic forehead. His mouth was wide, hiding his enormous yellow, stained teeth, and his eyes were sunken into his face, making his massive brow the feature most people noticed first. He was slumped forward slightly, meaning if he stood straight up, he would easily add another five inches to his frame. He didn't wear clothing. He was covered in a thick layer of black hair. Nix told Takis once that Feme had begged him to put on something to cover his massive penis. She explained to him that was the last thing people wanted to see after the tragedy of death. Still, he refused, saying he didn't like the feeling of anything against his skin and anyway he'd been doing this long before she arrived, and he wasn't changing for her.

Takis met Nix properly at Pompeii in the year 79. They were the only two tasked with ushering everyone into their rightful places, taking people to and fro, and trying to explain to them what just happened. All who met Nix were afraid of him, and Takis would have to drop what he was doing and explain to the poor soul that it would be alright and that this monstrosity wouldn't hurt them. It was just his job. Nix was grateful to Takis that day, and whenever the two got the chance to speak after that, they did.

"My friend!" Takis cried out and clapped Nix on the back. "Where have you been?"

"Working," Nix said, raising an eyebrow. "I see you haven't moved on yet."

"No, they've had me taking women to the crossing for a while now. Forget about me; why haven't I seen you around?"

"I took over Acquisitions," Nix shrugged.

"Really? I just thought the other day I hadn't seen you in so long."

"I think I got it about five hundred years ago; it's nice to work. I'm alone a lot of the time."

Takis thought that Nix had been punished for something. Feme and Nix hated one another, not just hatred, but disdain for the ages. They never had a kind word for one another or to each other. Whenever they were close, you could see it written on their faces. Feme was nasty to everyone, but she held a special type of cruelty for Nix. Not that Nix didn't give it right back. He was the only one who didn't put up with her abuse.

"That's great," Takis said. "You always hated being out in the field."

"I know, especially now. Could you imagine me picking up someone today?" They both shared a laugh. Nix studied Takis' face for a moment.

"So, what did she want?" Nix asked. Takis looked around and leaned in.

"I'm getting a partner," he said, hushed. Nix went wide-eyed and whispered back.

"Get out of here. Seriously?"

"Yes, a seventeen-year-old boy. I'm picking him up shortly."

"Grooming your replacement. You'll be out of here sooner than you think. I'm happy for you, Takis." Nix patted Takis' shoulder with his massive hand.

"You want to go with me? Scare the shit out of him?"

"No, I can't. I just had an important drop-off, and I have to see

Feme." His voice lowered when he said her name. He couldn't hide his already rising anger.

"Alright, Nix, but don't be a stranger. I can't believe I'm saying this, but I missed you." Nix smiled and brushed past Takis, opened Feme's door, and entered. The last thing he heard before the door closed was Nix speaking to her.

"Feme, I'm surprised you have clothing on!"

Takis watched the door for a moment before he said,

"Clayton Shaw final moment," and turned around 180 degrees. In front of him was a door, not a door to any of the offices, but somewhere else. He opened it slowly and stepped through to a gully.

13

THE WORLD

The sun was up, and Takis could see the trees were starting to regrow their leaves. He was happy to see some green, the last couple of places he'd been to were deserts, and Takis always hated the sand. He watched a deer run past him, unaware that he was there. His sandals didn't make noise, for he had no weight. This always made him chuckle because of his size. He could feel the sun, though, and the breeze was lovely, a tad chilly for the way he was dressed, but he didn't mind.

This was the spot. His senses had sharpened over the many years. His instinct was telling him Clayton Shaw would die a few feet in front of him, so he stopped and leaned against a tree. It wouldn't be long now. Something seemed familiar about this place, even though he knew he'd never been there before. He watched as another deer stopped and took a drink from a small stream. Takis wondered what Clayton would be like. His life list suggested someone innocent. He'd have to watch himself around him a bit; Takis wasn't known for his subtle ways. He lived his life that way, and he was boisterous even here in the After.

Takis was happy that he was outdoors, that this wasn't happening in some musty room somewhere. He loved the sounds of nature and enjoyed being out and about in the sunlight. It reminded him of when he was alive. The world was constantly changing, people were different, Takis didn't understand them anymore. He gave up trying centuries ago. But who was he to judge? After all, Takis' last living thought was how much he regretted his life.

He had always been flirtatious, and he loved wine, but he'd never strayed from his wife, Lipa, before. When he did, it was with his daughter-in-law. He tried to lie his way out of it, he denied the encounter ever happened, he swore on Zeus, he swore on anything that came to his mind, but she knew the truth. The letter was in her hand.

When the denials didn't work, Takis blamed the drink. He told her he didn't remember much of the encounters, but that was another lie, for this had happened while he was stone sober. Takis was never an attractive man, nor was his wife one of the most beautiful in all of Macedonia, but they were suitable for one another. They fit, and he should have appreciated her more.

Takis should have told the truth. He should have said it started with an innocent remark, that he realized he wasn't a strong or young man anymore, that he wasn't a gift from Aphrodite. He was Takis, the son of a butcher and the brother of a hero.

Takis lived in the shadow of that brother. He hid his insecurities with an outgoing personality. Takis was always trying to be the life of the party, the humorous one, the clown, but inside he was dying. His brother was one of Perseus' finest, a man of impeccable character. Lucius was a warrior of little equal and a legend among the army, the pride of his bloodline. Compared to him, Takis saw himself as an afterthought and a joke.

It started one evening at the kapileion he owned. Takis' establishment was the most successful around. He always mingled with the patrons, and it was extremely popular with soldiers because of his connection to Lucius. He had always taken care of the place alone, and it was wearing on him, so he brought his daughter-in-law, Phile, to work. They had a great relationship, and she was an excellent employee.

She had been with him every day for a month while Leon, his son, was training for Perseus' army. Leon wanted to be like Lucius; he idolized him, which weighed heavily on Takis. His son would beam with pride whenever he mentioned Lucius, and Takis never once heard Leon brag about the kapileion. He could only recall one time his son ever stepped foot inside the property. So, it was no surprise when Leon enlisted to fight for the glory of Greece. Leon had left for training, and Takis didn't want Phile to be alone at night. He'd needed the help, so he offered her a serving position, and she was remarkable at it.

They had closed for the evening, and she had remarked how a soldier had asked her to take him home. Takis snickered and told her if she wasn't so lovely, things like that wouldn't happen. He could tell she was moved by his response, and she asked him if he thought she was enchanting. Takis, at that point, should have said yes and left it at that.

Yet he couldn't resist. Instead, he showered her with compliments and even broke into song. Phile was young, petite, pretty, and very thin for a Greek housewife. There was hardly anything to her except her hair, which she kept braided and long, to the back of her knees. It was a source of great pride for her. People always mentioned her hair. She didn't come from much money. Her father and mother made bread.

Takis was playing the fool when it began, but when Phile reached out and grabbed his manhood and kissed his chest, things had gotten much more serious. Before Takis had time to reassess the situation, he was already in the act. They were together on a table in the back of his kapileion, and he'd never been with a woman this beautiful. Phile put on a show for him. She was loud, saying his name, telling him he was amazing, and moving with him in rhythm. He'd never experienced anything like that before, and when he finished, he was speechless. He stood there while she lay on the table covered in sweat, he wanted to say something, but it all seemed surreal. She went home without a word, and he did the same, confused and ashamed.

The next day his wife could tell something was wrong with him, but he was short and told her he didn't feel well. That evening Phile and Takis worked late into the night without a word between them. He intended to tell her it was a mistake and it should never be spoken of again. He wanted to apologize to her for what had transpired because he believed it was all his fault. He had done her a grave injustice and hoped that it would be left in the past. This was something that would ruin four lives, and he would never want to intentionally hurt Leon or Lipa. It was despicable. So, they worked in silence, and after the last customer had exited, Takis approached her in the back before counting the coin for the night. He opened his mouth as she turned to face him.

"Phile," he began, but she had moved towards him. Her hands were all over him, and again it happened. This time she shoved him down atop a table and climbed up on him, something new to him. His wife didn't do these things. Phile was aggressive, and Takis found himself swept away by her ferocity. From then on, each night they closed the taverna down, they made love. The more it happened, the less Takis felt guilty. He thought she was a fantastic lover, and he lusted for her every moment they were apart. Phile fed Takis' ego by telling him how attractive he was, that no one could make her laugh like he could. She called him infectious, and she made him feel wonderful.

He knew what they were doing was wrong, and if anyone found out, the empire would take his property, shame him, and she'd be put to death. He had thought about calling it off, but he was addicted to her. He couldn't bring himself to do it.

"Run away with me," Phile pleaded, her head resting on Takis's chest after a particularly memorable night together. "We could take what we need and leave Macedonia behind. Start something new. Together."

"You know we can't do that. We both have too much here." Takis kissed her head. Phile did not mention it again. Instead, she would bring love letters to him nightly, as she explained to him that it was hard for her to express herself in person. Her father had taught her to read and write, and she used it well. He couldn't believe that someone felt so strongly towards him. Takis loved getting her letters; she was poetic. That is until she told him Leon was to return in a week, and she could not face him. She couldn't be with him for the rest of her life. Takis wondered if they should leave together. His wife, Lipa, had always been there for him. She'd always taken care of him, but she didn't make him feel special. Phile made Takis feel like a king, and for once in his life, he felt he had something his brother would covet.

Takis was moving barrels to the front of the bar when his wife came in. Her face was hard as stone, and her eyes burned with wrath. That was the night she showed him the letter, the very one Leon had come home to find. He had injured his hip during training, and they sent him home to heal before being shipped out for a campaign in the north. His son read one of Phile's confessions of love and was devastated. He took the letter straight to his mother, and they both tried to make sense of it. Takis didn't believe that Lipa knew what Leon had planned as she confronted Takis in the empty taverna. Leon was silent as he came up behind Takis, apologizing profusely and stumbling over his words. The knife was cold at first, then Takis' lungs felt hot, and he couldn't take a breath. He fell to his knees, looking over his shoulder to see Leon, his hands covered in blood. He had been murdered by his son, and he thought rightfully so. What father betrays a son like that?

"Sorry," he croaked. His last word as he lay dying, staring up at his Lipa, whom he had failed spectacularly.

14

MARCH 25TH, 1805

THE WORLD

Clayton's lungs burned, he'd run until his body couldn't go any farther, and he knew he was no longer on the Ward property. His eyes stung from the tears. The pain in his chest was from his broken heart, not from physical exertion. He had not only lost the one thing in his life that made complete sense, but he also had nowhere to go and no one to turn to. Why didn't she tell him? Did she know she was pregnant? Who was the father?

He could see how Ruth jumped to conclusions. They were always together, and they were quite close, though not close enough, or she would have told him. Everyone in town would assume he did that to her. He couldn't believe she would lay with someone. *There has to be more to this,* he thought. There had to be something else, something that he was missing. He touched his lip but instantly pulled his hand away. It was already swollen, and it throbbed. His father had never struck him before, and he'd never seen him so angry. Jonas didn't believe him, and Clayton was telling the truth. The Reverend Price didn't have confidence in him either. If Amber thought the gift was too forward, why not just give it back? He would have understood. She told him on the front porch that it was wonderful. She was even wearing it. Did she lie to him?

All the thoughts about how much he cared for her, all the things he told himself, it was all shattered this morning. She was gone, and he was alone. He didn't have friends; little Eve wouldn't understand. He had no one to talk to, he had no one to turn to, all he had were the emotions swirling in his head and the feeling that he was going to vomit. His hands shook, and as his adrenaline was wearing off, a sense of hopelessness had ebbed in. He placed his hand against a tree and bent double. He'd run a long distance; he was almost a mile and a half from the Ward home.

He was struggling to get air. He just had to get away from all of them and their accusations. He kept replaying the thought of her looking back at him. It was the last time he'd ever see her.

"Why?" He asked aloud. Clayton had run to a spot above a gully where children played. He was standing in the tall grass on the overlook, a long way above the small creek bed. The hillside had eroded back at a sharp angle; most people never came up this far. It was quite breathtaking in the spring as the leaves were beginning to come back to life, and Clayton could see a fair distance. His father had taken him up here once or twice when they were hunting to see if deer were drinking water down below, and at this moment, one was.

He stood there, crying, looking out over the Virginia woodlands, filled with pain and regret. The breeze picked up, and he closed his eyes as his feet came close to where the ground abruptly ended. He had never dealt with emotions as powerful as these before, and it takes a strong man to push them down. Clayton wasn't a strong man; he wasn't a man at all. He was still a boy. A boy who had lost his mother, lost the respect of his father, lost the girl he thought was his best friend, and to top it all off, he was being blamed for her death.

His thoughts turned to God, and he wondered why the Lord had taken so much from him. He deserved better. He did as he was told and followed the scripture as best he could. He had no hate in his heart, he tried to show everyone and everything respect and compassion, and at the end of the day, all he was given was loss. That's when he heard it, it was faint, but it was there. In the back of his mind, he heard a small voice.

Just step forward.

Clayton tensed; he didn't understand what his mind had told him to do. But he heard it again, louder. The breeze was gone; there were no sounds of the birds, the leaves, nothing save the voice.

Just step forward; the pain will disappear.

Clayton's mind slowly began to wander. He was lost in a sea of thoughts. He felt as if he should step forward; it made sense. He was hurting in a way he couldn't describe. A pain so pure he'd give anything to make it go away. It was consuming every corner of his mind, and he couldn't make it stop.

It hurts, doesn't it?

"Yes," he answered himself.

You don't deserve this. What do you have to go back to? If you leave, where will you go?

"I know." He kept his eyes shut tight. Instead of turning, opening his eyes, and heading back to the road, Clayton stuck his left foot out over the hillside and hung above the gully. The voice called out to him one last time.

Forward.

15

He opened his eyes and snapped back to his senses, but he was already leaning forward, and gravity had taken hold.

"No!" He shouted and tried to pull his foot back.

It was too late. His weight pulled him off the edge, and he was falling down, face first, toward a large rock below. He was surprised at how quickly the ground was rushing towards him. He knew he was going to die; he didn't want to.

He wished he could go back to yesterday, and instead of taking Amber home, he would have taken her to Doctor Brown. She would still be alive, he wouldn't be about to die, and his father wouldn't hate him. He had let his mother down. The thought of her watching him from heaven, saying, "Oh sweetheart, why?" was gut-wrenching. He thought of Eve being alone with Jonas and growing up, slowly forgetting about him. How long before he would be found? Who would find him? Would anyone find him, or would he end up in the belly of some animal?

He hoped if anyone did find his body, they would think this was an accident. He didn't want Eve knowing that her brother leaned into his death and plummeted to this rock below on purpose. Suicide was a sin, he knew that, and he was praying for forgiveness as he was near the ground.

He tried to stop it; he tried to pull his foot back. He hoped God had seen that part. He hoped that it got him some sort of reprieve. Clayton feared Hell; he knew what was waiting for him on the other side. He didn't want his life to end like this; there was so much left to do. He thought of Amber; he hoped he would at least get to talk to her before he was cast into the Lake of Fire.

16

CHRISTMAS DAY, 1804

"Get away from me," Amber said through tears near the back of the church. She had just left Clayton standing alone, and she felt like such a fool. His mother had passed barely a month ago, and he'd shown such strength. He had just given her a beautiful necklace that belonged to his mother. It was the sweetest thing she'd ever heard of, something out of a fairy tale, and all she could think of was what this man did to her.

"Amber. If this is to stay between us, you cannot break down like this," he said, not looking her in the eye but gazing around the room to see if anyone was watching.

"I'm no-" She raised her voice.

"Keep your voice down, young lady," he warned.

"I'm not breaking down. We made a mistake. I should have never let you touch me. I am so ashamed of myself," she said in a hushed tone. Reverend Price looked Amber up and down.

"Now, dear, you know that's not true."

"It is true. This is not the way it's supposed to be. You're a man of God, and I think you lied to me. You don't love me; you don't think I'm beautiful. You said all those things to me, and I believed you. You only wanted me for sin." She was to the point of hyster-

72

ics. Her wide eyes poured tears, and her mouth contorted in a grimace of pain.

"I told you what I felt. I thought what was happening between us was special. You know I love you."

"Stop it, you horrible man," she cried into her hand.

"Shut your mouth, girl. You were there with me. You were just as much a part of that as I was," he sneered. She blamed herself; she hated herself for what she did with this man. She wanted him out of her sight. She wanted to take it back. What would her parents say? She was sure her father would disown her.

"I want you away from me. Now. I'll go tell my pa," she threatened. She had struck a nerve, he'd almost taken a step back, and for a brief second, she saw fear. He was afraid of her. He didn't want her to tell anyone, and she relaxed for a moment. She felt as if she had the upper hand. She was starting to regain control until he recovered his own composure and smiled at her.

"I saw you give Clayton that coat. That was a little much, don't you think?"

"Clayton deserved that coat. He works hard outdoors, he's a good man, and he cares about me."

"He gave you a necklace that belonged to his mother? His deceased mother?"

"What are you going on about?" She wasn't crying anymore; his tone had her frozen.

"Such a special gift to give a friend, wouldn't you say? I mean, what on earth would possess someone to give something so special? I'm sure if I told them I saw you two out behind this very church with his hands all over you, what would they say?" She looked hard at his face. He was serious. He would lie and tell her parents she was improper with Clayton.

"You wouldn't dare," she said weakly.

"Oh yes, I would, Amber. Who are they going to believe? Me, a man of the Lord? Or you and the boy giving you his dead mother's priceless jewelry?"

She looked for Clayton, but he wasn't where she'd left him.

"Listen, girl, I asked you if this was what you wanted, and you said yes. You never once told me to stop. If anyone should be upset, it's me. I thought you loved me."

"You are a liar," she could barely speak.

"And you are a whore. You tell anyone, and I will ruin you and that boy forever. You keep your mouth shut."

He's serious. Your reputation will be ruined. They will believe him over you. Your parents will hate you. Clayton will be shunned. This is all your fault.

The words felt like ice running down her spine. Her mind wandered to Clayton and how the town felt about him. How all the elders respected him. How they looked to him as what a young man should be. He would hate her. She would have to tell him why this was happening. She would have to tell him the horrible thing she did. She would have to say she laid with this man, unwed. He would lose his honor over her, and he did nothing wrong.

Guilt crept over her, and it was unbearable. She would give her soul to take it all back. She had given herself away to someone unworthy. She knew better. Why had she done it? What came over her that afternoon? She was sickened with herself after it happened. The same feeling she was having now.

"Just stay away. Leave us alone," she said, looking up into his eyes

"It never happened. Say it," he said forcefully and grabbed her arm.

"It never happened," she gritted out. Reverend Price smiled, nodded, and stumbled away as the whiskey started to take hold.

17

MARCH 25TH, 1805

It was over quickly; there was no entirety of his short life passing before his eyes. There wasn't even a moment to put his hands up. His forehead struck first, and Clayton felt a warmth spread through the crown of his head. He didn't feel pain but heat. His final living thought was of Amber's kiss before he exited life as he knew it, and the darkness enveloped him.

18

SOMEWHERE IN BETWEEN

"Why, boy?" Takis asked the lifeless body at his feet. "There are easier ways to do that." Takis stared at the mangled mess of what was Clayton Shaw.

The boy's face was almost unrecognizable, and his suit was covered in blood. One of the bones in his right arm pierced through the skin and cloth, and his legs were bent in unnatural directions. Takis put his hand up to his forehead and turned away. Despite all the horrors he had seen in life and the After, these sorts of things never ceased to disturb him. Life, Takis knew, was something too precious to simply give up on.

"Hurry up," he said, looking around. "I don't want to be here when someone finds you." It made the job easier when the deceased was alone, which often didn't happen. He hated being in a room where family and friends mourned over the death. It made talking to the recently departed even more difficult, and he didn't want Clayton to be found by someone who cared.

"I mean, most of you is on that rock; what more life could you have left?" Takis complained, tapping his foot impatiently. Takis had to wait until Clayton was completely dead. The soul wouldn't leave the body until the entirety of life was snuffed out.

This was the easy part. Once he met Clayton, the real horror began. The questions, the crying, the denial, and then, worst of all, when he realized everything he believed would be waiting for him, wasn't. Takis had seen that particular look of sadness that slowly rose across someone's face far too often. He thought of the day he died, and Hermes wasn't there for him. No Hades, no Acheron, just his handler, and his new existence of gathering the dead and sorting them along to their fates. He could still remember his first few days as a soul retriever. He thought Zeus was playing a trick on him. It couldn't be this boring or depressing, even if it was the Underworld.

Takis was looking up at the gloomy overcast clouds that had moved in when he heard Clayton's soul scream as it was ejected from his body. An exact duplicate of the young man flung violently off to the side. Takis turned, and his eyes shot down to Clayton laying beside his body, howling in excruciating pain. Dressed the same way as he was at death and curled up in the fetal position, Clayton was in intense agony.

"It's alright, boy!" Takis yelled. "It will pass." For the next minute, Clayton writhed on the ground, whimpering as the small rope of light that connected the Achilles heel of his soul and the one on his right foot were severed. He could feel the boy's pain. Everyone had to go through it. He reached down, picked Clayton up off the ground, and set him on his feet. Takis patted him on the shoulder.

It took time, but Clayton finally opened his tear-filled eyes as he tried to get his bearings. He wiped at his left eye first and stared up into the face of Takis, smiling down at him. He still had his hand on Clayton's shoulder, steadying him and making shushing noises. Clayton put his hand out and braced himself on Takis' chest.

"I -" Clayton began, "I fell."

"No, Clayton, my boy. You didn't," Takis sighed.

"I'm alright. I'm hurt, but I'm alright."

"No, you're not," Takis said softly. Clayton saw his body dead on the ground and tried to jerk away, but Takis held him in place with his hands on his shoulders. Clayton stared at the body, his eyes were wide, and he was trying to speak. Takis let him whimper for a while.

"I'm dead, aren't I?" Clayton finally spoke up.

"Yes, you are."

"Oh, no," Clayton cried. Takis took his hands off Clayton's shoulders.

"It's going to be alright. I'm here for you. Take a moment and get your wits, Clayton. I know you are a little off, and this is a lot. Just take a deep- "

"You're here to take me to Hell, aren't you?" Clayton interrupted, his voice rising in panic.

"Hell?" Takis asked, not prepared for the question. "Oh, right, right. No, I am not here to take you to the Darkness." Clayton stared blankly at him. The tears had stopped. He could tell the boy was confused.

"I killed myself. I'm damned."

"Yes, but you're not damned," Takis shrugged.

"I'm not?" Clayton sighed; a sound of relief crept into his voice.

"No." Takis knew all of this was coming. In the centuries he'd been doing this, he had perfected talking to people. It was where the skills he had acquired in life came in handy.

He knew to start quickly to take their mind off of things. He could deflect and occupy them to keep them from thinking about the ones they were leaving behind, the mistakes or regrets they had, to not dwell on the fact that they were no longer living. This would be the start of another chapter, a new beginning, a brand new existence.

"Alright, let's get the formalities out of the way. Clayton Shaw's life list," with a flick of his wrist, a piece of paper appeared in Takis' hand. Clayton was startled and took a step back. Takis looked at him and nodded. "Just wait, you haven't seen anything yet. Clayton Shaw, my name is Takis," he began with a comical bow. "I am here to retrieve your soul. I am here to help you along your way towards final rest. I'm going to begin by reading you the list of your transgressions." He looked down at the page.

"Wait, isn't St. Peter supposed to do that?" Clayton asked.

"Who?"

"You're supposed to take me to the Pearly Gates, and St. Peter reads off my sins. Right?"

"I don't know a St. Peter," Takis lowered his voice and tried to be as comforting as possible. "Clayton, I have been doing this for over two thousand years. I know you have questions. I will have some answers. Not many, but some. We will be together for a while, and I don't want to start out by lying to you. So, I want to begin this with honesty." Takis could tell Clayton was bracing for horrific news and instantly regretted making it sound so sinister. "A lot of the things you believe in aren't here, Clayton." He never broke Clayton's gaze and spoke in a hushed tone to try and keep Clayton from losing control.

"I know that you expected gates, angels, and trumpets. Maybe you even expect me to fly around with wings. Sorry, Clayton, that's not here. I hate to tell you these things. The After is different than anyone imagined." He saw Clayton slump. The boy closed his eyes tightly.

19

"I have to admit, I was underwhelmed." Takis grinned and clapped his hands together. "I'm here to teach you, Clayton. I've been looking forward to having a partner. But to answer the main question you have, everyone got a little bit right and a lot of things wrong." Takis waited for a response. He watched Clayton's eyes shifting from right to left as he opened and closed his mouth.

"Partner?" Clayton wondered aloud.

"I'll explain that in due time," Takis assured him.

"So, no heaven?"

"Heaven? Oh, no, there is definitely paradise waiting for you one day."

"Really?" Clayton beamed with a sliver of hope.

"Yes, really. Now can we finish up here? I'd like for us to be on our way." Takis looked around, making sure they were still alone.

"Sorry, go ahead," Clayton apologized.

"It's fine, boy, you just passed on. You're doing great. This should go by quickly. Where was I?" Takis scanned for where he left off. "Clayton, you've only lied eleven times since understanding right from wrong," he glanced up at him in amuse-

80

ment. "This is actually the lowest number I've ever seen. The same with stealing, only two instances." Takis looked to Clayton, an air of pride about him. "Little boring, don't you think?" He joked.

"I did as I was told," Clayton responded. Takis ran his finger down the list.

"Well, you weren't greedy. You wished ill will on no one and no mention of murder," he paused and winked at him, which got a chuckle out of Clayton.

"I honestly thought this was a mistake, but you've never pleasured yourself. I see no mention of you doing that." He looked up to see Clayton staring at him expressionlessly.

"Seriously?" Takis asked.

"What?"

"You're of age. Nothing? Not once?"

"I always assumed my grandmother was watching me from Heaven and would be mad," Clayton replied and looked away, embarrassed. Takis couldn't help but laugh. He waved and apologized.

"Alright, here we go. You were prideful and thought highly of yourself. That's not that bad. If I'd been able to keep my hand off my penis, I'd have an ego too," Takis teased, and Clayton smiled. "Finally, and probably the only reason you aren't riding the River, you committed suicide."

"I tried to stop myself," Clayton said. Takis felt for the boy. He was leaving a father and sister behind. He never experienced the embrace of a lover, would never have children to call his own. He would never have the moments in life a man was meant to. No one should die so young. It was there on the sheet that he tried to stop himself, but what was done was done. He wished he could turn time back, place the boy back up on the hillside, and let him walk away. He wasn't someone who deserved the punishment he was about to receive. This boy was good. Takis paused. He'd seen Clayton before.

"You alright, Takis?" Clayton's voice brought him back to reality.

"Yes, sorry. I was thinking of what to go over next." Takis studied the boy's face as he spoke. He was sure of it. This was the same person.

"The River?" Clayton broke Takis's concentration again.

"In due time," Takis ran his right hand across his bald head. "There is way too much to go over in this place, and I don't want to be standing here forever. We need to get back to the office. I am to bring you to Feme, our boss. Trust me, Clayton, it's easier to show you than explain it. You'll accept all these things better when you see them with your own eyes. So,are you ready to—" A twig snapped, interrupting Takis.

"Shit." Takis tried to stop Clayton as he wheeled around to see the man approach them. An unattractive fellow in a white dress shirt and black tie. His hair was almost cherry in color, and his skin was pale, with freckles dotting his face and neck. Takis took note of how tall and lanky the man was. He looked unhealthy, his skin-tight against his face, and his clothes looked a size too large for him. He was holding a Pennsylvania Longrifle, and as he stared at Clayton's body, he scowled. He took the barrel of the rifle and poked at Clayton's corpse.

"He can't see us, can he?" Clayton whispered.

"No, he can't," Takis whispered back, even though there was no need to. "We should go." The man gave the corpse a soft kick. He showed no remorse or regret for the young body in the gully. He smiled and spat on the corpse's blood-covered back. He seemed so pleased with himself, he even giggled childishly.

"That's for my sister," he sneered.

"Why did he do that?" Takis turned to Clayton, enraged. Clayton gasped, and Takis could see that Clayton was shaken. Tears had started to form in his eyes, and he was to the point of whimpering again. Takis put his hand onto Clayton's shoulder. Clayton was doing well for someone who'd just died, Takis had seen these moments go bad quickly, and he wasn't going to have the young man break down now.

"Easy," he started. "Clayton, why did this piece of shit do that?" Clayton didn't answer him. He was staring at the man reveling in his sadistic act. "Clayton!" Takis said forcefully, and Clayton finally pulled his eyes away from him.

"That's Amber's brother. He thinks I got her pregnant. She miscarried and died. That's why I ran away, why I was up there." He pointed to the cliff edge. "Everyone is blaming me, but I never touched her." Clayton was a wreck. Takis knew he had to do something.

"What's his name?" He asked.

"Huh?"

"His name, what is it?"

"Alan Ward," Clayton answered. Takis walked away from Clayton and towards Alan.

"Alan Ward life list," and as he finished speaking, several pieces of paper appeared in his hand. He held the last page up and skimmed it, and Takis' mouth hung open. He began to cackle with laughter, almost bending over completely. He walked closer to Alan, who was mumbling to himself about how happy his mother would be.

Who in Hades do you think you are, Alan Ward?

Takis' voice sounded hollow, as if it wasn't coming from his mouth, but somewhere in his throat. It sounded as if he was whispering, but at a full volume, and when his voice left his mouth, it had the slightest hint of an echo. Alan's head cocked to the side, and his smile started to fade.

You spit on this poor boy, you judge him, but it is you who deserves to be spat on. Before you judge anyone, maybe you should point that finger at yourself.

Alan looked away, but the look of anger was still across his brow. Takis rounded him. There was a forceful hush to his words, a calm but threatening tone.

Such a son, to be revered by his mother. Wonder how she would feel about your vices? You are a deviant, Alan. A man who lays with beasts. Is it because no one finds you desirable? The shame you must feel.

Alan's demeanor changed instantly; he looked like an animal caught in a trap. Takis had moved right next to his ear. Alan looked left and right quickly and back over his shoulder. Takis turned around and looked at Clayton with a wicked smile.

You are such an ugly man. You can't talk to women. They ridicule you behind your back. But you have desires, don't you, Alan? A man needs release, what better place than the barn with something that can't tell anyone. What if your mother or father knew?

He had to pause to control his laughter. Alan groaned, and shame was etched on his face, his cheeks redder than his hair.

You are as ugly on the inside as you are on the outside. You are twisted. You are rotten. You are diseased.

Takis was speaking forcefully now, and Alan was wincing from the power in every word. Takis was still close to him, his voice dropping to a whisper.

Oh, you can blame the whiskey all you like, but you know. You know what you are.

Alan's shoulders slumped. He looked ill now, and he turned away from Clayton's body and Takis.

"I should get someone," Alan said out loud. "Someone needs to see this." He stumbled forward, tripping over a log. He started back out of the gully the way he came in, cursing under his breath the whole way.

20

"He heard you?" Clayton asked, watching him leave.

"Yes." Takis paused to think. "No, it's hard to explain. He didn't hear me the way you are now. He...felt me."

"Felt you?"

"The life list shows your transgressions, all the awful things you've done. You are a saint compared to that guy." He pointed in the direction Alan was heading. "That man is..." Takis shuddered.

"So, what did you do to him?"

"Afterwords. One of the few perks of the job, if you can actually pull it off. You can use a person's emotions against them. Make them feel what you are saying."

"Like magic?"

"Yes," Takis thought about it, "you could consider it a magic trick. It's tough to do. Feme taught me how. I've tried to teach it to a few others, but they can't seem to pull it off."

"Could you do it to me?"

"Doesn't work on us, only the living. If it worked on us, this job would be easier. I could get people to calm down." He looked down and patted Clayton on the shoulder. "I'm impressed."

"Why's that?"

"You've handled yourself well here. Most people are begging me to send them back. Crying, can't accept that their life has ended. You have been unnaturally calm. I thought for a few minutes you were touched."

"My father told me when it was your time, it was your time," Clayton shrugged. "What would begging you accomplish? I'm dead. I want to cry. I want to scream. But I know I'm not going to Hell, so there's that."

"Nope, you're stuck with me." They watched Alan leave in silence. Once he rounded the bend from their sight, Clayton spoke.

"I wish he didn't hate me," he said weakly.

"Who cares? He fucked a cow," Takis crowed. Clayton huffed a laugh, and Takis beamed at him. He grabbed Clayton by the arm.

"Home," he roared. He turned around 180 degrees with Clayton and opened the door that appeared. "Let's get started."

21

THE AFTER

S ince Takis arrived, the hallway has had the same carpet, a musty brown to go with the white walls. Donning those walls were paintings of people who'd been in charge many years before, with Feme staring hatefully at the very end. The paintings were atrocious; the person the image portrayed was almost unrecognizable. It was as if a child with a small inkling of artistic talent had put brush to canvas.

"Feme has tried to throw that painting away so many times. I've even seen her spit on it." Takis chuckled.

"It's terrible."

"She would come down here and get it, and somehow it always found its way back. She blamed me for that forever."

"Why would she blame you?"

"She hates me."

"Oh," Clayton looked down the hall.

"She hates everyone, but she thinks I'm the only one with the balls to prank her. She had it sent into the world of the living. It found its way back. She even had a match brought to her and burned it, a short while later, here it was."

Clayton stared at the paintings. Takis pointed out the backgrounds in some of them. They didn't match the person. For example, Feme was dressed in an eloquent kalasiris. She was obviously of Egyptian descent, yet the background was Mount Olympus. It was as if the artist had no clue what to put behind her and just made it up as they painted.

"These paintings are shit," Takis said to him. "Don't mention that to Feme. It drives her crazy." He paused, touched the painting, and grinned. "I love this thing," he crooned.

"I won't. Thank you for the warning."

"Anyway, Clayton, welcome to home base." Takis made a grand gesture with his hand as if he was showing off something special. Clayton noticed the hideous brown carpet at his feet was stained everywhere, and the air had the scent of something ancient. It wasn't that these carpets were never cleaned, or the walls and such weren't dusted, but they aged. When something has worn on the way this place has, it develops a particular odor.

"Takis?"

"Yes, Clayton?"

"This is awful."

"I know. I see this every day and want to eat a sword." He winced after it left his lips. He made a suicide joke to a child who'd just taken his life. He glanced towards the boy and was relieved to see him with a slight grin. They stood in awe of just how underwhelming the After was.

"What are you wearing?" Clayton asked him.

"What?" Takis snapped back to attention.

"I see the way you're dressed. You look different. No offense."

"I'm Greek. I was born in Macedonia. I died two thousand years ago."

"You've been here that long?" Clayton stopped suddenly. Takis turned around to him.

"Yes, I have. Feme will explain everything to you," he said. Clayton hesitated. Takis could tell by his fresh look of panic that Clayton was wondering if he'd be here for that long. "It's going to be okay. I'm a special case. Let's go," he waved his hand, beckoning.

"I thought people across the ocean spoke differently?"

"That's a really neat trick here. I know I am speaking Doric, I never learned English, but you understand me perfectly. And I know for a fact you are not speaking to me in my native tongue, but I hear it that way. We just understand each other. That's how it works."

"That is remarkable."

"The same thing goes for written words."

"So, I can just read things in other languages? Like before the Tower of Babel where everyone spoke the same?"

"I don't know of any Babel or of a time when anyone spoke the same. I think it's because we have to go all over the world to pick up the people we are assigned to. When you get to the other side, you can ask." They continued up the hallway for a while, passing door after door with various names carved into each one.

"Does each door have someone in there?" Clayton asked.

"Every one of them."

"What are they doing exactly?"

"Be thankful you aren't in one of those spots, Clayton. There is some meaningless shit going on the other side of those doors. You don't want one of those jobs. Those people are miserable. The only joy they get is when someone visits them." Takis stopped walking and grinned. "You want to meet one?" Takis leaned down to Clayton.

"Sure," Clayton said cautiously.

"This one will do," Takis snickered. He stopped at the door and banged his heavy fist on it three times.

22

"Enter!" Clayton heard a woman yell from the other side. Takis opened the door and ushered Clayton in first with a shove. At first, Clayton had to get his bearings. The room was small, so the very first thing he noticed was that there were no windows, just two chairs crammed together in front of a wooden desk. A small lamp glowed there, and behind the desk was the largest woman he'd ever seen.

She stood as he entered, and her incredible height was on full display. Clayton had always thought his father was tall. This woman would have towered over him. She was at least a head above Jonas. She was thick in muscle. Her biceps were almost as large as Clayton's head, and her thighs were like tree trunks. She was intimidating, to say the least. Her long blonde hair gleamed in the light of the lamp, making it ash in color. It was a tattered mess, and she looked as if she'd been up for days. Her blue dress was disheveled and torn in a few places. Clayton imagined when she moved a certain way, her muscles ripped it. Her eyes were an ocean shade of blue, and her smile was wide with her teeth an off-putting white, almost unnatural. She was giddy to see him. Clayton could see that from the second the door opened.

"Clayton Shaw!" Her accent was thick, and he could not place it. She rushed around the side of her desk and picked him up in her massive arms, hugging him and planting a kiss on his forehead. As she set him down, he waved meekly and felt embarrassed by her reaction to him. "I was just reading about you," her eyes shone with a glimmer of sadness. "Tragic, absolutely tragic, but I am so happy you came to see me." She smiled at him as she leaned down and tapped his nose with her index finger. "By Freya, you are lovely. I would have eaten you alive back in the day."

"I bet you say that to all the boys," Takis chuckled.

"Just one's as beautiful as this," her massive hand went under Clayton's chin and tilted his face up. "Oh, your eyes. That shade of blue is delicious."

"How are you, Astrid?" Takis laughed

"So happy you brought him to see me." She rubbed Clayton's shoulders with her massive hands. "Clayton, I am Astrid," she took a step back and offered her hand. Clayton looked at it for a split second. He had read about this. He just couldn't remember where. He took it and kissed it quickly.

"Oh," she gasped, "such a gentleman."

"It's a pleasure, Astrid," Clayton said with a smile.

"Tell me this, am I the first person you've come to see since you arrived?"

"Yes."

"Oh," she grinned "I'm the first woman you get to see in the After. So, what do you think?" She arched her eyebrow coyly and posed in an attempt to be alluring. Takis started to interrupt, but before he could, Clayton responded.

"You are beautiful, miss. I've never seen a woman like you." Which was the truth. He'd never seen anything like her before. In fact, he was reasonably certain she was one of a kind. She clapped her giant hands together in delight. Clayton thought he saw her blushing. She leaned close to his ear.

"I've said this to many people here, but to you, I mean it; when you get off that boat, I'll be waiting, and you," she reached down and grabbed his left buttock, "are mine." Clayton jumped back and squeaked. He heard Takis laughing behind him. He placed his hand on Clayton's shoulder, and Clayton looked back at him with panicked eyes.

"Astrid, my love," Takis said as he opened her door, "he still needs to get his legs about him. I am sure we will see each other at the next meeting." Astrid's face turned sour.

"I hate those meetings. I am the one who always ends up with the most work."

"I know, dear. I promise we will come to visit more often." He gestured to Clayton in the direction of the door. "Could you wait outside for a moment?"

"Sure, Takis," Clayton answered and walked through the door and back into the hallway but kept right beside it to listen in since Takis hadn't shut it.

"Why were you reading upon him?" He heard Takis ask in a hushed tone.

"I heard you were getting a partner. Can't a lady be curious?" Astrid snickered loudly.

"Shh, I don't want him to hear," Takis whispered. "Don't you have enough to do during the day?"

"Shouldn't you be worrying about yourself?" She retorted. Clayton moved away from the opening and pretended to be enthralled by the office door beside Astrid's. Takis walked out and threw him a quick smile as he closed the door.

"What was that?" Clayton asked, feeling a little perturbed.

"Astrid. Scandinavian."

"She's," Clayton thought for a minute, "something."

"I was trying to laugh at your expense back there. You were great."

"I didn't want to be rude."

"Smart, I've seen her angry. You don't want to see her angry. I was shocked you didn't run out of there screaming."

They continued down the hallway, passing the occasional individual who said hello to Takis or welcome in Clayton's direction. The hallway was long, and Clayton had stopped trying to read the name on every door. He felt comfortable around Takis, even if he did look out of place. His voice was comforting, and Clayton believed that Takis cared for him and wanted to keep him safe.

"Takis, what's this?" They had reached an area in the hallway where large double doors were on the right. Wooden and foreboding with giant golden handles, there were no names or plaques on this entrance, just an ominous feeling. They looked much more worn and out of place than everything they'd passed so far. Clayton could swear it felt colder than the rest of the hall.

"That leads to the cells."

"Like prison?"

"No, boy, worse." Takis walked a few more steps forward and leaned against the wall. "The cells extend for as far as the eye can see and keep going after that. Each cell has a lone bed against a wall and nothing else. You can stand, but there isn't much room to maneuver. The bed isn't very large either. For someone like me, I'd spill over the side of it." He patted his belly. "No visitors, no breaks, no work like we are going to be doing, just your thoughts. And when you're tired of your thoughts? Images play out on the wall beside your bed of the people you hurt in life, the consequences your actions caused others. The horrible shit you've done, shown to you over and over again. Once you've finished there, one of us comes and gets you, and you're given an office job."

"That sounds horrible."

"Boy, you have no idea."

"Was Astrid in there?" Clayton asked.

"No. She used to have a job similar to the one you're getting."

"Were you in there?"

"No, but I've dealt with a lot of people who were, and it ruins them, it breaks them down. You can always tell when you meet someone who served in the cells. They are filled with guilt; it's all over their faces. They had to watch themselves inflict pain over and over again and then deal with the emotions of the people they devastated. They feel the pain they caused," Takis said. Clayton felt pity for those trapped in there, and at the same time, was thankful he wasn't inside that door.

"Will I be taking people there?"

"No, you are on a much simpler task. You'll find out soon. We're almost there." Takis was again moving down the hallway, which was almost at an end. The end of the hallway had a painting of the Earth, as terrible as the paintings at the entrance. To the left and right were doors. To the left was a light brown wood with the name "Feme" burned into it. To the right, the door was painted black with white etched lettering that said "Acquisitions." Takis was about to knock on the left door but noticed Clayton's curiosity about the one on the right.

"Oh no, I am not knocking on that door. Scary place," Takis told him.

"What's in there?"

"Doesn't matter," he waved dismissively.

"Come on, Takis." Clayton almost pleaded, his curiosity piqued.

"Alright," he said, defeated. "You aren't going to believe me, but I'll tell you anyway." He bent down to look Clayton in the eyes, his face stern as if he was preparing to scold him. "The man inside that room collects things, things that shouldn't be. Things people shouldn't mess with, and things that shouldn't be found. He keeps them out of the hands of the living by bringing them here."

"Things like what?" Clayton asked and watched Takis' face for a twitch or a sign of breaking.

"Holy things, evil things, things of incredible power."

"Are you poking fun at me like you did with Astrid?" Clayton snorted. Takis stood upright.

"There are things in the After even I can't explain, and the things in there make me afraid. I'm just trying to give you caution."

"I'm sorry, I didn't mean to offend you."

"It would take a lot more than that to offend me," Takis chortled. They heard a click, and the door to Acquisitions opened, slightly ajar. Clayton looked up at Takis, puzzled. Takis didn't move.

23

"Clayton, close the door," Takis whispered, his voice tinged with fear. Clayton was hesitant at first, but that subsided quickly. I'm already dead, he thought. What's the worst that could happen? So, he stepped forward and placed his hand on the doorknob.

At that moment, the door flew open, and a creature covered in hair, seven feet tall and somewhat resembling a man, roared in Clayton's face. It was naked, spit flew from its mouth in a rage, and it reached large arms out to grab Clayton. Clayton tripped over his feet and fell backward against the hallway wall. The monster roared again. It was deafening. Clayton tried to stand, but his legs wouldn't move. It was as if the primal noise had rendered them useless. It stepped out in the hallway, its massive feet making a thumping sound. Clayton closed his eyes, put his hands up, and screamed.

He waited for death to come again, its hands to pick him up and swallow him whole, or to be beaten by those massive fists. Yet Clayton heard nothing. He opened his eyes and put his hands down. Takis was laughing so hard he wasn't making any noise, and the creature whose face had been a contortion of rage and anger was smiling down at him.

"You must be Clayton Shaw," it said with its hand outstretched. Takis was gasping for air between laughter.

"Go on, kiss that one!" Takis howled, doubled over, his face a deep cardinal. Clayton stood up and took the massive hand, his mouth agape. What was this? A man?

"I'm sorry, Clayton, I knew it was childish, but he gets such a kick out of that, and we haven't done it in ages. I'm Nix," he shook Clayton's hand.

"What are you?"

"I'm Nix. I just told you." Clayton thought Nix was still toying with him. Nix pulled his hand back and twisted his neck to the left. It cracked loudly.

"No. I mean, *what* are you?"

"I'm you, just a lot older," Nix replied. Clayton left it at that. He would ask Takis later if the laughter didn't kill him first. Takis was starting to catch his breath.

"I'm sorry, I'm sorry," he gasped. Nix looked at Takis and told him to stop, making him laugh harder.

"Clayton, you'll have to excuse him. He's an uncultured swine."

"I love you, Nix, I love you!" Takis gasped again. "Did you hear him scream?" He lapsed into another laughing fit, bent forward with tears pouring from his eyes. Nix smiled at Clayton, but it was more horrific than friendly.

"I got the memo of your arrival. I'm sorry you got stuck with this guy over here," he cocked his head over toward Takis.

"We should have done the thing where you shook it at him!" Takis wheezed out while placing his hand on his crotch. Clayton looked at Nix, puzzled.

"We did that one time," Nix explained. "It was his idea. Anyway, I know it's your first day, and you have to meet the leader.

So, I won't keep you." Clayton was still somewhat speechless and kept staring at Nix in disbelief. Takis finally got a grip on himself and was calming down.

"Wait. Nix, you got a minute?"

"I was getting ready to go pick something up. What is it?"

"Well, I was wondering, once we get Clayton settled," Takis slapped Clayton on the back, "do you think we can get a tour? I've always wondered about that place and would love a peek in there."

"Why would you want to come in here?" Nix pointed a massive thumb at the door.

"I don't know, I'm bored? Curious? Something to do with the boy besides dead people all day? Who gives a shit why?"

"I hope you don't have to deal with him very long," Nix said and shared a quick laugh with Clayton. Then Nix's giant eyebrows shot up.

"Stay right here," Nix grinned and walked back into Acquisitions. Clayton and Takis stood by the door.

"That was pretty funny, Takis," Clayton said sarcastically.

"Look," he grinned and held up his hand, "I know it was a shitty thing to do, but I haven't laughed like this since maybe the year four hundred something. Just give me this, alright?" Clayton nodded but kept his face stony. He was still annoyed. Nix opened the door and stepped out into the hallway. Clayton wondered if he would ever get used to the sight of him. In his right hand, he had a gnarled piece of iron rusted through and through, about seven inches long. It curled upward at the end, so if he held it upright, it looked like an "L." Nix showed it to them both and handed it to Clayton, who turned it over in his hand and stared at it with confusion.

"What is this?" It was brittle and cold. He brought it closer to his face. It had tinges of rust at all the edges, and it had an odd smell, one he couldn't describe. It was much heavier than it looked, and Clayton could tell by how Nix had been gentle with it that it was old. Clayton had no guesses as to what he was holding.

"That is from the year 33. It was taken from a man named Caiaphas," Nix proclaimed proudly. Clayton gasped and handed it quickly back to Nix. Clayton knew the Bible well. Nix didn't have to tell him what it was.

"This was the nail for His right hand," Nix said with a tone of sadness. Clayton's eyebrows drew together, and tears welled up in his eyes. The corners of his mouth trembled, and he turned away from it.

"Oh, I'm sorry, are you alright? I thought you would find this interesting. I didn't mean to upset you," Nix said hesitantly.

"Yes, it's just...that isn't something I should be touching." Clayton backed away from Nix, who was holding the object behind his back in a poor attempt to hide it.

"I'm sorry, Clayton, I didn't mean to make you uncomfortable." Nix hung his head slightly.

"It's fine, but can I ask a question?" Clayton regained himself quickly, hoping to not show weakness to this giant of a man.

"By all means."

"Why bring those here?"

"As in this specifically?"

"No, but if you have that," he pointed to the arm that Nix was holding behind his back. "I can't imagine what else you have in there. Why take them and hide them away?"

"There," Takis joked, "there is a reason for me to want to go in there." Nix looked away from Clayton for a moment and shushed Takis.

"Clayton, I know you may not understand this, but this is a powerful weapon in the wrong hands," he produced his hand with the nail resting in his palm. "One day, I'll show you what I mean."

"Are we just going to waste the whole day out here? Some of us have work to do." Feme barked from her now-open door. Nix moved away from Clayton.

"He's all yours."

"The two of you get in here, now," she demanded Takis and Clayton. The two entered her office, but Nix spoke out.

"Feme, I know you've probably never heard this one, but be gentle."

"Shouldn't you be throwing your shit at something?"

24

Feme slammed the door and walked around her desk.

"Sit," she barked, pointing to the chairs in front of them. Clayton and Takis sat down, and Feme wasted no time.

"Do not interrupt me. I will not repeat myself." She scowled and looked at Clayton while rearranging some papers. "And don't start fucking crying. I don't care about your family. I don't care what you left behind. You are dead. You committed suicide, and as Takis probably informed you, that's why you are here.

"My name is Feme, and I am in charge of all things here in the After. The After is a place people are sent to when they have done things that keep them from going to one of two places you'll see in just a little while. You are being punished. This is not a happy place. This is a job and an important one. One that requires meticulous attention and that you stay sharp. One fuck up can cause serious repercussions, which can trickle down into the physical world. Actions here have caused the deaths of people on Earth, and that cannot happen, not on my watch. You have your responsibilities, and I am responsible for you.

"Takis has been here a long time, and typically when you get a

101

partner, it means your time here is coming to an end. I am sure the last thing he needs is you getting his sentence extended because you decided to do something stupid. Takis has never lost a soul. He has never had a severe violation. The less I see of someone here, the better, and I rarely see Takis. I need you to be like that. I don't want to see you in front of me.

"Every day, you will be given ten people you must collect. You must go to them, get them at the time of their death, bring them to the Fork, and send them to their proper place. You are new here, so you will not be putting people in or taking people out of the cells. The cells are purgatory. They are a place for people that have done worse but didn't deserve to be shoved into the Darkness. You do not want to go to the Darkness. There is no exception to the Ten Rule. You have to complete it. If you fail, time is added to your sentence. Added time is a Black Mark. Don't make mistakes, and I won't give you one. That is the description of your duties; this is all you have to worry about. Go, get, sort. You will begin on newborn detail. Sometimes children do not survive birth, it's a job here a lot of people don't want. They get emotional about it. Personally, I've always hated children, and I'm still glad I never had that assignment. I've read your life's report, and I must say you are kind of soft. So, before we have an issue. I need to ask you, are you capable of collecting babies and taking them to the Fork?" She paused, waiting for an answer.

"Yes."

"Yes, what?"

"Yes, ma'am, I can."

"Manners and quiet, I like that. Do you have any questions for me?"

"All of the souls I collect go to Heaven?"

"I am fairly sure all of them will be sent up the River inside the Brilliance. Or Heaven - call it what you want. I don't think I've seen a baby sent to the Darkness, but nothing shocks me anymore.

"So, the Darkness is Hell?"

"Nothing gets past you," she mocked. Clayton started to say something, but Feme stood. "Takis, I am going to walk with him down the hall. You can stay here, but don't fucking touch anything, am I clear?"

"Yes, Feme," Takis said without looking at her. He was staring off into the corner of the room as if bored. Clayton stood and waited for Feme to pass by and open the door. She stopped and glanced back at him.

"Well, I haven't got all fucking day." Clayton quickly got to his feet and hurried out the door in front of her. She closed it behind him, and they started down the hall together. Immediately, Clayton could tell that everyone was avoiding eye contact with them. Everyone they passed seemed to try their best to hug the wall, to stay out of her line of fire.

"So, when my time is done here, what happens next?" Clayton asked her.

"I have never seen the other side of the Darkness nor the Brilliance. I have no idea what is on the other side, neither does anyone here. It's still a mystery, just as it was in life."

"Takis said he's been here for two thousand years. Am I going to be here that long?"

"Everyone is here for a reason. Take this man here. Hello, Enrique." Feme stopped in front of someone in the hall, a younger, dark-skinned man with papers in his hands, a look of dread wove across his face. He stumbled and almost dropped his papers. Clayton could see sweat forming on his forehead.

"Hi, um, hello, Feme. Ma'am," Enrique said nervously and cleared his throat.

"Enrique had a thing for young boys. I mean, really young boys because he was a sick disgusting shit that I wish I could throw into the Darkness myself. However, he was a coward. He wouldn't act upon it. When he finally did get the nerve, he broke into a neighbor's house to take their son, but the father caught him and killed him. Isn't that right, Enrique?"

"Yes, ma'am," Enrique looked at the floor in shame.

"That's why Enrique is here with us, and I am sure he will be with us for a very long time." The three of them stood in the hallway, Feme with a look of accomplishment on her face.

"Enrique?" She finally said.

"Yes, ma'am?" Enrique asked, holding back his tears.

"Get the fuck out of my face," Feme ordered him. Enrique hurried away from them, almost tripping over his own feet. Clayton could hear him sobbing. They watched him scurry away as Feme continued.

"Everyone here has done questionable things. Things that many would consider immoral, and I guess someone higher up than me thought so too. So, they decided upon our punishment, and until we are finished, this is where we'll stay."

"What could possibly get someone two thousand years, though?" Clayton wondered. Feme's tone darkened.

"Don't ask anyone why they are here. It's uncomfortable. If they offer it up, listen if you want to, but everyone has a tragic story. I have my own. It's a sensitive subject. Avoid it." Feme started down the hallway again with Clayton in tow. He was trying to take in everything she was saying. She was so vicious in her mannerisms and words, Clayton found himself afraid of her. She was not someone to be trifled with.

"I am here to make sure this place runs right. I am not your fucking friend, I am not someone you can confide in, and I could give a shit less about your problems. I don't care if you don't like going and getting babies. I don't care if you and Takis can't get along. Do your job. I'll do mine. Unless it is dire, do not darken my door."

Clayton felt even more unease. He hadn't known this woman for more than six minutes and already disliked her. The tone in her voice was so naturally condescending he wondered if she was capable of speaking any other way. He couldn't wait for her to finish so he could get away from her. Takis was everything this woman wasn't. He wanted Clayton to feel comfortable and welcome. She made him feel stupid and like a burden. Feme stopped at an office door with "Lydia" etched into it. She seemed lost in her memories for a moment but continued.

"Remember that every person here is punished in one way or another. Yours will come too, I have no idea what that will be, but it will come. You may think this isn't that bad, that it's just a job and fall into a routine. This place will find something to hit you with. That is what it does.

I did not look like this when I got here. I continued to age. My sin was vanity, and I think that is why I have aged more than Takis has, or most people here for that matter. It's just a theory, but it's the only one that makes sense. Takis doesn't care how he looks, fat fucking slob." She opened the door, and an older woman who looked as disheveled as Astrid was working at her desk, papers piled high and strewn all over the floor.

"Way to get behind, Lydia. You really fucked up," Feme said to her. "Twenty black marks." The woman screamed and pulled at her hair before flinging the papers from her desk into the air. Feme smiled at her and closed the door.

"Just keep in mind time moves slower here, much slower," Feme started walking again, moving her finger back and forth like a metronome. "You won't get hungry, or thirsty, or sleepy. None of life's simple pleasures are here for your enjoyment. Tea, coffee, meat, none of that here, and you couldn't eat it or drink it if it was. There is one thing, you can still feel physical pain, so don't think you are invincible. You can be hurt. You cannot fly or pass through walls.

"I cannot stress this enough: Keep your head down. No one knows how long they are here. I don't even know. I get a golden sheet of paper that appears on my desk that will tell me your time is up, and I will send you on your way. So, the only thing you need to concern yourself about is your job and listening to Takis. Everything else is unimportant."

"Takis seems nice. I'm sure we'll get along," Clayton said with confidence.

"Takis is a fucking buffoon."

At this point, Clayton had nothing to say. She would be contentious no matter what he said or did, so he listened and walked. They reached the edge of the hallway where the paintings were, and Clayton watched as Feme curled her lip at her painting before turning and starting back at a quicker pace.

"The world changes constantly. We have staff meetings to catch people up on fashion, slang, and other matters of importance. Astrid is in charge of wardrobe changes so you can fit in more with the period we are in. Takis was supposed to see her today, and if he doesn't, I am hitting him with a Black Mark. You should let him know." Her voice rose slightly.

"I've met her. I will remind Takis, and we'll stop back after you and I finish."

"Good. Things keep changing at an alarming rate, so you'll be seeing a lot of her. We need to be able to reach and connect with people in our line of work, and we can't do that if we look out of place like Takis does or if we say things that make no sense to them.

"That brings me to your gifts. Takis will show you this, I'm sure, but I'll try and explain it. There are a lot of abilities bestowed on this line of work that give you the tools needed to complete your tasks.

When you leave this office, the back of your dominant hand will itch. Flick your wrist, and the paper for the individual you are supposed to pick up will appear in your hand. You can say certain phrases then turn around, and a door will lead to that destination."

"You don't have to worry about speaking or reading different languages. You'll understand those instantly, and no, I don't know why. This is why you can understand Takis and me. Even if the person was deaf in their lifetime, they would understand and speak to you upon their death. These things are invaluable to a soul retriever."

"It's a lot to remember."

"Well, you better remember real fucking fast."

"Yes, ma'am."

"Finally, we need to go over the things that make me upset. People can see you if you want them to. Only, and I repeat, only use this in extreme circumstances or when necessary. Would you like to know when it is necessary?"

Clayton nodded.

"It isn't. Moving on. We have a pretty high failure rate here. You have the capability to go to people you have known in the past, but you must not. Some people have gone back for revenge. If you do this, break this one rule, into the Darkness you go. You don't get a second chance or a moment to regret it. It's happened a lot more than I care to admit. You will be tempted. Clayton, I am warning you here and now. Do not go back to see anyone. Your life is over. It ended when your soul left your body. Let them mourn, let them miss you, and carry on."

They started past Enrique in the hall, who had his back turned to them, facing the wall.

"Enrique?" Feme taunted.

"Yes?" He answered without turning around.

"I thought I told you to get out of my fucking face?"

"Y-You did," he stammered.

"Black mark," she said triumphantly. Enrique huffed and ran down the hall in the opposite direction, sobbing.

"Clayton, there are rules. The rules are the same for everyone, the living and the in-between. Follow them to the letter, do not stray away from them in the slightest." She finished and looked at him, expecting a response.

"You'll have no problems with me," he responded. They returned to her office door. She opened it, walked back to her desk, and sat down. Clayton stood by the door.

"Are we done?" Takis looked up from his chair to Feme. She

looked down to her paperwork, picked up her quill, and began writing something.

"Yes," she answered without even looking at Takis.

"Clayton?" Takis cleared his throat. "Did you get everything she told you?" He asked sternly.

"Absolutely," Clayton responded. Takis stood.

"See, Feme, the boy is quick. He won't let you down."

"You better fucking not," she warned. "I don't expect to see you for a long time. Go do your jobs. Do you think you two can do that?" She growled, they were wasting her time, and she wanted them out of her sight.

"One question, ma'am," Clayton said and rubbed his hand on his cheek.

"What is it?"

"How come your painting looks nothing like you?"

25

Feme was still yelling when Takis shut the door behind them, and Clayton saw a twinkle in his eyes. He had asked about the painting innocently enough to play dumb. Clayton knew what he had done.

"Well, she hates you."

"She hated me before I got in there."

"That's not true. You just have to get used to her."

"Are you used to her?" Clayton asked. Takis smiled without looking at him.

"Good point." Takis looked up and down the hallway.

"What are you looking for?" Clayton questioned.

"I was hoping Nix was still out there. He'd love what you did. We'll have to stop by and tell him about it later. That was great."

Clayton smirked.

"Is your hand itching yet?" Takis asked curiously.

"It is, actually." Clayton hadn't noticed until Takis had mentioned it.

"Give it a try," he imitated the motion to retrieve the paper. Clayton gave his left hand a quick flick. He dropped the paper out

109

of shock, but it worked. He'd summoned it out of the air. The first person he had to retrieve. He tried not to let it show, but he was excited. He ran his fingers across the bold black lettering that stood out on plain, white paper. It was four simple lines.

Bruno Roth

Granted Passage to Brilliance
Cause of Death: Suffocation
No Sins to List

"Well, this seems simple enough. So we just go and get Bruno and send him to the Brilliance?" Clayton looked at Takis, who was leaning on an office door.

"Sure, but it won't be so easy for you to shut out the noise. It's your first time, after all."

"What do you mean?"

"The mother will be there. It's a hard thing, boy, not to get lost in the sadness. You think you'll get used to death, you'll get used to being in a room where someone is going to die or has died." He rubbed his chin with his large fingers. "I've been doing this for a long time, and there are times when the sadness is overwhelming. This should be easier on you because it's a baby, the baby won't question you, he won't wonder why, and he won't beg you for more time." He looked into the distance, deep in thought. "A baby dying is potential lost, happiness shattered. One of the worst things in this whole fucking place. Feme acted like this was an easy job, but it isn't. Every parent has their children's life planned out before they even arrive, and that's taken away. Wherever we are about to end up, it's gonna be bleak. Be prepared."

"I didn't think of it like that." Clayton felt apprehensive. He decided to stall for time. "Did you have children?"

"A son, and a wife, I left them behind." Takis's lips pulled back slightly. Clayton realized, too late, what he'd done.

"I'm sorry, I wasn't supposed to ask."

"You didn't ask me how I got here. You asked if I had children. Big difference, Clayton."

Takis and Clayton walked down the hallway, making small talk. Clayton wanted to know as much as he could about Nix. Seeing him was a complete shock. Clayton hadn't amassed much knowledge throughout his short life. He'd read the Bible, and Jonas taught him what he could. Mary Price was there for the kids with a makeshift school in the church, but when she passed, no one else was willing to take up that mantle. It wasn't that Clayton was dumb. He learned things faster than most; he just never had much of a chance to branch out from the tiny farm he was raised on.

There was so much to learn. They'd made it sound simple enough, but just how much about the world did he not know? What mysteries awaited inside these offices? He could tell Takis knew a lot just from his time here, but he wondered if Takis knew everything there was about the After. Clayton let his mind wander for a minute, and he thought of Amber and what she thought of this place when she passed through on her way to the Brilliance.

"I have a question," Clayton started.

"You've had several."

"I told you about Amber and her pregnancy and me being blamed for it."

"You did, and we met the friendly man with the odd sexual tastes."

"Is there a way to find out who the father was? Who did that to her?" Takis stopped, a look of worry flashing across his face.

"Clayton," he cautioned.

"No," Clayton stated, understanding, "I know we aren't allowed to visit our living relatives, and I don't want to end up in the Darkness, but she died this morning. She's already passed through here."

"There are measures in place, boy. You can get life lists for people you are assigned to and those you are in front of," he bent down to Clayton's face. "Meaning, to have Amber's list, you needed to be her retriever, or know who was, and there are so many of us, and our jobs change so frequently that's almost impossible." Clayton sighed. He knew it wouldn't have been that easy. They stared at each other.

"I had to ask," Clayton said

"I know you did." Takis gave him a moment and then clapped his hands together. "Are you ready?"

"As ready as I'll ever be."

"You need to say his name out loud and follow it with 'final moment.'"

Clayton looked down the hallway. No one was paying attention to him. He could have sworn his palms were starting to sweat. He was frightened but also a little bit excited. He took a deep breath and closed his eyes.

"Bruno Roth, final moment." He opened his eyes, and Takis stood in front of him, smiling.

"Now turn around." Directly behind him, in the center of the hallway, was a door. A plain white wooden door with no walls around it, nothing written on it, and no frame. Clayton reached out and touched it. This was different from pulling the paper out of the void. He had done this with his words. He could not believe what he was seeing. His hand making contact with the door finally made all this seem real. He understood he was dead, and he was standing in a hallway somewhere between Heaven and Hell with his hand on a door that he conjured. He was with a man older than Christ himself. The both of them were ready to go through, collect the soul of a dead child, and send it to a place called the Brilliance.

He didn't move, and he found himself holding his breath, keeping his hand on that door for what seemed like an eternity until finally, Takis spoke up.

"It's a door, Clayton. You are going to see things a lot stranger today. We need to go."

Clayton nodded and opened it.

26

MARCH 26TH, 1805

THE WORLD

The moment Clayton opened the door, he could hear screaming. His eyes took a second to adjust. The room he entered was dark. He closed his eyes and shook his head a few times, and opened them to see a woman lying on a luxurious bed. A man sat beside her with his sleeves rolled up, holding her hand, and his face pressed close to hers. The bed had no comforter but was adorned with many pillows to prop her up. She was covered in sweat, and the man was trying to speak over her cries of agony.

"It's ok, Beulah. Just push."

"I am pushing!"

Another man was barely on the foot of the bed, propped up on his knees. He was silent and looking unfazed by this woman bellowing at the top of her lungs.

"I think that's the doctor," Takis said behind him, pointing over his shoulder. Clayton looked back at him with amazement that Takis could think that he was that stupid.

"You sure?" Clayton said mordantly. Takis looked shamed by his gaze.

"Sorry," Takis muttered. The man on his knees was bald and

scrawny. He was wearing a white overcoat with matching gloves, and his face was expressionless. He looked nothing like Doctor Brown. This man seemed much more professional. He seemed completely and utterly in control. Clayton, however, couldn't stop staring at his mustache. It was thin above his lip, shaven in a straight line. Almost as if someone had drawn it on with a quill and ink. He'd never seen one styled that way.

"Beulah, I can see the head. The worst is almost over. She is almost here!" The doctor's expression changed to a smile. His mother had mentioned how difficult a birth he was and that she thought she would die. He felt sympathy for her.

"You hear that, Beulah?" The man holding her hand cried out. "She's coming. Our Olga will be here soon." He kissed her cheek.

"I think that's the baby's father," Clayton picked at Takis as he pointed at him.

"Shut up," Takis snorted. Clayton chuckled and winked.

Takis was taken aback at how well Clayton was handling everything and how calm and collected Clayton was in this madness. Takis was not. He'd always hated the sight of blood, it made him uncomfortable, but he loathed the birth of children. It was something he could not handle. He wasn't even in the same building for the birth of Leon. He had walked into his neighbor's house because he could still hear Lipa screaming out an open window while he paced the street. The idea of the arrival of a baby was enough to make him queasy in life, and here he was sick to his stomach in death.

"How in Hades am I feeling ill?" He thought. He hadn't eaten since the day he died, and here he was, feeling ready to vomit all over the floor. He could feel himself getting cold and clammy.

"What's wrong with you?" Clayton jostled him back into reality.

"I don't feel so good."

"You don't feel so good?" Clayton asked, confused.

"No, I might be sick."

"How?" Clayton took in the blanched look of Takis' face in disbelief.

"Shit, I don't know!" Takis exclaimed, terrified. "I hate this, babies and all the-" he gagged and clamped his hand to his mouth.

"Well, look away. Just tell me what to do when I ask, okay?"

"How are you so calm?" Takis asked him, rubbing his hands together nervously.

"I've seen many lamb births. I've seen things go bad. I've had to skin and dress a lot of animals. I've cleaned up a lot of muck in the barn. I'm just thankful I don't have to touch any of this stuff."

"Alright," Takis said, ignoring him and taking in breaths. "I'm alright." Beulah let out a blood-curdling scream, and Takis's eyes went wide. He leaned forward and gagged. Nothing came, but in Takis' mind, he was throwing everything he'd ever eaten up. Clayton looked at Takis with concern.

"Takis, do you, um, do you need to go outside?"

"It was her fault," he gasped. "It's killing her." There was a large tearing sound in the room, and Takis heaved again. Takis noticed a woman dressed in white, carrying a torn piece of cloth dripping with water, emerge from the corner.

"I hate this place," he spat and wiped his mouth.

"Here, let me give you this, Beulah," the midwife said, placing the wet rag on her forehead. "Excuse me, Mr. Roth," she apologized as she stepped in front of him.

"No need, miss, I'll stand back," he said.

"Takis?" Clayton asked. Takis looked up from his bent-over position, his eyes watery and his face flushed.

"Yes, Clayton?"

"Do you need to go?"

"I can't. We're trapped in this room. We can't walk through

walls and there's no open door. The doors disappear shortly after we use them," he took a deep breath.

"Can't you just go back to the hallway?"

"No, I need to be here for you. It's alright, boy."

The doctor stood, catching Takis' attention, his face much more serious.

"Dorthea, the umbilical cord is around the neck," he waved his hand. "Here now." Dorthea stopped what she was doing and rushed to his side. She put one hand over her mouth when she saw.

"What's wrong?" Mr. Roth asked. Dorthea put her hands up, palms forward.

"Mr. Roth, I need you to leave the room. The umbilical cord is around the baby's neck, and we may need to resort to trickier procedures, so if you please. I promise we know what we are doing." She gestured towards the door.

"She's lying. The baby is already gone," Takis said through clenched teeth. Mr. Roth placed his hands on his head, but he nodded and walked around her and through Takis. He looked back as he reached the door.

"I love you, Beulah," he said and left the room. Dorthea hurried back to the doctor, who was now guiding the little, blue figure out of Beulah's body. Clayton turned and looked at Takis, who shook his head.

"Doctor Hahn?" Beulah asked in exhaustion. "What's going on?" Doctor Hahn was looking Dorthea in the eye as he unwrapped the umbilical cord from the lifeless body's neck. There was no crying. The room was quiet. He cut the cord and stepped back from the bed. The child wasn't moving.

"What happens now?" Clayton asked as Takis was still trying to compose himself.

"She has to name him," Takis rasped.

"Why?" He turned to face Takis.

"You know how I told you I don't have all the answers?" Takis spit and gazed toward Clayton, his eyes watery. Doctor Hahn looked up at Beulah.

"My dear, it's a boy," he stammered, "but the umbilical cord was wrapped around his neck. In fact, there were several knots in the cord."

"What does that mean?" Her eyes filled with fear.

"Well, when there are knots-" he began, but Dorthea stepped in front of him.

"It means he was born still, Beulah. I am so sorry." Those words hung heavy in the room. Beulah began to cry softly at first, and then it filled the entire room.

"This is a wound that doesn't heal, a pain someone carries even past death." Takis put his arm around Clayton, who was staring at the ground.

"You were right. This room is unbearable. I just want to finish. I want to be far away from this," Clayton grieved. Dorthea turned and walked back to the baby and began cleaning him. She slowly wrapped him as if he was alive, carefully picked up the bundle, and walked to Beulah's side.

"Here he is, dear. He's yours," Dorthea said. Doctor Hahn walked through Clayton and hurried out the door.

"Oh, he's so tiny," Beulah wept. "He's my little boy." Dorthea sat beside her and brushed Beulah's hair out of her face.

"He's beautiful. Did you have a boy's name picked out?" Beulah looked up and nodded her head.

"Bruno."

———

Clayton rushed forward and saw Bruno's soul come flying out of the body. He dropped to his knees in a slide and caught him right before he hit the floor. He witnessed the thin line of light disconnect from the baby Beulah was holding. Bruno's eyes shot open, and he let out a cry. Clayton knew he was in pain, for he had recently felt that fire and rocked back and forth.

"It's fine. It will go away; it takes about a minute," Clayton murmured. He turned and walked towards Takis with the naked soul of Bruno Roth. He held him with great care as if he was the most important thing in the world, and Clayton caught a glimpse of Takis tearing up when he kissed Bruno on the forehead.

"Boy, you're going to be alright," Takis said with approval.

"What do I do now?"

"You need to say 'the Fork,'" Takis replied. The bedroom door flung open, and Mr. Roth rushed to his wife's side. He was in shambles, and Clayton didn't want to witness the two of them deal with the loss of their son.

"The Fork," he said with confidence. He turned around, and there was, now blocking his view of the Roths, the same door he saw before. He knew it led to somewhere new, and he couldn't wait to get little Bruno there as fast as he could.

"It's going to be fine, little man. You get to go home soon," he said to Bruno, who had started to relax. Takis opened the door, and Clayton, clutching Bruno, stepped through.

27

THE AFTER

"That's right, you'll be fine," Clayton trailed off. Takis outstretched his arms.

"Welcome to the Fork!" He proclaimed loudly as he turned and started away from Clayton. Clayton stood with his mouth wide open. He couldn't believe the scope of what was before him. It was as if he stepped into a painting. There was so much color above him in the night sky. No, not just any night sky; it was beyond comprehension. Stars littered it, glimmering so brightly it was blinding to stare at too long. If he were to begin counting, he'd be there for longer than his punishment. A purplish hue mixed in with the ink of night. There was no sky like this visible on Earth. A star shot across the sky, and Clayton watched it fly out of view. His eyes slowly panned to the ground where the grass was the deepest shade of green he'd ever seen. It was thick and lush, a living carpet that swayed in the wind. It went on forever. He knew if he began walking, there would be no end.

"There are no words," Clayton whispered.

"No. No, boy, there aren't," Takis said. To Clayton's right was a pond; the liquid inside resembled water but was golden and thick, as if someone melted thousands of gold bars down and poured them here. It sparkled and rippled in different places, hundreds of tiny lines moving in different directions. There were no waves. There were no patterns. It was random but perfect. At the front edge, it flowed into a river that traveled for another twenty-five yards into a cave on the side of a rock face. The cave opening was large, like everything else here. He could see the gold flow inside the cave to a blinding light.

"That has to be the Brilliance," Clayton said.

"You think?" Takis laughed. To the near side of the cave entrance was a pedestal with a giant book and quill. The pedestal was made of marble, and the feather on the quill was so white that it seemed as if it glowed.

"Praise be," Clayton uttered.

"I said the same thing when I first arrived. Well, something similar," Takis chuckled. Clayton stood for a long while, just watching the river of gold flow. He was proud to see this. After all the pain and suffering he'd witnessed, it was a calming sight. He knew something extraordinary was waiting for baby Bruno on the other side of that dazzling light. That's when Clayton turned around. For all the happiness and joy that the sight of the Brilliance gave him, it left him instantly when he saw the Darkness.

The grass died as it approached the cave on the left rock face. The dirt around it looked sickly, dry, and cracked. Clayton felt that if he stood on that dirt for very long, it would suck the life out of him too. He could not see inside the cave. Smoke rolled and swayed. It was a dense black, and he could feel the cold just looking into it. No light could escape this darkness. It was a manifestation of despair and misery.

"You've lead people to that? How?" He asked, shuddering.

"They're drawn to it. You don't have to do anything. They can't get away."

"I am so thankful I'm not going in there."

"Wait until you see it take someone," Takis grimaced. Clayton looked at him and saw the fear in his eyes but didn't ask. He didn't want to know. Bruno let out a wail, and here in the Fork, it echoed. It was deafening.

"Let's get him on his way," Takis yelled.

"Why is he echoing like this, and we aren't?" Clayton raised his voice.

"What?" Takis yelled. Clayton repeated himself. "Because, like everything else, this place makes no sense!" Takis yelled, irritated. Clayton followed Takis around the pond and over to the pedestal. Bruno was crying louder now, and the echo was growing in power. It started to hurt. A ringing took up in Clayton's ears, and it was hard to hear anything else but Bruno's cry. They hurried up the riverside towards the pedestal.

"I was going to have you do it, but I'll write his name in the book this time!" Takis yelled.

"What?" Clayton asked. Takis waved him off and turned to the pedestal.

"What do I do with him?!" Clayton yelled. Bruno's cries were ear-splitting, echoing louder and louder.

"I don't give a damn, but I'm about to pitch him in!" Takis bellowed. He picked up the quill. Bruno had sucked in a breath to let out another cry, so all Clayton heard Takis say was "pitch him in." Clayton looked at Bruno, whose entire face was red. His tiny fit was getting worse. Clayton was confused by what Takis had told him to do, but he was in charge, and Clayton wanted to make a good impression. He looked down at Bruno and kissed his forehead.

"Be on your way," Clayton whispered. He tossed the baby in the flowing gold. There was no splash. There was no noise. It was as if the liquid swallowed him. The crying stopped instantly. There was silence again. Clayton thought he would have floated up the river and was confused with how fast he sank. Takis put the quill back after signing Bruno's name on the page.

"Thank Zeus! I was getting a headache. How did you shut the

little man up?" Takis turned around to see Clayton peering into the river.

"So, what happens now? We go get the next one?" He asked.

"Clayton, where's Bruno?" Takis asked, looking around in panic.

"What do you mean? I did what you said," Clayton answered.

"What?"

"I threw him in."

"YOU WHAT?!" Takis' eyes went wide, and he threw his hands above his head.

"You said to pitch him in," Clayton imitated, throwing him in.

"Oh no, oh no. You didn't." Takis' hands came down to his lips. Clayton watched Takis shift back and forth, and his eyes looked down as if he were in a trance.

"Was I wrong?" Clayton asked.

"I said, 'I'm about to pitch him in,' not 'pitch him in!' Shit, Clayton." He started to pace.

"No problem, I'll just get him. How deep is it?" Clayton put his arm down to the surface.

"CLAYTON, NO!" It was too late, Clayton's fingertip touched the gold, and he was blown back by an unearthly force. The pain shot through Clayton's arm like lightning and seemed to hold in his chest right at his heart. Clayton hit the ground with a sickening thud. The air rushed out of his body when he landed.

"Boy? Boy, are you alright?" Takis screeched as he ran up to where Clayton lay.

"Why?" He gasped.

"You aren't worthy. It's alright. It happened to me a long time ago. I'm sorry, I should have grabbed you." Clayton closed his eyes and slowly got to his knees, still woozy, swaying back and forth

"Bruno. Oh no, Bruno. What are we gonna do, Takis?"

"Shit. Shit!" Takis yelled.

28

The boat emerged from the pond, a simple wooden gondola. The stern was littered with carvings of stars. It slowly rose through the gold, not a drop sticking to it. A lone hooded figure was seated in it as it surfaced and started moving slowly across the pond to the mouth of where the river began.

"Charon. Maybe Charon can help us," Takis said. He stood up and rushed to the shoreline. He waved his hands above his head, and the hooded figure glanced up. It raised its right hand. Clayton stood and fell back over. He was dizzy and was having a hard time catching his breath. He braced himself and tried to stand again. Somewhat successful, he stumbled forward a couple of feet before tumbling again. He was finally able to make it to Takis' side as the gondola pulled up to the riverbank.

"Something the matter?" Charon asked softly. "This better be important." Clayton could not see inside the hood. He had no idea what Takis was talking to. The voice was raspy but high pitched. He didn't want to lean forward for a closer look for fear of falling in again.

"Did the boy touch the river?" Charon asked, amused.

"Yes," Takis answered.

"Isn't this his first day?" Charon chuckled. Takis nodded but quickly changed the subject.

"We have a problem, and I need your help," Takis said. Charon stood up on the gondola and was quite short. In Clayton's eyes, the hooded figure couldn't have been more than four and a half feet tall.

"What happened?"

"The boy," Takis gestured toward Clayton, "threw the baby's soul in the river." Charon looked back and forth between Takis and Clayton.

"Are you serious?"

"Yes! That's never happened to me before. I don't know what to do. I can't call on Feme. You know what will happen. Can you help us?" Takis dabbed fretfully at the sweat on his forehead. Charon looked at Clayton.

"Why did you do that?" Charon asked.

"I thought he told me to pitch him in," Clayton explained, still rubbing his hand. Charon was motionless except for the gondola rocking up and down.

"This is new to me too," Charon sighed.

"Who can we call that isn't Feme?" Clayton inquired. Charon pulled the hood back to reveal her chubby face, round eyes, and long silver hair. Her features were feminine, but she looked so out of place to Clayton. It was as if she was carved out of ivory. She was beautiful, yes, but not in a way he saw his mother or Amber. She was unique to him. Something other-worldly, something odd. Her eyes bothered him, though. They were a deep shade of red, almost the color of blood, and lacked pupils. They were something out of a nightmare like they didn't belong on her face.

"I don't know. Maybe Acquisitions?" Charon suggested. Takis brightened up quickly.

"Yes! Yes, Nix will know what to do. Clayton, go fetch Nix.

Hurry," Takis said. Clayton stood up straight, trying to not focus on the pain.

"Okay, just say 'home,' right?"

"Yes. Hurry, before Feme finds out. I'll stay here with Charon. If Feme sees me, she'll know something is wrong."

"What if she sees me?"

"Lie to her. Tell her I'm with Astrid getting fitted. Damn it, boy, hurry!" Clayton nodded even though he knew perfectly well if Feme saw him, he would tell her the truth if she asked.

"Takis," Charon interrupted, her voice soft, "you go. It's the boy's first day. He's already scared out of his mind. He can stay here with me."

"If Feme sees me-" Takis began.

"If she sees either one of you, there will be trouble. You can handle it better than he could." She pointed a gloved hand at Clayton. Takis looked away and sighed heavily, mulling over what Charon had said.

"Home," he shouted and turned around and rushed through the door he called without looking back to them.

29

There was an awkward silence between the two of them after the door disappeared. Clayton was trying hard not to stare at Charon. He'd already made one blunder today. The last thing he wanted to do was anger this strange creature.

"It's the eyes," she said suddenly.

"What?" Clayton asked, confused.

"The eyes. No one can seem to get over my eyes." She smiled at him warmly. Clayton felt his cheeks flush. It was as if she was reading his mind.

"I, well..."

"Not many people see us with our hoods off, certainly not on their first day."

"No, no, you're lovely. This has just been a lot to take in," he admitted, snorting a laugh. Charon paused. Her eyes widened.

"I'm sorry if I offended you," Clayton apologized.

"Not at all." She walked around him in a circle. His eyes locked on her as she looked him up and down. "Usually, on the first day, there are a lot of tears and whining. You seem quite calm if I may say so."

"I'm sure I'll get to that. It's all happening so fast. One minute I'm asleep in my bed, the next I'm at the gateway between Heaven and Hell." Clayton ran his fingers through his hair and stared back at the Darkness.

"How did you end up here?" She asked him. Clayton jerked at the question. He didn't want to tell her that he had killed himself. He was ashamed at the very thought.

"I'm sorry," she said and put a hand up to him, "I'm not good with things like this. It isn't often that I get to have a real conversation with someone. Most of the time, I'm answering questions about the Brilliance." She gestured towards the cave.

"It's fine," Clayton wanted to change the subject away from his death. If he dwelled on it for too long, the reality of it all would hit him. "But let's not talk about me. I want to know about you." Even if her eyes were haunting, she was intriguing, and talking to her was taking his mind off the disaster of moments ago. "What exactly are you?" She placed her hands on her hips playfully.

"I am a ferryman," she smiled as she boasted. She wasn't loud like Takis, she wasn't cruel like Feme, and she wasn't as imposing as Nix. There was a softness in her voice, and something in her facial features came across as kind.

"How long have you been doing that?" He was thankful he got to ask this question so quickly. Maybe her answer would help him gauge how time worked in the After.

"Since my very first day?" She raised an eyebrow.

"No, I mean, when did you get assigned to your position?"

"Oh!" She exclaimed and put her hands together, almost clapping. "We aren't like you. I've been at this since this place was created."

"Really? We?"

"Yes, there are several ferrymen," she answered. Clayton paused.

"You won't get in trouble for what I did, will you?" He asked.

"No need to worry, I will be just fine," she let out a small laugh, and Clayton noticed her teeth. They were almost perfect.

"Since Creation?" Clayton asked incredulously. So many questions ran through his head. Was Charon created by God? Was this her only purpose? Did she ever get bored? These he kept to himself. He was just happy someone wasn't chastising him.

"Did you own a dog?" She asked him, a hint of excitement in her voice.

"Um, I had a horse," Clayton said and felt a slight sting. He would never see Charley again, and he would miss him. "I had sheep too." He felt sorry for all of them. His father would never give them the attention he did.

"I have a bird," she told him with too much exuberance. He found it charming. For someone who had been around since creation, she had a child-like innocence. It reminded him of Amber and how she could barely contain herself when she read the Lewis and Clark article to him. He could feel the sadness tugging at him. Everyone he loved and everything he enjoyed about life was at the forefront of his mind.

"I'm sorry," Charon said.

"Hmm?" He asked.

"You're crying," she pointed out. Clayton reached up and wiped the tears from his eyes.

"Oh, I, uh...."

"You know, maybe the baby is still in the River. I can go check." She quickly climbed back into the gondola and shoved off before Clayton could get his bearings to tell her it was alright.

30

"I'm back!" He heard Takis exclaim from behind him. Clayton stood on the shoreline watching the gondola out in the center of the river; Charon had her oar in hand and stabbed at the gold. Clayton glanced over to Takis and nodded at him.

"Nix will be here shortly. What the hell is Charon doing?" Takis asked, mildly amused.

"She's using her oar trying to find Bruno," he answered. Clayton watched Charon bring her oar up and down in a swift motion. He thought if she hit Bruno that it would have to hurt. Plus, if she did come in contact with him, what good was that going to do?

"Bruno isn't in the river. I think Nix said he would be somewhere on Earth," Takis reported. "Charon! Come on back, the baby isn't in there," he called out to her, his voice booming throughout the Fork. Charon looked back and waved. She steered the vessel back towards the shore.

"So, he said he could help?" Clayton inquired.

"Apparently, one of Acquisitions' jobs is to recover lost souls,"

Takis informed them both, as Charon stepped out of the gondola onto the solid ground with the two of them.

"I hope he finds him soon," she said. "We won't have much longer before it starts a paper trail."

"I know," Takis said to her, his voice too high. He was nearly shivering, and his motions were jerky.

"It will be alright, I'm sure-" Clayton began.

"Clayton," Takis started, "losing a soul is a serious offense. If Feme finds out, it could be the Darkness for the both of us."

"I'm sorry."

"We know you are, but that won't matter to her. I've heard the stories," Charon said. A chill came over Clayton. He had messed up his first retrieval. He didn't want to get Takis in trouble. Everything was coming at him so fast. He hadn't had time to mourn Amber. He hadn't even had time to worry about the effect his death would have on Eve. He had just made a friend in Takis and had already let him down.

"How's your arm?" Takis asked Clayton.

"I'm alright, just sore," he lied. It was a lot more than sore. It was throbbing.

"We can visit the doctor after this is over," Takis said. Clayton looked at him questioningly.

"A doctor?"

"Yes," Takis answered. "Doctor Peron."

"Isn't he the one that goes on and on about leeches, complaining that he can't work without them?" Charon piped in.

"Good point," Takis nodded. He patted Clayton on the back. "You're fine. We'll save the doctor for real emergencies."

"There are doctors here?" Clayton asked, stunned.

"Absolutely," Takis winced. "I got in a fight with a man here a long time ago. We were both laid up for a few days while my eye went back in, and his arms healed."

"Your eye?

"Yeah, the bastard popped it out with his thumb. It seemed like it took ages to go back into place. I was miserable. I don't remember the doctor's name, though. He was a few back. Doctors don't last long here. Every time I turn around, it seems like I'm being introduced to a new one," Takis said. Clayton didn't know how to respond to that. He had seen Mr. Roth walk through Takis, so maybe only ghosts could hurt one another. Clayton had expected so much from the tales he was told of the afterlife from Reverend Price and his parents.

The worn-down hallways, the tiny cramped offices, Feme, the fact that he could be injured and still feel pain, it was all depressing. There should be so much more than this. The Fork was magical, otherworldly, but everything else was so disappointing.

"What if someone comes here?" Clayton realized. "What if someone sees us waiting here?"

"We have our own set of rules," Charon answered. "There is more than one Fork and more than just me. This one just happens to be yours." She pointed a gloved hand towards the lake. "We have our own little slice of the After down there."

"So, no one else can get in here?" Clayton asked.

"Not unless they summon a door here, calling to find one of you," she assured him. "But we don't have time for this. Is there anything we can do to help Nix?" They all heard the sweet sound at once, a baby crying, and they turned to see Nix coming through a door.

"It's alright, I got him! You'll never believe this, but he was in Cleveland," Nix said, greeting them. "A family of four thought their home was haunted." He laughed and made his way to them through the high grass. He handed Bruno, who was still throwing a fit, to Charon. She boarded the gondola and shoved off from the shore.

"I'll see you later!" She called and put her hood up, hiding her face again.

"It was nice to meet you!" Clayton called and waved.

"I didn't log this one, Takis. You owe me," Nix exhaled.

"I know, friend, the debt keeps rising." Takis bowed.

"Clayton, you owe me too."

"Thank you, Nix. I promise I'll repay you someday," Clayton bowed too, which was awkward for him. Nix wasted no time, and he was out his door with a quick phrase and a turn. Clayton and Takis watched as Charon, holding the baby, rode into the cave entrance and out of sight. They turned and looked at each other and began laughing.

"I can't believe you threw the baby in the river," Takis chuckled.

"I thought you told me to," Clayton responded. They laughed a little harder.

"I bet Bruno was the most shocked of all," Takis said and wiped a tear from his eye.

31

AUGUST 9TH, 1855

Clayton was efficient in his work. They finished their days quickly, and outside of a minor snag here and there, they had time to talk before the daily ten reset on them. Takis, since Clayton was in training, only had to complete the ten Clayton was assigned. Clayton was determined and didn't waste any time doing his duties.

There was a small office set up with chairs against the wall that acted as a lounge for people who finished their work early. Clayton and Takis found themselves there almost every day. Takis kept everything light-hearted as they talked of everything from their love of food to how different life was for the both of them. They were rarely disturbed. Most of the others finished just in the nick of time. Clayton summoned all the doors and did all the work for them now, including signing the passage book in the Fork. Takis wondered on several occasions why Clayton needed him at all.

"You know," Clayton said as he stretched his arms behind his head. "This isn't so bad. The days just fly by." They had finished up much faster than usual and had taken their regular spots in the lounge.

"Shit," Takis cursed as he eyed the room. "Don't say things like that."

"What do you mean?" Clayton teased.

"This place will make it harder on you. Stop acting like you're having a good time." Takis' eyes fluttered around the room faster, and his voice grew quieter.

"Oh, I hate this place," Clayton mocked.

"Stop it."

"If this was any worse, I don't know what I would do! The torture, the horror," Clayton put his wrist to his forehead and pretended to faint in his chair.

"Clayton!" Takis exploded. "You're my friend, I'd do anything for you, but unless you want me to box your ears, you'll cut that shit out right now."

"I was just fooling," Clayton explained. Takis sighed. He held his hands up and shook his head. "I know. Shit, I didn't mean to snap. I've been here a long time, and I know what this place wants. It wants you to suffer, and you're mocking it."

"You act like it's alive."

"It is," Takis said. Clayton jerked in his chair as if he'd been punched hard in the arm.

"What's wrong?" Takis probed. Clayton dug at his left hand.

"My hand is itching something fierce."

"I was right. We only did nine." Takis rolled his eyes.

"No, we did ten. I counted."

"Well," Takis rose, "your digging at your hand tells me otherwise. Let's get this over with."

"I was sure we did ten," Clayton said and stood up.

Clayton was the first one through the door. He loved Takis like a brother, they had grown quite close over the last few years, and the conversation they'd had in the lounge solidified it.

They were friends, and Clayton hoped they'd be partners for a long time. Since he was stuck here, who better to be with than his best friend? Clayton wanted to make this quick and finish up the set. He thought they already had, but as Takis had pointed out, he wouldn't be itching like this if he'd completed all ten. Clayton stopped when he saw the New Mexico Territory night sky and the vast beauty of it all. He stumbled as Takis bumped into him.

"Well, move on, boy," Takis quipped.

"Sorry," Clayton said and stepped forward a little way. Clayton looked around confused and turned back to Takis. "Did I make a mistake?"

"I heard you say the name. The door was summoned. I mean, you did everything right." He looked around at the sand and cactus, trying to make out exactly where they were. "Check it again." Clayton looked down at the life list in his hand. He had said the name correctly, Cheyenne Hart.

"I called for Cheyenne's final moment. This is it."

"I see someone," Takis called back to him. Clayton squinted and tried to see in the dark.

"Where?"

"Come on," Takis pointed. "I can barely make them out, but that has to be what we are here for." Clayton followed behind Takis. Even for the dead of night, it was hot. They shuffled along through the sand a little way until Clayton could see the outline of a man hunkered down behind a large rock. Clayton sped up and walked past Takis to get a better view of their situation. Clayton was practically on top of the man when he finally got a full glimpse of him. He was young, likely in his twenties, holding a revolver. He knelt down, shaking his head. The man pulled a small cigar from his breast pocket and put it in his mouth with his free hand. He reached in the same pocket, produced a single match, and struck the match against the rock, and lit the cigar in one fluid motion. He discarded the match and took a long draw, slowly letting the smoke escape from his lungs and mouth.

"Listen, Maude!" He finally yelled out. "I've followed you for weeks. Just let me take you in. I'll treat you fair!" He put the cigar back in his mouth then wiped the grime from his forehead. He was covered in dirt and sand and smelled of the land. They heard a voice from a small way up the hill a few moments later.

"Horse shit, Sheriff! You'll hang me! You ain't hangin' me!" She yelled. The sheriff spit a little tobacco out and looked annoyed.

"Listen, woman! You have my word. I don't want to hang you out here in the middle of nowhere. Let me take you back. You can plead to the judge!" A few more moments passed.

"Ain't no way I don't hang," she cried back.

"You killed a man in broad daylight! In front of his kids! You deserve to hang, but I don't make that call. Please, Maude, I served with your brother. Don't make me kill you. I don't want to kill you!"

"If you take me back, they're going to kill me, so you might as well do it yourself!" This time Clayton noticed something in her voice. There was pain. The unseen woman was struggling with her words. Clayton looked down at the sheriff, all dressed in brown to the point he blended in with the dull tones of the land around him. Clayton walked around to the sheriff's front, saw the silver star on his chest, and the worried look in his eyes. He could tell this man didn't want this to end violently, he meant what he said, and the concern across his brow showed it. Clayton felt Takis tap his shoulder and turned to face him.

"You need to see this," he said and tilted his head in the direction of the hill. Clayton followed Takis up the hill and came to a second large rock. He could hear someone breathing heavily behind it. Clayton looked around the rock and saw a woman leaning against it. She was obviously in pain and holding a revolver, her blonde hair matted to her face and shoulders. Her eyes were wide with panic, and her belly swollen from the baby she was carrying.

"No," Clayton huffed. "This one is going to end badly."

"They all end badly."

"You know what I mean," Clayton fired back. He looked at the woman, who was clearly in labor, and wondered how long they had been in this standoff. How long had she been sitting here in pain?

"He deserved to die! You don't know what he did to me!" She yelled out through clenched teeth.

"I don't care what he did. You don't shoot a man in front of his family! You could have come to me. I would have helped you!" The sheriff answered from downhill. Clayton looked at Takis. He'd made up his mind. He was going to attempt to diffuse the situation using Afterwords. It was the only way.

"I'm going to try," Clayton said as Takis rolled his eyes.

"Come on, Clayton, this isn't how we do things."

"I just don't want either of these people to die, Takis. We know the baby is going to, but I don't want these two added to the tally."

"Whatever. Let's see it. Go ahead." Takis gestured at her.

Over the last decade, Takis had attempted to teach Clayton how to use the Afterwords, how to relax, and speak to a living person to convince them to do as you wish. It was only to be used in extreme circumstances, not for the parlor trick that Takis had done with Alan when they first met. It was a tool that very few in their position had properly used. Clayton flicked his wrist, and her life list came into his hand. He knelt down beside her and started reading.

"This is Maude Hart, twenty-two years old, from Boerne, Texas. She is unwed and actually a pretty decent person."

"Except for the whole murder thing, right? That kind of stuff keeps you from being a decent person." Takis joked. Clayton ignored the remark and kept reading. He dropped the paper and glanced back at Takis.

"She was raped by a man named Robert Miller. He hurt her

pretty bad. When she recovered, she shot and killed him in the street. He was with his kids. She's been on the run ever since."

"I'll go look at the sheriff's list. It's never easy, is it?" Takis walked slowly backward and started downhill. Clayton looked at Maude, who had tears streaming down her face. He thought back to the things Takis tried to teach him. He relaxed his muscles and thought of Amber's face. He thought of Eve playing in the yard at his father's farm. He thought of his mother's smile. He spoke softly and from deep in his chest.

He can help you deliver this baby. You can't do this on your own.

She jerked violently away from his direction. Clayton wondered if she heard him. Her eyes were even wider now, and she looked conflicted. He decided to try again.

You want this to be over, don't you? Why keep this up?

"I want this to be over. I just want it to stop!" She cried out. He could barely contain himself. He let out a triumphant *yes!* He had done it. She heard him, and she was responding. He stood up and started towards the edge of the rock just as Takis rounded it.

"The sheriff is a guy named Matthew Oakley. Good man. Killed a few people, but all of them were criminals he couldn't take in. Has a pregnant wife at home. Life list was fairly clean." Takis tilted his head at Clayton quizzically. "What are you all giddy about?"

"I did it!" Clayton gloated.

"You did what?"

"Afterwords! She's responsive."

"Oh shit, seriously?" Takis looked genuinely happy. "It took me forever to learn how to do it, and it still doesn't work most of the time."

"I'm going to try to get her to get...what's his name again?"

"Matthew Oakley."

"I'm going to try to get Sheriff Oakley up here to deliver Cheyenne. This does not end with them shooting each other. It's bad enough the baby isn't going to make it." Clayton turned back to Maude and leaned towards her.

Tell him you are setting the gun down and ask for his help.

Maude looked in Clayton's direction and wept. She couldn't see him, he was sure of it, but he knew she felt him.

"Sheriff! I'm going to set my gun down. I need your help! Please help!" There was a stillness in the air as they waited for what seemed like an eternity.

"What? Why do you need my help? This better not be some goddamn trick, woman. I don't need this."

"I'm with child! I'm having the baby right now! I need your help!" She winced in pain again and cried out into the night. "Sheriff?" There was no answer. "Matthew?" She called out once more.

"Son of a bitch." Clayton wheeled around to see Sheriff Oakley standing there with his gun drawn and his mouth agape. Matthew rushed over to her and knelt down in front of her.

"What the hell? You've been running all this time like this?" He pointed to her belly.

"Yes," she sighed and made another face in strain. "I'm seven months. With all the people I've hid out with, no one told you I'm pregnant?"

"No," he wiped the sweat onto his sleeve and laid his hat beside them. "I don't know how to deliver a baby."

"Me either. I know it's coming."

"We're alone out here. It's a two-day ride to the nearest doctor," he said. She screamed and laid down on her back. They were there for a while as Sheriff Oakley murmured words of encouragement, and she screamed in pain. Clayton stood in silence as Takis paced back and forth. Clayton knew that Takis had gotten better around childbirth, but he was still squeamish.

"Did Robert do this to you?" Sheriff Oakley asked her in a moment of silence. She nodded. "Goddamn it, why didn't you come to me? I'd have beat the skin off that man. I would have helped you. You didn't have to kill him."

"He took from me. I took from him." Tears streamed down her face through a layer of dust. Her mouth opened wide as if to scream, but nothing came out.

"Maude?"

"Help!" She finally exhaled and let out a scream that could wake the dead.

It didn't take long, and the baby came without much of a fight. She was tiny. One of the smallest Clayton had seen. She was crying, but it didn't sound strong. Clayton knew her time was short. They wouldn't have been there otherwise. Maude was holding her, still seated where she had been, sweat oozing from every pore.

"My little Cheyenne," she whispered softly.

"I have no idea how the hell I'm going to get the two of you back to town." Sheriff Oakley said, smiling at the baby wrapped in the blanket he had on his horse.

"You can't take me back," she said to him. Her face was serious, and her tone sharp.

"Maude, I have to do my job. Tell your story. You'll have your day in court."

"And they'll hang me, and what happens to her then?" She rolled her eyes weakly. Sheriff Oakley stood.

"You have a mother and a father who are back home. They don't understand what happened to you. Let me take you home. They'll watch the baby for the trial. This isn't going to—" He began.

"I will be tried by a jury of twelve men. They'll think he was having an affair, I was trying to destroy his home, and when he wouldn't leave them, I killed him."

"Listen, I can speak on your behalf. I know you. They may not be willing to hear you, but they will hear me."

She shook her head at the sheriff.

"I'm too big of a coward. You're going to have to do it." Maude's right hand slowly started for the gun beside her.

"What the hell are you doing? Don't do this," Matthew ordered, his left hand resting on his revolver. "Please."

"You know it's true, but you always have to play nice, keep your head in the sand. I'm not dying like that." She gripped her gun. Sheriff Oakley pulled his revolver.

"Don't. Think of the baby. You are holding your baby. Don't make me kill you while you're holding her."

Clayton felt the panic rising. He leaned into Maude and looked between Sheriff Oakley and Maude.

"Boy, you need to calm down. You have to be relaxed." Takis warned Clayton. Clayton glanced back at Takis and to Maude again. He tried to keep his voice commanding but soft.

What are you doing? Let him take you home. There is a chance.

It wasn't working. Clayton wasn't calm. He wasn't thinking clearly. She didn't hear him at all. Clayton looked at Takis, pleading with his eyes for help.

"I don't think she'll listen," he told him.

Clayton tried one last time.

Maude. He can help. He didn't-

She pointed the pistol at the sheriff, and he acted on instinct. The shot rang out in the night air. It only took one; the bullet struck Maude between the eyes. She was gone in an instant. The sheriff rushed over to take the baby away from her. She stared at him, lifeless, her back still against the rock.

"Why?" Sheriff Oakley asked. "Why the hell did you make me do that?" He repeated the phrase over and over. He stepped away from her. Sheriff Oakley stood, holding Cheyenne as the sun peeked over the horizon, Clayton beside him the entire time.

"I'll bury your momma, then I'll get you back home,

Cheyenne." Matthew looked down at the blanket and shook her gently. "Cheyenne?" He whispered. Clayton caught her as she left her body. He was close enough to the sheriff to smell the cigar on his breath from earlier. Clayton peered into his eyes and saw they were filled with fear. He watched as the sheriff dropped to his knees and unwrapped her. His right hand held the back of her head while he rubbed her chest with the other and repeated no, over and over again. Clayton felt sorry for him. The sheriff didn't want any of this, and Clayton had tried to help him achieve that. Matthew stopped rubbing her chest and pulled her into his body. He sat on his knees, clutching her. Clayton knelt beside him.

You did all you could.

Sheriff Oakley looked in his direction. He slowly gathered his composure and got back to his feet, still clutching Cheyenne tightly against him. Sheriff Oakley kissed her forehead.

"I'm so sorry. You didn't deserve this." He walked back towards Maude. "I'll bury you together." Takis and Clayton stood off in the distance and watched as Sheriff Oakley began to dig a grave.

"Who picks up Maude?" Clayton wondered.

"Hmm?" Takis appeared to come out of a trance. "Oh, in situations like this, we can't see her soul or her handler, and they can't see us. Could you imagine the fight she'd give you to get that baby?"

Clayton didn't answer him; he just stared at the sheriff, watching him dig. He felt the heat of the sun on his face and realized how hot the day was going to be. The sheriff was in for a rough time burrowing into the earth.

"I hate this job," Clayton finally said.

"Me too, boy," Takis shuffled his feet. "This place wants to punish us."

"Let's get her home," Clayton nodded and gave one last look towards the sheriff.

"We spent a lot of time here. I bet our next set has already started," Takis mused. Clayton called the door to the Fork, and they passed through.

32

THE AFTER

It was a few days later that Clayton opened up about himself. Something with Maude and Cheyenne had affected him. Takis didn't need him to explain it. He was withdrawn and quiet. He seemed to have lost a bit of his shine. When Clayton started talking about his sister, Takis listened and let him vent. He didn't interrupt him. He wanted him to get it all out.

"I left her behind, all alone with Papa. She didn't deserve that."

"You can't look at it that way."

"How else am I supposed to look at it?" Clayton asked, looking flustered.

"Let me ask you a question," Takis leaned forward in his chair, "did you ever tell that little girl you loved her?"

"That's a stupid question, Takis." Clayton rolled his eyes at him.

"Answer the question, Clayton."

"Of course I did."

"That stays with a person. You don't seem like the man to use that word lightly." Takis leaned back and looked upward.

"I hope she remembers me," Clayton spat in frustration.

"She will," Takis reassured him. Takis talked about losing his

145

mother at an early age, and Clayton discussed Emma. He spoke about how she was the glue that held the family together and of her tenderness and the love she had. Finally, Clayton brought up the subject of her death, about how scarlet fever took hold and how he sat with her. He described how terrible she looked and her suffering.

"She called you good," Takis interrupted. Clayton stopped.

"How did you know that?"

"You sat with her that entire night," he spoke as Clayton looked at him suspiciously. "That seems like such a long time ago."

"Takis, you were in the corner?" Clayton stood.

"I remember it because I was afraid I'd made myself visible, that she could actually see me," Takis explained, rubbing his eyebrow with his index finger.

"She did see you!" Clayton exclaimed.

"That's not possible," Takis dismissed with a shake of his head

"She was talking to you, straight to you. Was she looking right at you?" Clayton pointed at Takis' chest.

"Clayton," Takis admonished. He wanted this conversation to end. He was growing uncomfortable.

"Was she?" Clayton persisted.

"Yes, but I wasn't visible," Takis surrendered with a huff.

"What happened after she died?" Clayton asked, leaning forward, his eyes narrowed in intensity. Takis sat back in his chair, looking towards the floor. He was trying to remember everything about that night. When one takes ten people a day for as many years as he had, the faces run together. He'd told Clayton already that he remembered her because of how she spoke to him directly and his fear that in his emotional state, he'd allowed himself to be seen. He told Clayton that he was called to her that night, and he was in the corner, watching as the young boy held her hand and that she spoke in his direction. He reminded Clayton that she was at the end, and her eyes didn't follow Takis when he moved. He remembered the boy falling asleep in the chair and the woman passing shortly after. He said she was upset about leaving her children behind. He took her to the Fork, where she asked if her mother would be waiting on the other side, and Takis turned her over to Charon, who took her upriver into the Brilliance.

"And?" Clayton asked.

"And what? I did my job and sent her on her way. I completely forgot about the whole thing."

"When did you realize you knew me?"

"Clayton, I don't know what you want from me here. She passed on. I took her where she was meant to go." Takis was trying to defuse this situation. He didn't want to tell Clayton he'd recognized him the day they met. Takis knew if he mentioned it on their first encounter, Clayton might not have reacted as well as he did. Takis had forgotten about it as time went on, but he was afraid to tell Clayton now.

"Let me see her life list," Clayton demanded and held out his hand.

"Why? What peace will that give you?"

"I want to see it," Clayton said and pointed to his palm.

"No," Takis told him flatly.

"She's my mother."

"She may be, but how is looking at her life going to make you feel any better? You'll see a part of her you aren't meant to. It isn't fair to her, Clayton. You wouldn't want someone doing that to you.

"I need to see," Clayton insisted.

"No, what you need is to take solace in the fact that your mother was good enough in life to make it to the Brilliance. What the Hades has gotten into you, boy?" He asked. Clayton's eyes widened, and his fists clenched. Takis found himself wondering if Clayton would swing on him. Takis placed his hands in his lap. If Clayton did step forward with intent, he was ready to take him to the ground. Takis found himself praying it didn't come to that.

"When did you realize you knew me, Takis?" Clayton asked again. Takis finally gave in.

"The day I met you." All the anger seemed to disappear from Clayton's face. It was replaced by the same expression of shock he had when they met, and Clayton saw his body on the ground. "Clayton, you should be happy. She was wonderful, and now you know I took her to the Brilliance. Your mother will be waiting for you. It's more than most get." Takis tried to smile at him.

"You could have told me. All this time, you could have told me. I would never do something like that to you," Clayton said. He turned and started for the door. "I'm going for a walk." Takis called after him, but he was out the door with a bang as he slammed it shut. Takis sat in silence for a moment.

"Of all the ungrateful shit. It wasn't like I was mean to her. I wasn't hiding anything. Oh, and why should I have told you, huh? Look at how you acted!" He said to the empty room. "I deserve a little more from you, boy. I've done nothing but treat you with respect." He leaned back in his chair and folded his arms in anger.

33

Clayton left the room and was out in the hallway. He was seething, but he couldn't tell why. He wanted to see his mother's list. It was the only connection he had to his past. Clayton wanted nothing more than to feel the way he did when he was alive. The After hadn't crushed his soul like everyone had warned him it would. He enjoyed getting the souls of the young and taking them to the Fork. He felt like his job was essential and that he was a special cog in the gears that made existence flow. The problem was boredom. He had so much time to reflect on what his life should have been, how much he missed Amber and Eve.

He looked down the hallway at all the nameless faces, people he'd never met but had been around for almost a decade. That leveled a little sadness on top of his anger. This was the first time since he'd gotten here that he was frustrated with the entire situation. A lot of the rules made no sense, and the overall dullness of this place made it worse. He just wanted to go home, to sleep in his bed, see his father again, and to play with Eve and her dolls. He started to feel sorry for himself. He shuffled down the hallway, not really knowing where he was going or why he was going there. He wasn't paying attention when she called out his name. She had to raise her voice to almost a yell before he heard her.

"Clayton, clean your ears! I need you in here now!" Feme called from her doorway.

"Shit," he muttered under his breath. He'd never been called into Feme's office before. He already felt like garbage and having her yell at him over something trivial was not what he needed right now. He faked a smile and started toward her office.

"Shut the door and have a seat," she said as she sat down. Clayton crossed the threshold, and he noticed instantly that she was not herself. She wasn't angry, she wasn't yelling, there was no chill in the room from her icy demeanor. There was something else in her face. He could have sworn it was fear, and he could see the worry in her brow.

"What's going on, Feme?" Clayton asked.

"I have a job for you. I am going to pull Takis into some meetings and have Astrid finally get him out of that terrible outfit. While he's busy, you are going to do this for me." She motioned to the paper in front of her. Her hand was shaking. As he reached across her desk to touch it, Feme slapped her hand onto the paper.

"Clayton, I need your discretion," she warned. Clayton stared at Feme. She watched him without blinking. This was something big. He nodded slowly, and she lifted her hand. He picked up the sheet of paper and sat back down. Feme looked down at her desk, pretending to be involved in something else to avoid his gaze after he read it. He looked at the instructions before him, then looked back at her.

"I don't know who this is," he said, confused.

"That's Takis' son." She didn't raise her eyes. Clayton reeled.

"Why would you put this on me, Feme?"

"This came from someone up above. I don't make the rules, Clayton, but I was ordered to have you do this. So I am."

"Fuck that, I'm not doing it." Clayton had never said that word before in his life. Feme pinched the bridge of her nose.

"Clayton, this isn't a suggestion."

"I don't care. I'm not doing it. He's my friend, Feme. What you're asking me to do is horrible." He slammed the paper down on her desk and stood up. "I don't know who you were in life, Feme. I want to think you loved people. I want to think you cared about someone. He's my partner, my friend. Get someone else." Clayton glanced down at the paper again to make sure he'd read it right, that he was making a stand for the right reasons. It ordered that Leon be retrieved from the cells. His rehabilitation was a failure, and he was to be sent to the Darkness.

"You can't punish a person with the cells only to cast them into the Darkness. That's cruel. That's not how this is supposed to work."

"You've been here for less than a hundred years, and you're lecturing me on how things are supposed to work?"

"No, but I sure can lecture you on right and wrong." Clayton's voice lowered. He was serious, and he wasn't going to budge.

"Sometimes the cells don't work, Clayton, and I don't need a lecture from you." He could see her face twitch slightly. She was angered but hadn't let loose on him.

"Well, who's above you? Let me talk to them. I'll tell them no too." He stated, and he meant it. Celestial being or another office manager, he was going to stand his ground.

"I've never met them," Feme sighed, "but I do know what happens if you deny them. I don't want you to suffer, Clayton. You're a good person. You don't belong here with us. Please do this. Don't incur this place's wrath," Feme said. That gave him pause.

"Why is he in a cell anyway?" Clayton questioned. What had Leon done that deserved so many years in solitude?

"He's a murderer. He killed two people and still pleasures in it. The more time passes, the more he savors it." There was something in Feme's voice as if she didn't want to have this conversation.

"Who'd he kill?"

"Takis, and Phile. Phile was Leon's wife," Feme said. She told Clayton the story of Takis's infidelity and his death at the hands of his son and how Leon waited for Phile to arrive and attacked her, showing her Takis' dead body before dragging her to an open wine barrel and drowning her in it. He set fire to Takis' establishment, burning Takis' life's work to ash with the bodies inside. He spent the next five years of his life on the run, stealing from whoever he could until he was killed by Lucius, his uncle.

"I don't care. You're looking at the wrong man for this job. Get someone else." Clayton stood to leave.

"Wait," she said forcefully and held her hand up.

"Feme, you can scream your head off, you can Black Mark me for another thousand years. Stick me in a cell. It's not happening." He looked her in the face, his expression stone.

"Clayton, we will all get punished," she said quickly.

"What?"

"If you refuse, we will all be punished, in some way or another." She sat back down. "Look, what will it take? What is it you want? Please, don't extend my time here. I've been here for so long." He could tell she was out of her element asking someone for anything, he had her in a rough position, and she would do damn near anything to get out of it. He understood that there was no one else. It had to be him. He sat back down.

"So he can't know?" He didn't want Takis to know that he was the one who condemned his son.

"No, it's on the order."

"It has to be me?" He recalled Takis' warning that this place was a punishment and that it would put more on his shoulders than he could handle.

"It has to be you. That's also on the order."

"I want two things," he said. He'd already made up his mind.

"If it is in my power, they are yours."

"The first is," he leaned forward, "I want to know what your problem is."

"What do you mean?" Feme seemed taken aback a little by this.

"Why?" He threw his arms up. "Why are you always screaming at us, making this even more miserable than it already is? I'm shocked you haven't raised your voice once during this entire thing. I mean, Feme, this is awful for all of us. Why do you treat us this way?" Clayton saw something he never thought possible; Feme looked like she was about to cry.

"If I tell you, it stays here between us. No Takis, no Nix, not a soul," she said. Clayton agreed, and Feme leaned forward.

"When I was given this position," she took a second to regain her composure, "I didn't want it. I just wanted to go get souls, serve my time, and get the fuck out of here." She looked over to the wall, lost in memory. "I've never gotten over what happened to me. I was someone. I was important. I did it all on my own. I built everything with my own hands, and it was all ripped away."

"Oh."

"Call it vanity; call it whatever you wish. I have sat at this fucking desk, watching myself wither away. What was I guilty of in my lifetime? I sold happiness." She paused to gather her thoughts. "People left me in a much better state than when they walked in." She sighed and slumped in her chair. "Do you think I want to yell at these people? You? You actually give a shit about people. Even after being completely fucked over, you still care. I don't want to be the biggest bitch in the afterlife, but I'm soured. I hate it here more than you could possibly imagine. If I didn't think my time was getting close to being fulfilled, I'd have walked into the Darkness a long time ago," she finished. They sat silently for a long time. He didn't want to say anything to her. She looked as if she was going to cry, and the last thing Clayton wanted to happen today was to watch Feme break down in tears.

"What's the second?" She broke the silence. He looked her in the eye.

"I want to know who hurt Amber."

"I was afraid of that," she sighed. She picked up her quill and kissed the feather, it changed color from yellow to blue, and she tore a small scrap of paper from a larger sheet. She wrote something on it, picked it up, and put it to her lips. She slid it across the desk to him. He looked down at it.

"There's nothing written here," Clayton told her with disappointment in his voice.

"When you finish the job, the name will appear." She looked down at the quill.

"You already knew who it was?" Clayton was taken aback that it would be this easy.

"I've read the files on everyone here, Clayton. I know your life inside and out." Her eyes locked onto his.

"Okay," he said and stood.

"You'll do it?"

"Yes." He looked away from her. He felt shame for giving in so easily.

"Okay, all you have to do is say his name and the word 'cell.' Your door will take you there. The same way you get a life list that will give you the key to his door." She looked relieved.

"Flick my hand?" Clayton asked.

"Yes, from there, take him to the Fork, and lead him to where the grass fades to dirt. The Darkness will take over from there," she said. Clayton stood and started for the door. "Thank you, Clayton. Please close the door on your way out."

34

Clayton exited her office, but before he shut the door, he looked back at her, and she had her head on her desk. She was in obvious torment, and Clayton finally felt sorry for Feme. Her job was the worst of all. He crossed the hallway to Acquisitions and knocked on the door. He looked towards the other end, scared that at any moment, he'd see Takis. The door opened a crack, and Nix looked out. His face brightened, and he opened the door.

"My boy, Clayton! How are you?"

"Shh, I need to ask you a question." He was trying hard to not draw attention to himself, and he didn't need Nix yelling into the hall.

"What is it?" Nix's expression changed to one of concern.

"If someone is sentenced to the Darkness, can you get around it?"

"Get around it?" Nix snorted.

"Is there a way to keep someone from being sentenced to the Darkness?"

"Clayton, what's going on?" He asked. Clayton looked down the corridor. He didn't want anyone to see him, much less hear.

"I'm being asked to take Takis' son to the Darkness."

"This damned place," Nix growled and stepped back. "Come in."

To say Acquisitions was massive was an understatement. Clayton could see items spilling out of boxes piled on shelves reaching to the ceiling. It was dark, a little too dark for his comfort, and with all these things just laying around, he was afraid he was going to trip over something. He followed as close to Nix as he could. There was so much to his left and right, he had no idea how deep the room was, but it was high, and even then, with the way items were stacked on one another, he felt claustrophobic. There was very little room to move.

"You collected all this stuff?"

"Mostly. I have a list of items that need to be in here."

"Does the list keep adding things?"

"No, I've been working on it all this time. I'm almost done."

"So, you tracked these things?"

"Yes, and I take them from whoever has them, or I unearth them."

Clayton almost forgot why he was in here, but the hair on the back of his neck prickled. He had to save Takis' son, but he was also in a room where the nails that held Jesus to the cross were stored. Who knew what marvels were inside these boxes or just lying around.

"Can I save him, Nix?"

"I don't know if we can, my friend. I've never heard of a sentence being overturned."

"I can't do this to Takis. He'd be devastated if he knew his son was deemed unworthy.

"I have an idea, but Clayton," he said skeptically, "I can't guarantee this will be a success."

"I'll do anything, Nix. Anything," Clayton said. They continued through the maze of wondrous things. Clayton saw spears leaning against shields, jars filled with organs that didn't look human, a book that looked as if it had a face carved into its leather cover, and in a pot, a small tree with black bark and red lettering carved into it. It looked like the lettering was alive and bleeding.

"What kind of tree is that?" Clayton asked with a nervous laugh.

"That tree was used by a witch for necromancy. A man had wronged her in life, and she was trying to bring him back as a slave."

"You can do that?" Clayton should have been used to finding out about things he didn't know existed.

"No, she brought something back, but it wasn't what she bargained for." Clayton decided to leave that one alone. He felt apprehensive about being in here. Nix's collection felt wrong as if most of these things should be destroyed. A cold feeling ran up Clayton's spine. They came to a clearing in the junk, a desk sat in the corner with two lit lanterns, and several lanterns hung from the ceiling. The desk was oversized and filthy. Tools and pieces of things Clayton didn't recognize were scattered atop it. The chair was broken. The back had a large crack running along the wood, probably from years of this gigantic man sitting in it. Clayton looked around at the debris near the desk and saw weapons and paper, lots of paper. This place needed to be organized. It was a literal mess.

"The list was so long when I got it," Nix said as if reading Clayton's thoughts, "I just started grabbing it all and throwing it in an empty space. Soon I was running out of empty spaces." Nix approached the desk, opened the leftmost wooden drawer, and started rooting around. He pulled out vials of ink, all in different colors.

"Light blue, light blue, ah-ha! Light blue," he produced a vial of cloudy light blue ink. He hurried over to Clayton. "Take this with you to the Fork, and dip the pen in this vial and write his name in the book. In theory, this ink should be allowed to be written on its pages. If it does, Charon will appear. With Takis' son's name in the book, it should grant him passage on the River." Clayton took hold of the vial, but before Nix released it, he said, "You are playing a dangerous game, Clayton. If she finds out, you both could get pitched into the Darkness. Are you sure you want to risk this? Is this man you don't know worth that?"

"He's been in the cells for two thousand years, no person deserves that only to be told 'sorry, but it's off to Hell with you.' It isn't fair." He took the vial. Nix backed away from him. "I owe you so much," Clayton said.

"You could always clean this place up?" Nix chuckled and looked around.

"Anything else, and you got it, my friend." They shared a laugh.

"Leon, cell," Clayton called out. The door appeared behind him. He waved goodbye to Nix and walked through.

35

THE CELLS

Leon was smiling when he heard the lock click on the door to his prison. The images on the wall had just finished showing him drowning his wife for what was easily the thousandth time. He enjoyed that one, it was always last, and it left him with satisfaction. He had been in this tiny room forever. There was no way to tell day or night. He'd lost track so many years ago. At first, there was nothing here with him but sadness. He had died at the hands of his uncle, who'd tracked him deep to the east of Thebes to seek revenge on him for killing his brother. Leon tried to reason with Lucius before he struck him down, but it was no use. Lucius adored Takis, even though Takis had unforgivably wronged Leon. Lucius didn't believe it. He thought Leon had killed his father to take ownership of the bar because he wasn't cut out to be a soldier.

Leon felt a sharp sting when he recalled Lucius telling him he was soft and weak before plunging his sword into his stomach. He told Lucius that Phile admitted to the affair before he killed her, but he was having none of it. Lucius thought Takis was a man of honor, which made Leon hate him even more. Leon sat in that room for a long time before the images began. The first was of his mother and her grief. She loved Takis dearly, and with his death and her son on the run, she lost them both. He would sit and listen to her cry. He would see people point and laugh at her for what had happened to her family. Lucius gave her a home, and he took care of her until her death, but she was miserable. Her life was shattered that day, and she mourned until her last breath. The second was his father dying, the anger in Leon's face, and the blood everywhere. He watched his father perish again and again, and for a while, this broke his heart. After all, this was his father he killed. The images would morph into him being held by Takis as a baby and Takis letting him sip wine at a very early age.

Leon was infuriated that day; he had been betrayed by his wife. Worse yet, he was betrayed by his father, the lovable man who raised him, clothed him, and tried to teach him about the world and the ways of it. Leon should have kept his anger in check. He should have gone to Lucius first and let the jury handle it. Instead, he murdered them both and became an outlaw. The third image was of Phile, their wedding, their smiles, and the first time they lay together. He could hear her telling him she loved him. He could hear her crying and begging not to die. Then her head was under the wine, his hands holding her there. For years Leon cried and regretted his actions. He wished he could take it all back, go back to that fateful day and tell himself to not go to the tavern, to go somewhere and let his anger subside. Just when the show ended, and he had cried himself senseless, it started anew.

That was until recently when different images were shown on the walls. These were of Takis and Phile in the middle of their union. Takis told her how weak his son was and that he'd never amount to anything, and she agreed, letting Takis know that he was a better lover and a better man. The following images showed them lying naked in Leon's bed, in his home. They plotted to kill Leon and his mother; that way, they would always have each other, and nothing could stand in their way. The images of them together were graphic, and every time Leon would turn away, the sounds of their copulating would just get louder till it echoed throughout the room. They had plotted his death. They were going to end Lipa too. It was beyond infidelity. It was evil. He spent the next few years wondering why he was being punished and not rewarded for his actions. Why had the gods sentenced him to this when he was in the right? He had vanquished them before they had gotten him. They deserved what they got. He thought it was unfair and cruel. He couldn't wait to get out of here and ask why. The images in the last week only showed him finishing them both, which made him happy. He had grown to love how swiftly he stabbed his father and the brutality of how Phile was drowned.

"Not so weak now," he repeated. He couldn't wait to watch them die. He was thrilled every time it started over. His mind raced when he heard the click. Would it be the giant monstrosity that put him in here coming back to get him? Would it be his father? He was ready to strike. He tensed up on the bed, ready to attack whatever opened that door.

The door slowly opened, and a young teenage boy looked in.

"Leon?" He asked.

"Who are you?" Leon looked at him, confused. This was not the person who sentenced him to this private hell. The boy stepped into the doorway and let the light shine in; it was blinding. Leon covered his eyes.

"My name is Clayton Shaw. I am here to take you home," he said with positivity.

"Did my father send you? My wife?" He narrowed his eyes as he stood. Clayton gave a small chuckle.

"No, your father didn't send me," the boy said. That eased Leon. He was sure this child was telling the truth. Maybe he would move on, and this wasn't a trick. Leon stepped towards Clayton, and he moved out of the way to let him out in the hallway filled with doors as far as the eye could see.

"Are there prisoners in each one?" He asked.

"I guess so. You're the first one I've come to retrieve from here," Clayton said. Leon could tell by Clayton's voice he was telling the truth. The boy was confident and sure.

"I need to get you out of here," Clayton declared.

"Why? Is something wrong?"

"No, I have a quota. I have so many people that I have to process in a day." That was a lie, but Leon let it pass. This boy was nervous, but Leon had no idea why. Maybe it was Leon himself, he thought. He was being very dry and overly cautious.

"The Fork," Clayton said, and a door appeared. He slung it open and said, "Paradise awaits."

"After you," Leon gestured politely. Clayton smiled, nodded, and went through first. Leon followed after him and shut the door.

36

THE FORK

Clayton was already making a line to the pedestal when Leon arrived. Leon was in awe, just as everyone else was when they saw the Fork.

"Don't go anywhere near that!" Clayton called back to him. He pointed to the Darkness.

"I won't!" He heard Leon call back. Clayton quickly made it to the pedestal, reached inside his pocket, and withdrew the ink. It swirled around as if it was alive, and Clayton kissed the bottle. He had no idea why he did it, maybe it was because of what Feme did earlier, or perhaps it was for luck. He popped the top off the bottle, grabbed the quill, and dipped it in. He had written so many times in this book that it was second nature. He scribbled Leon's name on the next available line and placed the ink back in his pocket. That was it. He had done his part, now he prayed it would work. He waved at Leon to come on over. Leon was slow, watching the river with his mouth half-open.

"This is beautiful," Leon said aloud.

"That's what you'll be riding on. You'll head upriver here into the Brilliance," Clayton told him. Clayton watched as Leon relaxed, his shoulders slumped, and he let out a satisfied sigh. He

163

could see in Leon's eyes that he was thankful. So far, things were going well, and Clayton wanted them to stay that way. "The boat will be along shortly."

"Thank you. Clayton, was it?"

"Yes, Clayton Shaw." He extended his hand. Leon took it, and they shook. Leon pulled his hand back and went back to gawking at the Fork. Clayton noticed he wasn't a very tall man, and he was round like his father. He was already balding at the time of his death, and he couldn't help but notice how strikingly similar the father and son were. If Leon had lived to Takis' age, Clayton guessed he'd have been a shorter, fatter version of his father.

"I'm just glad it was you that opened my door and not that thing," Leon said.

"Thing?" Clayton asked.

"It was a monster, covered in hair, twice my size."

"That was probably Nix. Good fellow," Clayton smiled. Leon raised an eyebrow.

"Really? He was quite aggressive and maltreated me, threw me in my cell without a word."

"He's been here a long time. We all have good days and bad days. I'm sorry about that, and I can promise you if he was here right now, he'd apologize too," Clayton said, trying to reassure him. Leon looked at him.

"Are my sins forgiven? You know what I've done, right?"

"I know about your father and wife, yes," Clayton replied, avoiding his gaze.

"Were you the one showing me my crimes?"

"Excuse me?"

"The pictures of me stabbing my father, drowning my wife, were you the one that forced me to watch those?"

"No," Clayton shook his head. "No, I have nothing to do with that."

"I was just wondering. I wanted to thank them for showing me the truth."

"The truth?" Clayton looked at Leon, confused.

"That my father and my wife were plotting to kill me," Leon said through clenched teeth.

"I don't know anything about that. That wasn't on my list." Clayton was stunned by what he was told, but he tried to keep his emotions in check.

"I just wanted to ask why I was being tortured when the two of them were planning to do away with mother and me." The gondola surfaced and headed their way. Clayton could see it past Leon. Charon was sitting near the back. He was trying to grasp what Leon had just said, so instead of speaking, he just pointed. Leon looked back.

"Is that the ferryman?"

"Woman. Charon."

"Fantastic!" Leon clasped his hands together. Clayton felt the hair on his neck stand up.

HOW DARE YOU, it said, and when it spoke, it hurt. It was as if his brain was pulsing. Clayton grabbed his head as Charon pulled the gondola up to the shoreline. She pulled her hood back, her round face puzzled.

"Clayton, are you alright?" She asked, a look of concern flashing across her face.

"Yes. Just a headache." He was shaking off the effect when it came roaring again.

HE'S MINE. HE BELONGS TO ME. This one rang in his ears and almost caused him to drop to one knee.

"Clayton, you don't look so good. Do you need to lie down?" Charon asked. Clayton looked at Leon, his eyes pouring tears.

"Get on the boat, now!" He ordered. Leon, who was watching curiously, nodded and went to step aboard. Clayton watched him lift his foot to step on, and then he froze, his foot hanging in midair inches away from the gondola. Clayton couldn't see his face, only his back. It looked as if he wasn't breathing. Charon stepped off the gondola and stood beside Clayton, her face awash with fear.

"Clayton, he's just staring into nothing. What's going on?"

"Leon?" Clayton slowly approached him. Leon wheeled around to face them. His pupils were gone, his eyes only white, his mouth frothing with a grimace of anger and pain. He grabbed Clayton and slammed him to the ground hard, and with spider-like, unnatural movements, crawled atop him.

"HOW DARE YOU!" Leon roared. "YOU DON'T GET WHAT'S MINE!" He grabbed the sides of Clayton's head and slammed him hard into the ground twice, screaming, "MINE! MINE!" Charon reached out to pull Leon off him. Leon backhanded her, and she flew over the river to the other side. She landed on her head and laid still. A shiver ran down Clayton's spine as terror engulfed him. His stomach twisted into a knot, his senses a jumbled mess. He could swear he tasted his own fear. Was this the Darkness manifested? Clayton had no idea what to do. How does one confront the Deceiver?

"Get off of me!" Clayton screamed. Leon was holding him down, and Clayton realized struggling was pointless. It got nose to nose with him. Clayton could see nothing but white in his eyes, the veins in his neck pulsing and blue. The devil made flesh.

"This one is mine! He's a killer! He earned his place with me!"

"He served his time. He deserves to go on!" Clayton yelled.

"NO!" Leon screamed. "No! He gets to suffer. He gets what he deserves. This one stinks. His soul is rotten."

"Let him go!"

"You!" Leon grinned at him. "You don't get to make the rules. The rules are written. I should take you too for this. I want to. The things I want to do to you," Leon closed his eyes for a second in ecstasy.

"But you can't," Clayton guessed. Leon rubbed Clayton's cheek.

"No. But you failed, you failed your friend. Poor little Clayton, you always seem to let everyone down."

"Fuck you," Clayton spat as he tried to push up.

"That's the spirit!" It crowed and hopped off of him. Clayton rolled over onto his side, still facing Leon.

"He doesn't belong to you!" Clayton cried out.

"No time to argue. I've planned a huge reunion party. Leon and his wife have a lot to catch up on!" It scurried along the ground, Leon's limbs bending in awkward ways. It was quick, and Clayton couldn't catch it if he tried. It reached the Darkness and turned back to Clayton.

"You pull a trick like this again, and you'll pay. I promise." It leaped in, the smoke quivering as it enveloped Leon. Clayton sat in the grass, staring into the Darkness. His face was wet with tears he hadn't even realized were there. The Darkness was right. He failed Takis. He was unable to save his friend's son. He thought he could outsmart this place. He thought he could slide one past a system that didn't seem to make much sense anyway. Leon trusted him, and now he was literally in Hell. Clayton stood and limped around the pond to the other side, where Charon was. She was lying on her back, dazed, and taking shallow breaths.

"What did you do?" She asked him, looking up from the ground.

"I'm sorry, Charon. I didn't know that would happen," Clayton apologized.

"What did happen?" She asked, refusing his hand to help her up. She continued to lay there.

"I made a mistake. He was supposed to go into the Darkness and not on the River," Clayton said. Charon rolled onto her stomach and rose slowly to her feet. Her dark robe was covered in dirt, and her chubby face started to swell.

"So, you throw a soul in the river, and now you write an unauthorized name in the book? Why would you do that? Why would you try to deceive me? I thought we were friends."

"We are friends," Clayton interjected.

"What were you doing here with that man anyway?" She asked, patting dirt from her robe.

"I can't—" Clayton stalled.

"Clayton," she paused, "You can tell me. You know, if this was anyone else, I'd have called Feme in by now." Clayton sighed and pulled out the ink vial. He handed it to Charon and told her everything. He was angry at himself now, and it showed. He lost Leon to the Darkness, and as he told her, he watched it. He could swear it was laughing at him.

"I understand why you did this," Charon stuttered. She put her gloved hand out, took his, and looked up into his eyes. "Clayton, there was no way that was going to work. You shouldn't have done it. I couldn't have allowed it."

"I had to try. For Takis." He found himself fighting back the tears. He could see out of the corner of his eye. Charon hesitated, then she leaned forward and hugged him.

"Not many people would do that for someone," she said. He had no idea why but he embraced her back. He felt terrible for trying to trick her. He should have called upon her in the first place and asked for her advice.

"I'm sorry. You've been one of the best things about this place, and I messed that up too," he said. She didn't say anything for a while, just gazed at him. He could tell she was mulling something over. She opened her mouth to say it but then smiled. She handed him back the ink.

"You better get back," she told him.

"Thanks, Charon."

"Your secret is safe with me, Clayton. No one needs to know about all this," she said as she boarded her boat, not looking back at him.

THE AFTER

"I hoped it would work," Nix said as he opened the door and saw Clayton.

"I know. It didn't. The Darkness possessed him and took him." Clayton said, defeated.

"Are you going to be alright?"

"Yes, I just need to get myself together before I see Takis." He pulled the ink out of his pocket, and he noticed a scrap of paper fall out. It tumbled to the ground. He had completely forgotten about it. He handed Nix his ink and picked up the tiny sheet from the floor. He looked at Nix.

"I'll see you soon, and thanks again," Clayton said, feeling heartbroken.

"We'll win the next one," Nix replied, and he shut the door. Clayton stared at the door, wondering what his next move should be. He still had a crushing feeling of hopelessness on his shoulders, but nothing could have prepared him for what happened next. He looked down at the note Feme gave him and read the name.

Donald Price.

He stared at it in disbelief. Amber had been hurt by the Reverend Price. He had accused Clayton of all of it, knowing he was the culprit full well. This man stood on that road and lied, which led to Clayton's death. He was responsible for Amber's fate as well. Clayton had trusted him, his father trusted him, and he was sure Amber trusted him. This was all too much to take. How could one man cause so much destruction?

"Are you still mad at me? Because we have work to do, so I suggest you get over it." Clayton looked to his left to see Takis. Takis looked as if he was ready for a confrontation.

"I'm sorry, Takis."

"Well, then that's-" Takis began. Clayton threw his arms around him, buried his face in Takis's chest, and started to wail. He cried like he never had before. Takis stood stunned for a moment before embracing him. "There, there, boy," he cooed and patted Clayton's back. "It will be alright."

39

THE CELLS

Amber Ward sat on the bed in the corner of her tiny room, just as she had been for God knew how long. She was miserable. The bed was rough and uneven. No matter how Amber tried, she could not sleep. There was a chill in the air, and while it was dark, she could still see. The wall across from her bed would light up and play moments of her life or someone else's life that were impacted by her decisions. It was excruciating. She never knew what it would show, but when she was placed inside her cell, the jailer warned her that they would come. Amber's mind wandered back to the first time the wall sprang to life. It was a replay of what happened between her and the Reverend Price, and it filled her with shame. She had felt so strongly towards the reverend before it happened as if it was impossible to love someone more than him.

Still, feelings of doubt and regret crept in once it was over. It was after she left his home and headed to her own that she felt it in the back of her mind. She hated herself for what she'd done.

That hatred festered as the days went on, and she turned it towards the reverend himself. She avoided the Reverend and would not glance up at him in church. When he would call to her outside of her home, she would make excuses for why she couldn't visit with him. Seeing it, all play out before her brought all those feelings back to the surface. She tried to turn away, and when she did, it felt as if what was on the wall played behind her closed eyes. Why had she allowed this to happen? She didn't love Reverend Price. It played endlessly, each time filling her with more and more disgust. When she felt she could take no more, she pounded on the door and begged to be let out. No one came. She loathed Donald Price and didn't want to see any images of him at all, much less those of him touching her.

As time wore on, she began to get used to the show. Amber no longer felt shame but instead was full of anger. She knew better, and she knew when this had transpired, she didn't love him. She had respected and trusted him, but she didn't love him. She would never know love. That chance was long gone. Again the wall showed her giving herself to Reverend Price. She watched with a look of indifference on her face. She had already cried every tear she would shed over this. That was when she noticed something in the right corner of the room. How had she not seen it before?

Someone was sitting on the leather chair by the window, out of focus and just out of view. She leaped from the bed and came close to the wall to study it. Who was that? Why couldn't she make them out? Was that a person? She wasn't sure of it, but she could swear someone was in that chair watching them. No one was there when she was alive. She was positive about that. The chair was in full view of the bed. There was no way either of them wouldn't have noticed a person sitting there. She thought she imagined it at first, or it was a trick of the light until the figure in the chair stood and the image faded away.

"Wait!" Amber called out to the ceiling. "Go back! Someone saw us! Who was that?" She moved around the room, calling out to the air. "You can't do that! I need to know who that was! ANSWER ME!" She yelled at the top of her lungs, her temper rising. The wall brightened again, and she was prepared to find the person in the chair, but this time was different. This time it was Clayton Shaw. She watched as Clayton sat in silence on the cart ride to her home. He never looked up from watching the road. Eve tried to speak to him a couple of times, but he wouldn't answer, and Jonas had to tell Eve to leave him be. They pulled up in front of her house, and she lived through the moment as Clayton was blamed for killing her. She winced when her mother slapped him.

"No," she whispered, covering her mouth with her hands. She bawled as Clayton explained himself. He loved her. He wanted to marry her. He respected and cared about her. He was devastated by her loss, and when he found out what she'd done. He was the one person she didn't want to ever hurt, but she watched him break. That's when Reverend Price lied to everyone. He insinuated that Clayton had taken her honor. Since Clayton was already a suspect, the group was now sure of it. When Jonas struck his son's face, she cried out, and Clayton landed in the dirt. His Sunday best was ruined, and blood trickled down his chin. She yelled out to Jonas that it wasn't Clayton as he accepted what the Reverend Price said as fact. She looked on as Clayton stood and took off running, and she cheered him on. He stopped by a tree and wheezed for air. She could see the pain he was in. She stepped to the wall and touched his face. He was talking to himself, but she couldn't make it out. She ran her finger down the wall, wishing to wipe the tears away from his cheeks.

"I will see you again," she whispered. "I will make this up to you. I am so sorry. I know you loved me. You deserved better." She leaned into the wall and closed her eyes. "I promise you, I will make this right." She opened her eyes, and the image panned back to show him on the ravine's edge. She glanced down and noticed his foot hanging above the emptiness.

"What are you...Clayton?" She questioned as panic crept in from all sides. He tipped forward, and she screamed, a shriek so loud it shook the room. She slapped the wall before she closed her hands into fists and pounded on it. Her fists slammed down against the image of Clayton's broken body. When she'd worn herself out, she slid down the wall, her eyes burned from the tears, and her stomach ached from heaving. She groaned, and that's when she felt the pain. Her right wrist throbbed. The ache went all the way up her arm to her elbow. She touched her wrist and winced. "How?" She asked as she held it up to her face and noticed the nasty bruise forming all around it. "How can this be? I'm dead!"

She laid against the wall for a while. Her mind reeled from watching Clayton take his own life. Her sins had landed her in this room. All she'd done was give in to temptation. Clayton had thrown himself to his death. He was in Hell. He was burning, and it was all her fault. She could have told him what happened with the reverend. She could have told him that she was pregnant. She wanted to, but she didn't know-how. Her panic began to fade, and soon she was overcome with guilt. This was her doing, and it all could have been avoided. What happened to her was on her, but Clayton certainly didn't deserve any of what happened to him. She put her head down. She didn't mean for this to happen. Why did she do this? What she had done to Clayton was unforgivable. He was dead because of her. He was her best friend, and his existence was over in the blink of an eye.

The feeling of guilt was overwhelming as if it had taken a life of its own. She told herself over and over again that she deserved the lake of fire. This was too good for her. She might as well have pushed him over the edge herself. Clayton would have done anything for her, but now? He was gone, forever lost. She heard the lock click but didn't look back when she heard the door open. She saw the light from the opening wash over her and the shadow of someone standing in the doorway against the back wall.

40

"Are you alright, miss?" She heard a masculine voice call out to her. She shook her head no, still balled up and not facing the doorway. "Can I come check on you? I got a report that you are hurt." She turned her head but couldn't make out the figure standing there. The light was hurting her eyes. He stepped in and knelt beside her. The first thing she noticed was his hair. It was long for a man, flowing past his shoulder blades and a dark shade of brown. It fell around his face. His beard was full and neatly trimmed. She could tell even from this angle that he was tall and stocky. He was wearing a suit, but it looked nothing like any suit she'd seen before. It was gray, of the highest quality, and very clean. His eyes were a piercing blue. They were kind and had not even the slightest hint of aggression. The soft expression on his face put her at ease. He smiled kindly, and his brow raised in curiosity.

"Why am I in pain?" She moaned and held up her wrist.

"Oh," he pulled out a set of oval, wire-rimmed glasses from his breast pocket and put them on. "Let me have a look."

"I hit the wall, and I- ow!" She yelled out as he gently began to examine her.

"Well, hitting the wall will do that, miss...?"

"Amber," she hissed through the pain. "Amber Ward."

"Well, Miss Ward, I think you may have broken your wrist. I'm fairly certain." He stood and motioned for her to sit on the bed. She moved across the floor on her knees and climbed upon it. She held her arm back out to him.

"I'm dead."

"Yes," he chuckled, "you are."

"How do I feel pain? How do I feel anything? I'm a ghost," she said. He laughed at her, though she could tell he didn't mean to by the way he clapped a hand to his mouth.

"A ghost? Miss Ward, who put you in here?"

"A rather large woman, terrifying. She was kind, though. Why do you ask?" She gasped as he touched her wrist again.

"I don't know whom you speak of, and I know most of the people on retrieval. I'll ask around. Obviously, you weren't told much of your predicament here?"

"No. I was told someone would get me one day, and this was my punishment."

"That's it?" He asked her in shock, and she nodded. "Well, you're right about one thing. You are dead."

"So? Pain is for the living," she said, matter of fact.

"And that, my dear, is where you would be wrong. You can feel all kinds of pain here. You can bleed, you can break a bone, just like the one here," he pointed to her wrist. "My job here is to patch people up who seriously injure themselves and get them back on track."

"You're a doctor?" She asked him excitedly, even though she had no idea why.

"I am. You can call me Doctor Rynerson, or Phillip, whichever makes you comfortable."

"Are you dead too?" She inquired.

"Wouldn't be here if I wasn't," he smiled at her again.

"Are you going to take me out of this room?"

"I am not allowed to do that," he began, the laughter leaving his voice. "It's just a break, not that serious," his smile faded.

"Oh," she said, dejected, looking down into her lap. He paused and took a more cheery tone.

"But hey, I have a few minutes with you while I wrap your wrist, so we can talk if you want before I have to go."

"I'd like that, Doctor Rynerson."

"You know what, Amber? Call me Phillip."

"Phillip," she acknowledged before gritting her teeth when he touched her wrist again.

"So, Amber, why in the world did you hit the wall?" He asked as he pulled out a cloth bandage from his pocket and slowly began to wrap her hand and wrist. She quickly told him everything about her pregnancy, death, and knowing her actions led to Clayton's death. She felt she could trust Phillip, and she didn't know when she'd be able to talk to another person. He listened as he carefully wrapped the cloth around and around her wrist.

"That's tragic, I'm sorry," he mourned. She paused for a moment. He really was kind. She wondered if he was this way in life or became that way after arriving here.

"Thank you."

"You have to be careful, Amber. Don't think of yourself as a ghost."

"Then what am I?" She asked. He looked her in the eye, then cocked his head to the side in thought.

"I would say you are somewhere in between. All of this is a punishment. This place exists only to hurt us."

"Why would this place want to hurt you? You don't seem like a bad man." Amber scoffed.

"I killed two men," he told her with barely any inflection in his voice. She gazed at him for a second. His expression didn't change; he looked unaffected by what he'd told her as if he'd told her that it was raining or that he was making coffee. Was she wrong about him? Was he an evil man?

"Really?" She tried to hide it, but she was taken aback by this. He certainly didn't seem the type. Her voice gave her away, but he smiled as if he understood her confusion.

"Three outlaws came to my home, two of them needing immediate care. They'd been shot robbing another home. They were brothers, nasty men; thieves, rapists, not a good intention between the three of them."

"What did you do?" Her interest was piqued. Doctor Rynerson looked at his hands, an amused look on his face.

"I rubbed feces in the wounds before stitching them up. They were both in pretty bad shape when they got to me. When I stripped one of them down, he'd soiled himself. I dirtied up my hand and went to work. I knew of them. Everyone did. They'd killed men, women, and children; I couldn't let it continue. I knew what I was doing. I knew the wounds would get infected, and they would die."

"Did they?" She leaned forward.

"Considering the third brother came weeks later and shot me in the back, I am going to say they did. I figured making sure two evil men never got a chance to ruin another person's life wouldn't condemn me. I was wrong," he sighed. For a moment, he let that hang in the air before his eyebrows dropped into a scowl. "That's fair, isn't it?" He hissed. He took a breath and forced a smile as he tucked the cloth in tight and sat back to admire it. "There. Keep it like that, and you should have zero problems. It should heal fast. That's one of the few bright spots here."

She studied his face. He was bitter one moment and nurturing the next, but she could tell he was trying very hard to keep himself from exploding. She could feel his anger but thought he had dealt with many patients and put this facade on daily. She pulled her arm back.

"I understand why you did it, but the Bible-" she began.

"I was doing the world a favor," he said coldly. She looked into his eyes. He was lost in thought, looking right through her. Could he really believe there would be no repercussions for killing two men? She wasn't going to prod and find out, so she sat in silence until he was ready to speak again.

"Amber," he smiled at her again, "promise me you won't go hitting the wall again. As I told you before, you can bleed, you can break a bone, you can hurt and ache, you just can't die. So, if you were to really injure yourself, you'd lie around in despair until it healed." He brushed a strand of hair from his face. "I didn't understand it all either. I know you might not think so, but believe me when I tell you this could be a thousand times worse."

"I won't do anything like that again," she looked away, saddened knowing he was about to leave her.

"Good," he patted her knee and stood. "I hope you aren't here much longer. It's time for me to go. I have others to attend to." As he got to the door, she called out to him.

"What year?"

"I'm sorry?" Phillip asked and turned back to face her.

"What year did you die?" She asked, hoping to get a feel for how long she'd been in this room.

"1892. It was nice to meet you, Amber." He left, shutting her back in her cell and locking the door. She laid down on the bed and began to weep. She had been dead for at least 87 years, and who knew how long it had been since his death. Her parents were gone by now, and her siblings too. She had been here far too long, and she began to question how long this punishment would last.

The wall lit up and played Clayton's death again.

41

NOVEMBER 7TH, 1922

"Nix was right all along," Takis said one evening while they waited for the soul of a baby boy. The pregnant mother had fallen down the steps of her building in Chicago. She laid on the sidewalk with a broken leg, in the cold snow, and in labor, screaming at the man beside her that something was very wrong.

"What do you mean?" Clayton asked.

"To just go around naked," Takis pointed to the gawkers and passersby. "Look at these people. They look ridiculous. Every man is covering his head. Why wear those things? It's not that cold. They aren't working in the field and need shade. It looks silly. Don't even get me started on the tie." Clayton didn't answer at; first he just nodded. Takis felt that Clayton envied the people living in the now. Takis knew that Clayton was fascinated by the music and films; he could see the excitement bubble up in the boy when it was time for them to be played in the meetings. There were so many wonders that didn't exist for him, and he talked about them all the time. The automobile, entertainment, it was all different. Nothing seemed to stand still; there was no time to relax. Everything and everyone seemed to be in a constant rush.

"I'd love to eat a steak, go dancing, maybe see a movie," Clayton said wistfully as a couple dressed for a night on the town stopped to see what all the commotion was about.

"Not my thing," Takis dismissed.

"Are you telling me you wouldn't want to drive an automobile?" Clayton asked.

"Nope. People are becoming lazy if you ask me," Takis answered.

"You're crazy," Clayton gritted his teeth. "I want out of here. I don't want to be around death anymore. How many more of these do I have to do?" He paced behind Takis, not looking at the woman screaming in pain. "I want to see my family again. I want to see Amber."

"And you will see them again. This wasn't meant to be enjoyed," Takis explained.

"I don't belong here."

"Clayton-"

"I pulled my foot back. I remember trying to pull it back. I didn't want to die. I didn't want to kill myself." Clayton became more and more irritated with each word. "I didn't sell my body. I didn't indulge in drinking. I didn't lie with anyone out of wedlock. I want to get away from all of this!"

You want to get away from me, Takis thought. He heard the contempt oozing from Clayton's speech as if he was disgusted when speaking to him. At first, Takis dismissed it as him being paranoid, but as time passed, it became apparent. Takis had grown to love Clayton, but Clayton had grown bitter. He was no longer the young man he had met in the ravine in Virginia.

"I made one mistake in my life, and I have to deal with dead children. It isn't fair, Takis," Clayton said.

"I heard you the first twenty times," Takis tried joking back, but Clayton wasn't listening.

"You understand, right? Am I wrong? I did what I was supposed to. I was a good person. I tried to live a decent life. I mean, look at Feme," Clayton raised his voice so he could be louder than the crowd.

"What about Feme?" Takis asked, puzzled.

"She was a whore," Clayton spat, disgust dripping from each word.

"Clayton, you don't know anything about how the world was back then. You have no idea how respected and revered she was." Takis felt his chest tightening. If Clayton didn't stop, this might go in a direction he would regret. The woman on the sidewalk broke the moment between them.

"It's not time! It's too soon!" She repeated at the top of her lungs.

"What's happening to her?" Takis asked Clayton. "Why are we outside in this mess?" He pointed to the sky.

"The baby is already gone. She's felt sick for days. Her husband hits her. That's why she waited till the last minute," Clayton told Takis, his voice emotionless. Clayton held his hand out to the snow. Takis observed him for a moment, trying to get a read on whether any of this bothered him anymore or if Clayton had grown numb.

The woman threw her head back and cried out into the frigid air. Takis snapped to attention and watched her grip the back of the man's neck who kneeled on the walkway beside her. Takis turned away as he heard someone yell, *it's coming!* He didn't want to see another dead child, and Clayton's attitude made the situation almost unbearable.

"Sad thing," Takis commented with his back turned.

"People die," Clayton answered. Takis recoiled in disgust. He couldn't believe Clayton would say such a thing.

"It's a baby. A baby should live a full life," Takis said as he turned to face Clayton. "I think you're missing the point of all of this."

"Oh, and what's that?" Clayton asked.

"This is supposed to be sad; you're supposed to feel for these people."

"How's that working for you?" Clayton quipped. "How long have you been here? How long have you been doing this? I mean, you must have done something bad to be here all this time." There was something behind his inflection, as if Clayton was looking down on him. As if he felt he was better than Takis. Takis shot an icy stare at Clayton.

"Boy," Takis warned, snapping his fingers and wagging his index finger at him. It would be the only warning Clayton would get.

"I just want her to hurry up so we can get out of this snow. I'm cold," Clayton complained as if nothing had happened.

"You sure are," Takis said. The snow continued to fall all around them, and Takis hovered near the woman, who was now in hysterics asking why the baby had not cried. Takis knew Clayton wouldn't speak to this infant. Clayton stopped talking to the babies while he retrieved them a while ago. There was no enthusiasm for his work. In Takis' eyes, there wasn't even enthusiasm for his existence either. He had shut himself off, and with each passing moment, he grew more distant.

Clayton had stopped asking for lessons on Afterwords. Takis offered for Clayton to continue trying to use them, but he refused. He'd offered to go into the offices and meet other people; again, Clayton refused. He didn't even want to go see Nix anymore. He just wanted to finish his ten and sit in the break room, and it was driving Takis mad. He wondered if the Civil War had been the breaking point. Takis knew watching his countrymen slaughter each other, brother versus brother, and in one instance father versus son, had been especially rough on him. The two of them had been called upon to handle the influx of new souls. Gettysburg alone claimed fifty thousand.

At first, Clayton seemed fine, but as the battlefield became littered with the freshly dead, Takis saw how shaken and disturbed it made him. The souls just kept arriving, still arguing with one another, still swinging their fists with voices raised. Clayton flinched at the sounds of gun and cannon fire. Takis had asked Clayton several times if he was alright, only to see him nod his head slowly. Still, the utter sadness in his eyes told a different story.

"Such a waste," Clayton muttered to himself as they stood in the middle of the battlefield and ushered men through an open door, some of them no older than Clayton himself. Takis had been brought into battlefields before. Clayton wasn't a fighter, so after getting hit a few times trying to separate soldiers still locked in their feuds, he stopped trying. Takis didn't mind. He enjoyed a scrap every now and then in his lifetime. When one of the soldiers got really out of hand, Takis got to throttle him a little bit.

Takis asked him afterward if he wanted to talk about it, and Clayton just shook his head. Since then, he never looked well, a frown permanently across his face. He was lost, and despite all of Takis' attempts and jokes, he couldn't pull him back. He'd seen this place rip a person apart, shatter even the toughest souls, and Clayton was just a young man. It had gone beyond that. He didn't seem sad. He seemed angry. Takis wondered if Clayton would lash out at him if it would finally come to a physical altercation. He hoped not, but if Clayton continued to talk to him like he was, Takis wouldn't be able to help himself. Clayton picked the baby's soul up off the cold concrete after it was expelled.

"The Fork," he said without acknowledging Takis and walked through the door. Takis stood for a moment, watching the mother cry while holding her baby. His heart ached for this woman. He knelt beside her.

It will be alright. He is in a better place now. He didn't stay to see if his Afterwords worked. He rushed through the door, livid at his partner.

"I've signed the book already," Clayton called back to him. "Did you get lost?"

"I gave the woman some comfort. She just lost her child," Takis replied angrily.

"That was mighty nice of you, Takis," Clayton said, but his tone was condescending.

"You got something to say, boy?" Takis asked, his voice rising. Clayton shook his head.

"I used to be fulfilled by this, Takis. I liked knowing I was sending children to God." He paused. "Now I feel like this is a useless job. Everything is so pointless," he finished, annoyed.

"The feeling will pass. You are doing good things, " Takis softened and tried to reassure him. It was the first time Clayton had opened up in a decade or two. Takis wanted to use this as a way to help the boy and get an understanding of what was rattling around in his head. He prayed Clayton would snap out of it. He was afraid the boy hadn't dealt with his death properly, and it was weighing him down. The more Takis attempted to get Clayton to open up, the more he would close himself off. Every time Clayton started to rise out of his funk, something would happen to slap him in the face; a baby named Eve needed to be gathered, or they would end up in his hometown of Clover. Every chance the After could kick him when he was down, it would, and it never held back.

"Charon is on her way," Clayton pointed towards the middle of the pond. "We don't want her to worry." Takis saw Charon emerge and drift towards them. He hoped Clayton would still be in the mood to talk after she left. For so many years, Clayton had been friendly with Charon; their rapport was refreshing. Charon always pulled her hood back to speak to them. At first, it unnerved Takis, seeing her this way. He didn't know what or where the ferrymen came from. He knew they were ancient and had been here for as long as the Fork existed. She had mentioned others, so he reckoned they looked as she did, though he'd never dealt with any of the others besides her. Her silver hair, eyes, and skin were quite the mismatch, but Takis found her adorable.

She didn't have many lines to her face, but Takis noticed her dimples when she laughed, and around Clayton, she laughed more than she should. Takis didn't know if she was sweet on the boy or if she just took a liking to him. He never was very good at reading the reactions of women. Takis was lucky to pick up that Lipa was interested in him when they met. Still, watching Charon throw her arm around Clayton's waist and hug against his side or be interested in Clayton's stories of where he got the newest soul was amusing.

These were a thing of the past now. Clayton was almost as rude to Charon as he was to Takis. She'd try to start a conversation with him, but Clayton wouldn't speak. She would watch him as she pulled away, Clayton not even waving goodbye, and in some instances calling a door and leaving her staring at him. Charon waved as she approached the shore, and Takis waved back and gave a hearty laugh.

"How goes your day, lovely lady?"

"Thank the stars, it's you two," she eased the gondola right up to Clayton. As usual, he didn't say a word.

"Why's that?" Takis asked.

"My boss decided it was my turn," she reached out for the baby in Clayton's arms, and he handed it to her quickly.

"Your turn for what?" Takis raised his eyebrow.

"Well - shh now," she rocked back and forth to soothe the baby who'd started to fuss. "You know how you told me Feme likes to tear you guys apart any chance she calls you in?"

Takis nodded.

"We have this supervisor, an awful woman," Charon snorted. Takis nudged Clayton.

"I think we know a little about that," Takis said. Clayton smirked but turned and walked away from both of them without a word.

"She's literally our equal, but every so often, she pulls one of us in and tells us how we are doing a shitty job, how we can be replaced, and how she hates us. We just smile and nod. It's not like she can do anything to us, really. She needs us."

"Well, Feme needs us, but she can ruin us," Takis said, his face falling.

"I know, but hey, do you want to know the silliest part?" She asked, leaning over the edge of the boat.

"You know I do," Takis said playfully.

"She used to be worshipped under the banner of comfort and mildness. It's like Feme being worshipped on Earth as the Goddess of Celibacy." Takis laughed, bellowing long and hard. Clayton stood away from them, his back turned and his hands on his hips.

"Clayton!" Charon called out to him. Clayton looked over his shoulder at her. Takis could see the indifference on his face.

"Have you been doing alright?" She asked, her tone light.

"I'm fine," he snapped back at her.

"You sure?" She asked, taken aback by his response. He nodded and turned away from her. The baby let out a squawk.

"Oh, there there," Charon said as she laid the baby in the front of the vessel. "I better take care of this. I'll see you, Takis." She pulled her hood back up, and Takis noticed the quizzical look on her face as she looked at Clayton. "Is he okay?" She asked in a hushed tone.

"Feme is so hard on him, really breaking the boy down. He'll be alright. He just has to get used to her hounding him." Takis lied. He didn't want Charon to worry about him. She'd probably seen several retrievers lose their sanity and do something stupid.

"Anything I can do?" She whispered.

"I got him. I won't let anything happen," Takis reassured her with a big toothy grin.

"You better not," she smiled back, but Takis could tell it was forced. She meant it. She was giving him a warning.

"You have my word," Takis put his right hand over his heart. She smiled and did the same.

"Be well, Clayton!" Charon called. He waved with his left arm but never turned around to face her. Charon took her oar and shoved off from the shoreline. Takis walked over to stand beside him.

"Do you want to finish what we were talking about?" Takis asked him and folded his arms. Clayton didn't answer at first.

"I've been dead for over 100 years," he sighed.

"How do you know that?" Takis asked.

"There was a newspaper, a man beside me in the crowd had one folded under his arm," Clayton responded.

"Really? So when are we?"

"November 7th, 1922." Clayton sighed again.

"Clayton," Takis took him by the shoulder and turned Clayton to face him, "are you alright?"

"Did I do something wrong?" Clayton asked.

"Charon tried to speak to you, and you were quite a shit."

"Does it even matter? Charon doesn't care about me, and I just want to get out of here." Clayton whined.

"You should be thankful you weren't cast into the Darkness," Takis said, anger rising up in his stomach. "You took your own life, and I've never known of another soul to commit suicide and then end up in the After. It just doesn't happen." He stepped in front of Clayton to make sure they were eye to eye. "They were always cast into the Darkness, but you got a second chance."

"Lucky me," Clayton looked away, not meeting his gaze. Seeing Clayton be so unappreciative of the opportunity for redemption bothered Takis. Still, he did understand that the boy was feeling the loss of his love and his family. Takis had been depressed too for a long time after his own death, and he had no one until Nix became his friend. He was trying to be patient with Clayton, but it was wearing thin.

"Shit," Clayton huffed.

"What is it now?" Takis asked, getting irritated at Clayton's tone.

"We have a meeting, don't we?" Clayton shook his head. "I forgot."

"Let's go. If we get there early, we can get fitted first."

42

No one finished their daily tasks as quickly as Clayton and Takis, so they were the first in the meeting room, and they would be alone with Feme and Astrid for a long time. Astrid measured both of them as soon as they entered the room, and Takis could swear Astrid took way too long getting Clayton's measurements, but he didn't speak up. She disappeared to work on their clothing while the barber gave both men a shave and haircut. They'd come ready to learn about the changes the world had gone through, not just in speech and mannerisms but fashion as well.

Astrid returned by the time both men had finished their shave. Takis had always assumed that, like most things in the After, Astrid's abilities had some kind of magic to them. She could have clothing ready in a matter of minutes, and they always fit with never a stitch out of place. She always did her work in her office, away from prying eyes, so no one knew her secret. They both received sack suits from her. Clayton's was gray with a morning coat, and Takis reluctantly accepted his suit, jet black with a matching frock coat. Neither man had looked so professional in their lives. The suits fit perfectly and hugged their forms without being too tight. Takis' suit even hid some of his girth. Feme grinned at Takis for the first time in eons.

"I would have let you into my bedroom, Takis," she proclaimed upon seeing him.

"Really?" Takis stammered.

"Why, yes. You could have watched a real man ravage me," she smirked.

"Oh, shut up," he grumbled. Astrid was off in the corner talking to Clayton, who seemed disinterested in what she was saying. Takis made his way over to them and put his arm around her.

"What are you talking about, love?" He teased.

"Our little boy has grown into a man," Astrid proclaimed. Clayton had grown two inches or more since his arrival. He was still thin, but he had lean muscle across his frame. He no longer looked like a young boy but a soldier to Takis. It was in his eyes; his stare reminded him of Lucius.

"He sure has," Takis reached out and ruffled Clayton's hair. Clayton huffed, pulled away, and walked to the other side of the meeting room.

"Is he alright?" Astrid asked with concern.

"He's having a bit of a bad decade. Nothing to worry about. We all go through it," Takis explained.

"I figured he was missing Amber," Astrid said but stopped short. Takis looked up at her sharply. A look of shock briefly lit her face. She hadn't meant to say that. She tried to turn away from Takis.

"Well, I hope you like your clothes. I think the color looks good on you-" Takis grabbed her arm. She looked down at his grip and back to him, anger formed in her eyes.

"I think the world of you, Astrid. You are one of my favorite people here," Takis lied. He'd actually always found her annoying, but he had to know how she remembered that girl's name when he barely could. "I don't want to cause a scene. I don't want us to start yelling and let Feme in on whatever is going on here," he whispered. Astrid relaxed.

"Then you can loosen your grip," she said. Takis released her arm and smiled at her.

"Shall we take this out in the hallway?" He asked her, his smile still wide.

"Well..." She looked back to Feme and the others sitting at the table.

"It will just take a second." He started for the exit, hoping she would follow. She did, staying right behind him, but when they made it to the door, Feme called out to them.

"What the fuck are you two doing? Everyone is arriving. We're about to start," she hissed.

"I want to talk to her about this color," Takis fibbed.

"Are you serious? You walked around in that rag until it stunk like a chamber pot, and now you care about how you look?" Feme complained.

"It'll just take a second."

"Hurry up. You know how I love to fucking repeat myself," Feme waved them off hatefully. Astrid closed the door behind them without being asked.

"What is your connection to Clayton?"

"I don't have one."

"Oh, bullshit, Astrid," he huffed. "I've been with him every day for a hundred years, and if you asked me to name the girl he pined over, I would get it wrong nine out of ten times. But you know it, and all I want to know is why," Takis explained, leaning against the wall and keeping his voice low.

"I read up on him," she answered quickly.

"Come on, Astrid. We get new workers and partners in this place every day. You're telling me you wanted to read about this boy?"

"He's not much of a boy anymore," she grinned.

"Stop changing the subject," Takis was annoyed now, and he

let it show. "What are you hiding, Astrid? You and I are friends. What is it you aren't telling me?" Takis asked.

"It's embarrassing, and maybe I don't want to get into it," she growled and stepped forward aggressively, her voice rising.

"Astrid," Takis said firmly, his hands up, "I just want to know. It's hard to trust people in this place. It's... I just want things to go smoothly. I'm sorry I upset you." Takis shook his head and looked away. He was trying to play on her sympathies, and when she sighed, he knew it had worked.

"I've been with many men," she glanced away from Takis, "but I've never been in love."

"What?" He huffed a laugh. "Are you in love with Clayton?"

"No, don't be silly," she ran her fingers through her unkempt hair. "What I mean is everyone I was with was only for pleasure. We didn't have stories like Romeo and Juliet."

"Who?" Takis asked.

"Shakespeare. Forbidden love?" She asked.

"Nope, don't know it. Sorry, go on." Takis waved his hand.

"We were mostly together out of need. We didn't have courtships or romance."

"I'm still not following," Takis told her as she fidgeted with a tear in her dress.

"I was the one ordered to pick up his love," she said quickly. Takis froze. He felt something he hadn't since he was living: fear.

"The girl," Takis whispered.

"Amber," Astrid confirmed.

"Why in the hell were you in the field?" He kept his voice hushed. This was entirely out of the ordinary.

"I was in my office, and it appeared on my desk. I was tasked with retrieving her. I have no idea why I was chosen. I've never retrieved anyone before. When I picked her up, she was a mess. You know how it is. There was begging, a lot of tears. Did you know she was with child?"

"I did, and it wasn't Clayton's."

"She was riddled with guilt. I'd seen it before, but something was different this time. She kept on and on about him," she pointed toward the door. "She told me the story of his mother's necklace, their horse ride, their only kiss. I know when you retrieve, you can ignore their stories, but I couldn't help but listen to her."

"Shit, that was why you were reading up on him." Takis realized.

"Yes. After we finished and I got back to the office, I got his life list. I even snuck out and watched him until he fell asleep that night. He had no idea she was gone. My heart ached for both of them."

"Astrid," Takis said. He sympathized with her. He knew how decent Clayton was at the time of his death. He didn't have the heart to tell her that person was fading.

"I sit in my office and read all these stories about love and romance, and that's all they are, stories," she paused. "This was pure and real, and I realized I wanted that. I want someone to think of me that way, to look at me that way. I don't care who it is." She chuckled. "Look, I know it's stupid-" Feme flung the door open, her face contorted into a scowl.

"Why the fuck don't you take all day, Takis? No color can fix fucking stupid," she growled.

"Sorry, Feme-" Takis started.

"Oh, I don't give a fuck. Get in here so we can start."

43

JUNE 12TH, 1985

THE FORK

Clayton turned away from the River after giving Charon his final soul of the day, a little girl named Abby. She hadn't cried or moved much, and Clayton didn't speak to her at all. He handed her off in silence and watched Charon disappear into the tunnel. Nothing was out of the ordinary during the pickup or delivery. Everything had gone smoothly, and once again, they'd finished quickly. Clayton always stared at the Darkness when he came to the Fork. Even though Leon's possession happened decades ago, being in proximity of that swirling smoke made him uncomfortable. He wanted to get away from it as quickly as possible. Takis watched the stars, not paying any attention to his surroundings when he tilted his head.

"What's happened to you, boy?" Takis asked

"What do you mean?"

"I've seen enough of your moping. For decades now, you've acted like a right shit." Takis looked down at him, his face turned to stone. Clayton felt his own face flush with anger.

"I don't know what you're talking about," he hissed.

"Oh, you don't? You don't speak. You used to kiss the children on their way, but you don't even acknowledge them anymore.

Charon has been more than friendly to you, and you ignore her. What's happened to you?" Takis asked again as he approached him.

"I don't owe you an explanation-," Clayton began. The punch hit him in the jaw, and he dropped to the ground, flat on his back. Takis was powerful. Clayton felt like he had been kicked by a mule. "What the fuck are you doing?" He cried out and grabbed his chin.

"See, right there," Takis pointed at Clayton. "You never used to say that word." He knelt and reached out his hand to Clayton. "I've been where you are right now. This feeling of helplessness, of hopelessness, I had that for a thousand years. It was numbing. It dulled me. You have no idea how many times I almost ended myself, just appearing naked in London and running through the streets, let them chuck me in there," he pointed his other hand towards the Darkness. "I care about you, boy. I do. There is a cloud above you. You were such a good kid. You can still be the man your mother wanted you to be. Please, stop this," Takis said with sadness. Clayton sat up and looked at him. He knew Takis was being sincere. No one had spoken to him with honesty since Feme. He reached out and took Takis' hand before pulling as hard as he could and head-butting Takis across the bridge of his nose. Takis grabbed his face and fell sideways.

"You little bastard!" Takis cried out, his eyes watering. Clayton fell backward, holding his head while trying to get to his feet.

"How dare you talk to me like that, about sadness, about hopelessness? You actually belong here. I don't." Clayton struggled onto his knee, still holding his forehead. He'd done about as much damage to himself as Takis, if not more. Clayton finally stood and put his fists out in front of him. He was ready for a fight. He wanted it. He needed it. Takis was bent over, holding his nose.

"I can't believe you hit me," he stood up tall and faced Clayton, who was motioning him to come on.

"You have some nerve to talk down to me!" Clayton spat. He

took the palm of his hand and rubbed his head. His eyes poured tears.

"I wasn't talking down to you," Takis explained. "I want to help you, boy, but I am warning you right now. Don't do this. We both know you're not a fighter. I don't want to hurt you."

"Fuck you," Clayton said and charged.

44

Feme had just finished her paperwork for the day. She was going to sit back and brush her hair when three sheets appeared on her desk. Two were regular orders to retrieve from the cells, and one was a paper made of gold. She knew what that meant. It was a ticket out of here. Someone was granted passage to the Brilliance. She leaned in and picked up the pass. She read it aloud to herself.

Takis
Time Has Been Served
Granted Passage to the Brilliance Upon Completion of Cell
Retrievals
Orders to Follow

Her heart sank. Takis was finally going home. He would get to see his wife again. He would get to give the apology she knew he yearned to say. He'd been here for what seemed an eternity, and now whoever was in charge was setting him free. She didn't hate Takis, no matter how much grief she dumped on him. He was somewhat respectable and rarely caused her any issues. She felt a pang of jealousy in her chest. He'd been here so long, but she'd been here longer. She found her mind racing into dangerous territory and suppressed it. She wanted to explode on someone over this. She wanted to yell, but Takis made his goals and was a good worker. She hated to lose him, but they would be alright by the reports from the field on Clayton's training.

"Takis!" She called out and twirled the paper in her hand, waiting for him to come barreling in, apologizing before he even knew what she wanted. Moments passed, more than usual. He never kept her waiting. "Takis!" She called again, louder and impatient. She slammed the golden sheet down on the desk and picked up the other two. She should have read the orders first because her heart sank further when she did. This was the most outrageous thing she'd ever been asked to do, and she wasn't sure how to proceed.

"This is bullshit." She stood and stared at the orders on her desk. She couldn't believe what she'd just read. She slammed her hand down on the desk. "The fucking gall!" She yelled out to no one. She began to pace, trying to control her anger. "This isn't fucking fair. It's as if you want us to fail!" She hissed. She picked up the orders, walked around her desk, and stormed out the door. She slammed it with a mighty bang, which caused everyone in the hallway to stop and stare at her. She marched across the hallway to Acquisitions. She raised her hand to knock and paused. Did she want Nix to help her? She despised Nix. She was afraid of him. Nix was an abomination, something that didn't belong even in a place as mind-bending as the After. He was a monster. She remembered meeting him for the first time.

"Is this the whore?" He'd asked rudely. He was belligerent to her from the start, not that she was known for her pleasant demeanor, but Nix was different. She hated this place and what had happened to her. She didn't hate the people here at first. It was Nix that was the driving force of her aggravation. She found herself wondering why this beast despised her so. The centuries had let the wounds run even deeper as the two of them were more hostile with each encounter. When Feme was granted her position, Nix was vocal in his displeasure, going as far as to warn her that she had no say over him. Nix was like a nightmare come to life. She made her rude remarks but did her best to avoid him. When he took Acquisitions, she was ecstatic that she wouldn't ever be dealing with him. She chalked his distaste for her up to him, thinking a woman was beneath him and left it at that.

This would be the first time she would be civil with Nix. She was uncomfortable, and the sight of him would make her queasy. All she needed was to find Takis and Clayton, explain the orders, let them vent, and get back to her desk. She thought about turning around and finding them on her own. Feme allowed the thought to roll around in her head for a few moments before she rapped on the door four times. Nix cracked the door and peered out.

"What the hell?" He asked and stepped out into the hallway, closing the door behind him. "To what do I owe the pleasure?"

"I have a problem, and I need your assistance," she said as professionally as she could, holding back her contempt.

"Why would I help you with anything? I hate you. You hate me. If it's something that gets you in trouble, I'm all for it."

"Clayton Shaw and Takis, it's about them. What I've been asked to do is just-" She stopped herself. "This place is like cancer. It eats away at everything until there is nothing left."

Nix was expressionless.

"What's going on?" He asked.

"I got a release for Takis."

"Well, that's not a bad thing. He's finally getting out of here," he said in delight.

"That's not all," her face turned sour. "They have two final jobs before he gets to leave." She gave Nix the two orders she had in her hand. Nix scanned them over, and a look of shock ran across his face. She watched him reread it.

"I can't believe this. This shit is cruel even for this place. I know these names. Whose idea of a sick joke is this?"

"I thought the same thing. You know what happens if I don't do exactly what that order says?"

"I do."

"Will you come with me to tell them?"

"I should tell you no, tell you to figure it out on your own," Nix said and looked at her.

"Yeah, yeah, and this place is my fucking responsibility, not yours, but Takis and Clayton don't deserve this." She noticed something in Nix's expression change, she couldn't read it, but there seemed to be less hostility in his eyes.

"If things get out of hand, I could help handle it."

"That's why I'm here," she said to him, looking away.

"Alright, I'll help," he agreed and handed back the paperwork. She was relieved to hear him say that. Nix was respected by both Clayton and Takis. They would listen to him, maybe even more than her.

"Are they with you?"

"No, why would they be?" Nix looked confused.

"I've called a few times, and Takis hasn't answered."

"Well, I guess we better find out what those fools are into," Nix smiled.

45

THE FORK

When they both came out of the door into the Fork, Takis was huffing over Clayton, his face red and his nose dripping blood. It was apparent to Feme that they were fighting and that Takis was winning. Clayton's suit was covered in grass stains and dirt, and his face had begun to swell. He turned on his side and was trying to stand.

"Stay down, or the next one will keep you down!" Takis warned.

"WHAT THE FUCK ARE YOU TWO DOING!" Feme screamed. They stopped instantly. Clayton rolled onto his stomach to look up to her, and Takis glared at her. Nix stepped around her.

"Hey, Takis! Are you guys doing alright?" Nix asked. His voice was playful.

"Just a misunderstanding," Clayton gasped out.

"A misunderstanding? You told me I belonged here and that you were better than me!" Takis stepped over Clayton and started walking towards Nix. "I guess things look a little different from down there." Clayton stood slowly as Takis walked away. Feme watched as Clayton spit blood. She was stunned. She thought the two of them were her best pairing. They seemed so jovial around one another, but she could see the embarrassment on Clayton's face. Takis had bested him, and pretty easily from the looks of the two of them.

"No, it looks the same as it always has," Clayton said as Takis turned to face him. "A man who coveted his son's wife, and after he had her, he plotted to kill both his son and his own wife. You're a piece of shit, Takis. Hit me all you want. It doesn't change that," Clayton snarled.

"Damn it," Nix said and took off at a run, his long legs quickly covering the distance. He reached Takis before he could react. He tackled the Greek and held him pinned to the ground.

"Easy, friend, easy. The boy is out of his mind," Nix grunted as Takis struggled against him.

"I'm gonna kill him! Get off me! I'm gonna kill him! No one talks to me that way! Not about my Leon, not about my Lipa!" If it had been anyone else, he would have easily broken free and may have hurt Clayton, but nothing in the After was as strong as Nix. No one currently residing among the living was either, Feme reckoned. Feme started towards Clayton. Their eyes met, and Clayton looked away. Clayton had gone too far, and for what reason? She damn sure was about to find out.

"He started it. He hit me first," Clayton said, pouting.

"He started it," she mocked. "Like I give a fuck who started what." She looked over at Takis, crying and screaming at Nix to let him up. "How could you do that to him?"

"His son told me the images in the cell showed them plotting to kill him. If Leon hadn't got him first, Takis would be in there by now," Clayton said as he gestured toward the Darkness. Feme looked Clayton's face up and down. She was fuming.

"You are not here to judge people. That is not in your job description. And for the record, he did no such thing," she stated. Clayton started to say something but stopped. He looked back at her.

"Leon said," he insisted.

"Like I give a fuck what Leon said. Takis life list," she commanded and flicked her wrist. The papers appeared in her hand, and she shoved them into his chest. "I check all my people. I know how they think, I know what they've done, I know everything." She walked away from him and over to Nix and Takis. "Fucking despicable," she muttered.

———

Clayton looked down at the papers. He'd never seen a life list that had any substance to it since he only dealt with newborns. In black and white were Takis' sins, and they were all quite timid before he got to the end. Takis led a relatively clean life. He'd fornicated, he'd drank, and he was guilty of tall tales. Until he betrayed his son and his wife and kept it hidden, he was mild. There was no mention of a plot to kill Leon and Lipa.

"And before you ask," Feme called back to him, "yes, that would definitely be on there." Clayton dropped the life list in the tall grass and watched it fade away. He stood with his head down. Why would Leon lie to him? Was he just trying to justify what he'd done? That had to be it, but Clayton had done severe damage to his relationship with Takis. He'd hurt him in a way that he doubted he could undo. Takis was the only true friend he had here, and Clayton had spent so long being angry at him. He wasn't better than him, far from it. Clayton started to walk towards Nix and Takis, but Nix shook his head at him.

"Just get out of here!" Nix yelled to Clayton. "You'll make this worse!" For a few seconds, Clayton thought he didn't know where to go, but then it dawned on him.

"Eve Shaw," he said. A door appeared behind him. He turned and went through. He stepped into the sunlight in the woods somewhere, not a building in sight. The light felt good on his skin, and a soft breeze came in from the east. A little wrought iron fence surrounded a graveyard. He had no idea where he was. He didn't care. He was just happy to be somewhere that felt peaceful with the sounds of leaves rustling and the chirping of birds. He felt warmth from within. He looked down at his feet, and there she was, a grave with a headstone and etching that had worn away. He knew she was there, though, that she was laid to rest in this place. This was all that remained of his baby sister. This was all he had to hang on to. He had missed her life. He hoped it was a good one. He reached down and touched the marker.

"Eve King," Feme said behind him. He turned and looked back at her. "Born Eve Shaw 1800, to Jonas and Emma Shaw of Clover, Virginia." She walked up and stood beside him. "Married 1818 to Edward King, a military man, who passed away from pneumonia in 1850. He was 50 years old. Eve had three sons with Edward; Robert, Jonas, and Clayton. She named them after the three men she adored most in her lifetime; her father-in-law, her father, and her brother."

"Shit," Clayton said, trying to hold back tears as he looked up to the sky.

"She lived to the unbelievable age of eighty-eight, living out her final years with Clayton, her son, and his family. She was happy and never questioned the scriptures. She was granted passage to the Brilliance where she resides to this day."

"I'm sorry," Clayton rubbed both his hands through his hair before pinching the bridge of his nose with his left hand, "thank you."

"That was fucking stupid, Clayton."

"I know, I know. I knew better."

"Yes, you did, and now Takis is a wreck, and I have to figure out how to keep the two of you from killing each other."

"I'll tell him the truth," Clayton said weakly.

"You can't."

"But I have to," he begged.

"Takis cannot know that Leon was sentenced. It was on the order." She reminded him as she took a handkerchief from her pocket and handed it to him. She made a gesture towards her chin. He took it and wiped away some of the dried blood. He handed it back to her.

"Come on, Feme."

"He cannot know. You break the order, and we all get punished, remember?"

"How can I make this right?"

"Takis got his pass. He is free to go after the two of you complete two more orders."

"Really? It's over for him? That's great!" Clayton straightened up. Immense joy overtook him. His friend was leaving.

"It's not that simple," Feme sighed and looked off into the distance. Clayton looked at her, confused.

"What's wrong?"

"You have to pick one person up from the cells and take them to the Brilliance, and the second is his replacement who's also in the cells. Meaning you are being issued a partner."

"Doesn't sound too bad," he scoffed. Feme breathed heavily, and Clayton could feel how distraught she was.

"Well..."

"What is it?" He could feel his mouth going dry. If this bothered her, it had to be terrible.

"The soul you are sending on to the Brilliance..."

"Yes?" He braced for it.

"It's Donald Price."

46

THE AFTER

Feme opened the door and stepped inside her office. Nix was leaning against her desk while Takis sat in the chair in front of him. He was still hyperventilating, pulling in air in massive gulps. Nix acknowledged her with a slight nod and went back to watching Takis in silence. Feme stood for a moment, trying to make sense of the whole situation and deciding her next move.

"You should have let me hurt him," Takis argued, breaking the chill in the air.

"Why?" Nix asked. "What would that have solved?"

"He accused me of wanting to kill my son, Nix. He said I wanted to hurt Lipa." Takis slammed his hand down on the armrest of his chair.

"I know," Nix conceded.

"Where the hell would he get an idea like that?"

"How should I know?" Nix asked.

"He's a spoiled little shit. I hope he rots here."

"You don't mean that, Takis," Nix sighed.

"How do you know?"

"Because you're not a spoiled little shit," Nix grinned.

"I can't work with him anymore, Nix. I don't even want to see him. I don't care how much time it adds. I don't give a damn if I'm stuck here forever. I'm finished with him."

That was her cue. She walked past Takis, raising her hand to pat his shoulder as she went by, but thought better of it and stopped herself. She rounded the edge of her desk past Nix and sat down.

"How are you holding up?" She asked, concerned.

"Reassign me, Feme," Takis ordered. Nix had gone to the door and was about to leave.

"Nix?" Feme called out. He turned around and met her gaze.

"Thank you," she began, "I owe you." He nodded, ducked on his way out, and shut the door. Feme sat in silence for a minute while Takis stared at her. She had planned everything in her mind before she entered the room. She knew how she was going to approach him on this. She just had to wait for the right opening for his guard to be down.

"I need you to listen to me."

"Feme- " Takis began. She held her hand up.

"I need you to listen to me, please."

"Go on," Takis said, leaning back in the chair and folding his arms in anger.

"People in this place, they say things. Rumors. Lies. Jealousy. We are here because of the things we did in life. Let's be honest. I know what happened to you. I know how you died and what led up to it," Feme said. He squirmed in his chair. "I was a prostitute, Takis. I can sit here and say all the right things to justify it, but I accepted items and coin for sexual pleasure."

"I knew that, Feme."

"Did you know I also lied and convinced a man to kill another man that was causing one of my girls grief? I used my body to seduce him and used that power to get him to end someone's life. Again, I can sit here and say all the right things about how this person deserved it. I can say how evil the man was and that by killing him, I might have saved that girl's life, but at the end of the day, I used my body to persuade him to do it."

"That doesn't make you a bad person," Takis said and leaned forward.

"Actually, when it comes to this place, it just might. I knew he would kill him once I made the offer, and once the deed was done, I gave that man what he wanted. I might as well have cut the man's throat myself. I lived a good life, Takis. I was fed, wined, and beloved. I never gave anything back, though. Sure, I brought some girls into my home, and I got them off the street, but all it did was feed my ego and my purse. I loved feeling like they owed me."

"I'm sorry," Takis mumbled.

"What happened with you and your daughter-in-law, was it all your fault? No. No, it wasn't. You should have stopped it. She was your son's wife. You *could* have stopped it. You weren't a child. You knew it was wrong." She folded her hands together. "Did you deserve a knife in your back for it? Believe it or not, Takis, I don't think you did. But there are many people on the other side of that door that do. The residents here are not exactly angels."

"What are you saying?" Takis asked. She had him now. She wanted this to be over with. Get Takis out of here, get Clayton back to his work, and get some semblance of order back to the offices. All of this conflict had to be reflecting poorly on her, and the last thing she wanted was to get an order of reprimand on her desk.

"Someone out there must have told that young boy that you plotted your wife and child's death. They told him to not trust you, that behind that lovable facade is a cunning, evil man who would step on him to get ahead in this place. I mean, look at what he did to his own son."

"Why would someone do that?" Takis asked, shocked.

"Who knows?" she asked. "But I will tell you this, what that boy is willing to go through for you is more than should be asked of anyone."

"What?" Takis asked, confused.

"How much do you know of why Clayton is here? How much do you know about what happened?"

"I know enough."

"You think you do. Did he mention the girl to you?" Feme inquired.

"Amber."

"And the man who got her pregnant? The incident that led to her death? It was an older man, a reverend from his village, his name was Donald Price. To cover his own ass, he lied about Clayton and blamed him. Clayton had just lost the love of his life, and everyone thought Clayton was responsible based on this man saying so."

"He didn't tell me any of that," Takis bowed his head as he said it.

"You never know someone's full story, Takis. All of us have something underneath that eats away at us. This brings me to our current predicament. Takis, I have your golden pass. It came today."

"REALLY?!" Takis stood up, his eyes wide with shock.

"Calm," she put her hand up again. "Sit down. There's a catch." Takis sat slowly, but Feme saw the way his hands shook as he clutched the armrests of the chair.

"You have two jobs left. You have to complete them, then I will escort you to the River myself."

"What are they? Let's do this now. I'm ready."

"They have to be completed with Clayton."

"I don't care. I don't have to talk to him. Hell, I don't even have to look at him."

"No, you don't, that's true, but I want you to know what he will be going through while you do these tasks."

"I don't care," he shrugged.

"The first is to pick someone up from the cells and take them to the Brilliance."

"Who are we retrieving?" Takis leaned in.

"Donald Price," she answered.

"The man that ruined his life?" Takis said, bewildered.

"Yes," she folded her hands in front of her.

"Does Clayton know?"

"Yes."

"And he's okay with this?"

"I believe his exact words were, 'if it gets him out of here.'"

"Shit!" Takis stood up and flung his chair backward. His voice boomed. "I want to hurt this kid! How can I hate him when he does something like this? I want to hate him, Feme!"

"I guess you can't?" Feme replied and scratched the back of her neck.

"Let me go to the break room for a day, let me think. We'll do it tomorrow. I don't like this. Just keep him away from me. I don't want to see him right now, and I don't want to do this today."

"What's one more day? It's alright with me. I'll get you both later, and you two can finish up."

"You're coming too?" Takis questioned.

"I've left too much to chance already. I'll be there. No more fuck ups, and no surprises." She nodded to him. Takis stormed out of her office and closed the door with a bang. Feme opened her desk drawer slowly and reached in for her brush. *Please*, she thought, *please just once, let everything work out fine.*

47

JUNE 13TH, 1985

They stood in front of the cell together; neither had spoken a word since Feme had gathered them both. Takis held the key in his hand with disgust. He had no idea why this man was getting a ride to the Brilliance. This man had committed a serious sin. He'd been with a young girl barely older than Clayton when he arrived, and to cover his crime, he blamed this boy beside him. It wasn't fair. Clayton stood still and emotionless. Takis couldn't get a read on him at all. He had no idea how the boy would react to seeing the man who ruined him. Takis hoped this would go fast, and there would be minimal chatter. He didn't want the boy to suffer any more than he already had. Takis was still angry with Clayton, but he'd been led astray by someone in the After. Takis was relieved that this would be his last day here. He couldn't wait to ride the gondola through the Brilliance and start making things right with Lipa. Takis placed the key in the lock.

"Hey," Clayton started before Takis unlocked the door, "listen." Takis paused but didn't turn around. "I messed up, I know that, and I'm sorry. I am happy for you. I'm glad you're getting out of here."

"Just let it be," Takis replied, looking down at the handle.

"No, I don't want to let it be. I want you to know. I was angry, and I'm sorry. I wish I had listened to you when you warned me about what this place does. It got to me, and I took it out on you. I was wrong." Embarrassed, Takis changed the subject quickly.

"I know how this is for you, Clayton. I know who's in here."

"If it gets you out, gets you away from this shit, that's all I care about," Clayton said with conviction. Takis could feel the sincerity coming from Clayton and soaked it in.

"Thank you, that means more than you know." He opened the door.

Clayton stood to the side as Takis went in. He felt sick to his stomach. He had spent a long time devastated by the actions of this man. Now he was about to take him and lead him to paradise. Reverend Price had been dead for less than the time Clayton had, and here he was coming out of a cell and rewarded. Clayton heard Takis speaking, but he wasn't paying attention to what he said. He was breathing slowly, trying to keep calm. He didn't want to see him, but he was doing this for Takis. Takis deserved to see his wife again; he earned his redemption.

48

Takis emerged first. He looked Clayton in the eyes as if to tell him everything would be alright. Clayton nodded. Next came the Reverend Donald Price, who shockingly looked almost precisely as Clayton remembered him. He must have only made it a year or so after Clayton. He was even dressed in the same outfit Clayton had seen him last. Donald saw Clayton, and his face lit up.

"Clayton, my son!" He reached out and hugged him tightly. Clayton didn't raise his arms and didn't move. He could see the anxiety in Takis' face, but Clayton closed his eyes and let it happen. "Finally, a friendly face! How are you?" Price asked, keeping his hands on Clayton's shoulders.

"That's enough," Takis said forcefully. "Donald Price, we are here to escort you to the Brilliance."

"Heaven?" Donald asked.

"Yes," Clayton answered.

"Thank you, Father." Donald praised, looking upwards.

"Feme's Fork," Clayton said, and the door appeared behind him. Donald jerked backward in surprise.

"That is amazing! Oh, the Lord and His ways!" The reverend

lifted his hands in praise. Clayton said nothing, turned, and opened the door.

"After you," Clayton said as he gestured for Donald to walk through. He was hesitant at first, but Donald crept through the entryway to the Fork. Takis was watching Clayton the entire time. Clayton nodded to him and tilted his head for Takis to go next. Takis started through, and when he walked by Clayton, he stopped and patted his shoulder.

"You're a good friend."

"Thanks."

"I'm kind of hoping you hit him," Takis chuckled.

"I'm okay."

"This isn't right, boy," Takis lamented and stared at him for a moment.

"I know, but you going home is all that matters," Clayton answered. Takis shook his head and went in. Clayton followed behind and shut the door. Donald was admiring the Fork when Clayton stepped through.

"Look at His glory," Donald said, laughing and twirling around like a toddler. Clayton could feel the hatred bubbling up, but he pushed it back down. He didn't want to hurt Takis' chances of seeing his wife again.

"Are you doing alright, kid?" Feme asked from behind him. Clayton turned around to see Feme and Nix, the latter of which was wearing shorts with geometric patterns of different colors on a leopard print. He looked ridiculous, and it made Clayton grin. It was the first time he'd seen Nix clothed.

"What the hell are you wearing?" Clayton asked him.

"Jealous?" Nix beamed.

"No, those are awful," Clayton laughed.

"I look good," Nix smiled, and Clayton wondered if he really felt that way. Clayton laughed again and turned to see Donald Price pointing at Nix in horror. Takis was whispering in his ear, probably trying to calm him down. Clayton couldn't make out what he was saying.

"He put those on just for you," Feme joked to Clayton.

"Nix, please," Clayton chuckled, "don't do me any favors."

"I don't do favors. So, are you good?" He asked with concern.

"Yes. Will everyone stop asking me that? This is for Takis. I got this."

"Look at that smug son of a bitch," Feme said, looking over Clayton's shoulder. Clayton nodded and almost started to cry but reigned it back in.

"Let's get this over with," Nix said and guided Clayton toward them with Feme in tow. Donald was staring at Nix in fear.

"You are something else," Donald said to Nix. "This place is filled with such oddities."

"Reverend Price," Clayton spoke up quickly, "here is how this works. One of us," he pointed to himself and then to Takis, "will walk up to that pedestal and sign your name in the book. After a few minutes, Charon will appear with her boat and take you into that cave, into the Brilliance."

"I knew I would make it. I knew He hadn't forgotten me." Donald followed Clayton's hand and leapt upon seeing the light in the tunnel. Takis was watching Clayton. Clayton nodded again to show he was still in control, but this was torture. This man was scum and the lowest form of it. Clayton amused himself by thinking he wasn't just a good friend. He was a saint. When it was Clayton's time to enter the Brilliance, Takis had better be there with a horn to announce his arrival. He couldn't take much more. He needed this to be over soon.

"How are you, dear lady?" Donald said and looked excitedly at Feme. Feme recoiled.

"Little too old for you, isn't she?" Takis asked out loud. Donald turned to Takis.

"Excuse me?" Reverend Price feigned insult.

"No, I don't think I will." Takis flicked his wrist and said,

"Donald Price life list." Multiple papers appeared in his hand. Donald looked at the papers, then back to the group.

"What is this?" He asked. Feme said nothing, Nix smiled, and Clayton understood what Takis was doing. Takis cleared his throat.

"Donald Price!" He boomed. "You have been granted passage to the Brilliance, however before you go, your transgressions must be read."

"Transgressions?" Donald expelled a nervous laugh. "There is no need for that. We can just get this over with."

"Oh, I'm sorry, but this is part of the procedure. You understand I'm sure." Feme smirked at him.

"I'll tell you what; let's skip ahead to the last page or two since it makes you uncomfortable," Takis said while pulling the last two sheets forward.

"Honestly, there is-" Donald began.

"Donald Price, you self-pleasured yourself. A lot." Takis whistled. "More than most, actually, while dreaming of your neighbor's daughter." Donald looked around, his face red, trying not to look at Clayton directly. Nix and Feme were glaring a hole through him.

"You abused alcohol, you had extremely lewd thoughts, and were prone to violent outbursts." He paused. "Well," Takis shook his head in disgust. "You used your position of power to lure and abuse one young Amber Ward."

"Now, you wait just a minute-"

"SHUT YOUR MOUTH!" Takis yelled at him. Everyone startled. Takis was enraged. "You," Takis held up one finger and pushed it violently into Price's chest, "you impregnated her. Then you threatened her if she told anyone. You shifted the blame to her and a young boy named Clayton Shaw."

"Son, that's not-" Donald began, looking at Clayton.

"I'M NOT FINISHED!" Takis bellowed, the echo deafening. Donald looked back at Takis.

"Please stop. Just stop. He doesn't need to know these things,"

Donald begged. Takis looked back at the page and paused. A look of confusion washed over his face as his eyebrow raised and his mouth turned down into a grimace. Clayton could tell he was struggling with what he was reading. Just how terrible had this man's deeds been? Takis looked up to Clayton, back to the paper in his hand, and continued.

"She perished through miscarriage. You seized the opportunity to blame Clayton Shaw so no one would suspect you. You turned his loved ones against him, which led to his death," Takis spat. Donald wasn't saying anything now. His head hung. "You presided over both funerals, did you not?" Takis asked, then waited for an answer. When one didn't come, he yelled again, "DIDN'T YOU?!"

"Yes, yes I did."

"At Clayton's funeral, you asked the whole village to forgive him for what he had done. You told them that we all make mistakes, that they should not judge him by one deed. So, I have one question, Reverend. What did the boy do?" Donald Price was silent. "You didn't live much longer after that, thank Poseidon. You choked to death on your own vomit, too drunk to roll over. But at least your secrets died with you. You got away with the crime."

"Crime?" He finally spoke, his voice rising. "I did not hold her down and take her if that's what you are implying," he said, his face turning purple. Clayton felt his stomach twist into knots. He gulped air. He wanted nothing more than to walk away from all of this. He hated this man. Clayton had never had this feeling before. He felt himself shaking. There was no way Amber laid down for this man willingly. He had done something. Clayton was sure of it.

Clayton envisioned killing Donald right then, holding him down and strangling him. A feeling of shame fluttered in his chest, but he dismissed it. Clayton thought about all the things the reverend must have said to her. How he must have used his position as a trusted man of God to get close to the girl Clayton loved and hurt her. She didn't tell anyone of the pregnancy, and it seemed to Clayton that she died because she never asked for help. If she had told him what the reverend had done to her, he could have gone with her to Doctor Brown. He could have helped her shed light on what Price had done. He could have seen the man punished, and maybe the doctor could have saved her when she became ill. Clayton could only imagine the things that must have gone through Amber's mind; fear of how the town would blame her, how they would label her a whore, they would cast her out. *That's why she never told me*, he thought.

Clayton thought of Amber's kiss and tried to calm himself. This was for Takis. No matter how much he wanted this man's existence snuffed out, he still loved Takis like a brother, plus he owed him. If it meant controlling himself in this situation, he would. He wanted Takis to reunite with Lipa. Takis had been here far too long, and he deserved to go. Clayton kept his feelings inside, thinking of the good this moment would do.

"This mother fucker," Feme groaned; she shook her head and walked a few feet away.

"What!" Donald protested. "I'm sorry. My wife was gone. I was alone. She never asked me to stop. She-"

"Then why blame the boy?" Takis stepped forward, and the reverend shuffled back a step in fear. Reverend Price looked at Clayton for a moment.

"I wasn't thinking clearly," he said. Takis made a quick jerking motion at the reverend, and he flinched. He held his hand up. "Clayton ran away. He could have stayed and-"

"Stop talking," Nix interrupted. "If you say one more word, one more word, I'll take your other eye." The reverend didn't move. His face went from purple to white. Nix looked terrifying with his eyes focused on Donald. Clayton thought it was the look a wolf might have before pouncing on sheep. Takis stood there smirking, and Feme stepped forward to stand beside Nix, shaking her head in disappointment.

"Thank you, Takis," Clayton said. "I'll go sign the book for him now."

"You're welcome. I'm almost inclined to turn the Brilliance down if they let hunks of pig shit like this in," Takis said. Clayton walked towards the pedestal.

"Clayton!" Price called after him. "Clayton, son, I want you to know-" Clayton spun around fast and smashed Donald in his eye patch. With a sickening crunch, he went down sideways.

"Don't," Clayton said to him. "You are evil. You should be going in there," he pointed to the Darkness. Donald Price laid on his side, glaring at Clayton, clutching his eye and muttering curses. Clayton turned and walked away.

"I will pray for you, Clayton!" Price spat, his voice quaking with anger.

"I'd be more concerned with what I was going to tell my wife once I got there," Clayton called back, which got a chuckle from his three companions. Clayton had almost reached the book when he felt the hairs on his neck stand up. The voice wasn't as loud or as mind-melting as before, but he heard it whisper.

What are you doing? The Darkness called out to him.

"I have to sign the book and let him on the boat," he replied quietly so that no one would hear.

I warned you not to take what is mine.

"This one isn't yours," Clayton said back.

He's mine.

"He's been in the cells. I have an order to put him on the boat."

He was supposed to be here over a century ago. He never belonged in a cell. Clayton stopped moving and glanced back at everyone. Nix took notice and nudged Takis.

"What the hell do you mean he didn't belong in a cell?" Clayton asked, turning back around.

"Hey, Clayton, are you alright?" Takis called nervously.

"Yeah!" He bellowed back, then he dropped his voice back to a whisper. "What do you mean? I have an order."

I don't care what you have. He belongs here with me. Clayton's blood ran cold. Could the Darkness be telling the truth? Was Donald Price always meant for the Darkness? Was Clayton being led astray?

"Leon...was he shown the images of his father plotting his death?"

Yes.

"And they weren't true, were they?"

No.

"Do you want me to sign his name?" Takis called out again.

"No, no, I got it! I'm just upset! Give me a minute!" He dropped his voice again. "What do I do? If I don't sign this book, Takis doesn't get to go into the Brilliance." There was no answer for a while, and Takis called out again.

"Clayton?"

"One more minute!"

I can do it, the Darkness finally answered.

"What?"

I can do it for you. Just say the word. Let me take what's mine. You won't be blamed.

"You can do it?"

Yes, I'll make him suffer. It's what you want. I win, you win.

"Just like last time?" Clayton asked. He could feel the Darkness contemplate its answer.

No, it will be something worse.

"It's ok, Clayton. I'll come sign it." Takis started walking towards him. Clayton had no idea what was about to happen, but if Donald Price belonged in Hell, and if Hell was willing to reach out and take him there, who was he to argue?

"Do it," he said. Clayton's mind went utterly blank; he wasn't conscious inside his own body anymore. The Darkness slid in.

49

"What are you doing, Clayton? Let's get rid of this piece of shit," Takis said to him, taking note of a change in Clayton's mannerisms. He was hunched forward, and he was giggling, but it didn't sound like him. Something felt wrong. Takis told himself to go sign the book as quickly as possible and get Clayton out of here, let Nix put that bastard on the boat, and Takis could take care of his friend. Clayton spun around, and Takis stopped dead in his tracks. Clayton's pupils were completely white, and a sickening grin flashed across his face.

"TAKIS, GIVE ME WHAT'S MINE!"

"Clayton?" Takis asked. He felt a chill and shuddered at the sight of the boy. He put his hand out but withdrew it immediately. He didn't want to touch him. He felt disgusted by his appearance and a need to get away from him. The whites of his eyes were terrifying.

"NO," it smirked, "NOT CLAYTON!"

"Clayton, are you alright? What do you need me to do?" He begged. Takis stepped backward. He was shaken to his core. This wasn't Clayton. It was something he'd never encountered.

"Get away from him, Takis! Clayton isn't in there!" Nix yelled.

Takis looked back at Nix, who was standing in front of Feme, shielding her with his giant arm across her frame. Takis didn't have to be told a second time. He took off running for them. He didn't look back at Clayton until he got to them, running right past Donald, still on the ground.

"What's happening to him?" Feme asked, puzzled.

"The Darkness is inside Clayton," Nix explained.

"What?" Feme asked, her voice trembling in fear. "How the fuck do you know that?"

"Stay behind me, Feme. Don't get in its way," Nix commanded. Clayton's neck craned upwards at a sickening angle, and he started to move forward, leaping, not walking or running. He wasn't behaving even remotely human anymore. The Darkness had total control of his body.

"REVEREND!" Clayton leaped and landed on Donald, straddling him. "YOU ARE MINE!"

"Clayton, what are you doing?" Price barely got the words out before Clayton's fists began raining down on him like pistons.

"MINE MINE MINE MINE," he cackled. "WOULD YOU LIKE YOUR EYE BACK?" Clayton bellowed. He regurgitated an eye up into his hand and smashed it into Donald's forehead. It made a squishing sound, oozed off his forehead, and fell onto the grass. Clayton began gyrating his hips back and forth. "WHAT'S WRONG, DONALD? I THOUGHT YOU LIKED THEM YOUNG?"

"Takis, do something!" Feme called out, and Takis looked at her, confused. What did she expect him to do? He pointed at Clayton and shook his head no.

"We can't stop that, Feme," Nix said. Clayton stood and kicked Donald in the gut several times.

"YOU THOUGHT YOU COULD GET AWAY FROM ME? I'VE WAITED A LONG TIME FOR YOU, HOLY MAN!" Clayton picked Reverend Price up and flung him over his shoulder, carrying him like he was nothing more than a child. "LET'S GO HOME!" He boomed and started towards the Darkness, whistling and saying mine in between bars. Takis started to worry. If the Darkness took Reverend Price, what would it do to him leaving? He began to walk towards Clayton to cut him off, but Nix grabbed Takis' arm.

"Listen, Takis, that is evil personified. It'll destroy you. I can't stop it. We can't stop it," he said. Takis looked back and saw Clayton take the Reverend Price off his shoulder. He grabbed the backside of his pant's waistline with one hand, his other gripped the back of his collar, and he tossed him inside the Darkness. Clayton stood there for a moment, then turned and walked towards the group. His eyes were white as snow, his face delighted. Nix stood entirely in front of Feme now.

"Stay behind me," Nix said. Takis stood still. He didn't want to catch Clayton's eye. Clayton stopped in front of them and bowed.

"I warned him, and I'll warn you. Don't ever try to take what's mine. He belonged with me, so I took him."

"What about my order?" Takis asked the Darkness. "I just want to leave." Clayton's neck popped as he moved it left to right, making an awful crackling sound.

"It's fine. Consider it completed. Job well done, Takis."

"So that's it? We were told to send him to the Brilliance," Takis said.

"Paperwork errors happen all the time here. Things get lost or forgotten. Right, Feme?"

"All the time," Feme squeaked, looking around Nix.

"Feme, Amisi hasn't stopped screaming since she became mine. She regrets, oh does she regret."

"Thank you?" Feme replied, her face pale.

"You're welcome," it said and moved in front of Takis. "Your boy."

"You have my boy?" Takis blanched.

"I do," it grinned. Takis looked at the ground. The world

started to fade, and he almost fainted. This was what he had feared since his arrival. He didn't want Leon to suffer for hurting him.

"Let him go. Take me instead. Let him go, I beg of you," Takis cried with the pain of a father who had lost his son. He knew he'd never see him again.

"Clayton tried to sneak him past me to the Brilliance. He tried to save your son."

"What?" Takis asked as he fell to his knees.

"You can't steal from me. What's mine is mine. You don't cross me," he moved in front of Nix. "Isn't that right, Nix?"

"Get away from me," Nix spat, a primordial snarl on his face.

"I figured he'd be happy to see me," the Darkness said to Feme.

"I'll figure out how to kill you one day," Nix threatened. "You will die by my hand. I promise you that."

"Your tribe, your people, they scream every second. They wait for you to save them, but you've never come. Why is that Nix? Why haven't you walked beyond the Veil and faced me?"

"I'll get you," Nix threatened as he stepped forward, bending down so that their noses almost touched.

"With what?" It laughed. "Your trinkets? Are you going to find some magical item that will give you a way to get them out? I am Forever, Nix. You can't beat me. You can't stop me. I'll have them all."

Nix opened his mouth to speak again, but Clayton slumped to the ground. He fell to his knees, bending forward at the waist with his arms at his sides and his face in the dirt.

"What did it mean, Nix?" Feme asked.

"Nothing."

"What do you mean nothing? It... knows you," she said.

"It does," he confirmed and walked off. Clayton was starting to come to and laid down on his stomach.

"Oh God, it hurts." Clayton gasped.

"Clayton, my boy, can you stand?" Takis asked and reached

out to touch him but withdrew his hand. He was still afraid of what might be lying there. He wiped the tears from his eyes.

"I feel like someone tore my skin off and put it back on."

"Clayton, what did you do?" Takis asked and sat down in the grass beside him.

"The Darkness told me it wanted him. That's all I remember."

"It took you, boy. It was inside you. Is it gone?" Takis asked with concern. Clayton nodded.

"It's gone. I felt it come, and I felt it leave."

"Do you remember anything?"

"No," Clayton answered. Takis recounted what had happened. Clayton rolled over on his back, his face was flushed, and his eyes were bloodshot.

"I tried. I swear I did."

"I know. I know you did," Takis put his hands to his face and cried.

50

THE DARKNESS

The first thing Donald noticed was how cold he was, then how wet and sticky the ground felt beneath his palms. His eye was still hazy from the brutality unleashed upon him. If he had been younger, he would have taught that little bastard a lesson. He rubbed his forearm against his eye, trying to bring the world back to focus, but it wasn't responding. He slowly got to his hands and knees and looked up. It was a blur, but someone was in here with him, wherever here was. He could hear sounds, but they were muffled. His ears were still ringing. His brain wasn't processing anything correctly. He grabbed his jaw and moved it left to right, trying to get the sting to ease, but that just made it worse. When he took his hand away, he noticed his chin was wet and cold. He stared at his left hand, trying to get his bearings, and finally, the color red came into view. His hand was covered in blood, dripping with it.

"Shit," he spat. "Wait till I get my hands on you." It was faint, but through the ringing, he heard laughter. He squinted his eye, but all he saw was red and shadow. "You can laugh all you want. It's my turn," he spat again. Donald focused on the laughter. It was growing louder and clearer. It was not Clayton but a woman. He

228

pushed up to his knees, he could feel the wetness soaking through his pants, and he shivered at the frigidness of the room. He shook his head, and the spots started to dissipate. He wanted to get to his feet, but his legs stopped listening. He took the palms of his hands and rubbed his thighs, trying to get them to respond.

"I don't think you'll be hurting anyone, Reverend." He heard her say. "At least not anymore." He looked in the direction of the voice, and at once, everything was clear. The room, if you could call it that, was encased in a layer of thin blood. The walls and floor looked like skin but sickly and blotchy as if sewn together in different hues of red, yellow, pink, and brown. It made his stomach turn.

"Where...?" He asked, but he knew. He knew damn well where he was. Clayton had sentenced him. He was in Hell. She stepped out into the light from the shadows, still laughing at him. Her long hair was matted to her skull, caked in blood, her face rotting away. One of her eyes was gone, the other rolling around in the socket. She wasn't staring directly at him, which made it all the more horrifying. Her naked body was ghastly white, the flesh sliding away, and greenish sores littered her waistline. Her veins were black, thin, and looked drawn onto the paleness of her skin. She wasn't slow or hunched over. She was exactly the opposite, upright as if she was proud of her appearance. Her feet made splashing noises in the half-inch of blood on the floor. She made her way towards him, one hand out. A few of her nails were missing, but the fingers were still there. He scrambled backward, on his backside, kicking blood up everywhere.

"You stay back!" He commanded. She stopped and smiled, and when she did, he noticed the skin on the right side of her jawline was missing. He could see inside her mouth at her yellowed teeth.

"You have no power here, Reverend."

"In the name of the Father, I order-"

"You order?!" She cackled. "You are in my world now, Donald."

"I do not deserve this! I was a man of-" he stammered.

"Ah yes, you were a man of many things. Were you about to tell me you were a man of God? A man of the cloth? A man deserving of the kingdom? How many, Reverend? How many?"

"But all the good I've done!" He was afraid now.

"Six. There were six."

"I tried to stop."

"No, you didn't," she smiled.

"I was weak."

"You forced yourself onto those poor girls in Georgia. Did you know one of them killed herself? You had to flee. They would have killed you if they'd caught you," she said with a playfulness in her voice.

"I'm sorry."

"It's a little late for that," she admonished. He got on his knees and placed his hands in front of him in prayer.

"That won't work. I tried that when I got here," she said. He opened his eye and looked at her.

"I could have stopped you, Donald. I knew what you'd done. I knew about Edith, but I did nothing. I didn't want the shame on me. I didn't want to admit you were rotten. As I was dying, I said to myself, it's just a matter of time before he does it again. I just hope it isn't little Eve. I had no idea you'd hurt sweet Amber," she hissed. He recognized her then. He knew what his punishment was. This hideous monstrosity, this thing was his wife. She had been waiting for him.

"Mary. Oh, Mary," he gasped. She was in front of him now, staring down at him. She smelled toxic. The scent flooded his nose and tasted like acid in his mouth. Her face twisted from a smile to a pained grimace.

"When I first got here, I prayed like you are now. I wanted to die, but I was already dead. There is nothing that can stop this, and it will only get worse."

"Please let me go," he begged. Tears streamed down his blood-covered face.

"You don't like me this way?" She leaned down and snatched his face with her hand. Her grip was like a vice, her strength supernatural. "I chose this for you. I want you to please me, Donald. Can't you look at me the way you looked at them?" He started babbling, trying to break her grip on his face. He couldn't stand her touch. "The things I am going to do to you," she smiled, and her cold, rough, black tongue darted out and licked the blood from his cheek.

He screamed. It was the first in what would become countless.

51

THE AFTER

Feme slammed her door and walked around her desk. She sat down and opened her mouth, then closed it. She was trying to get her bearings and needed some semblance of calm. She placed her hands in front of her and took a deep breath.

"Ok, who's going first? It's all coming out here. Right now. I am tired of being kept in the dark. Do I need to remind any of you that this is my house?" They looked at one another. "I am fucking waiting."

"I'll go first. I probably have the least to tell." Clayton started. "The Darkness broke the order, not me." He took it slow and started from when Feme asked him to take Leon to the Darkness. "I wasn't about to send my friend's son to Hell. This place was trying to get me to betray Takis. I was going to try my hardest to stop that from happening."

Feme wanted to explode at his direct defiance of her order, but she kept it in; she wanted to end the trouble happening in the After. She was tired of all the problems and just wanted things to run as they did in the 1200s, where most of her days were spent reminiscing about a lover or brushing her hair.

"One of my jobs in Acquisitions is to refill the ink at the

pedestal. There are many different colors of ink, each has a specific purpose. I gave him light blue because one of my texts said it would override an order, so I hoped it would work for the passage book," Nix added.

"I know about the ink and the colors. It's part of my job. If you had let me in on the plan, I would have told you that wasn't possible. Light blue allows me to write notes on an order to add to it. That's all," Feme sighed. She was livid that her people were doing things behind her back.

"When I got to the Fork, Leon thanked me for the things shown to him in his cell. He was shown his wife and father plotting to kill both him and his mother," Clayton continued. Takis wrung his hands together.

"That's why you said those things?" Takis asked through gritted teeth.

"Yes, I'm sorry," Clayton apologized, and Nix patted him on the shoulder. "I tried to get him on that boat, Feme. He had one foot in the air when the Darkness spoke to me."

"It spoke to you?" She asked, raising her eyebrow.

"Yes, in my head. It's loud. It hurts. He told me Leon was his and then took control of him and went into the Darkness after beating me," Clayton said. Feme sat in silence for a moment, letting that sink in. Takis was looking off to the left wall in silence. She could only imagine what he was thinking. Clayton put his soul at risk for Leon.

"I was upset because I lost Leon. I was torn apart thinking you plotted the death of your wife and son. Feme was no help either. Everything was a confrontation. I felt like I made one mistake and would be here thousands of years, and I never hurt anyone. It's why I acted like I did. I just hate this place."

"No one likes it here," Nix said.

"Then today, when I was walking to the book, the Darkness told me this was the second time I tried to take something from him. It told me Reverend Price was supposed to be with it over a century ago and that he never belonged in a cell."

"But the order-" Feme interrupted.

"That's the thing. He said the order was wrong."

"That's not possible. They come straight to my desk," Feme scoffed.

"The Darkness wouldn't have said it if it wasn't true."

"How do you come to that conclusion?" Feme asked.

"I wasn't able to put Leon on the boat because the Darkness had a claim to him, right? Wouldn't it work the other way too? You can't just stick someone in there that didn't earn it," Clayton said. Takis stood and started to pace, and Clayton turned to look at him. "I'm sorry," he apologized. Takis shook his head and continued pacing.

"That makes sense," Nix said. Feme stared at Clayton for any sign of dishonesty, any sign that there was more. There wasn't.

"And you trust that fucking thing?" Feme asked. "Takis?" Feme tried to get his attention.

"Yes?" He asked, not stopping his pacing.

"What do you have to add?"

"Nothing. I have nothing to add. I just want to be done with this place," Takis replied.

"Go on. We need to figure this out. It's tearing this place apart."

"Clayton shouldn't be here. I get it, the kid killed himself, but I've personally delivered people to the Brilliance with worse shit lists than him. We all have. Something here isn't right. He's only doing what any good person would do. He was just trying protect me. I'd have done the same in his shoes. I'm supposed to be his partner, his mentor."

"More like family," Clayton muttered. His eyes were wide. He hadn't meant to say that out loud. Takis placed a hand on the boy's shoulder and cleared his throat.

"Something here is hellbent on making sure he suffers. The

babies, your shit-for-brains son, and the dickhead priest we just dealt with..." Feme started

"With the biggest 'fuck you' being Clayton's new partner from the cells," Nix finished the train of thought. Feme panicked.

"Wait," she said.

"New partner?" Clayton asked.

"Alma? Emma? I've never been good with names," Nix mused.

"Amber?!" Clayton shouted.

"Ah, yes," Nix snapped his fingers, "that's it."

"The cells? We need to get Amber right now!" Clayton panicked.

"Clayton, listen. You are overreacting right now," Feme interjected. "I am not going to have another fuck up just so you can see some little girl you were infatuated with two goddamn centuries ago. You can fucking wait until we are done here," she hissed. Clayton fell silent. "And you, Nix. Do you know the Darkness? Because it sure knows you."

"I'll tell you everything if you answer one thing for me," Nix said, leaning against the wall.

"What's that?"

"'Things get lost or forgotten, paperwork errors,' what did it mean?" He asked. Feme glared at Nix.

"Shit," she said softly. Flushed with a mix of shame and embarrassment, Feme opened the front drawer of her desk and leafed through some paperwork. She produced a golden sheet. She laid it in on the desk and scooted back in her chair.

"What is that?" Nix frowned.

"It's your pass to the Brilliance."

"How long has that been in your desk?" He asked flatly. Feme looked at him. She was going to lie, she wanted to lie, but she couldn't. Nix had protected her. It certainly didn't make up for the millennia of words and almost coming blows, but it was a start.

"Since the day you took over Acquisitions," she sighed.

"Oh my God, Feme!" Takis exclaimed.

"I don't need a lecture from you," she spat at him.

"No, what you need is some decency!" Clayton yelled.

"Who the hell do you-" she began.

"No, who the hell do you think *you* are, Feme?" Clayton interrupted. "This man has been here for God knows how long, and he's been able to leave this whole time? Why would you do that? Have I been able to leave too? Did Takis' note come up in the 1500s, and you decided to screw him too since he's good at his job?" Clayton threw his hands in the air. Feme stood up, her palms on her desk, and leaned towards him.

"Let me tell you something, I will not be spoken to like that, and certainly not by you," she said through clenched teeth. Clayton stood up and leaned toward her.

"Who gave you this job? Because you sure as hell weren't qualified for it. Why don't we go out there in the hallway and let everyone know you've been holding back passes."

"Clayton," Nix spoke up. Clayton turned and looked at Nix and then back at Feme. She was furious.

"It's alright, Clayton," Nix told him.

"No, it isn't."

"Yes, it is. I wouldn't have left anyway," Nix said, matter of fact.

52

? BCE

Nix was easily the biggest in his tribe. He towered over the other males, and his skill with a spear and making fire were second to none. He would leave at first light and come back with enough meat from his kills to feed everyone. He loved to hunt, and he relished the praise of his tribe. Nix was close with his people. He had mated with the females, and the males looked to him for leadership even though his father was the chief. Nix was born to be his father's successor; his brothers were nothing compared to him. They challenged him several times for his place, but it was like a man flogging children. His mental acumen and strength were too great.

One morning, Nix left on a hunt. While near the river they gathered water from, Nix encountered an unusually large pack of wolves at the edge of a forest. He'd heard them coming well before they were upon him, and he had no choice but to flee. He counted over ten, and he knew that was a fight he just might lose. He didn't want to lead them back to the tribe, so he went into the woods while they gave chase. Here he had cover, could get into the trees and have a fighting chance. Nix wasn't afraid of the wolves, and he wasn't afraid to die, but he was going to die on his feet like a warrior. He scrambled up into the trees to gain an advantage.

From above, he killed two and was moving from tree to tree when he realized the pack numbered more than ten. They were at least thirty. He was trapped. They were everywhere, and they knew where he was. If he were to fall from the branches, or if they broke, he would be devoured instantly. He sat in the tree while they circled and howled. It was almost as if they were laughing at him. They knew they had him, and it was a matter of time. Seconds turned to minutes which turned to hours, and night had fallen.

The moon was full, and Nix ached from sitting in the tree. It wouldn't be long now. He wanted his chance to be chief, but it looked like that would never happen. He wanted to lead. He was vain and arrogant and thought this was a stupid way to die. Nix was not going to die falling from this tree and not have the strength to fight back. So, he stood, prepared to leap down and kill as many of them with his hands as he could. He sucked in the night air and braced for his glory when the wolves all turned their heads sharply.

A few started to whine and put their tails between their legs. They began to scurry away, slowly at first, until all of them were running away from him. He watched as they hurried off into the distance. Nix was overjoyed. He couldn't believe his luck. He thought he was a dead man for sure. As Nix began to climb down the tree, though, a thought dawned on him. If thirty wolves weren't afraid of him, and they all ran away instead of facing whatever was coming this way, what could scare them so? What was so vicious and terrible that they didn't even try to fight it off and claim the prize they earned? Nix rushed back up the tree and held still.

He heard rustling in the distance and kept himself low against the branch. Nix was practically fearless in his lifetime, but what he saw scared him beyond belief. It was a man, but it wasn't moving like a man. It was hunched over, almost on all fours and moving cautiously through the foliage. Its eyes glowed white and without pupils. Its veins were black, thick, and shown through the thick layer of hair covering its body.

It was whispering things, making strange noises. It walked directly underneath the tree Nix was in and stopped. Nix could smell it now. Its odor was foul and much like that of death, like a carcass out in the sun for days. Nix held his breath, and he hoped for it to pass. The fear had reinvigorated Nix, and his strength was back in full. He wanted to drop from the tree and run as fast as he could, but he knew it would catch him, and whatever it could do would be a fate worse than death.

He stood still as it slowly crept on, calling out over and over again as it stalked. Nix watched as it got to the edge of his line of vision and disappeared out of sight. He stayed still, even after he heard nothing rustling. It was almost morning before he climbed down. Nix decided to not make a straight line back to his tribe from the tree. He circled wide and moved slowly so as not to draw any interest. He didn't want to see that thing again. He didn't have the word evil yet, but he knew the concept. He wanted nothing of it.

Nix had made it back to the river south of where his tribe was when he saw her. She was drinking from the river and looking left and right in panic. She was covered in mud and blood, but to Nix, she was beautiful. She was tall, not as tall as he, but for their kind, she was massive. Her hair was not dark but light. Her body wasn't covered in hair like the females in his tribe were. She was different, unique. And she was afraid. Nix slowly came out of the tree line, and she saw him. Her eyes were blue. He'd never seen that before. He put his finger up to his lips, and he looked around and approached her with his hands up. He didn't want to frighten her away, she had a spear beside her, but she didn't pick it up. She watched him as he got closer. He waved his hand around and tried to mimic the creature by hunching down to imitate its walk, and she nodded her head. She knew what he was talking about. She was avoiding it too. Nix wanted to see her to safety. She stood and got close to him. She took her fist and bumped her chest.

"Rae," she said.

"Nix," he responded, patting his own chest. He took her hand and guided her across the river to the other side. They made their way back towards the caves where Nix called home. He knew something was wrong the second he got close. He could smell it in the air, that familiar metallic smell. He heard nothing, no voices, no laughter. He snuck around to some bushes and saw the carnage first hand. They were dead, all of them. The men, the women, the children, they'd all been torn to pieces. Their insides laid bare, strewn from cave to cave. The rocks were caked in blood and gore.

At first, he thought the wolves had made their way here, but he knew better. This wasn't a kill for food or survival. This was a kill for pleasure. This was to make them suffer and how they must have suffered. He was angry with himself for a moment. Maybe if he'd been here, if he'd confronted whatever that was in the woods, they would still be alive. Perhaps he could have fought it off, but then he thought of how the wolves ran. How they didn't even attempt to fight. He would be as dead as the rest of them. Rae grabbed his hand.

"Go," she said, and she began to pull. "Go." Nix looked back at the remains of his tribe. He was sorry. He left them to the animals. They ran for days, putting as much distance between themselves and where they came from as they could. It wasn't until three weeks later that they let their guard down when they came into a valley. They found a small cave with a nearby stream where he brought several fish back for them to eat. She mimicked the creature and let him know that it had done the same to her people. They didn't stop moving. For months they withstood harsh conditions, through valleys and atop of mountains. Nix wondered if they'd ever be far enough away from that monster. Just when he felt comfortable with how far they'd gone, a noise in the night would cause Rae to look at him with worry.

Nix adored Rae. She was strong, charismatic, and took charge of the hunts. He treated her with kindness, for he had never seen such traits in a female before. He'd also never felt attached to someone this way. He never wanted to be away from her for very long. He would protect her with his life. He would hold her in the night as they slept. They never stayed in one place very long, and they had traveled many seasons before he was with her intimately. He didn't use her the way he had the women of his tribe. He was delicate with her as if she was fragile. He loved her. She was his queen. They needed no tribe; they had each other.

They continued onward until they both smelled salt in the air. They had reached the ocean. Neither had ever seen it before, the waves pounding against the sand, the breeze. They stood in awe, holding each other's hand before they both decided this was where they would stay. This was where they would live out their lives together. They found a large cave inland, a small way up the coastline. It was there they made their home. They spent every moment together, never tiring of each other. Rae was pregnant after their first few months there, and along came a baby girl. Nix would go to the ocean and fish or go further inland and hunt for the family, never leaving them alone for too long. Soon a son followed, and they had their tribe.

53

THE AFTER

"My son was still an infant when he came. My daughter couldn't have been more than four," Nix continued.

"The Darkness?" Feme asked.

"Yes, the Darkness. It came for us in the dead of night. I awoke first and saw him standing at the entrance of our cave. His eyes were white, he had no pupils. I walked calmly to the Darkness. I couldn't beg. I didn't have the vocabulary for that. I held up my hands, and I offered myself in exchange for them," he said. Clayton shifted in his chair, Takis turned pale, and Feme looked away. "He spoke to me. I didn't understand at the time, but I eventually got to ask the Darkness what it said to me."

"What did it say?" Clayton asked.

"It's not personal, but you have a higher calling." Nix recited. He swallowed past the lump that formed in his throat and took a deep breath before continuing. "The last thing I remember feeling was his hand inside me. It was like ice. He tore me open in front of my Rae and children. I could do nothing but lie there and watch as it slaughtered the only family that had ever been mine," Nix finished. He watched as Feme sat back. Her eyes searched his face. Was that pity? How rich.

"Why was the Darkness on Earth and not here?" Clayton asked.

"We were your ancestors, and She liked the newer model better," Nix shrugged.

"She?" Clayton asked.

"The Almighty. The Creator."

"God?" Clayton asked again.

"Whatever you want to call Her. Here is the truth: We, well, my kind, we were an experiment. She was testing this place. She was creating, like a painter or a writer, everything in the land of the living. That was her masterpiece. She was always creating, always making things, churning out everything from grass to tiny hairs on insects. She tried to make Man three times. We were the first. My Rae was part of the second generation. You were the third, the ones she wanted to keep."

"So you were killed off?" Takis asked, shocked.

"No," Nix scoffed. "We had served Her well, so as a reward, she was giving us the After and the Brilliance. We were to be the caretakers ushering souls in and out of here and run the Brilliance, a place of true paradise."

"You guys have done a shitty job," Feme joked.

"Our creator is also a Mother. She has a Son, and that Son hates us. He hates you. He loved His Mother and wanted Her attention all to Himself. He didn't want anything to come between them, and here we were. She spent all her time making the world perfect, making the After just right.

"So, She sends her Son to collect us, to bring us here so She can get this place built and mankind can be on its way, but the Son doesn't come and get us quietly. He hunts us. He tortures us. He slaughters us like animals."

"He killed all of your kind?" Clayton asked.

"Every last one of us, and where did we go when we died?"

"The Darkness?" Takis answered.

"We came to the Fork, where He would show up and throw us into the Darkness. See, the Son was creative too. She had made a world of paradise for us to live in eternal bliss. He created one of eternal damnation." They all stared at him in disbelief. He smiled at them and scratched his chin. "He's terrifying when you actually see Him, so tall and imposing. Makes me look like a child. I mean, He is the son of a God, so there's that."

"Is He human?" Clayton asked. "The Son?"

"Nothing about Him is human. I tried to stop Him from throwing my Rae and my children in there, but I couldn't. He laughed as He cast my tribe into the Darkness. He wanted me to suffer, to beg. Finally, there were two of us left, me and another male. The Mother finished the Brilliance and came to check on Her Son to see how He was progressing in Her grand plan."

"You saw Her?" Feme asked.

"Oh yes. She was everything you'd envision, rays of light, skin the color of gold. She was the most amazing thing I've ever seen." Nix began to pace. "She was furious, and when She asked Him what the Darkness was, He explained to Her it was a place to put the bad ones who didn't deserve Her. It wasn't exactly a lie," he chuckled. "If He was left to judge, no one would deserve her. She started to calm down, She was listening to Him, and I couldn't take it anymore. I jumped in between them and started to cry. I didn't know who She was. I still didn't know what was happening to me altogether, but I knew She could save me. She looked at me and reached out and touched my face." Nix reached up and touched his cheek, and was, for just a moment, lost in the memory.

"And?" Feme asked, snapping her fingers in his face.

"She lost Her temper. Through me, she could see what he had done. She witnessed it all, and in His fear, He attacked Her. She yelled at Him in a voice I will never forget. 'How dare you raise your hand to me?' She grabbed Him by the throat. She was ashamed of His cruelty, baffled by His viciousness. While She had love and wanted to create, He hated and wanted to destroy. She said if this was a prison for the ones unworthy of Her, the ones who didn't deserve Her, He belonged there most of all."

"She put Him in there?" Takis finished for him.

"Yes, She did."

"And then what? She just left?" Takis asked.

"No, She threw Herself back into Her work. She told us what to do. She created the River, the doors, the halls. We put it all together for Her, but She wasn't the same after losing Her Son. She would never leave the Fork. She had punished Her child, but She wanted to bring Him back to try and reason with Him. He wouldn't let Her inside. She tried for centuries while we worked to make the place She wanted this to be.

"One day She was crying. She was begging Him to answer Her, but the Darkness was silent. She was heartbroken. Her Son was truly lost; irredeemable and could not be saved. She turned away from me, stepped on a ferryman's boat, and She floated off into the Brilliance." The room fell silent again.

"And?" Clayton asked, barely above a whisper.

"And nothing. That was over ten thousand years ago. This place is unfinished. The Son has my children and my Rae. I collected souls until I was put in charge of Acquisitions. I had hoped She'd left something behind there or on Earth, some clue as to what I should do next."

"S he left us?" Clayton asked dejectedly.

Nix scanned over their faces, all three stunned into complete silence. He'd never opened up this way before, he'd not told anyone of how he came to be here, and he definitely had never mentioned his family before. He knew that they all perceived him as something different from them. Not just physically but emotionally as well. They probably just assumed he took what he wanted and was more like a beast than anything else in existence.

Rae and the children had brought a feeling of peace to Nix he'd yearned for. A feeling he had been chasing ever since his death. The blank looks on their faces said everything to him. They needed a plan. They had to do something; they just didn't have any idea what.

Nix knew this was his time, his moment to take charge and do what needed to be done. He let them sit for a while longer. He had given them the origin of the After, the origin of everything. They walked these halls every day and had no idea of the secrets they held.

He finally spoke.

"Well, Takis, this isn't your problem anymore," Nix slapped him solidly on the back and mustered up the best smile he could.

"What do you mean?" Clayton asked.

"He's out of here after we get Amber," Feme reminded him.

"Amber! We have to get her. She's still in the cells!" Clayton remembered and stood.

"Right. Takis, take Clayton and get her. She is to be brought directly to me, she has to have a meeting with me on her job, and I'll have to catch her up to speed before releasing her into Clayton's care." Feme ordered.

"How long will that take?" Clayton asked.

"It takes however long it fucking takes," he replied firmly. Clayton couldn't hide his disappointment, but he nodded.

"As for Takis, after you drop her off to me, you are free to go. I will take you to the Fork," Feme said. "And you, Nix, I suppose you expect an apology from me?"

"I expect nothing of the sort. We've been at each other's throats for a millennia, maybe you could dial back on being a bitch?" Nix said.

"Is that all?" Feme rolled her eyes and looked at him.

"No. I want one more thing. It's Takis," Nix said. "We've had good times together, and I want to see him off." Feme handed Nix the pass, he pocketed it, and she looked at Takis.

"I guess you will be leaving as soon as possible."

"I have to. I have to see Lipa. I hope all of you understand."

"I do," Feme told him. Nix walked towards the door.

"I'll go to the Fork and wait for you there. Clayton," Nix clapped Clayton's shoulder, "I'll talk to you later."

"Yes, sir."

"Takis, it hasn't all been miserable. I will miss you," Feme said. She stood and offered Takis her hand. He took it and stood, shaking her hand.

"You will?" Takis chuckled. She sighed and walked around her desk and hugged him.

"I mean it," she said. Takis didn't move for a moment, but then he put his arms around her.

"I don't know what to say."

"You could try, 'goodbye.' Maybe, 'I'll miss you too.'"

"What's going on here?" Takis asked, laughing in shock. Feme let him go and looked into his eyes.

"I'm pissed it's you and not me, but you were one of the better ones here. You fucked up slightly less than the others which made my job easier. I won't forget that."

"Damn, Feme, lighten up," Nix said, joking.

"Fuck you, Nix," she laughed and started back towards her seat. "I still hate you."

"I hope you are right behind me, Feme," Takis told her and nudged Clayton. "Let's go, boy."

54

THE CELLS

They stood together again in front of a cell. Clayton wasn't motionless this time. He was rocking back and forth on his heels, tapping one hand against his leg; his other hand was up by his mouth.

"Stop chewing your nails," Takis ordered.

"Sorry," Clayton took his hand away from his mouth.

"Stop apologizing," Takis ordered again.

"Sor- I'm a wreck, Takis."

"I know. Relax."

"What do I say to her?" He whined. Takis looked over at him.

"Welcome her here, don't overwhelm her. She's getting a friendly face, but she's still been in here for damn near two hundred years."

"Right," Clayton started. "Takis, I'm going to miss you. You know that?"

"Yes, boy, I do."

"I mean, I am really going to miss you. You're more than a friend to me," Clayton confessed. Takis stared at Clayton for a moment.

"Don't make this hard on me. It's killing me already to leave you here."

"Sorry," Clayton apologized and looked down at his feet.

"Clayton, listen to me," Takis' voice echoed through the hall. "Look at me." Clayton raised his gaze to match Takis'. "What you did," he started, "you risked your soul for my son. You didn't know him. You weren't friends. You did that for me, and you could have wound up in the Darkness."

"Takis-" Clayton began. Takis held up his hand.

"Shut up for once, and let me finish. I had a brother. He was a soldier. Beloved by thousands, respected by a king. I envied him. He was everything I wasn't; brave, strong, a hero. I owned a bar," Takis chuckled. "He was a fierce warrior. I watched that man kill a lion with a sword and shield."

"Why are you telling me this?"

"Why do you never let me finish?" Takis mocked. Clayton looked abashed. "I don't think even he would have done what you did. It was foolish. In fact, it was stupid, but it was brave. I don't want to leave you, Clayton. You're family to me, but there is one thing I can take with me into the Brilliance that puts me at ease."

"What's that?"

"You'll follow me soon," Takis stated.

"I hope so."

"You will," he unlocked the door. "Your mother was right. You are good."

Clayton stayed outside while Takis went in. She was sitting on the edge of the bed, staring at the doorway in surprise. Takis noticed immediately how gorgeous she was. Her hair was rose red and her face full. She was dressed in the nightgown she passed in.

"Hello, Amber Ward, I'm Takis," he said softly and with a wide smile. Just on her appearance alone, he could see why Clayton was so smitten with her. She had aged as Clayton had and didn't look older than nineteen.

"Hello."

"I am here to take you to a woman named Feme who is going to explain what you are doing here. I mean you no harm, I promise."

"Am I going to Hell?" She asked.

"No, dear, you aren't going to Hell."

"How do I know I can trust you?" She questioned as she scooted herself back towards the wall.

"Because I brought you a present. It's right outside the door," he gestured. "Amber, just step out the door. I swear to you on the soul of my wife, you will not be harmed," Takis said with conviction. She moved across the tiny bed and placed her feet on the stone floor. She stood, watching Takis the whole time, and Takis moved away from her towards the back of the cell against the wall.

"Go on."

———

Amber stepped backward, focusing on Takis the entire time until she cleared the doorway. Her gaze went to the left, and a young man was standing there, looking at the floor. She blinked hard to make sure she wasn't dreaming, to make sure it wasn't a cruel trick. He looked older, his jaw more defined and sporting the beginnings of a beard. He was taller, and his body was muscular and thin. The outfit made him look ridiculous, and even though he was drastically different from the last time she saw him, she knew it was him.

"Clayton," she whispered. He didn't move. He nervously chewed his bottom lip, and his eyes stayed focused on the ground. She turned to fully face him.

"Clayton Shaw," she whispered again. This time he looked up.

"Are you okay?" He asked. She grabbed him, almost knocking him over, and embraced him as tight as she could. The smell, the voice, he was real.

"Clayton, I'm so sorry," she sobbed. All this time, she thought he was lost. She was torn between happiness and guilt. Amber was glad he was here with her, but he could have had a full life. She needed him to understand just how sorry she was, how much she wished they could go back so she could tell him what happened. She was the reason he was here, and that thought scratched at the front of her mind as she held on to him.

"It's okay, I've got you," Clayton shushed, his voice breaking. Amber opened her eyes and saw Takis leaning in the doorway.

"Thank you," Amber said to him.

"Don't mention it," Takis waved his hand dismissively. "You two deserve a few moments alone. I'm going to go. Make sure you take her to Feme, but seriously, don't take too long."

"Takis, wait," Clayton pulled away from Amber.

"No, it's ok. We said what needed to be said. No need to draw this out. It'll make it worse. I need to go," he pointed to the two of them, "I'm a little late for a reunion of my own."

"Thank you. For everything," Clayton said.

"Boy, take care of her, and when you get to the Brilliance, I'll give you a tour," Takis quipped.

"I'm looking forward to it," Clayton grinned.

"Goodbye, Clayton."

"Goodbye, Takis," Clayton said. Takis walked a few feet forward.

"The Fork," he said. He turned around and took his final door.

55

THE FORK

"**A**re you crying?" Nix asked as Takis came through the door

"Shut up," Takis sniffed.

"What happened?" Nix asked him, laughing.

"It was beautiful seeing those kids together. It went better than I thought it would, and I had high expectations."

"I'm glad," Nix said. Takis stepped forward into the tall grass and stared up at the sky.

"This place was always special to me. The one place where it felt like the stories we were told. The magic, the wonder, you know what I mean?" Takis said.

"I do."

"This place was hard on me, Nix. It did everything to break me. I'm so glad I got the kid when I did. I don't know what I'd have done without him. I was at my wit's end, and you were always busy. I guess in the end, I was lucky."

"I know," Nix sighed.

"It's over," he said as he watched a star shoot across the sky. "I get to see Lipa again."

"No," Nix stated, putting his hand on Takis' shoulder. "You don't."

"Wha-" Takis started. Nix punched Takis in the stomach as hard as he could. The air left Takis' body in a loud whoosh, and he fell to his knees. He gagged and gasped as tears streamed down his face. Nix held the back of Takis' head and slammed his palm down on the bridge of his nose before making a fist and hitting him three more times. It made a sickening sound as Takis' nose and front teeth shattered. Takis opened his mouth to try and get his breath back, and when he did, Nix gripped his forehead and pulled Takis's head straight back. He fished in his pocket with his other hand and produced a sealed ink bottle. The ink inside looked like black smoke, swirling as if alive, like he'd trapped some of the Darkness inside the tiny bottle.

Nix slammed the bottle into Takis' open mouth. It shattered, and the ink and bits of glass went down his throat. Nix released him and let him fall forward in the grass. Takis clutched at his throat, gagging. A moment later, he clawed at his chest and rolled over on his back, ink and blood oozing from the sides of his mouth. His eyes began to change, not the pure white Nix had seen before, but swirling black like the concoction Nix forced down his throat. Takis was glaring at him with those eyes, his face a mixture of confusion and pain. Those eyes reminded Nix of the Darkness, the place where his wife and children were rotting away. Nix felt pure rage; he hadn't allowed himself to lose control like this since he arrived in the After.

He roared, grabbed Takis off the ground, and held him aloft. Nix pulled him in and breathed in the scent of fear. It was delightful.

They stayed in that position for a few moments as Takis stared at him, pleading with his eyes. Nix snarled again and took off at a run with Takis held in front of him. Takis tried to fight, but that only made Nix angrier. Nix got two feet from the Darkness, skidded to a stop, and released Takis, whose momentum carried him into the thick black sickness. It enveloped him quickly, and he was gone. It was over. Nix stepped back and wiped the spit from his facial hair. He was still growling, his anger rumbling in his chest. He wiped his hand on his shorts and walked to where he broke the vial. He picked up a few pieces of broken glass and watched as the ink turned to vapor and floated back to the Darkness.

I'm impressed. That was vicious, the Darkness spoke. Nix stared at it for a long moment. *You didn't even think twice about it. I was right in asking you to do this for me.*

"Just keep your end of the bargain," Nix said and spat on the grass.

You still owe me two.

"You'll have them, just hurry up. I'm tired of waiting." He placed the glass in his pocket. "After you get Clayton and Feme, I get Rae and my children."

I know, and you will. Don't you trust me?

"Hell no, I don't," Nix chuckled mockingly, "but I have no choice."

No, you don't. You are so close to getting them back, Nix. A family reunited after thousands of years. How romantic.

"What was that shit you pulled earlier, mocking me in front of them like that? Are you trying to ruin this?" Nix was annoyed and still breathing heavily. His nose had begun to bleed. It did every time he spoke to the Darkness. It hurt, and on top of that, his pure contempt for it made this a battle of will to try and stay civil.

I didn't want them to suspect you. I thought I did a good job. Don't you agree?

"Are you the one that sent the orders for the Reverend Price? What are you playing at? Why have me put him in the cells in the first place? Why not take him then?" Nix paused and rubbed his forehead. "Are you the one releasing the girl from the cells?" There was no answer. "I can't help you if I don't know everything," Nix complained.

You worry about what I tell you to worry about. The girl is not your concern. The Reverend Price is not your concern. Clayton and Feme are what you should be focused on. Once Clayton chooses me, you hand me Feme, and this will all be over.

"Clayton and Feme won't be a problem. Clayton's weak. We're close. Why can't I just do to him what I did to Takis? Why do I have to jump through all these hoops?"

I told you, he has to want to be in here with me. I want him broken. If you cast Feme in here before Clayton, the entire After will know it was you. Patience, Nix, you need to learn patience.

"This is taking too long. I hate games."

This is no game. Soon we will both get what we've worked so hard for.

56

MARCH 25TH, 1805

Nix watched Clayton sob; the boy couldn't see him. To Clayton, he was all alone with nothing but his heartache. He pulled at his tie, loosened up the collar. Nix watched as the boy cast the tie to the side and wondered why anyone would wear such a ridiculous item. He had been waiting in this spot. He knew Clayton would be here. Takis was waiting for Clayton below, so he couldn't get too close. He had to stay behind him. If Takis saw him, the plan would be ruined, and the chances of getting his family back would be shattered. So, Nix watched him, waiting for the perfect moment to talk to him, to use his gift to try and nudge the boy along.

"Why?" Clayton asked out loud. *Why indeed*, Nix thought. Why did the Darkness want this boy? What was so special about this tiny human? He wasn't important at all. Nix got the feeling if he'd lived his life, he would have died without achieving anything of note. He was a nobody. Just like the girl he watched die last night. She was easy to manipulate. He didn't even have to repeat himself with her.

He loves you, it will be fine.
Love is love.

He is an honorable man.

Such a stupid species. He had perfected the use of Afterwords as the first century came to be. He could push a human to do damn near anything. Afterwords came easily to Nix because he was always in control. He'd been through and seen more than one person should, it left him cold and emotionless, and that was the secret to the Afterwords. One had to be calm and suggest with no feeling behind it. It certainly helped that humans were flawed in their design. They were too quick to allow emotions to dictate their actions. He had easily convinced Amber Ward to let that old man have his way with her. When it came time to convince the reverend to put pennyroyal extract in Amber's drink, it took practically no effort.

It will kill the baby. It's what you both want.

No, a few drops more won't hurt her.

If they find out it was you, they will see you hang.

Nix was sure if he hadn't suggested it to the reverend, he would have come up with a similar plan anyway. The man had already been plotting a way to kill the child. He just didn't know how. Nix made that simple and killed the girl in the process too. Everything had fallen neatly into place, and he'd reached the most challenging part of the plan. He was here with the boy, Clayton. He had to die, and the death had to be a suicide. It was what the Darkness asked. If Clayton didn't die by his own hands, he would be granted passage to the Brilliance. The Darkness had explicitly asked for Clayton to be sentenced to the After. Nix thought this would be harder because Clayton had faith, and it was strong. Obviously, something was going to happen here. Takis was waiting for his partner below. Clayton Shaw would die. Nix just had to be the one to make sure it went his way. He relaxed his senses.

Just step forward. He saw Clayton tense up. He had heard him, and Nix knew he had him when the boy didn't recoil in disgust.

Just step forward. The pain will disappear. He gave Clayton a moment to roll the idea around in his mind.

It hurts, doesn't it?

"Yes," Clayton said in his trance.

You don't deserve this. What do you have to go back to? If you leave, where will you go?

"I know," Clayton responded weakly. Clayton moved towards the edge and stuck his left foot out.

Forward.

He saw the child snap out of it at the last second, but it was too late. He was toppling over the edge and on his way down. Nix almost jumped in the air for joy. This was the one variable he was unsure of, but it worked like a charm. Clayton wouldn't survive the fall. He'd be in the After where the Darkness could manipulate things. It wouldn't be long now. He'd have his family back. He smiled.

"Acquisitions," he said and turned to his door. All that was left for him to do was meet Clayton, the newest member of the After. He stepped through, proud of the work he'd done.

57

1985

THE AFTER

"I have to get you to Feme. We'll get in trouble if I don't," Clayton finally said to Amber. She was still holding onto him with a vice-like grip.

"Who is Feme?" She said in between sniffles.

"I guess you could say she runs this place."

"Do we have to go now?" She asked, almost pleading. "Will you be there?"

"No. You've been locked inside there for almost two hundred years, Amber," he pulled back and looked her in the eyes. "Feme needs to tell you what has happened to the world. She needs to explain what you'll be doing here."

"Will I be here with you?"

"Yes, you will be here with me," he smiled. "We'll be together. You're my new partner. The man who just left was Takis. You're his replacement."

"Thank God," she laughed, and a few more tears streamed down her face.

"Well," he pulled away, "I feel the same way."

"Where was that man going? Your friend?" She looked around, but there was no one in the endless hallway of doors besides them.

259

"He's going to Heaven. It's called the Brilliance. His time has been served. I was his last assignment. He trained me."

"Oh, so you're important?"

"No," he shook his head and laughed. "I'm far from important. Listen, we might get in trouble if we don't go. We can talk about this later."

"Will I be alone? Don't leave me alone." She locked her hand in his. "I was in there for so long. It was awful. It showed me what they accused you of, and I'm sorry. I should have come to you. I should have-" Her voice caught again. She reached out and touched his face with the palm of her other hand. "You're not in Hell. I thought you were suffering." Amber gasped for breath in between hiccups.

"There are a lot of people here, and you don't have to go back in there. You will not be alone. Someone will always be with you. I know you're upset. Trust me, I'm fine. This place hasn't been great, but I had Takis, and now you have me. We have to get to Feme, though. The last thing I want on your first day is for us to get in trouble," Clayton said as softly and calmly as he could. His heart broke, watching her cry. Being alone in that room must have felt like an eternity. She pulled her hands back, wiped her cheeks, and took a long, stuttering breath. She forced a smile and shook her head, trying to regain her composure. He smiled back and gave her a moment.

"Alright, let's go," she said.

"Feme's office." The door was behind him. He led her through and followed closely behind.

Feme's door was open, and she was actually smiling when the two of them came in.

"Clayton, good work," she said as she stood. "Hello, Amber, I'm Feme."

"Hello," Amber answered cautiously.

"Why weren't you changed from a nightgown before being put in the cells? I will get Astrid to fit you for something else as soon as I can." Feme stepped around her desk and took her elbow. Clayton stood in the doorway. When Amber glanced back at him, he nodded.

"It's fine. Feme is great."

"It's going to be alright," Feme reassured her. Feme was going to try and do right by this girl. She was going to be firm but less abrasive. She felt that maybe a lot of the resentment towards her here was because of her bitterness, and perhaps the reason Clayton had adjusted so well was that he had a friend. The time she'd spent with Clayton, Takis, and Nix had done something to her. She enjoyed having them around. She felt a shift somewhere down deep. She couldn't explain it, she didn't even notice it at first, but it was there. She had taken young girls out of living in their own filth in her living days, and she loved the feeling she got from helping them. Did it feed her ego like she explained to Takis? Yes, it did, she liked the feeling of being owed, but it also gave her a warmth she hadn't felt in a very long time.

She had lied to Clayton. She would work in the field with this girl for a while. Obviously, he could handle it, he was more than capable, but she wanted time to see the world. She wanted time out of her own prison. She wanted to be with someone she could talk to that wasn't afraid of her. Amber didn't know the Feme that yelled at the top of her lungs. She didn't know the Feme that would add a hundred years to someone's sentence for looking at her the wrong way. She had a blank slate with this girl, and she was going to take advantage of it.

She didn't think she and Amber would become close, but if she tried to keep the hostility to a minimum, maybe things would flow smoother. She couldn't change a lot of the people's opinions on the other side of that door, but she didn't care. Most of the people out there honestly didn't deserve the chance they'd been given in the After. Some of their crimes were terrible. She just wanted a change. The monotony had only added to her anger and bitterness. Was it gone? No, not in the least, but maybe she thought she could make the rest of her time here less about stress headaches and sore throats from screaming at people.

She was of the mindset to rule by fear, and what had it gotten her really? People still disobeyed orders, and things like the Darkness manipulating behind the scenes continued to happen. She had already served a lot of time here; everyone she'd known outside of Nix had moved on. She had to be next. Nix's story had broken her heart. He'd stepped in front of her when the Darkness took Clayton. He'd protected her. After all the garbage they'd done to each other, he wasn't going to let her get hurt. It was admirable, and she was embarrassed by a lot of what she had done.

The four of them had a common enemy. Someone was fucking with them. They were stronger together, and now Takis was out of the equation, so Amber would have to suffice. She was a part of this. Feme wasn't going to treat this girl poorly. Amber had been dragged through enough. This was going to be new to Feme, who'd spent the last two thousand years ready to strike. Her first instinct was to tear a person down and keep tearing until they had nothing left to give. She was already annoyed by how timid Amber was being, she wanted to tell her to toughen up, or this place would eat her alive. Baby steps, Feme thought.

"Clayton, can you get the fuck out of here, please? We have a lot to cover."

"How long will this take?" He asked her hesitantly.

"Bye," Feme smirked.

"But-," he started, but Feme shot him a look.

"Amber, I will see you soon, alright?" He finished. Amber was eyeing him with such sadness that Feme felt a slight pang of guilt for cutting their time short, but she pushed it away.

"I hope so," Amber agonized.

"You will, but this has to be done," Feme told her, and Clayton left her office.

***

Clayton paused for a moment and closed the door. He leaned his head against it with his eyes closed, lost in the thought of seeing her again. She was everything he'd remembered and more. He had gotten her back. She would be his companion, and together they would retrieve the souls of the dead until they had paved their way to the Brilliance. His mind snapped to Takis and Nix. Maybe he could catch Takis before he left. There was so much more he wanted to say to him, so many things left unfinished. Nix was the one signing the book, so he'd try him.

"Nix's Fork," he said and hurried through his summoned exit.

58

THE FORK

Nix was standing in the grass looking over at the Darkness when he heard Clayton come through a door.

"You're too late. He's already gone," he called out and smiled at him. Clayton looked around and threw his hands up in the air.

"Shit, I really wanted to talk to him before he left."

"The Greek bastard made quite the impression on you, didn't he?"

"More than you know. I just wanted to tell him goodbye," Clayton said downheartedly.

"Don't look so glum. You'll see him again soon," Nix grinned. Clayton approached him.

"Was he happy to go?"

"Actually, quite the opposite. He was really broken up about it. I think he was apprehensive."

"You could have gone with him."

"I could have, but I have unfinished business," Nix stared into the Darkness, his hatred bubbling to the surface.

"I know, and I'll help you any way I can," Clayton said. Nix was almost touched by this statement. Clayton did have a good heart, even if it made him weak. Nix didn't want to hate him. This wasn't a personal vendetta, wasn't him wanting to hurt this boy. It came down to Clayton or Nix's family, and Clayton didn't have a chance.

"I know you will," he patted the top of Clayton's head. "I can't believe how much you've grown. How was she?"

"She looked great."

"Good, good. I hate to tell you this next part," Nix started. Clayton leaned back with a look of worry.

"Everything was going great. Here comes the spoiler. What is it?"

"You know that we can't..." He placed his hand on the back of his head. "Well, here in the After, there's no..." He decided to spit it out. "You can't touch her, Clayton. We can't feel any form of pleasure here."

"But I was just hugging her," Clayton shrugged.

"This boy, I swear," Nix muttered to himself and looked off in the distance; he chuckled. "I mean, you can't mate with her."

"I wouldn't disrespect her like that," Clayton smiled. Nix couldn't help but laugh at him.

"You are the real deal, Clayton."

"So, what do I do now?"

"I'm taking you until Feme finishes. You're going to help me clean and sort stuff in Acquisitions. Are you up for that?"

"Absolutely," Clayton's eyes widened. Nix could tell he was excited to be invited into his world. Plus, it would be wise to keep an eye on him, maybe figure out why the Darkness felt Clayton was so special. Maybe Nix could get a clue to what underlying motive the Son had for him.

Clayton and Nix worked for several days unboxing and cleaning piles of items, finding some of history's lost treasures lying underneath mountains of things.

"I should have handed these to Takis," Nix said, looking into a box filled with scraps of papyrus.

"What is it?"

"Sappho's poems," he held one up carefully and then sat it back down. "He would have loved these." He sat them in the corner and sighed.

"Who's Sappho?" Clayton asked. Nix looked over at him and shook his head.

"Doesn't matter," he replied and went back to picking through things. Clayton had found some fascinating relics in this place.

"What is this?" Clayton asked as he pulled an exquisite sword from its sheath. He held it up to the light, captivated by its gleam.

"That is the Honjo Masamune, a Japanese sword. One of the finest items crafted by Man," Nix said with pride.

"Why keep this here?" Clayton asked.

"They were going to melt it down. I couldn't let that happen, so I took it. It is an amazing weapon, Clayton. In fact, give that here. I love that blade." He held out his massive hand. Clayton put the sword in Nix's grasp, a puzzled look on his face.

"Didn't take you for a collector."

"Really? I always thought I gave off a he-has-a-collection-of-priceless-artifacts-of-war vibe."

"So, I have to ask, what is the most impressive thing in here? I mean, I've seen ancient swords, poems, a woman's stone head with snakes for hair," Clayton shivered a little at that revelation. "Come on, Nix, really knock me out." Nix seemed lost in thought for a moment and then placed the sword back in its sheath. It made a swish sound as it went back in. He walked over and leaned near Clayton's ear.

"Come on, I have just the thing," he whispered. They headed through the large path they'd made back to Nix's desk. Nix looked around and found a large crate. He dumped the contents to the floor and turned it over. "Sit," he commanded, and Clayton did as he was told. Nix went to the left of his desk and carefully began moving items. Clayton could tell these meant something to him. He wasn't flinging things to and fro as he did with ninety percent of the items here. He was gingerly picking things up and laying them carefully to the side. Most things he looked at with indifference, but not these.

"There you are." He turned to Clayton with a book in his hands. It was gigantic and considering it looked big in Nix's already oversized paws, Clayton knew the word large wouldn't suffice. Nix placed it carefully at his feet and stepped back. He sat at his desk and faced Clayton with a smirk. "You'll never be the same after this, Clayton."

"What in the world?" Clayton wondered aloud. He was so captivated by the sheer scope of it, he was only half paying attention to Nix. The book had a cracked hardbound material covering its innards. As far as he could tell from looking at an angle, the pages were of the same material as the life lists. It smelled old. A thick layer of dust was on the brownish-orange cover, except for where Nix's elongated fingers had been. Clayton reached down and gripped the cover. He let his finger slide down and took a few pages, then opened the book. Inside was art, but unlike anything, he'd ever seen before. There was a meadow. The colors were vibrant, the sky filled with stars, the ground covered in grass waved in the wind. The ink was moving. The picture flowed as if it was alive.

"Wait," Clayton said. "This is the Fork, isn't it?"

"Yes," Nix answered. It was the Fork, but the cliff faces didn't exist in this picture. Otherwise, it looked exactly like this. The grass swirled and swayed as if being drawn right then.

"This is unreal," Clayton gushed. He turned a few pages and saw the ocean, the blue waves crashing down on the shore. Birds flying in and out of view. Clayton swore he could almost hear the water breaking. The ink rose and fell with the tide.

"What is this, Nix?"

"It belonged to Her," he sat back and stretched out his long legs, "it's where She came up with Her ideas. Everything She created for you, for me, our father's father, it's all there. When She left, She cast the book out of the After, along with Her inks and quills. I found them all."

Clayton took his hands away from the book in fear of doing something wrong. This was the sketchbook of the Creator. It held Her meticulous, thought-out visions. He reached down and turned pages again and opened it to the human heart. It beat in a steady rhythm, and blood flowed in and out of view.

"Nix, this is the most amazing thing I've ever seen."

"So, did I knock you out?"

"Unconscious," Clayton brought his left hand up and imitated, getting punched in the jaw. "Have you looked through this whole book?"

"No," Nix became bleak. "It's excruciating to see all the things She had planned for everyone and never finished. I love that book and hate it at the same time. Plus, the back half constantly changes. I can't keep up."

"I don't follow," Clayton looked back down to a drawing of ants in their little hill, working away.

"Halfway through the book is where it keeps records of all human life. The book records what you do. That's the source of the life lists."

"No shit?" Clayton started flipping fast towards the back of the book until he got to a page where text was scrolling as if being written by an invisible hand. "Will you look at that..."

"Don't bother looking up someone in particular. It's impossible to find anyone in that mess. Believe me, I tried. It's writing a million things at once."

"Thanks for showing me this. This is the greatest thing I will ever see," Clayton said and closed it. Nix leaned forward, a playful grin came to his face.

"If you promise to be careful with it, you can come to look through it anytime."

"Really?"

"Sure, it makes you happy, and who am I to dump more shit on you?" Nix waved his hand at him.

"I don't know what to say," Clayton was truly touched. Nix stood up.

"Don't say anything, just help me clean out the back some more until you're called back to duty."

"Sure thing," Clayton said, leaping to his feet.

59

Amber had trouble for the first three days with Feme in the meeting room. Things had changed so quickly, and when Feme showed her the airplane, Amber thought she was lying. It took days for her to absorb shopping malls, automobiles, modern medicine, politics, and candy bars; it was just one thing after another. Nothing was simple anymore. Few people were getting up in the morning, getting their eggs from their own chickens, and cooking their own breakfasts. Even fewer went out in the fields and worked on their property.

Now people flew down interstates, got food at drive-thrus, and bought clothing off racks in megastores. They got their milk from a place that sells all kinds of different foods, and they put it in a closet that keeps everything cool. They worked in factories and on giant boats out on the ocean; they worked in massive warehouses where they put together a box that displayed moving pictures to people for entertainment. Music confused her too; she had gotten to the 1970s when she asked Feme to stop. It was too much. Hard rock had done her in. It made her head hurt. She told Feme she couldn't understand how anyone could listen to "Lead Zeffan," as she put it. At least she now looked the part, dressed in acid-washed jeans and a white button-up shirt. She kept fidgeting with her shirt and remarked how it felt odd against her skin. Her hair had been trimmed, and she sported a ponytail. She looked like an ordinary young woman from the 1980s.

Feme had given her typical spiel, albeit much nicer this time, about her duties and her job. She told her they would be going out in the field and to watch her every move. It wasn't as hard as it sounded, but she had to toughen herself up. She'd see some gut-wrenching things. She had to learn how to handle herself with compassion but with firmness.

"So, I'm going to be collecting souls?" Amber asked her.

"Yes, but you will be gathering women from eighteen to thirty-five," Feme explained.

"Really? So, we are separated into groups?"

"Yes, you are," Feme answered. "I have to find a replacement too, which is another pain in my ass," Feme complained.

"Oh?"

"Yes, newborns who don't make it," Feme caught herself as it left her mouth. "Oh, I'm sorry. I hope I didn't upset you."

"You didn't," Amber said quickly and looked away. Feme followed her gaze to the wall.

"Amber, I read the life lists of every person here. I know my people. I know who works for me. I know every tiny detail of their lives," Feme said. Amber slowly turned back to match her stare. "You know why you are here. I know why you are here. I am not here to judge you, but a word of advice: Come to terms with it quickly or this place will beat you over the head with it."

"I understand," Amber nodded.

"Good, and with that, I think you are all caught up," Feme changed the subject quickly. "It's time for you to leave the nest," she smiled warmly. "Time for some fieldwork; you've done great so far, all things considered. I'll tell you this, I'm terrified of having to get someone from the 1400s from the cells and try to explain today to them." Amber snickered and leaned back in her chair. Feme could see she had finally relaxed. Amber had been so meek and afraid when they started, and she had asked Feme several times if Clayton could sit in. Feme knew the cells could have affected her sense of trust.

Amber seemed to respond well after Feme took her out of the offices to teach her. Feme started to feel after the fourth day of retrievals that Amber could take point. She let Amber summon her own lists and allowed Amber to speak while she stayed watching in the background. The people they'd been assigned to weren't very difficult, and Amber didn't seem to mind being around death. She didn't get shaken easily, and Feme was overjoyed by that. Amber was firm but soft-spoken and easily convinced the departed to follow her through the door. She had followed Feme's instructions to the letter, and that made all their journeys to the mortal world quick and pleasant.

She liked having Amber around; she was Feme's first semblance of a friend. Feme hardly ever trained anyone even before she was promoted. This wasn't so bad, and it finally got her out of that dingy office and into the world at large. Instead of seeing images in the meetings, she was up close with the people and all of their fancy new things. Mankind was moving at a breakneck pace, and she was finally witnessing it. Feme felt a small glimmer of happiness when they went out together. She decided they would take their time before she listed her as ready. She wanted to savor this tiny speck of relief.

She gave Astrid temporary control of day-to-day operations, and off they went just the two of them. Feme hadn't realized how much she missed the company of another person, and Amber didn't treat her like the boss. Sure, she was obedient, but she would talk to her about things that didn't pertain to the After. She seemed generally interested in Feme as a person, which made Feme feel a connection to this young woman.

60

THE WORLD

"So, what do you miss the most?" Amber asked Feme as they walked through the hallway, almost stride for stride.

"What do you mean?" Feme looked over at her with a grin.

"About life, you know? What do you miss?" Amber stopped and looked around at the red wooden doors, a gold block number on each one. Feme had mentioned earlier that this would be their last day of training, and Amber was more than prepared. Amber didn't want to leave Feme; she had a fondness for her. She was the strongest woman she'd ever met. She always held her head high. She was in a position of immense power. She was in charge of seeing her people ushering souls to Heaven or Hell. There were many moving parts to Feme's job, and Amber found her mastery impressive.

Feme walked a step further and turned to face her. She paused and looked down at the ground. Amber could tell she was somewhere else. She imagined Feme had a lot of things in life to call upon. Amber was curious about her. Feme and Amber had spent every moment together for several days now as she learned the intricate details of her work. Amber savored the moments they had to talk to one another.

"Baths," Feme said finally. "I loved a nice hot bath. The stream flowing around the room. Looking at my feet up on the lip of my tub." She put her foot out and turned it from side to side playfully. "A lot of people hate the smell of lilies, but I used to have blue water lilies brought in an hour before my bath. I loved the scent of the water and the flowers. I had the tub specially made too. It cost me a lot of coin," Feme laughed. "My people didn't do that in my day. I hired someone to make it for me and had two of my girls heat my water every evening."

"You had someone whose main job was to heat your water?" Amber asked. Feme held up two fingers and nodded.

"They were both older women that had nowhere to go. I let them live in the house. They cleaned, prepared my flowers, and drew my baths."

"My God, were you spoiled!" Amber bumped into her playfully.

"I really liked to pamper myself. Nothing wrong with that," Feme said, looking down at her hands. Amber closed her eyes and let her mind drift to what Feme had described. The warm water soothing her skin, the heat rising up past her face and her hair. She was sure her baths in Clover were nowhere near what Feme experienced. The wash they had back in her home was a large basin that she stood in while the water barely came halfway up her shins. Amber was jealous. She wanted one of those baths.

"Nothing felt better as the moon was rising," Feme continued. "I would lay in my tub, look out the window and watch it float past. I have a thing with smell. I can't stand for something or someone to stink." She crinkled up her nose and shuddered.

"We had cows. I hated that smell. It's why I would go on walks. I had to get away from all that." Amber confessed as they started walking down the hallway again.

"Have you ever smelled perfume made from the lotus? I wore

it every night," Feme said, her voice soft as if she was admitting a dark secret.

"No."

"One day, you and I will sneak off and try to find something similar." Feme nudged her as they rounded a corner with more doors on both sides.

"I'd like that," Amber grinned. Feme had let her guard down several times with Amber and talked about herself. Amber had always been told by her mother that she was easy to talk to. She liked to listen to people and enjoyed it when someone confided in her. She never wanted to betray their trust. If a person felt strong enough to share a secret with her, she felt she owed them to keep it. There weren't very many girls in Clover her age to speak to, but many of the women would have Amber around. They wanted her advice or would just complain about their day to her. She didn't mind because it usually came with complimentary tea, which was a weakness of hers. Plus, she got a tiny thrill from hearing Esther tell her how Loraine's cooking wasn't very good and vice versa.

"What about you?" Feme asked, bringing Amber back to focus.

"What do I miss most?" Feme nodded at her as they passed two women running down the hallway screaming. Amber watched the women around the corner, still shrilling at the top of their lungs.

"Food. Oh, God, how I miss food."

"Really?" Feme chuckled.

"I would try anything I could get my hands on. Mom always yelled that I was going to get too heavy. Eating so much wasn't very lady-like," she mocked.

"Oh, fuck that. Food is fantastic. What was your favorite?"

"That's a tough one." Amber let her mind wander towards the things she'd eaten in the past. She could swear she heard her stomach rumbling. It was either that or the building they were in. "I'd have to say apple pie."

"Never had one," Feme sighed. "I'd eat the fuck out of grapes."

"Oh, grapes are great," Amber squeaked with a little too much excitement. They went through an open doorway as a woman rushed by, crying. Her arms were wrapped around her torso as if she was embracing herself. Feme moved out of her way, Amber assumed from instinct. Feme glanced back at the woman for a moment before turning and walking on, and Amber waved her hand in front of her face as the smoke started to grow thick in the air.

"I forgot, what are we doing here again?" Feme stopped and made a bitter face as the smoke was swirling all around them now.

"The woman's name is Crystal, um, Crystal...wait..." Amber flicked her wrist and brought the life list into her hand. "Okay, it is Crystal, but with an 'O.' Crystol? That's different. She is about to die in this fire caused by her cat knocking over a candle."

"Seriously? Nothing crazy or nefarious? The last three were pretty intense," Feme said. Amber rolled her eyes and nodded her head. Today alone, they'd retrieved a woman who was attacked and killed by a shark, another who'd been moving a piano up some stairs with her sisters when it slipped. She rode it down a flight, only to have her skull cracked open as it pinned her to the wall. The one before this had been electrocuted by a faulty hairdryer.

Having Feme there made the terror of death easier. Amber always turned away from the gore, she had a weak stomach, and the sight of blood and viscera were enough to bring on a panic attack. She called doors quickly so they could get away from whatever had befallen the recently deceased. Amber would take deep breaths and tell herself over and over again to think of it the way Feme told her to; *This is a part of life, someone has to do it, and each one of these you finish is one step closer to you getting out of here.*

"Well, I hope the cat makes it out. If I see a fucking dead cat, it will ruin my day," Feme complained, snapping Amber's attention back to the moment.

"Wait, what happens to the pets?" Amber asked, putting her hand on Feme's shoulder.

"Nothing. They just die. Isn't that some fucking joke?" Feme scowled.

"No, really?" Amber questioned, hoping it wasn't true.

"Really," Feme said chillingly. Amber put her hands up as if to say she'd given up.

"So, my dog won't be waiting for me?"

"I know! Why let us get close to the fucking things? I had so many cats in my lifetime, and when I was told no one gathers their souls, I was livid."

"Okay, that right there is too much," Amber joked half-heartedly.

"Believe me, it's one of the reasons I'm so cheery," Feme shot back. Amber waved her hand in front of her face again.

"Why is this stinging my eyes?"

"When we get away from here, it will pass. You'll heal quickly." Feme answered. "Just don't get too close to the fire. I've had people get badly burnt before, and that takes a few days to heal."

"That's something I've been meaning to ask you." Amber coughed as she spoke and rubbed at her eyes. Feme moved closer to her, her eyes visibly starting to water too.

"What is?"

"Why can I feel pain and be hurt?"

"I haven't a clue," Feme scoffed, "that was something that always pissed me off, but I know someone who might have that answer. Remind me when we get to the Fork to call on Charon." Amber nodded her head but couldn't tell if Feme saw her or not for the thickness of the smoke. Amber knelt down and saw a cat zip past her. She couldn't help but be elated. At least the cat might live to see another day.

"Good news! I saw the cat!" There was silence for a while, and Amber felt slightly uncomfortable. She stood and put her right hand out to feel where Feme had been, but she wasn't there. She bent down below the smoke again to see if she could see Feme's legs. She wasn't in front of her anymore, and Amber felt afraid for a moment.

"Feme?" She called out. "Feme, are you there?" She felt Feme wrap her hand around her right arm from behind her and yank her to her feet.

"We fucked up! We have to go back!"

"What did we do?" Amber choked on the smoke as it irritated her lungs.

"We were a little late. The woman that went past us crying was her. She's been dead for a few minutes and has no idea what's going on."

"Oh, no!" Amber took off in a run back down the hallway to look for her. She tried several doors but remembered that she was unable to open them. She turned the first corner and saw some firemen waving people on as they made their way to her and then passed. Amber racked her brain, trying to remember what the crying woman looked like. Did she have jet black hair? No. Was she a brunette? She couldn't recall.

"Damn it," she said out loud. Feme was standing beside her now, scanning the hallway and all the people flooding out. She took several steps forward.

"She can't open any doors. She's just like... There!" Feme yelled and pointed. Sitting at the far end of the hallway on her knees was a crying woman. She was trying to touch the cat Amber had seen earlier, but her hand kept going through it. Every time it happened, she would let out a squall. Her dark hair was pulled up into a ponytail, and she was clad only in a faded Baltimore Colts shirt, a pair of socks, and underwear.

"Crystol!" Amber yelled out, and the young woman's head snapped up. When Amber reached her, she fell to her knees and wrapped her arms around her. She shushed her and told her it was okay. She let Crystol cry into her shoulder while she stroked her hair.

"I'm dead. I saw myself. I SAW MYSELF!" Crystol screamed.

"I know." Amber soothed.

"I WANTED TO TAKE A NAP. I HAVE TO WORK THIS EVENING! SOMEONE GET MY MOM! CAN YOU CALL MY MOM?" She yelled into Amber's chest while clawing at her back. Amber kept patting her. She had no idea what to do. Amber looked to Feme, who was cursing under her breath because she had attempted to pet the cat and her hand went through it too.

"What do I do?" Amber asked, starting to feel the weight of Crystol's emotion.

"Want me to handle this?" Feme asked her.

"Yes, please," Amber nearly begged. She hadn't had a soul be this emotional yet, but she'd also been there at the time of death. This woman had crossed over alone, and no one was there to greet her. Amber couldn't imagine the horror of going through the pain of death, and no one was there to tell her what was happening.

"Is she going to the Brilliance of the Darkness?" Feme asked Amber.

"Brilliance," Amber answered.

"Fuck, that's easy. The Fork," Feme called out, and a door appeared behind her. Feme turned and opened it. "Crystol," she whistled and snapped her fingers. "Hey, Crystol." Crystol looked up from Amber's chest, her face covered in tears and her eyes almost glowing red from the irritation of both crying and smoke. Amber scooted back from her but held on to her hand.

"I know this is fucked up. You're dead, and we're sorry we weren't there to get you when it happened, but I need you to listen to me," Feme said to her. Crystol nodded, though she gasped for breath and her body trembled.

"Behind me, inside that door is where we need to take you. You made it. You are going to Heaven. But we," she pointed to Amber and then to herself, "have to get you there as soon as possible. So, I am going to need you to stand up and walk-in." Feme smiled and held her hand out to the open door. "Can you do that for me?"

"I don't want to be dead..." the young woman trailed off.

"I know, no one does, but the cat knocked over the candle and...." Feme told her with sorrow in her voice. Crystol stood and walked to her.

"This is real, isn't it? My life is over."

"I'm afraid so, but you get to go on to the Brilliance, paradise. You won't suffer anymore, nor will you feel pain or want. I envy you. I wish I was going," Feme said. Amber stared at the two of them and felt Feme's words tug at her heart. She had no idea Feme could speak this way or be this compassionate. Feme looked as if she was about to cry, and as Crystol stared into her eyes, she started to calm.

"I'm sorry. I just- I'm thinking of my family. There are so many things I wish I could tell them right now." She leaned and glared into the open door. "That door there?"

"Yes," Feme responded. "Go on through; we will be right behind you. Just stand in the field." Crystol nodded and carefully shuffled towards the door. She held onto the frame briefly, then closed her eyes and walked through. Amber flicked her wrist as she approached Feme, and Crystol's life list appeared in her right hand.

"That was amazing, Feme. I'm sorry I froze."

"It's okay. I just wanted to show you how to handle a situation like that. You have to be ready for when they are in a state of panic. It's difficult, I know." Feme turned to the door, "Let's get in there, and you sign the book. We'll finish this up and head back home. I think you are ready," Feme said. Amber looked down at the life list to find Crystol's last name for the book and froze in terror as she read the last line. Feme must have noticed Amber's face.

"What's wrong?" She asked.

"Oh, I screwed up. I screwed up bad," Amber said, looking at her.

"You're losing color. What did you do?" Feme commanded.

"She's not going to the Brilliance. She's set for the Darkness," Amber's voice shook. Feme grimaced. "What do we do?" Amber asked her.

"Give me the list," Feme said, rolling her eyes. Amber was taken aback by Feme's dismissiveness towards the situation. Feme held out her hand forcefully, and her eyes widened. "Come on, we need to get this over with." Amber handed it over, and Feme turned and walked through the door with purpose. Amber walked behind her, her head hung low in shame.

61

THE FORK

"This is beautiful," Crystol said in awe. She stood in the grass of the Fork, giggling at the sky. Feme continued to march right towards her looking down at the life list and not speaking. Amber had to speed up to match her stride. Feme stopped a foot from Crystol and put her hand on Crystol's shoulder.

"I'm really sorry about this."

"About what?" Crystol said as Feme walked past her and looked toward the Darkness.

"Hey!" Feme called out in its direction and waved the life list. "Do your thing." Crystol made a slight jerking motion, and her eyes widened. Feme's sudden coldness had caught Crystol off guard. She stepped to Feme and then a step past her. Amber rushed over to Crystol and started walking beside her towards the Darkness.

"I am so sorry. I was flustered, and honestly-" Amber began.

"What's happening to me? Why can't I stop? Why can't I move my head?" Crystol asked, fear trickling into her voice.

"You're heading inside there," Amber pointed towards the Darkness.

"The giant cave filled with smoke?" Crystol asked, panicked.

"Yes, I am sorry," Amber apologized.

"Heaven's in there?" Crystol questioned, her eyes straining towards Amber.

"No, I mean, no that-" Amber stumbled.

"Bitch, are you telling me I'm going to Hell?!" Crystol cried out.

"I read it wrong. I-"

"YOU READ IT WRONG?!" She screamed as she was halfway to her destination.

"Oh," Amber wrung her hands together as she pleaded with Crystol. "I know. I really wish I wouldn't have gotten your hopes up. I..." Amber trailed off.

"If I could strangle you right now, I would," Crystol growled. Amber could see she was straining, trying to turn her head towards Amber.

"I-" Amber started.

"Stop talking! You and that lying bitch back there can go fuck yourselves. I WISH YOU WERE COMING WITH ME TOO, BITCH!" Crystol screamed at Feme. Amber looked to Feme, who was waving for Amber to come back to her. Amber sighed and gazed at Crystol's back as she continued towards her fate. Amber started her slow trek back. She could only imagine what was going through Crystol's mind. To have that kind of joy ripped away from you, to realize you are heading to a place where true evil dwells, she must feel horrible. Amber was almost to Feme when she heard Crystol call out one last time.

"AT LEAST KILL THAT FUCKING CAT!" Amber glanced back over her shoulder as Crystol stepped through and into the abyss. Amber stood in front of Feme, still hanging her head and her cheeks flushed with shame. She peeked up quickly at Feme standing expressionless, her arms folded.

"You can't make a mistake like that," Feme hissed.

"I know." Amber was crushed. She felt she had destroyed their friendship in one swoop.

"Look at me," Feme ordered. Amber looked up and braced for Feme to start yelling.

"You listen to me, and you listen well," she barked. "I'm certainly not killing a fucking cat." Feme started walking towards the book on the pedestal, howling with laughter as she went. "It's alright. I've seen a lot worse." Amber wanted to join in with her laughter but couldn't. After Crystol had wished death upon the cat, it made her guilt ease considerably, but to joke about eternal damnation seemed almost cruel.

"Amber, you didn't lose her. You didn't get her hurt. She was mad at you, but the minute she crossed into there, she had a lot more on her mind." Feme said, still chuckling.

"What are you doing?" Amber asked, ignoring what she said.

"I'm writing a request to speak to Charon. She'll be here shortly." Feme stepped up to the pedestal, removed the quill, and started writing. "You have to let it go, Amber. You can't dwell on things here." She said aloud as if she was reading Amber's mind.

"I know, but-"

"Done." Feme placed the quill back in its holder.

62

Feme was standing on the shore of the River. She knew her training with Amber had come to an end. She hoped for a little more time together, but it was time to let her go back to Clayton. She would dismiss Astrid when they returned and get back to the monotonous grind. She cracked the knuckles in her right hand. They were stiffening up.

"I'll call Clayton after this," she said.

"I can't wait to get started," Amber told her gleefully. "I just want to see him again and tell him I'm sorry."

"Amber," Feme dropped back into her boss persona, her voice taking on a stern tone. "This place is a punishment. You are being punished. Now, I don't know how being with the love of your life could be considered that, but I am not one to judge. There will be moments of hardship for you. Somehow, someway, this place is going to hurt you, and when it does, it will be brutal. Keep your chin up, do not falter, don't let it win. One day, just like Takis, you will get the fuck out of here, and when you do, it will be glorious."

"Love of my life?" She asked. Amber blushed and worried at her lower lip.

"Clayton," Feme smirked and looked over at her, noticing the confusion on her face. A sickening realization slowly came over Feme. "Wait."

"He was my best friend, and I'm responsible for his death. But if I loved him, I wouldn't have done what I did with...." Amber looked away, "Donald." *Oh fuck*, Feme thought as she smiled at Amber, hiding the uneasy feeling welling up inside her.

"I'm sorry, I always assumed," she said.

"Oh no, I get it. I kissed him the night before I died. I knew I was sick. I wasn't thinking straight. I remember going inside my house and thinking that I'd made a mistake, that I shouldn't have done that," Amber said. *OH FUCK!* Feme thought again.

"I didn't know," she said, again doing her best to cover her genuine emotions.

"I'm just glad the two of us are together, you know. He was always such a gentleman, and I loved his family to pieces. I know that Clayton had feelings for me. He told me as much," she trailed off, looking for the words to say. "He's like a brother to me."

"This is a fucking disaster," Feme thought to herself.

"I think you both will do great. It's good to have a friend you can count on." She lied, straight-faced. She saw Charon off in the distance, paddling towards them. "Charon!" Feme cried out, a little too loud. She was relieved she had someone to interrupt this awkward conversation. Charon slowed as she got near the shore, her hood still covering her head. She tilted her head slowly to the right.

"What's the problem?" Charon asked.

"There's no problem, Charon. I actually have a question for you," Feme said, her tone kind and warm. Charon pulled her hood back, her silver hair fell around her face. She brushed it back with her hand and propped her left foot on the front of the gondola. Her red eyes were burning a hole in Feme. She could tell by Charon's blank expression she didn't like her much, if at all. She glanced at Amber, who looked away, and then back to Feme.

"A question?"

"How much do you know of the After? I've been here for a long time, not as long as Nix, of course, but he only knows the how. I want to know the why," Feme said. Charon sat down in the front of the boat. Feme had never noticed how small Charon actually was. The ferryman was no bigger than a child, and it reminded her of how much she disliked children. She was glad to see Charon, though. They'd known one another from when she was collecting the dead. Still, they were never friendly, and the hesitation she saw in Charon now was probably because Feme had never tried to have a conversation with her before.

"What do you want to know?" Charon leaned forward, her eyebrow raised in curiosity.

"Amber and I just collected a woman from a fire. The smoke burned our eyes, and we both got choked up. I've stubbed my toe on my desk, I have pain in my joints, I can pull a muscle." Feme explained. She could see Charon's face lighten a bit, a smile forming across her lips. "We even have a doctor. There are people I know that have bled, broken bones. I had one man mangled to the point I couldn't tell he was human anymore." She stepped closer to the River's edge. "I know we can't die. I assumed the pain was just an addition to our punishment, but now I'm not so sure." Feme shook her head. "You'd figure I would have found all this out by now, but I just consumed myself in my work. I really would like to know. We both would like to know."

"This is why you called me in here?" Charon shrugged. "Really?"

"Yes, really," Feme said. Charon stood and grabbed her oar.

"Because you aren't really dead. Can I go now?" She asked, annoyed.

"Wait, what do you mean we aren't really dead?" Amber interjected. Charon turned to Amber.

"You aren't alive, and you aren't really dead. You are something in between. You can't interact physically with the living, but you can talk to them."

"Afterwords, right?" Feme answered.

"Yes, but you can't touch them. You aren't a true spirit yet either, like the ones in the Brilliance." She placed her oar on the shore, ready to shove off.

"Same for the Darkness?" Amber wondered aloud as she stared back at its entrance.

"Don't know, I've never been there," Charon snapped and gave Feme a look of anger.

"There's no need to be rude," Feme warned Charon.

"Kiss my ass, Feme," Charon retorted.

"Excuse me?" Feme gasped. Charon blurted it, and with such vehemence that Feme was stunned. Charon had no reason to act like this. Feme gritted her teeth, prepared to lash out.

"No, I won't," Charon fired back, "and watch your tone with me. You have no authority over me, and it's taking everything in my power to not crack your head open with my oar."

"I've done nothing to you," Feme told her. Charon scoffed.

"I've never had a friend here. People dropped a soul off, and away I went. Clayton would talk to me. I liked him. I watched as he withdrew, as he became something else. Bitter, hateful, just like everything else here."

"What the fuck does that have to do with me?" Feme asked her, confused.

"Takis told me how hard you are on him. When Clayton would show up to drop off a baby, he used to kiss their forehead and wish them well. The last few times I saw him, he practically pitched them in my boat. He doesn't speak anymore. His smile is gone. You broke him, Feme. You crushed his spirit." Charon stomped her foot, and she gripped her oar tightly.

Feme wanted to explode but held it in. Charon was extremely powerful, and she had a point; Feme did not have any say over that department. With Feme's reputation as a hard ass, Charon could say it was Feme that started an altercation and be taken at her word. Takis had clearly explained Clayton's odd behavior as her fault. None of them knew at the time that Clayton was breaking down because of outside influence. Feme took in Charon's frown, her bushy eyebrows pushed low over her eyes, and her lips were drawn back nearly in a snarl. Feme decided to try to diffuse the situation.

"Charon, this is Amber Ward, Clayton's new partner," she held her hand out in Amber's direction. "She knew Clayton from when they were alive. They've been put together to help him. I know he's-"

"Oh," Charon interrupted and turned to Amber, "well, I'll be sure to write you off too."

"Write me off?" Amber asked.

"I put in a request to not carry souls for Clayton any more. I can't stand to see him this way." Charon seethed. Feme took a few steps back and waved her hand for Amber to do the same.

"Just how close were the two of you?" Feme asked. Charon narrowed her eyes, and she pushed off the shore.

"Call me again, and I'll hurt you, Feme," Charon hissed. Feme and Amber stood together on the shore, watching as Charon rode back to the middle of the pond and slowly sank below the surface. Feme said nothing till she was sure Charon was gone.

"What the fuck was that?" Feme asked, puzzled.

"I take it that wasn't supposed to happen?" Amber asked, her mouth still open in shock.

"No," Feme barked and threw her hands in the air. "I had no idea she felt that strongly towards him. Takis never mentioned it." Feme said, rolling her eyes. "She obviously thinks it's more than a simple friendship."

"Yeah," Amber responded, her voice raised slightly in confusion. Feme could tell then that Amber was telling the truth. She didn't have feelings for Clayton. Feme had been around jealousy. She'd been around people trying to hide their feelings from her. They always revealed things to her in their tones. She could feel it in Amber's inflection. She didn't harbor anything of the sort towards Charon for her feelings towards Clayton. She really did look at him as a member of her family. Feme knew how Clayton felt about Amber, and this was going to be a problem that Feme wasn't prepared to deal with.

"We need to get back to my office. You need to get started," Feme ordered.

Feme rounded her desk and sat down. Amber sat across from her. Feme didn't want to make a big deal about them separating. She wanted Amber to leave her office chipper and ready to tear into her work. Feme was about to call Clayton to pick Amber up when an envelope appeared on her desk. She was going to dismiss it, but it was addressed to Amber in thick black letters.

"What is this?" Feme picked it up and looked it over. It was sealed, so she couldn't tell what kind of paper was inside. Feme was trying to hide any concern on her face. Something like this had never happened before, and it made her uncomfortable. She looked at Amber. "It's for you." She slid it across the desk, and Amber picked it up and quickly opened it. She pulled the folded parchment out, a dark blue with white ink, the color of a reprimand. Amber began to read it.

"Feme, what is this?" She said, her voice becoming shrill as she shot to her feet.

"I have no idea, Amber. You are the one looking at it," Feme joked, trying to break the tension that was rising in the room. Amber's face lost all color, and she stared at the paper without blinking. Feme stood and took the letter from Amber's trembling hands.

For failure on your last retrieval, Clayton Shaw receives a black mark.

For the Fork station replacement request, Clayton Shaw receives a second black mark.
For failing your training, Clayton Shaw receives a third black mark.
You are to stay with Feme and retrieve 20 souls in one day to be listed as satisfactory.
Every day you fail is another black mark towards Clayton Shaw.

"Are you fucking kidding me?" Feme slammed it down on her desk.

"What does this mean?" Amber asked. Feme noticed the sweat on Amber's brow and the way she trembled.

"That means at the very least Clayton just got another two hundred years on his sentence!" Feme yelled as she kicked her desk in anger.

"It was a simple mistake," Amber whispered.

"I know it was. There is no fucking reason for this! Why not black mark us? Why him?" Feme huffed around her office. "Why do the rules keep changing? I was told that following the rules kept everything in order. Why does this place keep fucking with us?"

"Feme, what do I say to him? I'm the reason he died, the reason he's here in the first place, and now he's stuck here longer because of me?" Amber asked, now violently shaking.

"I need to speak to Nix. Stay here. Breathe, just try to calm down while I figure this out." She rushed to the door, leaving Amber standing by the door.

63

Nix was at his desk, and Clayton sat on his crate, paging through the book. Clayton had been with Nix for days now, and they were taking a little break. Clayton adored going through the Creator's sketches. Nix told Clayton he would use this time to catalog things they had been sorting, but he was actually just doodling. He stopped caring about these artifacts long ago. The only thing that mattered to him was the few trinkets he had that belonged to the Creator and the great sketchbook. He had spent lifetimes trying to find something to combat the Son inside the Darkness, but nothing he found on Earth or in the After provided an answer. The Darkness spoke to him quite often, normally taunting him, daring him to come in and retrieve his family. It always ended the same way. Nix would curse for an hour or so while the Darkness laughed at him before Nix would break down and beg for his family.

Then the day came where it didn't taunt him. It made him an offer. *Do what I tell you, and I will return your family to you.* Nix didn't believe it at first. He left the Fork that day angrier than he'd been in a long time, but the more he thought about it, the more it made sense. He could beat the Darkness. He agreed, and his first order of business was to watch Clayton and then manipulate the entire situation the way the Darkness wanted it. The Reverend and Amber, everyone's loss of faith in Clayton leading to the boy's suicide. It was all meticulous and had to be done only when the Darkness told him the time was right.

Nix didn't understand the plans or the schemes, and he didn't care. It had been almost two hundred years since they started, and it needed to finish. He knew that the boy was an integral part of all of this but to what end? He had been around the boy for well over a century and still couldn't see anything exceptional about him. Clayton was weak. So what if he cared about people? There had been thousands of people who lived a decent life and thought of others more than themselves. Nix heard Feme's voice, calling for him in his thoughts.

"I'll be right back. Please don't touch anything while I'm gone.

"Mmhmm," Clayton acknowledged.

Clayton heard Nix leave but was still enthralled in the book. He wanted to see everything it had to offer and was anxious with every turn of the page. This one was of a whale deep in the ocean. It glided through the gloom and turned to face him. He was giddy when he turned the page and saw the sky and snowfall from the clouds, all in that magnificent art style. He flipped back to the very last page, curious to see what was there. He felt his heart sink when he saw nothing but emptiness. He'd expect the final page to have something glorious. He didn't know why. He'd always assumed the book was complete. He was about to go back to the art when his eye caught the small print in the lower corner. It was almost unnoticeable, and it was faint. It was upside down, so he stood and walked around the book to the other side so he could read it.

I miss you. Without you, I am lost.

Was this about Her Son? Why did She write this on the final page? Could He even see it? He couldn't imagine the pain of losing a child the way She did. He was without his mother for a few hundred years, and the mere thought of her left a lump in his throat. The handwriting was different from the other notes and writing in the book, and it seemed so out of place. He thought about what this book probably meant to Her. She discarded it. She left it. Did she feel empty and hollow? Incomplete? He walked away. He'd been looking at the book for a while now, so he leaned against Nix's desk and waited patiently. Her final note was depressing, and he didn't want to dwell on that anymore. He just wanted to see Amber again.

"Can you believe this shit?" Feme hissed and forced the order into his hand.

"What is it?" Nix asked, concerned. He stepped out into the hallway and closed the door to Acquisitions. He looked down and read the paper, and as he finished, his first thought was, this is brilliant.

"She's devastated. We fuck up, and Clayton suffers. Who knows how much time it's added to him already? I don't know if she can even pull this off. Twenty in one day is astronomical. What if we have to wait on a cross-over, a slow death? What the fuck is wrong with this place?" Feme leaned against the closed door of her office and shut her eyes. "He can't take much more."

"He'll be fine," Nix said. "He got Amber back. Sure, he can't touch her, but they are together. That will be enough for him."

"Oh, that's the worst part," Feme said, exasperated. Nix raised his eyebrow.

"It can get worse?"

"She doesn't love him," Feme admitted. Nix looked down at the paper again. *There it is, the one thing that throws him over the edge,* Nix thought.

"This is the last thing I need, Nix. I'm falling apart here, and now Charon wants me dead again," Feme moaned.

"What happened with Charon?" Nix asked, looking up and down the hallway.

"She's in love with him, and she blames me for his downturn. She requested not to retrieve any souls from Clayton or Amber. She even threatened me," Feme confessed.

"Well, that's unexpected," Nix began. He handed the paper back. "You didn't know this was going to happen, Feme. You can't blame yourself. This place does what it wants to."

"I know, but all this makes a volatile situation a lot worse."

"Do you want me to talk to Charon?" He asked her.

"No, just...tell Clayton Amber's not taking well to the changes in the world and that she's having a tough time. Tell him it will be a while longer before I turn her over to him. Charon will just have to get over it. She's not one of mine, so I couldn't care less."

"I can do that," he said.

"Do something to distract him before this all goes to complete shit," she said as she grabbed the doorknob to her office.

"Like what?" Nix snickered.

"I don't fucking know. Anything. Use your imagination, Nix," she snapped.

"I'll try." Nix turned away, and he heard her enter her office. He took out his key and opened the door to Acquisitions.

It won't be long now. He smiled at the thought and walked in, excited to tell Clayton they'd be spending more time together.

64

CHARON'S ROOM

Charon fell on her bed, her robe lying below her on the floor. She loved the feeling of her naked skin against the Egyptian cotton sheets. She sighed.

"Stupid," she said out loud. Nothing adorned her room besides her bed, which was extremely large for her petite body. A small desk with paper and a quill sat neat and tidy against the wall. She hated things to be messy. It made her uncomfortable to see anything out of place or disheveled. In the very corner of the room was a bed of hay, and this is where her dodo slept. She kept him as a pet, fed him, and cared for him. She loved him dearly, and as they dwindled to such a small number, she couldn't bear to know they would cease to exist.

She begged to have one, and her wish was granted. She'd asked for other creatures before but was always denied. So many were lost to time, either by the ignorance of the animal or interference by mankind. She would have taken them all if the powers that be would have let her. As long as he dwelled in her room, he couldn't die. This three-foot-tall, gray feathered bird with a yellow and black striped beak was the only one of his kind that remained. She simply called him Dodo since he was the last. She didn't want the name of the species to be lost. She was the only person to have one.

She laid on her back and stared at the ceiling. Dodo was her only real friend in the worlds. The other ferrymen didn't look like her, they didn't think like her, and they were cruel. They teased her for being too kind-hearted and caring for things they considered beneath their kind. She was an outcast, and she never felt as if she belonged with them. She never sat with any of them and never even attempted to know them personally. When she had her free moments, she would lay on her bed and talk to Dodo. However, this time, when he came over to her expecting affection and praise, she pushed him away.

"Not now, Dodo. I just want to lie here," she said, on the verge of tears. The bird tilted its head as if it was trying to understand her. She knew he didn't. For all the things Dodo was, he was not intelligent. Her icy demeanor was enough for him to take a hint, and he shuffled off towards his bed and his food bowl. She couldn't bear to see Clayton as he was anymore. He was so distant and vicious to her. It had been a while since she had seen him, and with each passing moment, the thought of the man he'd become tore at her heart.

"This is all my fault," she whispered. Her throat burned with the threat of tears. She knew why this was happening. She had a simple misstep, and now Clayton Shaw was all she thought about. There is a reason ferrymen wear gloves. They take them off to touch a passenger on their vessel to ensure the person is worthy of the trip. They are warned to only remove their gloves when they reach the cave and then touch a soul. It's usually a pat on the shoulder or something of the sort, and the ferryman gets a feeling of yes or no. She'd never experienced a no. She never heard of a ferryman who had. In fact, she didn't know what to do if there was a no. She was sure they told her centuries ago, but somehow it slipped her mind.

She had taken the glove off on the rise through the gold. Her hand was itching, so she removed the covering on her right hand and scratched it. She had emerged and saw Clayton and Takis, easily her two favorite retrievers in all of the After. It had been a little over a month since Clayton had attempted to sneak Leon through the system, and she respected what he'd done enough to keep his secret. She was excited to see them. Clayton was always so talkative and would stay and listen to Charon as long as possible before going back to his duties. He even knew of Dodo and asked after him all the time. The other retrievers weren't like that at all, including Takis. They were always such a depressing lot. She never put her glove back on. She'd forgotten. After speaking to Clayton for a while, he handed her a baby due to make the trip to the Brilliance, and their hands lightly touched.

She absorbed all his memories. She knew everything about him, all his emotions flooded into her. She saw how he missed his mother, how he ached over his father striking him, and how he regretted not being there for his little sister. She felt his pride in his work on the farm, how he cared about the livestock he watched over and hated to see them perish. She saw how he felt about Amber and the feelings he had the night before he died. Clayton had asked Charon if she was alright as she stood there holding the baby and taking it all in. She told him she had something on her mind and wished him well, and from that point on, he was always in her thoughts. She couldn't stop thinking about him, and she tried. She got to the point where she would come into this room and talk to Dodo. He couldn't understand her, obviously, but she could confess things to the bird that she didn't dare to say to Clayton.

Every time she saw him, it became harder and harder to contain herself. She wanted to whisk him away back to this room and let him read her work, and introduce him to Dodo. She wanted to tell him all the ways he made her feel special without doing anything really at all. He meant so much to her that watching him slowly break down, seeing the person that she admired, and yearned for slowly dying inside, was just too much to bear. She couldn't go to her superior. She would only have to listen to how she made a mistake by touching someone and how she was always daydreaming and never paying attention to her surroundings. Again, she would be told how no one understood why she was created for this role.

She glanced past her feet at the rest of her room. She was starting to hate this life. She honestly thought that maybe it was time to hang it up and take her retirement, head into the Brilliance and try to find happiness. She had her work and Dodo to keep her company, but she felt so alone at the same time. The one person she wished could be here with her wasn't, and that made her ache in a way she'd never experienced before. She rolled over on her side and closed her eyes. Maybe instead of retirement, she should try and be like the others, unfeeling, and let Dodo go. Perhaps she should stop wanting things that were unbecoming of a ferryman. She shuddered at the thought of letting Dodo back into the world.

She tried to focus on something else, but her mind always wandered back to Clayton. Maybe being away from him for an extended period would help her feelings dissipate. She felt a nudge against her back, and she turned to look over her shoulder. Dodo had enough, and he wanted her attention. She took her hand and ruffled through the feathers on his head.

"I wish you knew what to do," Charon sighed. He tilted his head again. She chuckled and then began to cry weakly. "Stupid."

65

JULY 14TH, 1985

THE WORLD

Clayton and Nix stood on a shoreline in Okinawa, watching an older fisherman cast his line from a dock in the distance. Rain fell in a steady drizzle, and everything was covered in mist.

"What are we doing again?" Clayton asked, boredom thick in his voice.

"I told you, I like to watch and see how man has changed. I love seeing people going about their day. This is one of my favorite spots."

"Why here?" Clayton tried to read Nix's face, but he seemed distant.

"I can't say. Maybe it reminds me of the home my family and I settled on," Nix said as if he was in a trance. "I wonder if we were given a chance to evolve, would we be as accomplished as your kind?"

"Do you think you would have?" Clayton asked, leaning on the rail in front of him.

"No, I'm just fooling myself. We were a violent lot. We would have killed each other off."

Clayton decided not to press the matter any further. This was a topic he had learned to avoid. In the time they had spent together, they'd talked about personal things, and when the subject of families came up, Clayton could see the pain on his face. Nix would grow silent and act as if something in front of him was exciting and deserved his undivided attention. Nix suddenly tapped Clayton on the shoulder.

"He's got something!" Nix pointed to the fisherman on the dock as he struggled with his rod against something in the sea. "Oh, it's big," Nix said gleefully, his eyes widening. Clayton watched Nix close his fist and mimic the old man's jerking motion.

"You're killing me," Clayton said as a small laugh escaped him.

"Why's that?" Nix faced him, his eyebrow raised.

"Getting excited over," Clayton held his hands out towards the fisherman, "that." Nix sighed and looked back towards the man on the dock.

"It's beautiful. One day you'll come to appreciate simple things," Nix said and put his hands in his pockets.

"I meant nothing by it," Clayton took a more serious tone. "You have all these amazing things in the office at your disposal, and yet here you are amazed by fishing."

"I taught my tribe how to fish. I guess that makes me the first fisherman," Nix proclaimed proudly. Clayton paused for a moment and cocked his head to the side.

"Why would you decide to eat one? Fish smell and look even worse. What would make you want to put that in your mouth?"

"I saw a bear grab one and bite in," Nix answered without missing a beat. "After seeing that, I had to try it. If they liked them, I mean, they had to be good, right? I spent the day grabbing like an idiot until I finally caught one and bit a chunk out of the middle of it."

"And?"

"And I spit that shit right out," he laughed. "I put the rest to the fire and tried again. Then I couldn't get enough of it."

"God, I hate fish. It makes me ill," Clayton said and shivered.

"That's terrible. Fish was my favorite food," Nix put a hand to his chest in mock offense.

Clayton. Feme's voice came through Clayton's mind, soft but insistent. His heart began to race. This was it.

"Feme just called me," Clayton said, his excitement turning to nervousness. He could finally see Amber again. He'd started to wonder if Feme was ever going to call on him. It had seemed like an eternity. He had enjoyed his time with Nix, but he was itching to be with Amber.

"Well, go on. Time for you to get what you wanted," Nix patted Clayton's shoulder.

"Yeah, I hope she's doing better," Clayton worried aloud.

"I'm glad you got your mate back," Nix smiled.

"I can't wait for you to meet her. Thanks again!" Clayton called as he took a few steps backward and called a door.

Nix watched the waves crash against the shore and breathed in the salty air. He closed his eyes and tried to envision Rae running up the beach with their daughter. He could recall every freckle, every expression, and for a moment, he swore their scent was mixed in with the fragrance of the sea and sand. He tried to imagine the feel of Rae in his arms as they lay wrapped together in their cave. His mind drifted, and now he only smelled the salt and coppery stench of Takis' blood as he choked on glass and ink. Instead of Rae's soft form, he could only feel the bones of Takis' face crunch beneath his fists.

Nix sighed and wondered what horrors the Darkness had conjured up for Takis. Was Leon a part of it? Nix thought he had to be. Takis' guilt regarding his son was his weakness. Phile was there too. He had checked on that some time ago. He pulled his upper lip back in a snarl as he remembered reading her life list. If Takis had denied her, she had planned to rid them both of their spouses. She was cruel, greedy, and she used people. Nix thought that the images Leon had been shown in the cells weren't far from the truth, but he wondered why Takis was a part of them. Takis had made a cruel mistake, but Nix didn't think he was a bad person. Takis had treated him as an equal, not a monster. Nix had liked him.

Nix had been cruel too. He had robbed his friend of the chance to make amends with his wife in paradise. Nix had always taken pride in his sense of honor, but there was none to be found in this act. The memory of Takis on his knees, bleeding, his eyes a mixture of pain and confusion came unbidden. Nix slammed his hand against the railing. Yes, Takis had been his friend, but Nix didn't hesitate when the Darkness came calling. He was consumed by the need to have his family back. He believed if he gave the Darkness what it wanted, the three of them would be returned to him. The Darkness had reached out to him after all, not the other way around. He tried to push the vision away and convince himself that he was just a pawn in some ridiculous game being played by the epitome of evil. He knew better. He had condemned his friend to an eternity of horror. Takis deserved better. Warm wetness trickled onto his upper lip. Blood.

"Get out of my head," he growled above the crashing of the waves.

Now, Nix, I thought we were friends. Nix closed his eyes; it hurt whenever it said his name. It hung on the "x" in a long hiss. It felt like his eyes were going to burst.

"You're too loud," Nix snapped. He made his way around the railing and started up the pier. He rubbed his forehead with his palm.

Pain reminds a person that they're alive. Oh, oh, wait.

"Cute," Nix growled, unable to hide his anger.

I find it amusing that you want to pin your sins on me.

"You have no need for Takis. You don't even need Clayton or

Feme, for that matter. You have millions of souls at your disposal. Why them? Hell, why do I have to be involved?"

Do you want your family back?

"That's not the point-"

DO YOU WANT YOUR FAMILY BACK? Nix almost dropped to one knee. He braced himself against the railing to his left beside the fisherman, who was oblivious to Nix's presence.

"Yes!" Nix cried out. "Yes! Stop hurting me."

I need Clayton Shaw. I need Feme. And thanks to you, I have Takis. Nix shook his head before staring at the old man in his yellow plastic raincoat. He cast his line out into the water, then took his hand and wiped the drops from his glasses. Nix was doing everything he could to concentrate on the elderly fellow's face, anything to stop the pounding in his skull. He focused on his wet mustache, how it was a little too long, and went over his lip. It was bushy and dark gray, and every so often, his face twitched. Nix focused with all his might, waiting for the next one to come.

Eiji Sato.

"What?" Nix asked, confused.

His name is Eiji Sato.

"Alright."

His wife died recently. Two years ago. He's been miserable ever since. See, Nix, he's not well. He's ill and doesn't know it. He has much suffering coming his way. Nix saw the man's face twitch again.

He loves this place as much as you do. He and his wife used to come to the benches near the end of the pier and have lunch together.

"I don't understand," Nix turned his back to the old man, and he dropped his voice down to a whisper even though he knew no one could hear the conversation he was having.

You know what's odd? For all his love of the sea, for all his love of this place, he can't swim. Nix was suddenly afraid. He could feel the playfulness in the Darkness, a taunting. Nix felt sick to his stomach.

"I should get back," he said as he cleared his throat.

This poor man will be bedridden soon. Kept alive with medications, not able to speak. Wishing only to see his wife because his ungrateful children, who are more worried about their careers and their own families, barely come to sit with him. It's terrible.

"Don't," Nix begged.

We should help him. All it takes is a little push, right?

After

66

THE AFTER

eme stood with Amber outside of her office, waiting for Clayton. As he exited through his door, his eyes locked onto Amber. Feme saw his face light up. He was walking as fast as he could without breaking into a run. She shook her head at the thought of him being smitten with this girl and having no idea the feelings weren't mutual. This was why she never let herself fall for anyone. Too many chances for the other person to let you down.

"Are you finally finished?" Clayton asked.

"I am," Amber smiled.

"She was great," Feme interjected. "Clayton, can I see you for a moment?" Clayton looked at Amber, puzzled, and stepped past her into Feme's office.

"Close the door," she ordered him. Clayton did as he was told and stood in front of her desk.

"Am I in trouble?" Clayton asked in a nervous tone.

"No, not at all, but I need you to be aware of something," she began. "You have to keep your hands to yourself, no hugs, no hand-holding, no patting her ass. I mean it, Clayton. Do not touch her."

"Why are you telling me this?" He asked. Feme wasn't about to tell him that Amber didn't feel the same way towards him, so she lied.

"Years ago, there was a fuck-up. A husband and wife were put together. Every time they showed physical affection, it added to their time here. I don't want you both staying here any longer than need be. I want to see you leave quickly."

"Oh, okay. I hugged her when I first saw her. Was that bad?" He asked, scrubbing a hand through his hair. Feme hated to lie to him, but she had to keep things running smoothly.

"Just keep your urges to yourself."

"Okay. Nix explained some stuff," Clayton said sheepishly. Feme felt relief that she didn't have to have that talk.

"Alright. She is assigned to middle-aged women. Most are bound for the Darkness."

"That's a big change from what I've been doing."

"It is. You are to observe. She's had trial runs, and she's done well. Try to keep that going."

"Anything else?"

"No, that will do. You're excused." Feme looked back down at her paperwork. Clayton tapped her desk with his hand.

"Thank you," he said.

"Don't piss me off. I am really fucking trying here." She waved her hand at him. Feme sighed after he'd closed the door. Clayton really was different. He wasn't like the other people here, and he certainly wasn't like the men of his age she had dealt with in Egypt eons ago. She felt for him. She wanted this place to let him go to the Brilliance and find whatever would make him happy. It seemed like the more time he spent here, the more she had to deal with. She was starting to miss only having mounds of paperwork.

"Are you ready to go?" Clayton asked Amber as he closed the office door. She was reading through a life list but glanced up when he spoke to her.

"Thirty-five-year-old woman named Ashlee Clark. I'm ready when you are," she nodded.

"There are only so many hours in the day. After you," he gave a slight bow. He spent the day watching Amber work. Ashlee had embezzled money from the wrong people and died in an alley from a bullet to the back of her head. Clayton had never seen someone actually submit to the Darkness before, so when they arrived at the Fork, and he witnessed Amber sentence her, it was a shock.

"Ashlee Clark, my name is Amber Ward, and you have committed too many sins in your life to be saved. You are hereby sentenced to the Darkness for eternity," Amber declared. The Darkness took over from there. Ashlee was drawn in. She walked towards it without looking back, without saying a word. It unnerved Clayton. It wasn't like with Leon. Instead, she walked in as if she wanted to. Clayton wondered what, if anything, was going through her mind.

Amber was fast and very short with the souls she collected. During a retrieval of a woman who'd murdered two husbands for insurance money, he glanced over to see Amber reading the life list as the woman was shuffling off towards the Darkness.

"What are you doing?" He asked curiously.

"Just wanted to make sure. I don't want any mistakes," she answered, her eyes glued to the list.

"You don't talk to them much," Clayton said as he watched the woman step into the Darkness.

"I don't want to take time to feel it," Amber told him, finally looking up. "I don't want to mourn them." Clayton stuck his hands in his pockets and stared down at his feet.

"I had it easy, I guess. The babies cried, sure, but I never had to see someone to that," he said and pointed to the Darkness. He'd known Amber his entire life, and she was always kind. He was relieved that her time in the cells hadn't dulled that part of her. He knew if he'd spoken to these people, knowing where they were going would bother him too. He was still torn inside by what happened to Leon.

"Are you alright?" He asked her after they finished that first day and sat in the break room.

"Yes," she started, "so, when we finish, we come here and what? Wait?"

"That's right. Takis and I would sit here and talk for hours till my hand started itching again," he told her, drumming his fingertips on the armrest of his chair.

"Fine," she sighed playfully. "Talk. Pick something. Anything." He appreciated her good humor. Taking those women to their demise was draining.

"Takis was the one who saw my mother off to the Brilliance." He had no idea why out of everything they could talk about, this was the first thing that came to mind, but he blurted it out.

"Really?" Amber said, taken aback.

"Yeah. Takis was in the corner of the room the night she died. He saw me there with her. He remembered her saying I was good."

"I always loved your mother," Amber said sadly.

"Mom always talked so highly of you," Clayton smiled. He pitched his voice high, trying to imitate his mother. "That Ward girl, such a sweet child." Amber laughed.

"Do you know what happened to Eve?" She asked.

"I do, actually, thanks to Feme. She named one of her children after me. She never forgot me," he boasted.

"I'm so happy! I always thought of Eve as a baby sister." Her tone darkened, "I wish I knew what happened to my parents, my brothers." She trailed off. Clayton leaned in. He spoke in a hushed whisper as if the After would hear.

"One day, when we finish early, we can go to their gravestones. You just have to think of them and call their names, and once we're in front of them, you should be able to call their life lists."

"Really?" She leaned forward too.

"Nix told me all about it when we worked together. I was telling him a story," Clayton paused. He didn't want to tell Amber about what happened with Alan and his body and how Takis retrieved his life list. "That's not important right now, but you have to be assigned to collect a soul to summon a life list without the person being present. Once they are in front of you, alive or dead, you can call it right there."

"No fooling?" She asked, surprised.

"No fooling," he reassured her.

"So, let me see if I get this straight," she looked away for a moment in thought, "we could go to the grave of President Jefferson and call up his life list and find out every bad thing he's ever done?"

"That's a little odd, but, well, yes. We could," Clayton pulled back and smirked. She gasped and put her hand over her mouth.

"You didn't see your mother's life list, did you?"

"No, Takis advised me against it. It caused a hell of a fight between us. I wanted to see it so bad. I made a fuss and told him it was my right."

"Really? What did he say?"

"I was so angry," Clayton looked at the ground; shame made his ears burn. "He made a good point, though. He told me that was her life. It was personal. She wouldn't want me to see those parts of herself."

"Was he right?" Amber leaned back and folded her arms. Clayton forced a smile.

"I never asked for it again. I hate to admit it, but he was. I don't want to see the things my parents did that would make me think less of them. I don't want to know Eve's sins. I want to know the parts they wanted me to know. It's silly, I know." He said and scratched the top of his head.

"No, no, it isn't silly at all," she said louder than she should. "I don't know what I would do if I saw my father's list and it said he was unfaithful to my mother or something else horrible." She bit her lip and looked away from him. He thought maybe he shouldn't have suggested getting her family's life lists after all. He cleared his throat and racked his brain for a moment.

"Hey, you want to hear about my first day? How badly I messed up and lost a soul?"

"Absolutely," her face softened, and the excitement came back into her eyes.

"Let me tell you about baby Bruno," he smiled.

67

The days started to go by faster and faster. Amber always seemed to be in bright spirits, and he somehow avoided discussing his feelings. Amber wanted to know all about what Clayton had been doing since his arrival, and he was happy to tell her all about everything, especially his friendship with Takis. There were moments of uncomfortable silence between them now and then, but Clayton tried to keep things cordial. He wanted to reach out and hold her. He wanted to kiss her again, but he'd been warned, and he knew what this place would do to him if he broke the rules.

They had finished the day with only one woman giving them trouble and still had time to go to the break room. When Clayton opened the door, he noticed Nix leaning against the wall.

"Nix!" Clayton called out in excitement.

"Hey, Clayton." Nix's eyes darted behind Clayton to Amber, and he nodded at her.

"What are you doing here?" Clayton asked him as he walked across the small room to shake his hand.

"I was hoping to see you," Nix confessed.

"Oh?"

"Well, you hadn't stopped by in a while, and I wanted to make sure you were doing alright," Nix said and rubbed the back of his neck. Clayton looked back to Amber, who was staring a hole through Nix. Nix frightened her. She had only really seen him in meetings, and she told Clayton in confidence that was enough for her.

"I'm sorry, Nix. I should have stopped by more."

"Well, having you around helping me out, um, made me realize how quiet that room is when no one else is in there. With Takis gone, I don't have many visitors."

"Shit," Clayton muttered. "Amber and I finish early all the time. I'll make it a habit to see you every few days."

"We just finished," Amber stepped up beside Clayton, her voice timid. She cleared her throat and spoke a little louder. "You can sit with us right now if you want."

"I'd like that," Nix said and looked down at her. Clayton could tell he was trying his best to be as non-threatening as possible. He clapped Nix on the back.

"Great!" Clayton took his regular seat and watched as Amber sat in hers. "You can tell her about the nail you tried to hand me."

The pattern continued smoothly for a while. They collected the women, and Amber sentenced them. They would finish early and spend the day laughing and talking in the break room, and every so often, Nix would drop by with stories of his time with Takis and Clayton. Amber warmed to Nix eventually. Her laughs became less forced, and she called his name with enthusiasm when he opened the door. Clayton was finally happy in the After. He had Amber, he had friendship, and finally, the world made sense again.

68

Amber sat with Clayton in the break room after a reasonably straightforward day. Amber had a chair that was all her own now, an oversized one without arms, where she would sit in the lotus position. She liked sitting with her legs up so she could remove her shoes. They were too snug, and this way, she could keep her feet off the floor. The carpet had seen better days.

"I hope Nix shows up today. It's been a few days, I think," Clayton remarked.

"How was it the first time you saw him?" She asked him, looking down, picking at her shirt.

"Takis and Nix played a joke. Nix acted like an animal. I thought he was going to kill me."

"Really?"

"Oh yeah, scared the shit out of me," Clayton laughed.

"He's not told that one," she giggled.

"Probably trying not to embarrass me. Nix has been there for me when I needed it. He was there when I screwed up with Leon."

"Who's that?" Amber frowned. Clayton sighed and recounted how the Darkness took Leon.

"I see the people you sentence. They seem like they're in a trance. Leon was, I don't know, possessed? The Darkness spoke to me through him. It was like he was just a shell," Clayton paused. "It happened to me once."

"What do you mean?" Amber asked, confused.

"The Darkness took me over once, and I don't remember anything."

"Wait," she said, stunned, "the Darkness went inside you?"

"Yes," Clayton scowled, "when I retrieved Reverend Price." Amber felt the air chill as the name left his lips. She hadn't thought of that man in a long time. She had kept his memory at a distance after the images of them stopped in her cell. She had been disgusted with herself for what she'd done, and she was equally nauseated by what he'd done to her. That wasn't how a man of the Lord was supposed to behave. She wanted to know the story, though, even if her conscience told her to change the subject. She had always been curious to a fault.

"You saw Reverend Price? In the After?" Amber asked. Clayton paused for a moment. She could feel his eyes scanning her face.

"I let the Darkness in so it could take him. We had been ordered to send him to the Brilliance, but the Darkness spoke up and said the reverend belonged with it." He finished. His tone was indifferent, but his eyes were sharp. He was watching her for a reaction.

"Jesus, Clayton," Amber whispered. She had no respect for the Reverend Price. She had even grown to loathe him in a way, but she felt a nagging sense of guilt at the thought of him in the Darkness. If she'd said no to him, could it have saved his soul? Would he be here in the After instead of suffering? She didn't know how to feel upon hearing of his demise. She had such strong feelings towards him before. She felt for just a fleeting moment that she couldn't live without him. How could things have fallen apart so quickly? All she could recall was the intense feeling of need, and then just as soon as that came over her, it was replaced by shame.

She tried to think of one moment between them that could have facilitated that kind of emotion, but she could not. He wasn't attractive. He wasn't funny. He didn't like to read anything besides the bible, and he had no passion for art. There was nothing in their conversations that even remotely interested her. Maybe she wasn't consciously blocking him out. Could it be that outside of that one moment of physical contact, there was nothing at all? She noticed Clayton shifting in his seat out of the corner of her eye. She'd almost forgotten he was there.

"You don't have to worry about him anymore. He'll never hurt you or anyone else again," Clayton said in triumph. Her heart sank into her stomach. Clayton knew what had happened between the two of them. It was something she'd hoped to never speak of, something she knew if it was admitted out loud, it would somehow be real again. She shuddered and wished he would change the subject, but that didn't seem plausible.

"So, how did he end up there?" She asked, trying to mask her discomfort. Clayton recalled the incident. He spared no detail. He seemed pleased with what happened to Donald and took pride in telling the story. Amber sat in silence.

"Just knowing he put his hands on you makes me sick. I would have thrown him in myself, but I was scared to hurt Takis' chances of leaving," Clayton claimed. His arrogance surprised her. Amber leaned forward.

"Clayton, don't you think you're being a little too harsh?" She asked. Clayton sat back in his chair, looking offended.

"He's a rapist. He hurt you. He deserved to go to hell. You should be happy."

"Clayton, there's a lot more to that than you know." She closed her eyes and took a deep breath. "He didn't rape me. He asked me, and I said yes. It was a mistake, but," she shrugged. Clayton paled. His mouth opened and closed as if he was about to speak and then thought better of it. "I wanted to tell you about what happened between us. I was going to, one night when you walked me home. I'm sorry." She reached out and put her hand on his knee, but he recoiled.

"Stop apologizing!" He blurted out, tears flooding his eyes. "He was to blame."

"Clayton," she stood and paced around the room. She had already gone this far. She wanted to get all of it out in the open, so they could get past this. "I was pregnant. He was the father."

"You say that like you actually cared for him," Clayton said, exploding out of his chair.

"Cared for him? At the time, I was so sure of it. I chose to be with him. I thought I loved him. I realize now I made a mistake. I'm sorry if this hurts you, but I refuse to lie to you," she stated. Clayton stared at her, his eyes wide. She could see the veins in his neck stand out as he clenched his fists so hard they shook.

"What about us?" He spluttered.

"What?" She wasn't prepared for that.

"Us. What about us?"

"Clayton, you were my best friend. You still are," she said. Clayton turned his back to her. She didn't know if it was out of disgust or shame.

"But I died for you," he said weakly. "They blamed me, he blamed me. I ran. I died. I'm here because of you," his voice grew in volume as he spoke.

"I wanted to tell you about the baby. Things were moving so fast, and I was so confused. What was I going to tell my family? What would the town think? I'd even thought of running away with him."

"He was evil. He hurt us both," Clayton spat as he turned to face her. His face was red, and his nostrils flared. "What about our kiss? I told you that you were my everything!"

"I shouldn't have done that," she said as she stepped toward him. "You do realize I died that night? I'm trying to talk to you.

You aren't listening." Clayton made no sound. She wasn't even sure he was breathing. He walked past her in a daze and exited the room. Amber sat back down and placed her head in her hands. There was no going back from this. She gave it a few moments, enough time for him to get to Nix. He would go to his friend, and she would go to hers. She left the break room and started for Feme's office. She'd know how to handle this.

Clayton stood in the hallway. Everything was out of focus, and his thoughts were jumbled. He had forgotten for a moment where he was. All he could feel was a sharp pain in his temples as it became harder to breathe. His chest tightened, and for a brief instant, he swore he could feel his heart beating. He needed answers.

"Amber Ward life list," Clayton spat and flicked his wrist. Nothing appeared. He scoffed and walked down the hallway a little way, then stopped. "AMBER WARD LIFE LIST," he said louder and flicked his wrist again. Again there was nothing. He balled his fists up and grunted.

"Clayton? Are you alright?" He heard Enrique ask from beside him. Clayton turned to him. His head was tilted to the side, a look of genuine concern on his face. Clayton let himself go. He grabbed Enrique by his shirt collar and slammed him against the wall hard enough to hear the air leave his body.

"If you ever speak to me again, ever, I swear to God the doctor won't be able to put you back together," Clayton growled, spit flying from his mouth and landing on Enrique's face. Enrique nodded furiously, and Clayton released him. Clayton looked both ways at all the people in the hallway gawking at him. "WHAT THE FUCK ARE YOU LOOKING AT?" He yelled, and everyone scurried away from him. He saw that he was close to the double doors to the cells. He marched angrily towards them and pushed them open with enough force for them to bang against the inner walls. He walked through and slammed the doors hard behind him. He could barely see for the hot, angry tears that blurred his vision. His mind was a series of images of her face, of their time together, and then of her and the reverend. The tightness was too much; it was like someone was sitting on his chest. He was sucking in air at an uncontrollable rate. No matter how much he took in, it wasn't enough. He was suffocating.

"AMBER WARD LIFE LIST!" He screamed at the top of his lungs and flicked his wrist as hard as he could. The air crackled around his hand. It sounded as if it was sizzling. He felt it, finally in his left hand. Her list was his. He felt a tickle on his upper lip. He reached up with his right hand and wiped the blood from his nose. He stared at it for a brief moment before wiping the blood on his shirt. He sniffed hard and looked down to his prize. Three sheets of paper, the story of her entire life. He clutched it tightly against his chest. He took a deep breath and started walking, trying to get his breathing under control. He started counting his steps to focus himself. He wanted the pain in his chest to subside. A ringing in his ears had started when he left the break room, and it had grown so loud it was almost unbearable. He had to keep going. The numbers began to add up. It took time, but the noise started to fade, and his feelings started to rush in. Amber was the one person he trusted and cared for more than anyone else. Hadn't he suffered enough?

As he walked, his anger was replaced by sadness. How could he have been so naive? Nothing ever worked out for him, nothing in his entire life, and it was even more so in the After. He just wanted a moment of peace, not where every second was spent with unease, constantly living afraid he would make a mistake and extend his time here. He longed for just one day where this place wouldn't throw obstacle after obstacle in his path to the Brilliance. He hadn't experienced a day like that, and he definitely wouldn't see one in the foreseeable future. He kept walking, forcing his mind to be blank. He was alone. He didn't want to speak to anyone, and he didn't want to see another soul.

Once he felt he was in control, he looked down at the three papers in his hand. He read through every lie she told and everything she'd stolen. She'd taken candy from a store when her father took her to Richmond when she was eleven. Clayton braced himself as he got to her relationship with Donald Price, the moment that set them on a collision course to the After. He continued through the second page that brought up her finding out she was pregnant and the lies she told to conceal it. Clayton turned to the third and final page, and his blood ran cold. He stopped and reread it.

"Oh," he said weakly. "Oh, no." He read it a third time before letting all three sheets fall from his hand and fade away. "No," he whispered. "No. No. No." He walked over and sat against the wall between two cell doors, his spirit broken, his heart in pieces. He put his head in his hands, and Clayton let go of all his hope. The After had won. It was a cruel joke. He sat in silence. He lost track of time, but he heard a voice in his mind. Feme was calling to him. If he didn't go, she'd just come to him, and there would be hell to pay. He stood and took a deep breath.

"Feme's office," he said, and he turned and took the door there.

70

"Clayton," Feme started as soon as he opened the door, "Is this going to be a fucking problem?" Clayton looked around the room. Amber was seated in the chair in front of him, doing what she could to avoid eye contact. Nix stood in the corner, leaning against the wall.

"No, Feme," Clayton said as he closed the door behind him.

"Well, it certainly sounds like a fucking problem. You attacked Enrique in the hall." Feme's voice was firm and tinged with anger.

"Oh, fuck Enrique," Clayton dismissed. Amber turned in her chair to face him, her eyes wide in disbelief, and Nix gave a soft laugh. Feme shot her eyes to Nix in warning.

"Oh, come on, Feme. He has a point," Nix defended.

"There is no point. Clayton, you do not, for any fucking reason, put your hands on anyone here, am I clear?" Feme barked as she leaned forward, her finger jabbed at him.

"Yes, ma'am," Clayton answered.

"Good," Feme eased back. "Now, this situation with Amber-"

"There is no situation with Amber," Clayton interrupted. "She's my assignment. I don't have to like it. I just want to get out of here, see my family and Takis again. She keeps doing her job, and I only intervene if needed. As far as I'm concerned, we don't even have to speak," Clayton explained. Amber shook her head.

"See? How are we supposed to work like this?" She asked, pointing her thumb in his direction.

"Quiet," Feme directed. "Clayton, I am giving you the benefit of the doubt here. You've been an asset to me since you arrived. I was beginning to like you. However, if you fuck up this girl's duties, I promise you'll be the last person on the boat to the Brilliance. Are we clear?"

"Absolutely," Clayton said. "You have my word."

"Alright," Feme motioned towards the door. "Now, the two of you go outside while I speak to Amber." Clayton turned and opened the door. He waited for Nix to exit before following behind him.

"I heard her story. Now I want to hear yours," Nix said to Clayton, who folded his arms as he leaned against the Acquisitions door.

"Nothing to say. She's a terrible person, Nix. I've been so stupid," Clayton complained, his voice quivering.

"I'm sure it's a misunderstanding-"

"You have no idea what she's done," Clayton said and shot Nix a cold glare. Nix held his hands up.

"I don't want to argue, Clayton. I just want to know you're going to be alright," Nix replied. Clayton stared at him, dumbfounded, his mouth slightly open. "What are you looking at?" Nix asked.

"Your nose," Clayton pointed, "it's bleeding." Nix's hand shot up and wiped the blood from his nose tip. He stared at it for a few moments hoping this wasn't what he thought it was.

"*Soon, Nix,*" the Darkness, said in the corners of his mind.

"Soon I'll have him and Feme, and you will have your family." Nix smiled at Clayton, trying to hide the excruciating pain.

"This happens, nothing to worry about." Nix wiped most of the blood away and rubbed his hands together.

"After the thing with Amber, I had a nose bleed too," Clayton trailed off for a second before snapping back to reality and continuing. "See, this is part of the problem. This place doesn't make any sense. We're dead! You've been dead for ages. You're a ghost. Why would your nose bleed? It's stupid," Clayton huffed, throwing his arms up in the air in disgust.

Because I make the rules here. Nix froze.

"What?" He said softly.

"I said, you're a ghost-"

"No," Nix waved his hand. "Clayton, I have to get in the office. I need to get this to stop." He pointed to the blood dripping off of his chin. Clayton nodded.

"Can you come by later?" Clayton begged. Nix was already fumbling for his key.

"Of course. Goodbye, Clayton," He quickly unlocked the door and hurried through, leaning against it with his arms out to his side once it was closed.

71

"You could have ruined everything," he whispered. The blood ran down his face to his neck.

Oh, shut up. He can't hear me. Only you can. It's almost time.

Nix stood upright from the door and started to his desk. His head was on fire, and his vision was blurry. Nix made it to his desk, took a cloth from a pile there, and wiped his face. His blood was thick and had already started to clot in his facial hair.

"You have to stop speaking to me like this. I can't concentrate." Nix threw the rag down on the desk.

"You're right," he heard from somewhere in the distance. Nix looked at a stack of items in the corner. He hesitantly walked toward them. He could feel the hairs standing up on the back of his neck, and the temperature in the entire room had dropped.

"Other side, Nix," he heard coming from the useless trinkets. Nix stepped slowly around the mound of things. He knew what was there. He passed by it every day. He confiscated a great mirror in 1670 from a group of Hungarians who worshipped it. It belonged to Countess Elizabeth Bathory. She would bathe in the blood of her victims then stand naked in front of this mirror, admiring herself. It was a massive piece of silver coated in a mixture of tin and mercury. The bezels were gold with symbols all around them. Nix never did find out what any of the symbols were. The back of the mirror was held by a gigantic oak brace that Nix himself had rebuilt entirely in the early 1900s. It was an exquisite antique, one of the finest mirrors produced in Venice from that period. Still, it always gave Nix an uncomfortable feeling. Several of the items here did. Some of them gave off an evil aura. Most of the time, Nix would chuckle to himself and move along, telling himself he needed to get out more, but he never felt that way about the mirror. There was something that made it rotten and unnatural.

He stared into the mirror but did not see his reflection. Instead, he saw his enemy, the one who took everything from him and taunted him from afar. The Son. He stood in the reflection, smiling. His skin was golden. His eyes were without iris or pupil, just white and frightening. He had no shirt on. His body was well defined and large. He only wore silk pajama bottoms in black and was barefooted. The only thing Nix could make out behind Him was a fire in a fireplace, but it wasn't clear. It was as if it was covered in a slight haze. His hair was jet black and unkempt as if he had just woken up. A five o'clock shadow accentuated his perfect jaw.

"You," Nix whispered, placing his massive hands on both sides of the mirror.

"Surprise!" The Son said as He held His hands out in glee. "You'll have to forgive me, I'm entertaining right now, but I got tired of you complaining. So, here I am."

"You," Nix repeated. The Son smirked and shifted His eyes left to right.

"Yes, it really is me."

"Why are you here?" Nix felt the left side of the mirror's bezel creak as he tightened his grip. The Son looked at Nix's hand.

"Careful, or we'll have to go back to the old way of doing things," the Son warned. Nix pulled his hands back. "Good, alright, we need to talk. I'm worried about you. You've changed, and not for the better," the Son tutted. Nix took a step back and tried to contain his anger. "When I made you this offer, you were all in. You killed Clayton, you killed the girl, you destroyed Takis. When he got here, I barely recognized him," the Son sucked in air through tightened lips. "He hardly had any teeth left."

"Your point?" Nix was getting impatient. He hated these games.

"Once you let me in, you gave me a free pass to your mind. I can tell what you're thinking, Nix. You've been having doubts," He admonished. Nix looked away. "You need to stick to the plan," the Son warned. "I am too close, and I will not have you mess this up because you feel bad for some hillbilly from Virginia."

"Clayton-" Nix started to argue.

"Is mine. He will belong to me, along with Feme, and you are going to help me as we agreed," the Son interrupted, his voice oozing disdain.

"What about Amber?" Nix asked. The Son chuckled and rolled his eyes.

"Who cares? She's not even supposed to be here. She should have gone into the Brilliance the night she died."

"What?" Nix choked.

"I interrupted the order and sent something different to the woman who makes the garments," he said, sneering in disapproval. "Clayton was supposed to leave with Takis too. I have his golden order around here somewhere." He looked around playfully. "Probably in my other pants."

"How?" Nix felt sweat break out on his brow, and his skin went clammy.

"You were here when this place was created. I was a major part of it until you ruined everything," the Son's brow dropped. His mouth frowned. He was getting angry. "Nothing goes through here that I don't see first."

"I ruined everything? You killed all of us. You were torturing us for fun. It wasn't what She wanted. She wasn't cruel," Nix growled. The Son closed His eyes and breathed in and out before opening them slowly and grinning.

"I'm not here to argue. I'm here to help you get your motivation back. I don't need this good-friend-Nix. I need the warrior. I need the hunter. The savage. I need the monster."

Nix was silent. He loathed the Son. Clayton could have been free, Amber could have been free, even he could have been free a long time ago. He allowed this thing to consume him, to drive him.

"I think I made a mistake."

"Oh?" The Son seemed genuinely surprised by this.

"Yes. I should have told you no. I can't believe I sent Takis to you." Nix put his palms to his forehead. The Son nodded mockingly as Nix spoke. "I'm out. I am not your puppet. I just wish I would have seen it before I lost my friend," Nix finished. The Son slowly brought His hands up and clapped.

"Bravo," He rubbed his chin. "Well, if that is your decision."

"It is," Nix said firmly. The Son sighed.

"Well, I guess this is goodbye. I'll just have to go back to what I was doing, try to find someone else."

"I guess you will," Nix finished, a feeling of trepidation coming over him. There was no way this devil would let him go so easily.

"Come, darling, let's go back to bed," The Son said while staring at Nix. He held out his left hand, and Rae came into view and took it. She was wearing a white nightgown that had several bloodstains on it. Her face and neck were covered in cuts and bruises. Her eyes were empty and dark. Nix leaped forward and grabbed the mirror again, almost knocking it over. His breath fogged the mirror. A guttural roar emerged from somewhere deep inside him.

"YOU BASTARD!" Nix screamed. The Son shoved her to the side and walked towards him in the reflection, their noses almost touching. His eyes went from white to red.

"That's right!" He screamed back. "She's mine! And I'll tell you what I'm going to do. I am going to wear your face. I am going to gather your children, and I am going to let them watch as I murder her over and over again!"

"Stop!" Nix pleaded as tears ran down his face.

"Then when I tire of killing her, she can watch as I kill your children again and again. I don't have many things here that give me joy, but this is one of them. Hey, did you know that there's a way out of here? All they have to do is ask me to erase them from existence. I can do that. I will make it my personal goal to get your family to beg me to end it." His breath fogged up the other side of the mirror.

"Please," Nix begged.

"Please," the Son mocked. "You are the reason I am here. If you had kept your mouth shut, none of this would have happened. You brought this upon yourself with our deal. You are going to get over whatever tug of morality you are having and do what I want. I will have the Shaw boy! I will have Feme! You will complete your end of the bargain, or they will continue to suffer! Are we clear?!" He boomed, the room shaking at the sound of His voice. Nix winced.

"Yes," Nix whimpered. The Son's eyes faded from red to white, but the scowl on His face didn't subside. "When next we speak, it will be the last time," He backed away a few steps.

"Good," Nix leaned into the mirror. "Please don't hurt her. Just put her aside till this is over, I beg of you," Nix sobbed. The Son paused, seeming to contemplate Nix's request. Finally, He smiled.

"No, I don't think I will." He put His hand back out, and she came into view and took it again. He turned to face her. He looked at Nix before turning and kissing her. Nix clutched the edges of the mirror, listening to the bezel snap. He screamed and pitched the mirror across to the back wall. It shattered and made a loud thud as it hit the ground. If He wanted a monster, a monster is what He would get. Nix tore through box after box, destroying priceless and irreplaceable items. He lashed out until he wore himself out. Gasping for breath, he lay in the mess and rubble of his own making.

"I'll kill you, I swear it," Nix muttered to himself. He reached up towards his face and felt his nose pouring blood.

There he is.

72

"If you can't say anything nice to one another, don't say anything at all. Am I clear?" Feme warned from her doorway as Amber left the office.

"You'll have no problems from me," Amber said, looking back.

"Like I have a choice?" Clayton said as he shrugged.

"You don't," Feme snapped. Clayton shook his head and stared at the ground.

"Well, let's just get this over with," he said. Amber wanted to say something to him. Maybe with Feme present Clayton would try to contain himself, but she thought better of it. Feme had enough problems within these halls, and playing sitter to the two of them was unfair. She told herself that she would find a way to do this on her own. She would fix this. This was Clayton. After all, she knew him better than anyone. He would come around eventually.

She looked his face up and down, and he bit his lip. She recalled, suddenly, the feeling of his lips on hers, and she believed it was that kiss that brought things to where they were now. She had regretted it the second it was over. She knew it when she pulled away from him. She was ill and vulnerable. He was the only person

331

she trusted, and she desperately wanted his help, but what could he have done? He was just a boy, and after she'd kissed him, how could she possibly approach him with the fact she was pregnant with another man's child?

She coasted through her memories back to when she closed the door that night, telling Clayton she'd see him the next day. She had to apologize. It was a beautiful moment between them, and he really did touch her heart, but he was her best friend. She had no idea what to say to him when she saw him again.

"That was a mistake," she said as she leaned into the door, touching it with her forehead.

"What was?" Her mother asked from behind her. Amber nearly leapt. She turned and faced Ruth, who was wiping her hands with a rag.

"Oh, just walking down the road. I still feel terrible. I shouldn't have done that. Clayton had to bring me home." She walked away from the door and approached the stairs leading to the second floor. "I'm going to retire early unless you need me?"

"No, go on to bed, dear," Ruth said back to her. "Do you need anything?" Amber shook her head no, and Ruth approached her. She placed the back of her hand against Amber's cheek. Ruth's hand felt so warm, she almost reached up to hold it there.

"You're cold. Awfully cold. Let me make you some hot tea," Ruth said, turning from her.

"No," Amber waved her hand. "I just need sleep. Plus, my stomach isn't well. I don't want anything on it."

"All right, I'll come check on you later," Ruth sighed. That was the last thing her mother said to her. Amber recalled the pain in her abdomen as she shuffled slowly up the stairs. Her legs were weak, and each step felt like a swift punch that sent a shockwave from her stomach down to her toes. Thinking back, she wished she'd told her mother she loved her. She should have called back to her mother from the top of the stairs and asked for help. She knew she was sick, but she had no clue she would be dead soon. She would give anything to return to that day and do it all differently.

Clayton had no idea how much guilt she carried with her. She felt like all of this was her fault, and she regretted it every second. She did care for him, she didn't want him to be in pain, but she was suffering too. All she wanted was for him to see it from her point of view. She left her family behind with so many questions. She never got to live her life. Amber wanted to see New York. She wanted to see the ocean. She wanted so much from life.

That's why she knew they would never work. Clayton had wanted a large family on the farm to raise livestock, and she wanted to experience everything the world had to offer. She wanted to take up painting. She'd once overheard a woman in Richmond talking about a great violinist that performed a concert in town. Those were the things she yearned for in life, and while Amber loved her mother with every fiber of her being, she always looked at her as a waste.

Every moment of her mother's life was spent raising her father's children. Amber felt there was so much more than that, and she would break free of Clover and find it. Her heart ached at the thought. She didn't make it out of Clover. She never heard a violin. She never saw the ocean, and she definitely never made it to New York. Not while she was alive anyway. She looked over at Clayton, who was still staring at the ground. She shook her head, called her door, and walked through.

73

1986

THE AFTER

Clayton took a seat across from Amber after an exhausting day. He hadn't spoken in a long time. He hadn't wanted to. He couldn't stand the sight of her. He prayed more than once that they would be separated or that he would be called up to the Brilliance. Amber didn't deserve him and being in her presence made his skin crawl. He was such a good person in life, surely he couldn't have much time left here. He'd counted each time they made it to the break room after their retrievals. The count was up to three hundred and eighty-three, so it was at least that many days. There were sets where Amber barely finished in time, but he didn't count those. Those days would have gone smoother if he'd have helped her, but he didn't. He didn't interact when she would retrieve souls. He would stay as far back as possible. If a soul was belligerent or feisty, he let her handle it. If she asked him a question, he'd nod or shake his head. If he caught her looking at him, he made a conscious effort to look away. The less interaction they had, the better he felt.

He hoped that when he finally left her behind in this place, that Nix would be the one to sign the book for him. He didn't want Amber to do it. He didn't want her to have the satisfaction of

334

it. He thought about Leon and how the After decided he deserved the Darkness even though he was in the cells, how the order had said he hadn't learned his lesson. He smiled to himself at the thought of Amber befalling the same fate. He knew that Feme was hoping they would at least be cordial, and Clayton had vowed not to make things difficult for her. Yet as the days began to pass, he also found himself angry at Feme. Why was she in the position she was? She was as morally bankrupt as Amber was in his eyes. He'd had enough of all of them.

Clayton had always been a reasonable person. He was never the type to hold a grudge, but the After was relentless. He knew that Amber wanted him to see things from her perspective, but he'd read her life list. He knew every secret she kept. He didn't know how much longer he could suffer this way. How could she do this to him? He always treated her with respect and care. He'd have done anything for her. She used him. She deceived him. All he saw was a liar. There was a wound on his heart that would never mend. The only thoughts that brought him comfort were his mother and Eve. He would see them again one day, and that day couldn't come soon enough.

"Are you ever going to talk to me?" She asked. He recoiled at the sound of her voice. He realized he'd been smiling as he thought of his family. Amber must have taken that as an opening to speak to him. He locked eyes with her, and he watched her lean back in her chair. Her eyes were soft and concerned. Her lips were drawn tight, and it looked as if she was pitying him. The feeling of rage that had been bubbling beneath the surface spilled over. Clayton felt a burning sensation through his very core. He hated her, and if she said one more word, he would make her regret it.

"You could at least say something."

"Shut up," he spat, "I don't want to hear anything you have to say," he said, his voice shaking in anger.

"Don't you talk to me that way," she stuttered.

"I'll talk to you any way I goddamn please," he chuckled.

"Listen-" She tried to interrupt.

"I don't have to listen to shit," Clayton said through gritted teeth. He was outraged. *She thinks I'm still just that boy from down the road, the one who'd give her the shirt off my back*, he fumed internally. *She doesn't respect me. She thinks she can manipulate me.* He wasn't the same person she knew. Clayton had changed the moment he read her life list. He stopped caring. He'd been good in life, and it landed him here.

"You're no better than the women you condemn. I died because of you," he hissed.

"What did you say?" She gritted.

How dare she, he thought. *Like she had nothing to do with it.* She knew. She said as much when he retrieved her from the cells. He wouldn't have been on that ridge if it wasn't for her.

"I hate you, Amber. I despise you. I would give anything to never see you again. With sins like yours, you should be sent to the Darkness. Hell, I would put you there myself now if I could, then maybe I could find some peace." Her eyes widened. He knew he'd crossed a line, but he was far from done.

"Go to Hell, Clayton," she spat back.

"I'm already in Hell," he laughed.

"Clayton," she took a deep breath, "are you so ready to throw away our entire friendship? Over what? Some misunderstanding? I was your only friend."

"You were never my friend," he said with disgust.

"Well, if that's the way you feel," she said with finality.

"That's the way I feel," he told her, his voice oozing sarcasm.

"You've gone too far, and I don't deserve to be treated this way." She shoved past him.

"Oh sure, leave everything ruined and walk away, just like you did before," he yelled after her.

"I didn't ruin anything," she wheeled around.

"Oh no? Reverend Price didn't give a damn about you. He just wanted to have you. And how stupid are you? You laid right down for him. Meanwhile, I'm up the road thinking about the life we could have had together. Your brother was going to kill me, did you know that? That perverted freak actually left the house looking to shoot me for something I didn't do!" Clayton let it all out. He didn't give a damn if it cost him a hundred years in a cell; she would know what she'd done to him. "My father hit me! Me! My sister lost her mother, but that wasn't enough, was it? She had to lose me too. None of this would have happened if you hadn't led me on."

"Get away from me," Amber warned, her eyes narrowed.

"Or what?" Clayton got right in her face, barely a few inches away. "You'll kill me again?"

"I DIDN'T KILL YOU! YOU KILLED YOURSELF!" She barked in his face. He smirked at her and shook his head. He turned and walked back to his seat.

"You will be here forever because you won't accept responsibility for your actions. What the hell is wrong with me? What did I ever see in you?" He ran his left hand through his hair.

"I had to watch you die over and over again. I watched you hit that rock. I saw my mother hit you. I saw your father hit you too. I can't imagine what you went through, but I hurt too. I made a mistake that killed me. I lost a child and my life. You didn't have to sit there and experience it over and over again. You had Takis. You had Nix." She stepped toward him. "I was alone."

He looked up at her. That was the last straw. It was bad enough to not take fault in the events that led to his death, but to be a liar too? All these years, he'd thought of her as this perfect angel, a beacon of hope in this sea of shit he found himself afloat in. How could she be so rotten?

"I've seen your life list," Clayton said with icy calm. "I've seen Reverend Price's too." Clayton leaned back. He kept his eyes on her. He could have sworn he saw her shiver. "He had a thing for teenage girls. You weren't the first. He got in trouble in North Carolina. One of the girls told on him. He and his wife had to leave in the middle of the night. If he'd gotten caught, he would have hanged." Clayton cracked his knuckles, his voice was breaking every few seconds, and he found himself fighting to keep it in check.

"What?" She whispered.

"Pay attention. This is important. If he told you he loved you or made you feel special, he used you, and he lied. But that's not what made me so angry. The reverend decided to get rid of your mutual problem. Do you know what pennyroyal extract is?"

"No," Amber whispered. Clayton stood.

"I had to ask Doctor Rynerson why you'd give a pregnant woman pennyroyal. He said it's used to get rid of a pregnancy, but here's the rub: Price gave you way too much. You didn't die from the loss of the baby. You died from taking too much of the poison."

"Are you sure?" Amber gasped. He felt a quick flash of fury at her response but continued on.

"It's in his life list. He didn't intend to kill you, but he did. So, I was angry that you could defend the person who deceived you and murdered you." Clayton said in a hushed voice.

"I didn't know," she said as her eyes welled with tears.

"Are you really going to keep up this charade?" Clayton's words hung in the air, and she jerked. "You're going to keep this up? Alright."

"Clayton-"

"You sat in his kitchen, and he gave you a cup of hot tea. You remember that? I mean, we just talked about it. It's what killed you." She didn't answer. She just looked into his eyes. "I would have never hurt you. I would have given you anything you wanted. You really were my everything. I meant what I said to you that day," Clayton continued.

"Stop, " Amber commanded.

"But you knew that," Clayton laughed darkly. "You met with

Donald, and he told you the pennyroyal would end the baby's life. You let him give it to you."

"Stop," Amber repeated, putting her hand up to her mouth. She started to cry.

"Oh, so now you're upset? All of this?" He waved his hand around. "It's because of you. I AM HERE BECAUSE OF YOU! You're my friend? Are you serious?"

"I was a child. I was afraid. I didn't know what to do."

"So, you let that man fuck you, then kill you?" He laughed and shook his head. "I'm glad I got to be the one to tell you. I'm glad you got to hear this from me. I get to see you realize just how stupid you really-" She slapped him across the face.

"You bastard," she choked out. He placed his hand on his cheek where her palm connected and rubbed it. He stared blankly at her. He was stunned; he didn't know she had it in her. He let his hand fall back to his side.

"Why are you mad at me?" He questioned. "I'm the good guy here. You've killed two people." She let out a small gasp, walked out, and slammed the door. He sat back down, livid. How dare she try to come up with more excuses! He wanted to hurt her. He wanted to see her cry. He wanted this place to punish her for her betrayal. The look on her face when she stormed out made him feel better, but it also made him feel shame. Clayton hardened his heart. The feeling didn't last long, but for a brief moment, he was content with what he'd done. Then the bitterness came bubbling back to the surface. His mother would be ashamed. He just wanted out of this place. He didn't care how.

"I wish you were here, Takis," he said.

74

F eme reached into her desk and took out a light purple sheet of paper and ink vial. She shook it till it was white and popped the top off, then grabbed her quill and wrote:

**Clayton Shaw and Amber Ward are failing as partners,
relationship irreparable
Requesting reassignment**

Feme sat back and watched the paper. Amber leaned forward, curious at what was happening.

"How long does it take?" Amber asked her. Feme held up her hand as she concentrated on the writing, and less than a minute later, words started appearing as if being written by an invisible hand.

Standby for new assignments.

Another minute passed before more words formed.

**Effective immediately, Astrid, daughter of Styrr, will be
promoted to Director
Amber Ward is found to be unfit for Soul Retrieval and will
be transferred to the role of Seamstress.
Feme will be reassigned to Clayton Shaw for his reeducation
within Soul Retrieval.
Black marks added to Amber Ward and Clayton Shaw for
failure to meet expectations.**

Feme read the words over and over. She was being sent back out into the field. She was being let out of this office and would be free of the shackles of leadership. She could see the world again, if only for brief moments. She didn't have to stare at orders and make decisions she always second-guessed. She held in a gasp. She didn't want Amber to see how happy this made her.

**Amber Ward is to tell Clayton Shaw of her new assignment
You should be present if any issues should arise**

Feme tossed her quill down. *Of course, there would be something stupid added at the end,* she thought. Feme handed the order to Amber, who was seated across from her. It didn't take long for her to read it.

"Oh, did I cost you your position, Feme? Forget it then. I'll make it work somehow," Amber said.

"It's fine, Amber," Feme dismissed.

"No, it isn't," Amber argued.

"Yes, it is. I need to get out of this office anyway, and Astrid will make a fine director."

"So, this has already happened?" Amber asked, putting the paper down on her desk.

"Yes, effective immediately." Feme stood and walked to the door.

"Let's go get Nix," Amber said, standing.

"Why?" Feme asked her, pausing at the door and looking back curiously. "Do you think Clayton might try to hurt you?"

"Clayton wasn't raised that way," Amber said, sounding sure.

"That wasn't a no," Feme retorted.

"He wasn't raised that way," Amber repeated.

"Then why do you feel we need him?" Feme inquired.

"Just in case," Amber added. "He could defuse the situation. After all, they're really close." Nix had stopped by two or three times to chat with Feme, nothing serious. He would just tell her he was "checking in." For the first time, they were actually friendly. He'd even made the suggestion of helping out more. They'd spent so long hating one another, it was a pleasant change. She had spared more than a few moments feeling sympathy for his loved ones and his tribe. She had no idea the pain he had endured and felt a pang of guilt for some of the fights she'd started with him.

"Would Nix help you? Are you two close?" Feme turned to face Amber.

"We get along if that's what you're asking." Amber looked lost in thought for a moment. She cocked her head. "And if Clayton were to lose his temper, Nix being there could go a long way. There is no way Clayton would try and challenge Nix."

"You expect him to attack you?" Feme asked.

"No, I don't see it coming to that. I was just making-."

"This place changes a person," Feme interrupted. "I know it changed me. I know he acted awful, and I do plan on ripping his ass properly. Let's get this done, but I need you to do something for me." Feme put her hand on the doorknob, her back to Amber.

"That is?"

"Don't let what that boy said get to you. This will all be over soon enough," Feme reassured her.

"Okay," Amber sighed.

"Alright, let's go get Nix." Feme turned the knob and heard Amber following in step with her across the hall. They knocked on Acquisition's door, and it didn't take long for Nix to answer. He opened the door just a crack and peeked out.

"Ladies, how are you?" He was quite chipper. His eyes lit up, and he seemed pleased to see them both. "What can I do for you?"

"Clayton and Amber have been reassigned, and Amber has to break the news according to this order," Feme said and held the page out to him.

"So, you want me there for...?" He snickered and jerked his head back slightly. "What, in case he goes crazy and tries to hurt her? Tries to hurt you?" He pointed to them both in turn, then rubbed his eyebrow and laughed. "This is Clayton we're talking about. He wouldn't raise his hand to anyone."

"He did to Takis," Feme said in a matter-of-fact tone. Nix looked lost for a moment.

"That was different."

"Was it?" Feme asked.

"Absolutely, but I'll go if it makes you feel better," Nix shrugged. Then his brows knit together. "Let's do it at my Fork."

"Why?" Feme asked.

"Because if he does lose his temper, it will just be the four of us," he suggested.

"That's...actually a great idea," Feme agreed. "I don't want anyone else involved in this mess."

"I'll be along in a moment," he smiled. "You go on ahead. I'll meet you there."

75

Nix closed the door and started to his desk. He retrieved the denim jeans Astrid had made for him. He never left Acquisitions anymore without wearing pants. He'd finally felt a moment of shame. It was bad enough that he was different and stood out, but running around naked made it worse somehow. He also tried to wear shoes, but they were too uncomfortable. The same could be said for shirts. He felt constricted while he wore one as if he was suffocating. It took time to get used to pants.

Now.

He froze. They hadn't spoken since He'd come to Nix inside the mirror. He felt his anger rise and snorted.

"Really?" He said out loud and a little more aggressively than he meant to.

Yes, really. Don't forget the ink.

He yanked the bottom door of the desk open and picked up a vial of orange ink. He turned it over in his hand and took a deep breath in an attempt to calm himself. The thought of the Son abusing Rae had not left his thoughts since their last encounter. What was he doing to her when Nix wasn't able to see? He pushed the feeling down, almost as if he was swallowing it. This was it. Everything would end today. He would get everyone in the Fork and trap them there. Two women and a young man throwing a temper tantrum would be nothing for him. He would have his family back today. His anger subsided and was replaced with excitement. He thrust the ink into his pocket, along with a second vial that contained the same concoction that he used against Takis, and headed out into the hallway.

Clayton was sitting alone in the break room. When Nix opened the door and beckoned him to come, Clayton stood silently and followed. Nix didn't even have to raise his voice. Clayton didn't look like a man on the verge of hurting anyone. His head hung, and his shoulders slumped forward as if some invisible chain hung around his neck. He was pale. Broken. Nix could snap him in two. This was precisely what he needed.

Nix's Fork

Feme tapped Amber on the shoulder and pointed to Nix and Clayton as they arrived at the Fork. She felt a tension growing behind her eyes. She had a sinking feeling in the pit of her stomach. Her mind had raced to so many horrible outcomes; Clayton attacking Amber, Clayton attacking her, she even imagined Clayton striking Nix. Things didn't always run smoothly in the After, but she knew keeping them together would escalate this situation.

Feme remembered a young stone maker who became addicted to one of her girls. He spent every dime on her, and his lust turned into a delusion of love. He asked that girl to leave the comfort of home. He promised her the world and was angry at her rejection.

Feme had the man banned from the house. A year later, he crept in and killed the girl and himself. She also recalled how a scorned man twisted her friend's mind, which caused her to end her own life. She knew people could take love to a dark place. She liked Clayton, but he was in love with Amber, and he wasn't taking her rejection well. She had no idea if Clayton could be that extreme, but she wasn't going to find out. At the end of the day, she was tied to these people, and if something horrendous happened while she was in charge, it reflected on her, and she'd already been here long enough. She squeezed her hand into a fist and then slowly let it relax. She breathed out as she tried to find her center. She watched them approach. They were moving slowly, and Nix was talking to Clayton, but she couldn't make out anything he was saying.

"What was that?" Feme asked.

"Nix told me to show you respect. He reminded me you aren't my enemy that you're worried about me." Clayton said, keeping his eyes on the ground. Nix gave a slight smile to Feme. She nodded in acknowledgment.

"I'm not your enemy," she agreed, "but I need you to understand why we came out here, why I wanted Nix here. I want nothing but the best for you." She liked Clayton, but was she wanting the best for him, or what was best for her? She was about to break the cycle of her everyday routine and throw her responsibilities onto someone else. Plus, she was about to have a partner, and she knew that meant she was close to leaving. She had to be the closer of the two.

"Can we get my punishment over with?" Clayton interrupted. Feme looked at Amber and nodded. Amber took a deep breath and began.

"Clayton," Amber said to him calmly. He was nervous. He knew he was in trouble. He just didn't know how much. Feme felt herself relax. If he was nervous, there was less chance he would do something drastic.

"I've asked that we no longer work together. It's obvious you, and I can't do this anymore," Amber continued.

"And?" He asked.

"Astrid will be taking Feme's position. I will be the new seamstress, and Feme will be with you from here on out." Amber finished. Clayton scratched the top of his head.

"Is that it?"

"I guess so," Amber answered cautiously, turning her gaze to Feme.

"Fine by me," Clayton said as he walked a few paces away from the group. Feme let out a sigh of relief. She was grateful that he was taking this so well and that there would be no incident. Nix winked at her, and she felt the muscles in her neck relax.

"I have to ask one thing, though," Clayton said without turning back to them. His voice was hollow, like someone who had lost all their strength during an illness.

"What's that?" Feme questioned cautiously.

"How is this fucking fair?" He looked over his shoulder at Feme. "Can you answer that one? From the day I was born, I've been told I was 'good.' I've been told to do the right thing, and outside of one instance, I did. I obeyed the word of God. I listened to my parents. I did my chores. I didn't lie. I didn't steal. I didn't lust after anyone. I certainly didn't do what she did," he pointed to Amber. "All I wanted was to live my life in Clover, on my farm, with my wife and a couple of kids. Be a good father and husband, die, and end up in Heaven," he choked on the last word.

"Clayton, I know you had your life planned out in your head. I know what it's like to think you have it all figured out," Feme attempted to console him.

"I always thought we would be together. I thought it was destiny or fate. I always thought of us as we." He attempted to smile at Amber, but it came off insincere and forced. Feme watched as Nix circled to Clayton's left, his eyes narrow, his body slightly forward. He looked as if he was ready to pounce. Clayton noticed it too.

"I'm not going to hurt anyone, Nix. I'm not going to go crazy. Why would you think that?" His voice shook. Feme could hear the pain in his words, and it stung. Nix stood upright. His eyes widened.

"I'm sorry, I just...." Nix walked back over to Amber and Feme, looking away from Clayton.

"The day before I died was one of my best. I finally got to tell Amber how I felt about her, and I thought she felt that for me too. That night I could barely sleep. I was so excited to see her the next day."

"I know I hurt you. I know you're upset with me, but I am trying to make amends here. You just keep making it worse," Amber said.

"I found out she died," Clayton continued as if he didn't hear her. "She was pregnant. I had no clue. I was as shocked as everyone else. Not only that, but later I found out our reverend had been with her, the same man who stood on the road in front of her house and convinced everyone that I had done it. My father hit me. You know he'd never done that before? He never had to because I was good."

"Clayton," Feme tried to interrupt, but he pressed on.

"I died that day because I'm stupid, and then I wound up here. But I kept my faith. Even when I realized this place wasn't what I had read about, I kept my faith because one day, I would be reunited with her, the one person I believed I was made for. Then I found out she's just like everyone else. She wasn't special at all. She didn't care about me. I died for nothing. I am here because I believed in something that wasn't real."

"Alright, that's enough," Feme said. Amber had long since put her hands on her hips, but at his last sentiment, she threw her hands up into the air. Feme didn't want this to escalate any more than it already had.

"In this job, all I've seen is loss. Life is terrible. You think you're going to get ahead, and all you do is lose. Nothing lasts, so you hold onto something; the promise of a happy ending, a forever with your family, friends, your wife. Then you get here, and you think to yourself, 'it can't be worse than what I just went through,' but it is. It's so much worse," he finished. He walked away from the three of them. No one moved to go after him.

"Feme, what should we do?" Amber whispered.

"I'm going to send you to Astrid and let her get you set up in your new office, and I'm going to sit here with him. I have a feeling we're going to be here for a while," Feme said softly in response.

"Should I try talking to him?" Nix asked.

"No," Feme decided. "You've done more than enough. I can handle this." She looked at Nix, who wasn't looking at her but off in the distance, worry on his face. Feme followed his eyes and turned to see Clayton had walked to the Darkness and stood mere steps from the threshold. She could hear him weeping despite the distance.

"Clayton! What are you doing?" Feme cried out. She heard Amber gasp. Nix stayed silent.

Clayton took a few steps forward and was gone.

76

THE DARKNESS

It was the farm. There was no mistaking it. He was home, but nothing seemed right. The colors were muted, awash in gray. There was no wind, but there was a nasty chill in the air, a horrible cold that bore into his bones. The sheep lay dead in the fields. They'd been that way for a while, rotting in the dulled light of the sun. He could smell them from the porch, and it made the acid rise in his throat. He'd never smelled anything so rancid. He'd been around death since he was a child, and this wasn't just the odor of decay. This was something much worse, and even if he held his breath, it seemed to pierce his nostrils and linger.

He started through the open front door. If the sheep were in such a state, he panicked at the thought of his family. The wood on the house was crumbling. Everything was falling apart. The front door wasn't open. It was missing, and when he went through, the air seemed even colder. He wondered why he couldn't see the clouds of his breath. He stepped into the main hallway, and Reverend Price greeted him as they passed one another. His skin was ghastly pale. He was wearing his Sunday pulpit outfit, but it was dirty and smelled of dust. He wasn't wearing his eyepatch, so

Clayton could see into the socket, and he could swear something was crawling around in there. In the dark of the hall, he couldn't be sure.

"Clayton, my boy! I just stopped by to check on your sister, Eve," Price grinned and patted him on the shoulder. "She's turning into quite the young woman," he said snidely. Clayton stared at him. He felt terror so pure he wanted to scream. He wanted to tell Price to get out of his house now, call for his father, and tell him what this man was capable of. Clayton opened his mouth, but nothing came out.

"I have to go, but I will let my Amber know you wished her well," he chuckled. "She's a handful, that wife of mine. Please tell Eve not to be late this Sunday. We have private prayer early that morn." He gave a playful salute to Clayton and started for the door.

Clayton watched him leave, his skin crawling. He bounded up the stairs looking for Eve. He tried calling out to her, but he still couldn't speak. He reached her room. Her dolls were there, but she was nowhere to be found. The room was in disarray, the sheets were torn, and there were no curtains on the windows. The dolls were all missing a limb or two, and there were scorch marks in random spots on all four walls. *What the hell happened here?* He thought. He had to find Eve. He hurried out of the room and down the hall to his parents' room. His mother lay in her bed, wheezing. Their eyes met, and she reached her hand out for him. He sprinted to her side and tried to ask her where Eve was, but again his voice wouldn't come. He grabbed his mother's hand, and it was cold and clammy. Her eyes were in a state of panic as she tried to catch her breath. He realized she couldn't take in any air at all. She was dying in front of him. He took her by the shoulders and sat her up.

She clawed at his arms, tears streaming from her eyes as she gasped for air. She was turning blue. He had to do something, but he had no idea what to do. He pounded on her back. He'd seen his father do that when Eve choked on a carrot once. He was pleading silently with her to calm down. She clawed harder. He couldn't hear her breathing anymore. She was convulsing violently in his arms. He tried once more to call out to someone, but made no sound again. He hit her back harder, but she still couldn't inhale. He felt her go limp, and he shook her. Her eyes had gone glassy. He wanted to cry out but couldn't. He held her close, his heart torn to ribbons. He'd lost her again, and this time her eyes begged him for help. He'd let her down, his father might've been able to help, but he couldn't get his voice to obey. He sat with her in his arms, trying to make sense of all of this.

"What did you do to Momma?" He heard from the doorway. Clayton wheeled around and saw little Eve holding a headless doll. Her hair was matted, and giant purple bruises lined her arms and legs. She was wearing a nightgown torn in the front, showing her tiny belly. He'd never seen her so filthy. He laid his mother back and stood, smiling through his tears and motioning for Eve to come to him.

"You hurt Momma!" She squealed. He shook his head forcefully at her, trying to tell her no, but Eve was angry. She bared her teeth, and her eyebrows hung low over her wide eyes. She threw her doll at him and barely missed. She ran out of sight, and Clayton stood to run after her. He crossed into the hallway, but he stopped, for coming towards him was his father.

"You hurt your mother?" Jonas growled, marching straight towards Clayton. "Answer me, Goddammit!" His eyes were red. There were no pupils, no iris. He looked like something out of a nightmare. It was a fierce growl when he spoke, and Clayton could see his teeth were rotten. This looked almost like his father, but like something was wearing his skin. Clayton put his hand up and shook his head no, but his father didn't stop. He came right at him, raised his foot, and kicked Clayton square in the chest. It made a loud thump, and Clayton felt like he'd been shot. He fell and tumbled down the stairs.

"I'll teach you!" His father pulled his belt off and started down the stairs towards him as Clayton scrambled to get away. Clayton was trying to get to his feet when Jonas swung the belt, it caught Clayton on the hand, and fire stung up his wrist. The belt came again and connected across Clayton's chest. The pain was immense. Clayton rushed backward out the front entranceway and fell off the porch. Jonas emerged from inside the house, his belt still in hand.

"Where are you going, son? Get back here!" Jonas commanded. He dropped down off the porch and raised the belt again. It came down on Clayton's outstretched arm, and he rolled back to his feet. His father swung wildly. Clayton felt the wind whip past as he missed. Clayton studied his father's movements. Jonas brought the belt down, left then right, then backhanded right to left. He waited on him to finish his swing left, and he punched with all his might. Clayton's fist connected with his father's jaw solidly, causing him to take a step back and turn away. Jonas held his chin and turned to look at Clayton.

"So, you're a big man now, ain'tcha?" He smirked. Clayton hadn't hurt him. He again tried to answer, but his throat stayed closed. "You were always such a disappointment," Jonas dropped his belt in the dirt and raised his fists. "First, you couldn't out peacock a sixty-year-old man." He grabbed Clayton's shirt collar and punched him square in the throat. "You couldn't keep the stock alive." Clayton's head jerked to the side as Jonas hit him in the temple. "You can't protect Eve." Jonas hit him in the stomach, and Clayton sank to the ground.

"Now you think you can take your old man? Look at'cha. You were a momma's boy through and through. You shame me. You shame my name." He pushed Clayton down on his back with a filthy boot. "You hear that boy? Nothing but shame." Clayton heard his father sigh. "I'm just gonna have to put you out of your misery."

Clayton rolled over on his stomach and crawled upright. He took off in a run towards the barn. That's when the screaming started. It was faint at first but grew louder as he approached the building. He couldn't tell which direction the screaming was coming from. It was as if it was all around him. Everything was wrong and falling apart. This was all his doing. Amber was married to Donald Price, and his father wanted to kill him. He reached the door and scurried inside, pulling both doors closed, and slammed the wooden latch down. The screaming was almost deafening. He backed away from the door and heard something hit it hard from the other side.

"Clayton, you open this door right now, you hear?" Jonas screamed. Clayton had no intention of opening the door. He was trying to keep focused. The screaming was so loud it rattled his teeth. He turned away and ran to the other side of the barn when he tripped over something. He fell on his side, and the dirt clouded around him. He gazed back to see what he stumbled over and saw Charley, the family horse, lying dead on the ground. His eyes were solid white too, and his midsection was torn away as if something had feasted on him. Charley's innards laid strewn across the floor of the barn. Clayton scrambled backward to the nearest corner and pushed himself against the wall. He was terrified. The screaming was too much to bear. He felt like he might lose consciousness. He put his hands up to his ears, even though he knew it wouldn't block out any of the sounds. He prayed for it to stop. He noticed movement over Charley's face. Something was crawling from his mouth. Clayton stood up, his back still to the corner, and squinted to see what it was. His father was banging on the door in rhythm.

"Come on out, Clayton! It's time for church!" He laughed sadistically. "Would you hook Charley up to the cart for me?" Clayton closed his eyes. He either stayed in here with whatever was coming from inside Charley or faced his father. It was a no-win situation. He was going to die regardless. And the screaming. *Please,* he begged silently, *stop, you're hurting me.* He dropped to his knees and put his hands over his eyes. He tried one last time to cry out, and this time he found his voice. He screamed in unison with the other voice, and then everything faded to white.

77

NIX'S FORK

"Did he?" Feme asked, seemingly to no one. Nix stood beside her, motionless.

"I can't believe it," Nix whispered.

"Oh fuck, oh fuck." Feme began. "I just lost Clayton." She ran her fingers through her hair as panic overtook her. She felt for Clayton, sure, but the real question burning at the back of her mind was how much trouble was she in? She had just been demoted, and before they could even get started, her partner committed soul suicide. Her first act as a soul retriever would be getting reprimanded by Astrid.

"He was already lost," Nix stared off to the Darkness, "this was just the tipping point." Nix reached into his pocket and took out an ink bottle. He squeezed his hand, and the bottle broke in his massive fist. The creamy orange ink, along with his blood, oozed between his fingers. He reached out and quickly grabbed Amber's arm. It left a bloody, orange handprint, and Amber jerked backward. Feme flinched as he stepped towards her and forcefully grabbed her wrist.

"Don't fucking touch me!" Feme cried out as she stumbled over her own feet, trying to get out of his grasp. Nix let go and turned back to Amber. He said nothing. Feme looked down at where his hand had been. The ink was slowly seeping into her skin. She'd never seen anything like this before, and for a moment, it broke the spell of dismay she was feeling.

"What the fuck did you just do to me?" Feme demanded, walking around in front of Nix. Nix shook his head. Feme looked over at Amber's arm, where the bloody ink was almost fully absorbed. "What did you do to *us*?!" She cried out. Nix finally met her eyes.

"The ink keeps you here," his brow lowered, and his voice deepened, "with me."

"HOME!" Feme called out, clutching at Amber's hand. She yanked on her and turned to where a door should have appeared, but there wasn't one. "HOME!" She called out again, and for the second time, nothing happened.

"No," he smiled, "you aren't going anywhere. It takes a long time to wear off."

"What are you doing?" Amber wondered, confused. Feme looked to the Darkness, then back to Nix.

"How could I have been so fucking stupid?" She cried out. "I knew it. I was right about you, wasn't I?" Feme could say one thing about her time in the After. She had always been in control. She always had her mind in the right place, and from the moment she met Nix, something about him seemed off. She spent lifetimes hating the very thought of him. People don't change. Nix was always a rude bastard. He had befriended Takis and Clayton, but she always thought he wanted something from them.

She never trusted Nix, centuries passed, and she only despised him more. When she received his ticket out of here and placed it in the drawer of her desk, she wanted to punish him for all the trouble he caused her. She told herself that day she'd regret that, but she didn't care. She knew better. Him opening up, coming to visit, helping out when he could? She should have been on her guard. She had gotten soft, and she'd played right into whatever this was. Nix sat down on the ground beside Feme and began picking shards of glass from his hand. Feme watched him in silence, shaking her head. If she'd been younger, she'd have kicked him in the side of the head, but she was too old for violence now.

"You didn't see that coming, did you?" Nix looked up at her.

"Fuck you," Feme answered.

"I can't believe it worked," Nix winced as he removed a large shard from his palm. "I doubted the whole time, and He was right all along. I never thought someone like Clayton would choose that. I guess this time, he actually did kill himself. But he did it. The hard part is over." His eyes widened at the size of the glass, and he chucked it towards the Darkness.

"What are you talking about? How can you be so calm?" Amber interrupted. Feme shook her head.

"I'm not a monster, you know?" Nix said to Amber.

"I never said you were," Amber said cautiously. Feme stayed silent.

"There were times that I wanted this to fail. To say it was out of my hands, to say I tried and blame myself, but it all fell into place one piece at a time." Nix wiped the blood from his hand on his jeans.

"She doesn't understand, Nix." Feme sneered. "Why don't you get to the point?"

"Alright." He stood and looked again to the Darkness. "I can't believe he sacrificed himself. I feel sorry for him. I'm almost ashamed of the things I've done. Almost. I want you to know, I didn't do this for the hell of it. At first, I admit that because of boredom, it gave me a thrill. Still, after a while, I realized Takis, Clayton, even you actually cared about me.

"I wanted to stop. I tried to. I was too far in, though. I had to finish. This isn't personal, but," he paused, "it's all about getting my family back. I would apologize, but I honestly don't believe I'd mean it. I shouldn't lie to you. I've done enough of that." He took a step towards Feme. The breeze picked up. Feme stood by Amber and watched Nix with caution.

"Nix, don't do this," Feme pleaded. "Please, don't do this."

"I don't give a damn if I ever make it into the Brilliance. I just want what's mine returned to me," he said, his voice rising.

"Clayton is gone," Amber whispered. "Nix, how can we get him back?"

"You can't," Nix scoffed at her. "I think this might have broken her too," he said to Feme.

"He shouldn't have done that. Why would he do that?" Amber pleaded to Nix and Feme. Nix sighed and ignored her question.

"That boy was good, almost saintly by today's standards. His soul was pure gold until this place tainted it. I mean, sure, he was a tad vain, but vanity is such a human trait. All of you have it in some shape or form. Did you know he apologized to the sheep his father had him kill for food? I mean, who does that? Now he's in there, trapped forever. Tortured." Nix pointed to the Darkness and chuckled. The hairs on the back of Feme's neck stood up. He couldn't kill her, but he could do a lot worse. Her old body couldn't withstand an onslaught from him.

"Are you alright, Amber?" He asked. "Do you need a moment before we continue? I need you to understand what's happening here." He cracked his knuckles.

"What is happening here, Nix? What do you want from us?" Feme asked him finally. She scratched at her wrist where his hand had been. She grabbed Amber's arm and slowly guided her backward.

"The Darkness asked for three souls in exchange for my family, which would have been simple. I was going to get you and pitch you in one by one, but the Darkness told me Clayton had to want to be in there. It wasn't going to be simple." That got Feme's full attention. He reached down, plucked a few blades of grass, and released them into the wind. "Isn't that always the way here?

There's a catch to everything. I had to wait. The longer it took, the angrier I got. Clayton had to be shattered, but I think we went one step further. That leaves you." His eyes locked on Feme as he paced around them.

"What are you going to do?" Feme asked him, her voice shaking in fear. She silently cursed herself.

"The Darkness wants you, and I want my family. I think you see where this is going." Nix's voice dropped to a growl. "I'm going to beat you relentlessly. I'm going to use a bottle of Darkness and shove it down your throat. Then I'm going to throw you in." He motioned towards Amber. "She's weak. She'll stand here in fear while I do it. She's terrified right now. I can smell it on her. Halfway through, she'll probably run, but where can she go?" Feme kept her face carefully controlled. Amber began to whimper. She needed to stall. She needed a plan.

"You give us up, and then what? The Darkness just hands you everything it promised?" She asked him.

"Yes," Nix nodded. Feme threw her hands up.

"You trust that...thing? Do you honestly think it will just keep its word? Have you lost your mind? You give us to it, and then it tells you to go get fucked, and then what?"

"Do you think I hadn't thought of that?" Nix started towards her again. "It's a chance I'm willing to take. They don't belong there. They belong to me."

"Clayton didn't deserve what happened to him either!" Amber yelled.

"You said it yourself. That boy was good," Feme added.

"SO WERE THEY!" He wailed as he raised his fist. "My daughter was a little girl. She was innocent! She never hurt another living soul. She was everything you could want, loyal, kind, and He took her!" He raved.

"That doesn't make it right, Nix," Amber said, staring at the ground. "Clayton was your friend. He would have helped you. We all would have."

"There is no help. She abandoned us! Left us here to rot! The Darkness won, He won, a long time ago. There is no fighting it. There is no hope. So, you know what they say. If you can't beat 'em, join 'em." Feme pulled Amber back faster, but he kept in step, slowly closing the gap. "The Darkness has power, Feme. It can manipulate things here," he growled.

"Like what?" Feme asked forcefully.

"It can change orders. I put people in cells that didn't belong there. Leon was supposed to be put in the Darkness well before he went, same with the reverend. He had Clayton get Amber from the cells. He told me. He planned the whole thing," he shrugged.

"Are you telling me you let Clayton hurt on purpose? You let Amber suffer in a cell?"

"That's exactly what I'm telling you," he acknowledged.

"You're fucking garbage," Feme spat.

"I persuaded Amber into her relationship with the reverend too. I told him to poison her. I enraged Jonas enough to strike his son, and finally —" Nix said.

"You convinced Clayton to kill himself," Feme finished.

"How?" Amber asked, tears streaming down her face. She clutched at her chest.

"Afterwords," Feme and Nix said at the same time.

"You are the lowest piece of shit, Nix. A real bag of fucking dicks, you know that?" Feme gritted through her teeth.

"I want my family. I need them." Nix glared at her. Feme felt as if she was going to vomit.

"This is all your fault?" Amber asked.

"It is," Nix said flatly. Amber cried out in rage and charged Nix. She screamed and swung her fist as hard as she could into his stomach. He didn't budge. He didn't even act as if it registered. She pulled back and did it again.

"You stole my life!" She yelled. He placed his hand on the top of her head and shoved her away as if she were a toddler. She landed hard but quickly rose to her feet and wiped her eyes.

"I did. I took everything from you. I told you, it's not personal." Nix turned away from her towards Feme.

"We're not finished!" Amber yelled back to him. Nix rolled his eyes.

"Okay, let's get this over with." Nix started towards her slowly, as if he was stalking her. Amber raised her fists and put her right foot forward. Nix smirked.

"Seriously?" He said, surprised.

"You think I'm just going to let you hurt us without a fight?"

"That's fair," he said, "but think about it. Feme would have done the same thing in my position. If the Darkness offered her the chance to get her girls back, she'd have taken it in a heartbeat. Do you think you're friends here? She would have served you up." He stalked towards her. She backed away, still guarded.

"No," Feme spoke up, "you don't know me at all." Nix stopped and looked to Feme.

"Do you understand what's happening there? What it is He created?" He waved his hand towards the Darkness. "That place is a prison. Nothing gets out once it goes in. Nothing! It is Hell. It is ruin. He bragged about it as he was sending my people in. He told them that the anguish they would feel would be worse than anything they had felt before. That every torturous moment would be amplified. Everything you suffered in life is given to you a thousand times over while it tears your mind and soul apart piece by tiny piece. Think about my son, an infant! How for eons that baby has endured the most twisted things the Darkness could imagine." The sadness in his voice was replaced by rage. His eyes narrowed, and he wheeled around and charged Amber, grabbed her by the throat, and hoisted her into the air. Amber clawed at his arm and kicked her feet. Nix tossed her, and it appeared for a moment as if she were flying. She hit the ground and skidded across the dirt, rolling head over foot. She slammed into the pedestal, rocking it, and the book fell, hitting her square on the head. She struggled to her feet, clutching her crown.

"You are a coward Nix, a damned coward!" Amber yelled. She wiped her brow and raised her fists again.

"I admire your courage. I really do," he laughed. His long stride ate the distance between them. "Look at it this way, Amber. You are a nobody, and she," he pointed violently in Feme's direction, "she's a whore. She belongs there with the rest of the degenerates."

"Come on, then. We can go together." Amber spit blood. Nix roared and hunched down. He rushed her again, grabbing for her throat. She moved out of the way and swung. He caught Amber by the arm and lifted her high in the air as she clawed at his eyes. He shifted his weight, tightened his grip, and slammed her hard onto her stomach, forcing the air out of her. He stepped on her back. She struggled underneath his weight. Amber cried out in pain.

Without thinking, Feme shuffled towards him and shoved at the base of his back with both hands. He gazed over his shoulder as she swung with everything she could muster. He caught her hand and swept her leg. She went to the ground with minimal effort. He laughed at her as he turned back to Amber. Feme tried to catch her breath. The pain of striking the ground was almost enough to do her in. She knew there was no way they could beat him in a physical fight. There had to be a way out of this; she just needed to think. As she rolled onto her stomach, her hand grazed the admissions book open on the ground.

"Get up, girl! Show me! Teach me a lesson!" Nix howled. Feme watched as he toyed with Amber. If she didn't do something, this would be over soon. He snatched Amber by the hair and lifted her to her feet. She pawed at him weakly and then kicked her foot towards him without even remotely coming close to his body.

"You're-" She gasped. "You're-"

"Spit it out, girl! I'm what? A bastard? Come on, get it out. Make it special because this is the last thing anyone will hear you say. Better make it count," he taunted.

"You're evil, Nix," she gasped again. He stared at her blankly, seemingly disappointed at her final words. He picked her up over his head and slammed her down to the ground again, and stood over her. He raised his fist.

"You'll see real evil soon enough," he spat. Feme's vision was hazy. She searched the ground for it, she had to find it. It was the only thing that might be able to save them. She reached across the grass, crawling on her hands and knees. Her left hand touched something, and she grasped it. The ink and quill. She scrambled backward to the book. She dipped the quill and wrote in giant sloppy letters.

Help us Charon Claytons in trouble.

78

She wrote it out and laid the ink bottle down. She pressed a hand to her chest, she was still having trouble catching her breath, and she closed her eyes. *Please come. I don't want it to end this way.* She felt a shove. As she rolled over on her back, she saw Nix standing next to her, a look of concern on his face.

"What's this?" He said as he bent down and picked up the book. "What did you write?" He scanned the book, turned the page, and then again. He knelt down beside Feme. "I saw you write something. What was it?" Feme smiled up at him. The words had faded into the book. She knew what that meant. Charon had seen it.

"Oh, you think this is funny?" He picked her up by her arm and set her roughly on her feet. "What did you write in the book?!" Nix shook the book in Feme's face. He pulled her head back by her hair, so her head tilted towards his face. "Answer me!" He yelled, his eyes wide and feral.

"I just fucked up your plan," Feme proclaimed triumphantly. She had no idea if this would work or if Charon would come at all, but it was the only shot she had. Amber had made it to her feet and was limping towards them. Feme fixed her eyes back to Nix. She feigned confidence and snickered.

"Oh, is that so?" He asked, baring his teeth and pulling her towards him. She felt the heat of his breath on her face.

"You have no idea how fucked you are," she taunted. Nix shook her.

"Tell me!"

"Clayton had very powerful friends, Nix," Feme lied. "He was beloved by more than just us, and when she finds out what you did, you're gonna pay." He looked confused, and worry flashed across his face. She knew he'd thought he'd won. She just needed to buy time till Charon could get here. Nix dropped her, and she almost fell, but she maintained her balance. She saw the gondola slowly emerging from the center of the pond.

"You're finished," Feme simpered and pointed. Feme knew Nix had worked on retrieval before his promotion, but he always sent people to the Darkness. Maybe he'd never dealt with the ferrymen much, or perhaps they were so powerful as to elicit fear. Whatever it was, Nix did look afraid. She'd bought Amber a reprieve from being beaten to a pulp, and she'd bought them time to maybe make it out of this predicament. Nix pointed to the boat coming towards him.

"Who is that?" He demanded. *Please be her*, Feme thought. Charon pulled the boat to the shoreline near the three of them. She was still seated, and her hood was pulled up. She held her oar.

"Why have you called me?" She asked, her voice stern. "That little message wasn't funny." Amber limped forward, blood trickled down her chin. She pointed to Nix.

"He did all this. He...he was the one who killed Clayton, betrayed him, he's been working with the Darkness. He broke him down. Clayton just stepped in," she said, sucking in air as she spoke. Charon jerked back. She looked towards Nix.

"Is this true?" Her voice cracked in anger. Nix said nothing, so Amber continued.

"It is. He pretended to be his friend. He's the reason Clayton jumped to his death." Charon ran her hands over the oar before dropping it. She rose and placed her hands behind her back. She stepped to the front of the gondola and then onto the shore. She walked to a mere foot from Nix. He towered over the tiny, hooded figure. She looked like a toddler next to him. She kept her hands behind her back but craned her head back to look at him. Feme began to wonder if she'd made a mistake. Feme motioned to Amber to come to her. If things went sour, she would usher them both into the boat and row out to the middle of the River. She would use Charon as bait if necessary. If she had to sit in that boat for the next century, she would. When Amber finally reached her, Feme tilted her head in the direction of the craft, and Amber nodded in understanding. Nix looked Charon up and down and then gave a soft chuckle. His chuckle broke into laughter, and then it became a fit. He was practically snorting, almost bent completely over holding his stomach. Charon remained motionless. Nix held his hands up as if he was giving up.

"Oh, no!" He mocked. He laughed harder at Charon. She was barely past his knees. Nix turned to Feme and put his hands to his face in a parody of terror. "Whatever will I do? She's so imposing." Nix continued to laugh as Charon stood still. Nix wiped tears from his eyes.

"What will you do, bite my ankles? This?" He pointed to Charon. "This is going to save you? Little Charon? I mean, you couldn't spring for Dante or Mortimer?" Feme's heart sank. They were doomed. Nix reached down with his right hand, picked Charon up by her robe, and brought her up to his face. Her hood fell back. Upon seeing her, Nix cackled even more.

"Look at you," he said playfully, "you are a scary one." Charon showed no emotion and kept her hands behind her back. Amber tugged Feme towards the boat, and Feme had started moving in that direction when she noticed Charon slowly raise her left hand. She pulled it back as Nix's eyes widened in mock fear.

"Uh oh," he said. Charon brought her hand around for a soft slap to Nix's face. When it connected, the sound reverberated across the Fork. It hurt Feme's ears, and she flinched at the boom. It was louder than thunder, and the echo amplified it. Nix dropped Charon and glided through the air. She landed on her feet and charged Nix, who was bleeding from his mouth and on his hands and knees halfway between the River and Darkness.

"My God, what did she hit him with?" Amber gasped. Nix turned his head to face Charon, who closed her fist and hit him square in the nose, making a sickening crack. Nix bounced against the ground and rolled away, putting his hands in front of him. Feme started towards them in awe. Amber tried to pull Feme back, but she yanked herself away. She wanted to watch him suffer.

"Hit him, Charon!" Feme screamed as she quickened her pace. Charon was raining blows down on Nix's head, which careened off the ground with each shot. Feme stood a few feet away, excitement in the pit of her stomach. Feme felt her heart leap with every punch, she knew Charon couldn't kill him, but she hoped she would make him suffer. He was finally getting what he deserved. Feme looked at Nix's face, a mixture of blood and gold. *Gold?* Feme wondered to herself. She looked at Charon's gloved hands. They were also covered in something golden. The River. Her gloves were soaked in the waters of the River.

"You did this to him!" Charon barked. "Why would you do this to him?!" Nix's face was already swollen, and blood poured from his nose, mouth, and ears. He was trying to get away from her, but she kept coming, hitting him in the head and face repeatedly.

"He doesn't belong there!" Charon screamed, waving her hand at the Darkness. She stopped, out of breath. Nix lay sniveling on his back. His eyes were almost swollen shut, and there was a wheezing sound permeating from his shattered nose. Charon stomped her way back to Feme.

"What do the rules say about retrieving someone who doesn't belong in the Darkness?" Charon asked.

"You can't," Feme said, staring at her. Her thoughts caught on Charon's question. Feme took a step forward and flicked her wrist. "Nix life list!" She yelled. Papers ejected from her hand like they blasted from the nozzle of a firehose. Sheets fell all around her, getting caught on the slight breeze and flying around the Fork in all directions. "Nix life list!" She yelled out again, and they came even faster. The papers continued to flow for a few seconds. Nix rolled over on his stomach and watched as they glided around him. One landed in front of him, and he took hold of it with a shaky hand.

"Wha' are you doin'?" He forced out, coughing.

"These are the horrible things you have done to people. Amber was right. You are evil."

"Mmm...famil... " He snarled. He slowly got to his knees. He put his hands on the ground and stood. Blood still poured from his mouth. "I wan' famil.'" He huffed. He swayed back and forth, and with his face battered this way, he looked like the monster Feme thought he was when she first saw him. There was nothing human in him now. She almost felt pity. Feme looked down at the last paper in her hand, the final page of his list. She held it up to show him. She released it into the wind and let it flutter away from her. *The rules apply to everyone, the living and the in-between.*

She knew what needed to be done.

"You can see your family, Nix," Feme told him as she dropped it to the grass.

"Wha'?" He coughed and wiped the blood from his chin. She kicked some papers out of her way as she walked towards him.

"So, let me see if I understand this. You got a man to poison Amber, killing her unborn baby and her in one fell swoop." Nix eyed her carefully as he still struggled to keep his balance. "You're a murderer! You may not have poisoned her yourself, but you said it. You told him to do it. You're a killer, Nix. Evil, if I've ever seen it.

You killed Clayton Shaw. You took everything from him. He called you friend."

"Stay back," he warned as he spit out a broken tooth. She ignored him and continued.

"You pulled strings and played with people's emotions. You lied and schemed, and now you are planning on passing judgment on Amber, on me. You want to send us to that unbearable place, just like you did to Clayton. That's evil."

"Sto…" He warned.

"I'm left wondering about your family, Nix. What happened to them was tragic, but the things you've done? Just to the three of us? You are a villain. Whatever soul you had is long dead. Whatever they remember about you? You aren't that person anymore."

"Sto…" He attempted again.

"You've beaten Amber, a girl a third your size, and you threatened me. Well, I have news for you. I'm not afraid of you, Nix. I feel sorry for you. You are a rotten creature. You don't deserve happiness, and you certainly don't deserve your family back," she said gravely.

"STOP!" He found his voice and bellowed. Charon and Amber were standing near her now, the three of them looking down at Nix. A once mighty warrior and feared figure in the After, defeated. Feme could see it in the eye that wasn't swollen shut. He had nothing left. There was only one thing left to do. She put up her hand.

"You did all these things. You have no one to blame but yourself." Nix reached up and put his hand to his mouth. A few more teeth fell into his hand, and he tossed them away.

"Who do you thin' you are? I'll rip yor tongue out." He proclaimed. He stood upright in defiance. "I wan' my famil.' How dare you talk dow' to me." He stumbled forward.

"Clayton doesn't belong in the Darkness, but you do." The Darkness made a high-pitched whine, and Nix turned to face it.

Feme never took her eyes off of Nix. This had to work. If it didn't, who knew what Nix would do, they could stick him in a cell, but one day he'd get out. What then? Nix's size and strength would make short work of almost anyone. He truly was a beast, one that Charon couldn't watch over forever. The Darkness looked more alive than ever. It pulsed and shifted like it was going to spill out of its borders.

"Wha' did you-" Nix wondered. The shadows swirled and leaped, hypnotic in rhythm. Feme had never seen the Darkness move this way. It made a bubbling, boiling sound. Amber placed her hand on Feme's shoulder and leaned in.

"What are you doing?"

"I got him," Feme said confidently. Nix turned and gawked at Feme. He seemed dumbfounded by this turn of events. He looked back to the Darkness and then to her and finally shook his head.

"I had a deal," he said. Feme braced herself, and with as much conviction as she could muster, she cried out.

"Nix, you are not worthy of the Brilliance, and given the sins, you have committed, you are hereby sentenced to the Darkness for eternity!" Feme's voice echoed throughout the Fork. The Darkness stopped moving as if her words had commanded it so. Feme looked at the Darkness and back to Amber, confused. Amber shrugged. Nix looked at both of them, and the eye that wasn't swollen shut went wide, and he scoffed. He almost fell over. He snorted, and blood spurted from his nose.

"You are a stupid creature. You can't judge me," he declared, wiping the fresh blood from his face. Feme felt fear raise the hair on her neck again. Nix started to walk forward, but then his face showed confusion, and his smile faded. He looked down at his legs and rubbed his right leg with his palm. He paused and tried to walk forward again. This time, though, he took a step backward towards the darkness. His eyes quickly met Feme's.

"Wait!" Nix cried. He took another step in the wrong direction. She could see him fighting with all of his might against an invisible force, but again he stepped backward. Then another step and another. Nix dropped to his stomach, and he began sliding towards the still Darkness, inch by inch. He dug his massive hand into the grass, down in the soil.

"We had a deal!" He screamed. He was able to hold fast to the ground. Feme could see him struggling to stay put. His massive arms shook. The veins strained in his neck, and his good eye was maddened with panic.

"You think you could have done that before he started kicking the shit out of me?" Amber called out to Feme, who was on her way to him.

"I thought of it after Charon-" Feme started, then waved her hand. "Doesn't matter." Feme reached Nix. She stood in front of his outstretched arms. His fingers were already starting to bleed as he kept his firm hold on the ground.

"Nix," she said to him with a somber tone. He cocked his head sideways and looked up at her. Blood covered his lips. His eye was bloodshot. He was losing his grip. For a moment, he looked as if he was pleading with her for help.

"I hope it's as awful as you imagined," she gloated, and she stomped on the knuckles of his left hand. He cried out in pain and instantly let go. The only thing left was his right, and he was gawking at it. Feme kicked at this hand.

"Fuck you!" She screamed after each strike. After the fifth, he couldn't hold on anymore, and he started moving again, much faster. He made it to where the grass turned to dry dirt, and he spun around on his back to face the Darkness. He planted his heels, and it stood him straight up.

"I won! You had them!" He cried out. He held firm, his body turning red from the strain. Then the Darkness began to move again, slowly as was normal, but it swelled in the center this time. It formed something resembling two fingers, then a hand. The hand was much larger than he was, and it reached toward him. It beckoned at him with its pointer finger and then snatched him. It pulled him in. Feme stood for a moment in silence, watching the Darkness return to normal.

79

"Well, that was satisfying," she smiled and turned back to Amber. Charon ran forward towards the Darkness.

"What about Clayton?" She looked to Feme.

"I don't know," Feme answered.

"This isn't fair," Charon said. "You hear that? This isn't fair!" She called out to the Darkness. She stood in front of the entrance, the veins pulsing in her neck. Feme put her arm around Amber, who looked like she was about to cry, and they started walking away from the Darkness.

"I wonder how long we are going to be stuck in this fucking place with that gunk he rubbed on us," she said, looking down at her wrist.

"Poor Charon," Amber said as she nodded in Charon's direction.

"I know," Feme said.

"She really does care about him," Amber whispered.

"I know," Feme agreed.

"I was going to tell him! It isn't fair! Give him back to me!" Charon screamed at the top of her lungs.

"Will you stop yelling, please," His voice called from within as He stepped beyond the veil.

The Darkness slipped from His body and back into the cave. He stood in a black suit with designer shoes. He was fixing his black tie and smiling at the three of them. His skin was gold, His eyes white. His black beard was neatly trimmed, and His dark hair was slicked back. He was even taller than Nix, and though he was clad in a suit, Feme could see that He was more muscular than any human. The suit was modern and looked tailor-made for His gigantic frame. His teeth were brilliantly white, lighter than even His eyes. His smile was warm and inviting. He was gorgeous. Perfect. Nothing was out of place. Feme didn't have to ask. She knew who this was.

The Son.

Even though He was looking in her direction, she couldn't tell if He was staring at her. He nodded and started towards them. Feme took a large step backward.

"Easy," He laughed. "I'm not here to harm you. If it makes you feel more comfortable, I'll stand right here."

"Please," Charon said cautiously.

"Such manners," He reached into His breast pocket and pulled out a cigar. "Can I offer you one?" The three of them shook their heads no, and He cocked His eyebrow as if to say suit yourself. He put His fingertip to the end and lit it in one swift motion. He took a long draw and blew the smoke upward. It curved and floated back into the Darkness.

"I really must thank you, Feme. That was quick thinking. I've wanted Nix in my collection for a long time. I am looking forward to dealing with him personally. I owe him," He said.

"Thank you?" She stammered.

"Don't mention it. So, I've come to you because I have a dilemma, and I think we can help each other out. I need you to do something for me. I mean, not that I don't appreciate what you've done already, but it won't trouble you much." The Son took another draw.

"A deal?" Feme asked.

"Yes. Don't be so apprehensive," He smiled.

"Like Nix?" Feme asked.

"No," He shook His head. "Nothing so insidious."

"Why?" Amber asked. He tilted His head towards her as if He was unsure of the question. "Why did you do all this?" She asked.

"Oh," He contemplated. "Nix hated me with a passion that has burned for well over ten thousand years. Every day he plotted and schemed in his little office to stop me. " He feigned a look of surprise. He was overly animated in His motions as He spoke with His hands. Every word emphasized by His massive fingers was mesmerizing. He walked up to them and bent down into Feme's face. He was beautiful and terrifying at the same time.

"I get more people that cross into my house on any given day than Hers. All shapes and sizes, all colors, it doesn't matter to me. The more, the merrier. It just proves my point. People have blamed me for so many things for years, claiming I was responsible for this or caused that; The devil made me do it.'"

"Want to know how many times I've reached out to the world of the living?" He stood up straight.

"How many?" Feme asked.

"Zero. I've let Man hang himself. This is the first time I've left my home to even come here. I'm busy most of my days coming up with things for the souls I already have. I don't really have the time to mess with humanity, but I've gotten impatient. I'm growing bored. I need something new, something different. Once you both arrived here, I wanted to see how far I could push it." He winked at Amber.

"So, we were just a game? A big joke?" Amber said, her eyes watering.

"No, you serve a higher purpose. Nix was a trial run, and now that I know what can be done, it's time to take it up a notch. This little game Mother and I have going? It needs to end. With no one else left, She'll see I was right all along. I want Her to realize Her little experiment is nothing but a failure like I told Her when this first started." He took a long pull from His cigar and blew it up in the air. The cloud lingered for a moment before it sped to the Darkness.

"Nix claimed you went against Her wishes, and She punished you," Feme interjected. He smiled wide.

"That's the problem. Everyone has their own spin on our tale. I didn't hate them, nor do I hate you. I've always felt She couldn't see the big picture. She tried to create you twice before getting you to what She thought was right," he chuckled. "I told her that by giving you free will, that by allowing you to make your own decisions, you'd be no better than animals. And Nix's people? Savages. Rape. Murder. She kept telling me to give them time, that they would learn. You still haven't learned. Even after She tried again, you're still just as awful as ever. You needed guidance. You needed purpose. I tried to give you that."

"Meaning?" Feme questioned. He turned and faced the Darkness.

"I always wanted to be like Her. To create. I wasn't as imaginative as Her, but like any son, I wanted Her approval. So, She went away to make a paradise for those who were good. If you weren't up to par, you served here and then were reborn to try again. I decided to surprise Her and make a place for the other end of the spectrum. Think about it for a second. If there is a terrible place waiting for you upon death if you don't behave, you will do your best to be decent throughout your life.

"Now, I have to admit, I became overzealous in my ambition. I wanted to test it. I had to know. She had already sent your kind out in the world. There was no place for Nix and his ilk. I hurried the process. I told Her it was a place for those who didn't deserve Her. Imagine my shock when she sentenced me to my own creation."

"Did you learn your lesson?" Feme asked. He laughed.

"She came several times asking me to apologize and to end this." He pointed to the Darkness. "She can't destroy my creation, just as I can't destroy Hers."

"So, at any time, you can end all this?" Amber asked him.

"Yes," He said and walked back to them.

"So, what happened?" Charon asked.

"I wouldn't talk to her. I shouldn't have to apologize for being right. One day She gave up and went into that tunnel, and that was the last I saw of Her." He looked lost in memory. The four of them stood in silence.

"What do you want from us?" Charon asked him. He reached in his pocket and tossed a key at her feet.

"That is the key to Acquisitions. I cannot leave here. I want you to go into that office and retrieve my Mother's book. It is lying open on the floor, in front of the desk. It's fairly large and has Her art in it."

"Why do you need that?" Feme asked Him cautiously.

"Believe it or not, I miss my Mother. She drew pictures for me in that book. Call it sentimental. All I am asking is that you retrieve it and bring it to me."

"Why would we help you?" Charon scoffed. He smirked and held up His left hand. A chain emerged from the Darkness and wrapped around His left arm. He gave it a soft tug, and from the Darkness, Clayton tumbled, the chain attached to a collar locked around his throat. His eyes were white, his skin pale, and his clothing was tattered.

"I'll trade you," The Son grinned. Clayton lifted himself to both knees. He didn't acknowledge them. He didn't speak or look in their direction. Feme's heart ached to see him like this.

"Deal," Charon shot back. Feme looked over to her and could see her shaking with anticipation. "I can do that."

"I have no use for him. Bring me the book, and he's all yours," The Son explained.

"That's it? Just the book for Clayton?" Amber asked.

"No tricks. You two run and fetch it. Feme and I have another matter to discuss." He smiled at her.

"Nix put ink on our hands. We can't leave." Amber added.

"Right, I forgot." He reached into His suit jacket and produced a handkerchief. He took Amber's hand and began dabbing the back of it softly. She watched as the ink from her skin was soaked up by the cloth. "There."

"HOME!" Amber yelled, Charon scooped up the key, and they both rushed through the door.

80

"What's the catch?" Feme asked after they vanished. He smiled at her.

"Catch?"

"Oh, stop it. I'm not stupid. The dramatic pauses, those were a nice touch, but this was the plan all along." He again feigned shock.

"Why, whatever do you mean?"

"This is about that book, isn't it? There's something extraordinary about it. I don't believe Nix would have traded his family for it."

"You think?" He asked, His smile fading.

"Or he would have asked for more than you were willing to give." She waved a hand at Him.

"Go on," He held His hand out and smiled again.

"You finally have all of Nix's kind, and you are about to get whatever this book actually is. Things are tied up too nicely. We get Clayton back, and everybody wins. But see, nothing ever just works out here. This has been about the book all along. A bit convoluted isn't it?."

"You don't know what it's like to come up with a few million different ways to hurt people in a given day. Convoluted? Anything but, my dear Feme."

"I know the rules. I've played this game for too long. So, what's the catch?" She looked around comically. "You can tell me," she whispered. He paused and wagged His finger at her.

"Won't be long now," He said. She found herself no longer afraid. If He wanted to kill her and chuck her into the Darkness, He would have by now.

"So, why me? Why did you want me to stay?" she asked. Feme always had a gift of knowing when someone wanted something from her. He looked at her with admiration.

"I've not been impressed with a human in a long while." He slowly reached in the inner pocket of His suit jacket and produced a sealed envelope. He handed it to Feme.

"What is this?" She asked Him as she turned it over in her hand.

"A letter you are to deliver to my Mother," He told her, holding His hand out as if telling her to be careful.

"What for?" She asked, shocked.

"It asks that She come here, tell me I'm right, and apologize," He answered with pride.

"Doesn't She want you to apologize?"

"She does," He nodded.

"So, this is kind of a pissing contest?" She laughed. He looked at her, confused.

"Don't know that one."

"It's where two people are trying to get the other to give in. Neither will budge," she said. He grinned.

"Pissing contest? I like that. I'll remember that. I guess you can say, yes, it's a pissing contest. If She does what I ask, then I'll release everyone. I'll destroy it," He motioned towards the Darkness, "and we can go back to the way things were." Feme pocketed the letter and studied his face.

"You want Her to bow to you? Is that it?"

"No," He said, amused, "but for once, I want Her to admit She was wrong. That you weren't perfect little creations. That you were flawed. I want Her to create again, move on. This thing with you is over." He dropped his cigar stub and put it out with His shoe.

"Just give Her your letter?" Feme shrugged.

"That's it." He picked the stub up and pitched it into the Darkness.

"This isn't a trick?"

"Like what," he said, bemused, "She'll get a paper cut, fall into a thousand-year sleep, and only the kiss of true love will wake Her?"

"Cute," Feme rolled her eyes.

"No, it's a simple letter."

"One problem."

"And that is?"

"Your Mother and I don't see each other very often, so I have no idea when I can get this to Her."

"Oh, I think I can help you there." He walked past her, leaving Clayton, and headed towards the overturned pedestal. It didn't take Him long. Every step He took was five of hers. He picked up the quill and the book from the ground and began scribbling.

"Clayton Shaw, Amber Ward, and Feme," He said aloud as He wrote their names. Feme was stunned. Could He do that? Could He send her into the Brilliance?

"Yes, I can," He answered her as if He read her mind, "and the three of you are going the second they return with my property." He walked back to her.

"So, I'm finished?" She asked, trying to contain her excitement.

"You're finished."

"Why do I get the feeling you did that to keep me from asking about the book?" He placed His hand on His chest.

"Why, Feme, if I wasn't mistaken, I'd say you don't trust me."

His tone turned serious. "Do you care about the book? Do you want to know what it is? Why I want it?"

"No. I'm leaving. You do whatever you want. All of this," she waved her hand around, "is someone else's problem now." He looked down at her.

"I like you, Feme," He grinned. "If you had been one of my Mother's first, things may have been different."

"I'll take that as a compliment," she paused. "Was that a compliment?"

"It was." He smiled. A door appeared and flung open. Amber walked through, holding the gigantic art book on one end while Charon had the other. They were barely able to keep their balance. It was obviously much too heavy for the two of them. They looked ridiculous trying to stay in step with each other.

"Oh my," He said and glided over to take it from their hands.

"You didn't say it was this big," Amber complained, bending forward and breathing heavily. He held it out in front of His eyes, almost caressing it.

"Back in the family," He said with glee. He looked down at Amber and Charon. "Thank you, ladies." He snapped His fingers. The chain around His arm that led to Clayton shattered into individual links, and the collar popped off. Clayton fell forward into the dirt and whimpered. Charon hurried over to him, ripping her gloves off as she ran. She rolled him on his back and clutched him tight.

"That's beautiful," Feme said.

"You have no idea," He smirked.

"One last thing," Feme interjected.

"What's that?"

"That isn't going to bring about the end of the world or anything, is it?" She asked, pointing at the book. "I'd feel pretty guilty if I was responsible for that."

"No, it is a memento of my time with my Mother," He snickered.

"Do you think She'll take you up on your offer?"

"No," He answered honestly.

"So, you're both stubborn?" She said in jest. He got down on one knee to face Feme.

"I was serious. I like you. Can I convince you to come with me?"

"Are you going to offer me a nice office job?"

"Something like that. I truly am impressed with you."

"I'll pass," she winked. He stood and playfully bowed before her.

"Then I bid you farewell, Feme."

"You too," she dipped her head, "I hope I never see you again."

He nodded, His wide smile showing the majority of His teeth. Feme couldn't help but notice how perfect they were. He started back towards the Darkness, clutching the book against His chest. "Thank you, all! Have a wonderful trip," He said.

81

Charon looked up from Clayton and shivered. Her face lit up brilliantly.

"I'm to take you to the Brilliance, the three of you."

"Wait. What?" Amber asked.

"Yes, I can feel it. Your names were entered into the book," Charon started rocking Clayton back and forth. He let out a moan. Feme watched as the Son went back into the Darkness. It stopped swirling again and sat still. She kept it in the corner of her eye as she approached Charon and Clayton.

"Is he ok?" Feme asked. Clayton opened his eyes and looked up from Charon's lap to Feme.

"It's so cold," he stuttered. He was sweating and shaking violently. "The screaming, there's always screaming."

"It's okay, you're with us now. Feme is here. Amber is here too. Nix is gone. His plan didn't work. We won," Charon cooed. She looked down at him and stroked the side of his face. His expression was stuck between pain and confusion. He knew he'd been inside the Darkness, but he had no idea what was happening now.

"Charon, it's so wrong," tears streamed down his cheeks.

"Wrong, wrong," he repeated. Charon stroked his face and whispered softly to him.

"It's going to be fine. I've got you. You're with me now," she cooed again. After a while, his shaking subsided.

"How did I make it out?" He asked. Feme slowly recounted what Clayton had missed.

"So, it was all a lie?" Clayton asked when she'd finished.

"All of it perpetrated by that fucker," Feme said with contempt.

"I didn't kill myself?" He asked. He felt the guilt ebb away, slowly being replaced by relief. He'd spent a few centuries questioning why he'd done something so heinous, and to find that he hadn't been in control was almost too much for him. He was spent from what he'd seen in the Darkness. It was taking all he had left to not curl into a ball and weep.

"No," Feme answered. Clayton closed his eyes.

"I trusted him."

"I know, and he'll never hurt anyone again," Charon said to him, shaking her head.

"What now? He asked.

"Well," she reluctantly released him, stood up, and moved out of his line of sight. "We get you home." Clayton looked over at the River, and there was Charon's gondola. "Let me know when you are ready," Charon said with a smile. She looked at Feme, who was smiling at both of them. Clayton couldn't take his eyes off the gondola.

"Feme, what's going on?" He questioned faintly.

"We're leaving. We got our names in the book. It's over," Feme proclaimed. Clayton rose from the ground and almost fell. Charon rushed to grab his arm, but he waved at her to let her know he was alright. He stumbled forward and turned to look at Amber. She smiled, a few tears drying on her face.

"I'm sorry for the things I said," Clayton apologized. She nodded slowly. She wouldn't look him in the eye, but Clayton understood. He had wished her to Hell. He'd told her he hated her. There was a glassed-over look in her eye, and she stiffened when he spoke. They were finished. That friendship was over. Whatever they were, it was gone. He'd allowed the After to break him. He should have been stronger. Nix was responsible for only so much. Clayton allowed the pressure to crush him. He walked through the threshold on his own. He let himself down, and it cost him dearly.

82

"We haven't got all day," Charon said, tapping his back.

"You're enjoying this, aren't you?" He said back to her. Clayton took a small step forward. He was getting his bearings back, and Feme offered her hand to help him balance. Amber walked behind them, staying a short distance away. Charon stepped onto the boat.

"I am happy for you, Clayton." She offered her hand too. He took it. "You look like shit, though. You need a minute to freshen up?"

"Give me a break! That place is no joke," he said as he pointed towards the Darkness.

"So, what happened there?" Charon asked him.

"Oh," he grunted. "I watched my mother die again." He paused, on the verge of tears. Charon paused to mull this over.

"You are the first I know of," she said.

"What's that?" He asked.

"To make it out." Charon and Feme helped Clayton to the last row of the vessel. Amber sat in the front, Feme in the middle, and Charon took her spot at the back. Charon put her hand on Clayton's shoulder. He reached up and put his hand on hers. He was attempting to put on a strong front. He was trying to wrap his head around everything he'd seen there. He wouldn't wish it on anyone. It knew what he was afraid of, it knew how to hurt him, and it was real. All of it. It wasn't in his head. It wasn't something he imagined. He found himself for a moment thinking about his Bible teachings and the lake of fire. Physical pain was one thing, but it wanted to break him apart, and he was inside for so little time. He couldn't imagine eternity there.

"You'll feel better once we get inside the cave," Charon offered, and she shoved off from the shore. The gondola sliced through the golden liquid and towards the center. The boat slowly moved up the River.

"This," Feme stammered, "this all happened so fast, I just realized." She turned excitedly to Clayton. "I'm leaving! No more office, no more painting, no more soul collecting, I'm free!" She looked at Charon and broke into tears of joy. "It isn't a dream, is it? My journey is over?" Charon nodded her head with a smirk, and Feme threw her hands up and kicked her feet up and down. She giggled like a child. This was the happiest Clayton had ever seen a person. He felt something stir in him. Her mood was infectious.

"What's the first thing I'm going to do when I get there?" She rambled. "Are all the pleasantries of life there, Charon?" She looked towards her.

"Yes?" Charon responded.

"Have you seen what's on the other side?" Feme had her hands out in front of her. They were shaking in excitement.

"I have," Charon answered.

"Has this been worth it?" Feme turned all the way around to face her. "Is it as wonderful as I hoped, as I dreamed it would be?"

"It's better," Charon sighed.

"Can I eat and drink?" Feme squealed.

"Yes, to your heart's content," Charon chuckled.

"Sleep?" Feme was again almost standing.

"Absolutely," Charon laughed. Feme paused, and her voice became gravely serious.

"Fuck. Please say I can fuck. If not, pull over."

"You can," Charon giggled. Feme leaned into Clayton playfully.

"You hear that?" She threw her hands up and let out a joyous, "Yes!" The boat passed into the cave, and a warmth came over him. Clayton's senses snapped to life, and his wounds healed. He looked down at his clothes and hands, then to Charon.

"I'm sorry for all the trouble I caused you."

"Don't be silly," she smiled and touched his shoulder again before slowly moving up the side of the gondola and touching the shoulders of Feme and Amber.

"You were always so nice to me, and Takis told me I was being such a prick to you. I was just so miserable," he said. She walked back and caressed his face. For a second, Clayton thought Charon was going to kiss him, but she looked deep into his eyes.

"It was fine. I should have talked to you about it. Maybe I could have helped you through it." She released him, blushing, and she went to her spot at the back of the gondola.

"Besides, you have forever to make it up to me," she teased. "I can visit you anytime."

"Forever," he said back. "Sounds good." He noticed Amber looking back at him. Her eyebrows raised, and she pointed forward to the light.

"Clayton, do you hear that?" She asked. He concentrated, and there they were. Voices. There were voices. He couldn't make them out at first, but as he leaned forward and really listened, they finally became clear.

"That's my mother! I hear you, Mother!" He gasped in excitement. The more he paid attention and listened, they came in as clear as a bell.

"He's coming, Jonas!" He heard Emma call out. Clayton

almost stood, but Charon pushed him on the shoulder with her oar. It was his mother. Emma was waiting on the other side of that light, along with his father. He would see them again, just as he was always told he would.

"Eve, your brother, look!" He heard Jonas echo in the cave. Clayton turned back to Charon, who was smiling at him.

"They're really waiting for me, aren't they?" He asked. Charon nodded.

"I'm going to miss you, Clayton. When I retire, I hope you and I stay very close." Clayton nodded and glanced at Feme, who was bawling her eyes out.

"Are you okay, Feme?" He asked her, concerned.

"My girls, I hear some of them. Some of my girls made it. They're there," she choked out. Amber reached back and grasped Feme's hand. The light was blinding now, they were mere feet from it, and the voices were getting louder.

"I can't wait for Takis to show us around!" Clayton called out.

"I hope he isn't the first person I see," Feme joked.

"Maybe you can sleep with him?" Clayton suggested, laughing. Feme rolled her eyes at Clayton.

"Well, now all my excitement has dried up," Feme said. Charon leaned in and looked at Clayton, puzzled.

"Takis?" Charon asked. "What about Takis?"

"Takis promised to show me around when I got here," Clayton smiled. Charon looked down, then back up to Clayton, her eyes narrowing. She tilted her head to the side like a confused puppy.

"Clayton, I never took Takis to the Brilliance."

"He got his pass ages ago, he-" Clayton began.

"Clayton, I have access to all names in the book. That's the rule. No one gets in without me or my kind knowing. Takis is not in there," Charon explained. Feme flew around and gripped Clayton's arms, a look of alarm in her eyes.

"Nix! Nix was supposed to bring him to the Fork and sign him over!"

"That mother fucker!" Clayton cried out. A terrible feeling hit the pit of Clayton's stomach. He again thought of his mother dying in his arms, the beating at the hands of his father, and the screaming that shook him to his core and curdled his blood. He heard the scream again in his mind, and now he knew who it was. It was Takis.

He was screaming for help.

"Charon! Stop, we have to go b—" He stood, waving his arms.

The four of them crossed into the light through the threshold of the Brilliance.

ACKNOWLEDGMENTS

To our wonderful Kickstarter backers- We would not be here
without you. Thank you so much for your support on this project.
We hope you enjoyed your time in the After.

Craig Hescht
Andrea Hough
Anna
Matt Oakley
The Devil
Brandon
Brian McKinney
Travis Shannon
Heather & Nick Andrick
MK
Michael Evans
Mike Hornyak
Jeff Colson
Kim & Phil Rynerson
Babette Meade
Andrea
Aunt Bobbie
Sergey Kochern
Myself
Gussie
Joe Clemente
Anonymous
Emily Walton

Chuck Norris
Rob Steinberger
Karissa Lawson
Nerdile Art
Broxxigarr
Mike Oxlong- The biggest piece known to man
Kelsea Addis
Shrader Family
Planet Plush
Stephen Bias
Ronald Sizemore
Gabysmama
Beth Frueh
Amber Ferguson
Sarah Ann Snyder
Crystol Perry
David Black
Kevin Luzuriaga
Loren Jordan
Tyler
Jennifer Bowman
Raymond Zelker
Kelly Skaggs
Stacey
Linda & Joe Phelps
Jamie Vensel
Hannah Gallian
Chris Adkins
Ashlee Sowards

Thank you for sharing this adventure with us!
We can't wait to share the next one with you.

The Henlo Press

ABOUT THE AUTHOR

White, middle-aged, hetrosexual, with no scars— Stephen Bias is quite boring. In fact, the novel you hold in your hands is probably the most interesting thing he's ever accomplished. Well I mean he does have three kids, and is married, but let's be honest how hard is that?

MORE BOOKS FROM

West By God by Tyler Bell

Deadly Choices: Will You Survive? | Camp Meltaway by Tiffany and Caitlyn Pace

304 Monsters by Stephen Bias

A Shade of Winter by A.B. Hooser

Nora the Narwhal and her Curly Horn

by Alan Maynard, Illustrated by Soma Cather

The Wonderfully Wild Adventures of Kana and Charlie | Monstrous Mo and the Stolen Apples By Josh Taylor, Illustrated by Jeremiah Morgan

Mumblings: West Virginia Horror Stories by Caitlyn Pace

Afterwords by Stephen Bias

The Dictionary Game by Mike Hornyak

The Genesee Letters by C.W. Phelps

To When It May Concern: And Other Poems by Ijan Brodrick